The Book of
CREATION
Book One of The Watchers Chronicle

Evan Braun
and Clint Byars

THE BOOK OF CREATION
Book One of The Watchers Chronicle

Word Alive Press
131 Cordite Road, Winnipeg, MB R3W 1S1
www.wordalivepress.ca

Library and Archives Canada Cataloguing in Publication

Braun, Evan, 1983-
    The book of creation / Evan Braun and Clint Byars.

ISBN 978-1-77069-461-3

    I. Byars, Clint M. II. Title.

PS8603.R3825B66 2012   C813'.6   C2012-901157-6

www.thebookofcreation.net
sherwoodbrighton@gmail.com

Cover illustration by Bradford M. Gyselman (http://occamite.com).

ACKNOWLEDGEMENTS

This book wouldn't be possible without the contributions of a lot of different people. First of all, I tip my hat to my coauthor, Clint, from whose mind this story was birthed. Thank you for bringing me on board; it's been a hell of a ride.

I also wish to thank Leigh Galbreath, for her careful attention to detail, and to all those who read drafts (or portions of drafts) at various stages and didn't hesitate to give me their unbridled opinions—Colette, Kylie, Moses, Dave, and Tom. And none of this writing could have happened without the support of many other friends and critique partners whose support and encouragement often made the difference between finishing another chapter and taking an early bedtime. Here's to you!

—E.B.

CONTENTS

PROLOGUE

Ercolano, Italy

SEPTEMBER 3

As an archaeologist, Noam Sheply didn't much care for Italy. On a personal level, he enjoyed it just fine; he'd grown up visiting his family's beach house in Palermo—a welcome change of pace from the dreary English countryside where he'd lived with his grandmother. When he closed his eyes he could conjure the Sicilian mountains of his childhood. How many mornings had he woken to the sound of gulls in a feeding frenzy? Perhaps it was just nostalgia that made him recollect that place so fondly. He hadn't visited in years.

But Italy had a lot of history, and that was the problem. Rome itself had kept archaeologists busy for centuries. The Romans left behind so many monuments, documents, and oral history that the most compelling mysteries had long since been resolved. Intellectually, the country bored him. Beautiful coastlines and fettuccine aside, Italy no longer had much to recommend it. But this—

But this.

This new business trumped whatever professional ennui Italy threw his way. This was a game changer. This was *something new,* and for a place that had been picked over almost literally with fine-toothed combs, that said something.

Sheply checked the GPS and confirmed that he was still heading southeast. Professor Agostino had said it wouldn't be more than a twenty-minute drive from Naples, but the clock on the car radio already read five minutes past the hour—though rental car time could never be trusted.

He was thoroughly unimpressed by the two-story building he pulled up to. Truly, the excellent work being conducted here was undervalued, and underfunded. He pulled past a small parking space along the curb, then shoulder-checked to make sure nobody was waiting behind him on the narrow lane as he backed in.

Sheply opened the door and swung his legs onto the uneven cobblestone. He took a long breath of air, comparing it to what he remembered from childhood.

He spat it out; it tasted stale and polluted, nothing like what he remembered. He surprised himself with the fleeting pang of homesickness. The air along the entire northern coast of the Mediterranean was much heavier than in Africa to the south. Egypt should never have been more than a quick stopover, yet in his third year in Alexandria he now had to consider the stay long-term.

"Doctor Noam Sheply?"

At the sound of his name, Sheply turned to peer at the short, balding man standing on the building's front stoop. He couldn't make out more detail than that with the morning sun hovering just above the man's head, creating a glare.

"Excuse me," the man's voice wavered in heavily-accented English, "but I do not suppose I am confusing you for someone else..."

Sheply took a few steps closer, passing near enough to the building to fall under its shadow. With the sun safely tucked around the corner, he saw the man more clearly.

The man looked to be in his mid-sixties, but his dark features made his age difficult to place. He wore a gray suit, threads fraying at the cuffs.

Sheply plastered a well-practiced smile onto his face and extended his hand.

"You must be Professor Agostino," Sheply said in his dulcet British tones. He expended much effort maintaining the accent; the smooth, lyrical rhythm engendered trust and respect. The accent was a gift.

The professor took his hand and shook it solidly. "Please, call me Andreas."

"Andreas, then." Sheply looked up and down the street. It was quiet except for a couple of scooters buzzing down a cross street two intersections away. He smiled at the Italian stereotype so proudly on display. "Have the others arrived?"

Agostino nodded. "About fifteen minutes ago."

"Sorry to keep you waiting."

"No, please. Perhaps it was the traffic." Agostino swung open the door, holding it back for Sheply to follow him in.

The front room held a small waiting area, lit by dim lamps. A man and a woman sat in foldable blue chairs, both of their faces turned to give the new arrival a onceover.

Sheply knew the woman. Elisabeth Macfarlane's long brown hair rested on her shoulders, forming ringlets that shifted as she uncrossed her legs. She smiled, but Sheply knew her well enough to realize the expression only masked an internal frown. She looked as though she couldn't decide whether to let her excitement run rampant or keep it under lock and key until the Italians' findings could be confirmed.

If they had been alone, the two of them would have had much to talk about. The last time he had seen Elisabeth, at a hotel in Barcelona, she had told him in no uncertain terms that she wasn't interested in a relationship. Neither was he, he had explained, but she either didn't catch his implication—a fling was all he wanted—or studiously ignored it.

He looked away before the moment became uncomfortable.

Sheply did not know the man seated next to Elisabeth, though he appeared to be local. His eyes narrowed at Sheply, as if he didn't have the faintest idea why he had been summoned so early on a Saturday.

"This is Enrico Calfo, from the National Library," Agostino said by way of introduction.

Calfo stood up. "I attended your lecture last April in Tunis, Doctor Sheply. It was very persuasive, but I hear there's nothing unusual about that."

Sheply inclined his head graciously. "You're very kind."

"And this is Doctor Elisabeth Macfarlane, from Brigham Young University in America," Agostino continued. "She's the director of the Herculaneum Papyri Project and—"

"Yes, I know," Sheply interrupted. "We've met."

"How have you been, Noam?" Elisabeth asked. If she felt any anxiety at seeing him again, she masked it well. "I see Egypt's been good to you."

"I can't complain," Sheply said. "How's Emery Wörtlich? I haven't heard much from him recently."

She frowned, her discomfort palpable.

"Emery and I are none of your business," her expression seemed to say. Instead she said, "Emery and I haven't spoken in some time."

Sheply wasn't sure if that was true, but changing the subject was the appropriate thing to do. "A pity. He would be interested in this. Especially now that they've found the index."

Agostino put a finger to his lips. "Please, don't. We are not certain. It must be confirmed." He looked down at his watch impatiently. "He should be here shortly. I do not know what is keeping him."

"Who are we waiting for?" Elisabeth asked.

"Our site coordinator, Dario Katsulas. We do not come in on Saturday, not normally. His assistant went to locate him."

Sheply rubbed his chin thoughtfully, peering back out toward the street. There was no one else around. He turned toward the professor. "Perhaps you have someplace more comfortable where we can wait?"

Agostino bustled them into a small conference room at the rear of the building. Interrupting the back wall were two windows covered with partially upturned Persian blinds which let in horizontal streams of morning light; they diced up the surface of the room's long wooden table like a backgammon board.

Once seated, Sheply tried to make eye contact with Elisabeth again, but the woman made a concerted effort to look away. She was probably nervous about the possibility of being wrong about all this. If there turned out to be nothing in Herculaneum but a two-thousand-year-old recipe for lasagna...

But if she's right, it would change everything.

The room's door creaked open and a young man with circular glasses stuck his head in.

Agostino breathed relief. He stood and clasped the newcomer's hand. "*Grazie per essere venuti, Dario. So che offi doveva essere un giorno libero.*"

Dario, the newcomer, nodded. "*Eppure, è proprio in questi casi che accadono le cose più interessanti, no?*"

The professor laughed uneasily.

Sheply could only make out a word or two from the exchange, but he could infer that Dario's attempt at an ironic joke had somehow hit the mark too closely to generate any actual levity.

Agostino led Dario to the table and introduced him to the group. Dario's eyes flashed with recognition when he saw Sheply.

"You are Noam Sheply, yes?" Dario took a seat across from him. "From the Egyptian Council of Antiquities?"

"Unofficially," Sheply said. "On paper, I'm an international observer. Doctor Menefee has been very kind to let me stay so long."

"Indeed. The Egyptian government does not normally approve visas for so long a period. They do not like oversight, especially from the British."

The Englishman shrugged. "Apparently, they like me."

"And, of course, I saw you in Tunis."

"Is that so?"

"Your work interests me. After all, we're both unearthing libraries."

"The Library of Alexandria is more than a mere library," Sheply pointed out. His eyes flashed as he added dramatically, "It's the crossroads of history!"

Elisabeth leaned forward, keeping the sun out of her sparkling green eyes. "I've been looking forward to meeting you in person, Dario. My colleagues were envious of my opportunity to see Herculaneum for myself. We've been working feverishly for weeks."

"Your speed has been very impressive," Agostino said.

"As Pompeii begins to lose some of its mystery," Elisabeth continued, "a number of interested parties are turning their attention to Herculaneum. It's becoming clearer every day that the next major discoveries will be found there."

Dario smirked. "It only took the archaeological community three hundred years to arrive at that conclusion."

"A fair point, Mr. Katsulas," Sheply said. "But I should think you would just be grateful someone is finally paying attention."

"Whatever this is about, it sounds fascinating." All eyes turned to Calfo, who glowered in confusion from the far end of the table. "An American," he tilted his head toward Elisabeth, "who flies overnight without so much as a notice on the Institute's calendar. And Doctor Sheply, who, begging your pardon, has better things to do than spend a day on the wrong side of the Mediterranean." He rested his hands on the table. "Is somebody going to explain to me what we're all doing here?"

"We have a few questions about the new excavation underway at the villa," Sheply said, turning his attention back to Dario. "From my understanding, you've been digging out the fourth terrace. Can you tell us about that?"

Dario cleared his throat. "As you are probably aware, just getting to the fourth terrace has been a three-year struggle. Obtaining permission from the Italian government to permit digging under a populated area was enough to—how do you say, drive us crazy? But the results justify our interest. There was no guarantee we would find any scrolls in the terrace at all, but what we found… it exceeded all our expectations. There are hundreds of new texts still waiting down there—"

"What about Scroll 3141?" Elisabeth cut in.

Dario paused, mystified. "I do not recall that one. One of the most recent texts, judging from the number. Apart from that, I'm sure we would have received a call from the university if there was any anomaly."

"I'm here, now," she pointed out. "Consider this your call. Trust me. There was an anomaly, all right. You have no idea."

"What did you find? You must have seen something quite early in the process."

The green in Elisabeth's eyes glinted as she leaned back into the sunlight. "It seems you've accidentally stumbled upon the greatest discovery of the century."

All Dario did was raise an eyebrow, a reaction completely insufficient to the claim.

"Did you know there were scrolls in Herculaneum that originally came from the Library of Alexandria?" Sheply asked.

Dario hesitated. "Well, no. It has been speculated before. But there is no proof."

"Julius Caesar sailed to Alexandria in 48 B.C., during his Egyptian conquests," Calfo said. "I have maintained for years that he brought back a cache of Alexandrian books and gave some to his father-in-law, Piso, on the occasion of his marriage. Piso resided at the villa at the time of the Vesuvius eruptions, so the theory 'holds water,' to use an English expression."

"Alexandrian books would have been an ideal complement to Piso's collection." Dario glanced across the table at Agostino, who was taking in every word like a sponge. "You knew about this, Professor?"

"Not fully, no."

Dario pushed his glasses back up the bridge of his nose, frowning at Elisabeth. "What is it about Scroll 3141?"

"At first it appeared quite ordinary," Elisabeth said. "I thought it was an index to a larger volume, such as the Septuagint, which would hardly have been a remarkable find." She paused, running a hand through her hair to push the curls behind her shoulders. Nervousness clouded her features. "I shouldn't say anything more until I confirm my suspicions. The matter is … potentially delicate."

"The professor assured me on the phone that we could have a look at where the scroll was recovered," Sheply said.

Dario balked at the suggestion. "That is a very bad idea. We could not accommodate so large a group. The site is highly sensitive."

"These people have come a long way, Dario," Agostino reminded him.

"Andreas, please," Dario said softly, almost under his breath. "You and I both know I could lose my position for this. Our sponsors could—"

Agostino shook his head. "I guarantee that will not happen. Especially if Doctor Macfarlane's suspicions can be confirmed. Look around at these people. They are not tourists, Dario. They are trained professionals. If anybody knows how to behave at a dig site, it's them."

Dario nodded, remaining in his seat as Sheply led the way toward the door.

"I assume you don't want us to head down without you," Sheply prodded.

Within minutes, Dario led a caravan of rental cars up the hill from the street, toward the ancient village of Herculaneum.

*   *   *

All that remained of the Villa of the Papyri was hidden away northwest of the town site, halfway up the slope of Vesuvius. As Dario led them along the narrow path that twisted up through petrified rock outcroppings, Sheply stole a moment to glance toward the sea. The view from the ridge was unobstructed, soaring over the urban sprawl as though it was all somehow inconsequential.

He snapped back to attention as Elisabeth brushed up against him, climbing ahead. Turning, he realized the others were now well past him, even the professor, who was struggling to catch his breath.

"The seaside retreat of Lucius Calpurnius Piso," Dario announced as they navigated a tight jog in the path.

Sheply looked up to where the young man pointed, affording him his first glimpse of the villa. A terrace of overgrown red paving stones flirted with the edge of a thirty-foot cliff. Over the centuries, dozens of those stones had come loose and rained down on the forest below. The stunted remains of broken columns littered the foliage as well, torn down by Vesuvius' fury and then scattered by the winds of time.

"It's beautiful," Elisabeth marveled. "More so than the pictures suggest."

Calfo put a hand up to his forehead to shield his eyes from the eastern sun. "Perhaps Mr. Katsulas would extend us the courtesy of a tour."

Dario stopped to let the others catch up. "Do not touch anything," he warned as they made the final ascent to the large portico.

Dario reached down, helped Agostino over a small ledge separating the site from the trail, then stepped comfortably between the foundations of two broken stone columns that announced the entrance to the villa.

Sheply surveyed the cold, rock-strewn excavation. This whole area had once been filled with gardens and vineyards, but they were gone now, buried under as much as sixty feet of molten rock where the pyroclastic flows had swept through.

Dario moved on through the columned atrium into a narrow peristyle. A slight depression in the center of the chamber was all that remained of a swimming bath. At the far end of the colonnade, two opposing statues stood in a gap between pillars. Sheply recognized the men depicted—Julius Caesar and Ptolemy II, one of Egypt's first Hellenist pharaohs.

Sheply stopped at the foot of the bath, gazing into a semi-circular enclosure. "This may have been a display area of some kind."

"Eleven fountain statues stood there," Dario explained. He pointed west toward a slope where three roughly-cut entrances tunneled deeper into the mountainside. "The villa is the largest ever discovered. Before the eruption, it sprawled over thirty thousand square feet, spread over four terraces, only the first of which was properly explored before now. Over two thousand carbonized papyri scrolls have been recovered."

"Scrolls which multispectral imaging allows us to read," Elisabeth added. As she spoke, she drew near to a wall mural. Between the columns were a half-dozen etchings and tableaus. "Quite impressive."

Calfo approached her. "You know what this is?"

"This looks very much like the court of Ptolemy II, who founded the Great Library," Sheply said. He pressed his tongue against his teeth, censoring himself. The display was hardly one of a kind. Frankly, there were more important things to see. He swiveled to face Dario. "I do hope you're going to take us down to the fourth terrace before the Institute calls to find out what the hell is keeping us."

"Absolutely. The fourth terrace is our most recent find. We've only begun excavating its contents," Dario said, focusing on the seaside corner of the atrium. Near the lip, where the ledge dropped precipitously toward the city, a hole opened up through the rock floor. Dario pulled a flashlight from his pocket. "Watch your step. It's a bit narrow in spots."

The descent was steep, but within a few minutes they all stood in the dark, clammy terrace chamber. The partially excavated room left them barely enough space to stand without stepping on each other's toes.

Cut into one wall was a length of recessed cupboards, or *armaria*, though no scrolls resided in them.

A surprisingly well-preserved wooden crate drew Sheply to the middle of the chamber. He edged past Calfo and Agostino, then knelt to shine his flashlight over the crate, looking for inscriptions. He found none.

"When the volcano began showing signs of an eruption," Dario said, "the scrolls were packed into cases in the hope that they, along with the residents of the villa, could be rescued in time. Unfortunately, history tells a different story."

Elisabeth took Agostino's flashlight and aimed it into the darkest recesses of the chamber. Dust hung in the air, sparkling in the flashlight's narrow beam. Two more boxes lay there, one opened, the other sealed. The back half of the opened box had crumbled in on itself.

"It's one thing to read about this in a report," she said. "It's entirely another to see it with my own eyes."

Sheply straightened and joined her. Looking inside the open box's cavity, he found a heap of undisturbed ash blanketing tightly packed scrolls. They were delicate, too brittle to touch.

Next to him, Elisabeth also inspected the box. He closed his eyes for a moment, catching the subtle scent of her fragrance. Lilacs, he thought.

"Fascinating," she whispered. "Over a hundred writings previously thought lost have been recovered from this box, including new plays by Sophocles, Euripides, Aeschylus... a range of Aristotelian dialogues, and over a dozen volumes of Livy's *History of Rome*, of which nearly a hundred others may still remain."

Heavy silence fell over the room. The blackened contents of the box seemed to stare back at Sheply, the light catching the edges of the papyri like the twinkling of watchful eyes.

"It's amazing that technology allows us to open these at all," Sheply said. "These books represent the greatest recovery of classic literature since the Renaissance."

"Are you jealous?" Dario asked.

"Immensely. In Alexandria, we've found lecture halls, auditoriums, and room after room of empty *armaria*... everything but an actual book."

Elisabeth looked up to Dario. "In which box did you find 3141?"

Dario stepped carefully around the crate in the middle of the room, his eyes hardening into a thoughtful expression. Finally, he reached down and tapped the edge of the other opened crate.

"It was in here. I will require several months to recover all the scrolls from this case. As you can see, some of them have suffered extensive damage." Dario continued to stare at the box, double-checking his memory. "Yes, this is the one. But if that is so, your scroll was retrieved just ten days ago, at the latest." His mouth opened to form a tight, perfectly round circle. "You could not possibly have digitized it already. The process should take months!"

"When I came to suspect its content, I gave it the highest priority." Elisabeth's eyes glinted with playful curiosity. "You still have no idea what you found, do you?"

"That's enough," Agostino said. "Now you're just toying with us."

"What have I found?" Dario asked.

Elisabeth's mouth opened and closed. She glanced over to Sheply, graciously handing off the pleasure of delivering the news.

"It's the index to the Library of Alexandria," Sheply revealed. "A record of every document known to the scholars of the ancient world. The scrolls themselves may have vanished into antiquity, but now we have a complete inventory of what was there!"

Dario's eyes widened as he attempted to absorb that. "Then we were right. Caesar brought these scrolls back to Italy after his Egyptian campaign."

Elisabeth nodded. "It stands to reason."

"We have to get the rest of the scrolls from this case to the university," Sheply said, dusting the dirt off his knees. "This will profoundly affect the work already underway in Egypt. In fact, it affects everything! Don't you understand? Everything we know about the ancient world is on the verge of staggering change."

ONE

Syracuse, New York
SEPTEMBER 3

W e live today in a world that is broken!" Six thousand eyes watched Ira Binyamin as his voice carried easily through the synagogue—but it didn't matter to Ira whether he spoke to three or three thousand; the message remained the same. "People are suffering debilitating hurt and despair in every area of life, both in the physical and spiritual realms. And I should know. After all, nobody knows suffering like Jews know suffering! For every one of us who experiences success, there are ten others who are destitute and unable to imagine themselves accomplishing the dreams and goals they once aspired to. That is because we are, all of us, broken.

"But we are not called to be a broken people," he said, taking a moment to smile. "We are called to servitude, yes. But to utter brokenness? No! Imagine for a moment an ordinary man walking down a street. Along the way, he comes upon a panhandler. Observing this panhandler, the man is so compelled by his way of life that he decides to sit on the stoop and join him."

Soft laughter rippled from one end of the congregation to the other. The rabbi waited for the moment to pass, then rested his arms on the podium.

"I know, it sounds ridiculous, but we've all been guilty of thinking like that, of ignoring our natural potential and settling for the bare minimum. It's time for us to put the principles of Jehovah to use. It's time for those around us to be so inspired by the ease with which we live, even through the most challenging circumstances, that they can't help but lay down their sin and dysfunction at the feet of Jehovah and follow him to the end of their days. After all, our Jehovah is a God of attraction!"

Ira's eyes shone brightly as his gaze roamed the sea of faces. The front ten rows didn't change much from week to week, though he privately wished they would. But as he looked to the far right, there was one face he did not recognize. A visitor certainly wasn't uncommon at Temple Emmanuel—as one of the largest temples in the state, there were hundreds of newcomers every week—but this man was different. Something about him tickled Ira's awareness.

The man stared right back at him, the two of them locked in a gaze that lasted three or four seconds longer than it should have. The rabbi blinked, then turned back to his message notes.

When the service ended, Ira retreated into a private corridor via the door at the back of the platform. He could hear the temple emptying behind him and felt a twinge of guilt for not making his usual appearance at the front steps as the people poured out onto the street.

But not today. Feeling tired, he slipped off his *kippah* and palmed it.

Ira closed the door of his personal study and leaned wearily on the edge of his desk. He closed his eyes.

His eyes fluttered back open at the sound of sharp knocking.

One of the office assistants poked her head in. "Rabbi?"

"Yes, Janene?"

"There's a man here to see you. His name is Wendell. Are you expecting him?"

He squeezed shut his eyes, wracking his brain for a recollection of that name. Had he forgotten an appointment? "Sorry, don't think so."

"Do you have a few minutes, now?"

"No, not today," he said. "Tell him to call back during the week."

Janene pressed her lips into a small smile. "Of course, Rabbi."

As she left, Ira slid down into the worn leather of his desk chair. He couldn't understand why he was so exhausted. It was normal to feel a little wiped out after a service, but this was different. Something felt... heavy, somehow, like a weight rested on his chest. Ira drew a few deep breaths to stir himself. He worked his fingers, trying to get the blood flowing.

Ira looked down at his watch and sighed. It was still early. "Wait, Janene!"

When she didn't answer, he stood up and walked out into the hall. "Janene?"

He froze in the doorway. Standing next to the office assistant was the same odd man he had spotted earlier in the auditorium. What was *he* doing here?

Janene turned. "Yes?"

"I've changed my mind. I have a few minutes, after all." Ira made eye contact with the stranger, trying to put his finger on what so interested him. "Come on in."

Ira let him in and closed the door. Without saying a word, the stranger turned his back to Ira and approached the room's only bookcase, brushing his index finger across the spines. He pulled out a narrow book and held it up for Ira to see.

"Ah, the Holy Grail," the stranger said, a hint of reverence in his voice.

Ira indicated the seat in front of his desk. The man silently accepted the invitation, all the while flipping through the pages of the book.

Ira focused his eyes, trying to make out the title on the spine. He recognized it. "The *Sefer Yetzirah*. A fascinating text. I take it you're familiar with it?"

"Oh yes. In English, it means 'Book of Creation.' The perfect blend of numerology and cutting-edge science. What could be more intriguing?"

Ira nodded, continuing to watch the strange man. The man held the book open to the first page. Ira was about to ask his name, for he had already forgotten it, when the stranger began to read.

"In thirty-two mysterious paths of Wisdom, Yah, Eternal of Hosts, God of Israel, Living Elohim, Almighty God, High and Extolled, Dwelling in Eternity, Holy Be His Name…" The stranger let the words trail off. "Heady stuff, don't you think? I've heard Abraham wrote it."

"Nobody really knows," the rabbi said.

"I'm told it lays out God's methodology for creating the universe, and that if you can decipher its meaning, you have the power to create and manipulate matter using nothing but your mind. I've also heard you personally use this power to manifest objects out of thin air." The stranger shut the book and set it down on the desk, taking a moment to study the rabbi's reaction—or lack thereof, Ira hoped. "By the way, the name's Wendell."

Wendell. Yes, of course. "My assistant mentioned that. It sounds like you've heard quite a lot of things, Mr. Wendell. Of course, you shouldn't believe everything you hear."

"Be that as it may, Rabbi, I'm sure you would agree that the possibilities are pretty... incredible."

Wendell's eyes darted around the room, perhaps taking a mental inventory of its contents, everything from the pictures on the desk to the diplomas on the wall. Ira shifted uncomfortably.

"I take it you didn't come here solely for the purpose of asking me about the *Sefer Yetzirah*," Ira said, pulling the book to his side of the desk and casually thumbing through its pages. "As far as texts go, this one is reasonably common. I'd hardly call it the 'Holy Grail,' as you put it."

"Yes, but understanding it is the key."

"You want to understand the *Sefer Yetzirah?*" A quirky smile played across Ira's lips. "You came here to mine from me the secrets of the universe? What makes you think I have any idea how it works?"

"For one thing, you're unparalleled in your studies of Kabbalah. Don't waste time denying it. I'm rather impressed, to tell you the truth."

Ira's smile faded. "You think I'm interested in impressing you?"

"No, I suppose not."

"As far as the scriptures go, and the mystical teachings, then, yes. I have an interest. As a rabbi, I cannot ignore the ancient writings. It would be ignorant of me to do so. But as for Kabbalah, I don't teach it from the podium."

"I think you're understating your interest."

"And I find your line of questioning curious."

Wendell leaned forward, his intense eyes catching Ira's and holding them fast. "What about the law of attraction?"

"What about it? I spoke on the subject this morning."

"Yes, I was paying close attention. But you didn't seem to go as far as you would have liked. I could tell. There were moments when you held back, stopping short of the point."

Ira sat up straight, surprised and anxious at the man's intuition. He wasn't far off the mark. "Now's probably not the best time to—"

"In the interest of full disclosure, Rabbi, I should tell you I'm not conducting this discussion on my own behalf."

"Oh?"

Wendell lowered his eyes to the floor, then raised them again. "My employer is Raff Lagati. I assume you've heard of him?"

Ira's surprise intensified. "The billionaire?"

"He would rather be thought of as a philanthropist."

"I doubt he gives his money away out of the kindness of his heart."

Wendell chuckled. "I wouldn't have pegged you for a cynic. Lagati believes he now has, in his possession, the original *Sefer Yetzirah*. The one penned by Abraham himself, thousands of years ago."

Ira's mind whirled at the very possibility. He struggled between wanting to laugh and wanting to cry, but managed to maintain a straight face.

"That's ridiculous."

"Is it?" Wendell asked. "He'd like some help authenticating and translating his find. He's come to the conclusion that there's no one better suited to the task than you, Rabbi Binyamin."

"I don't care what he thinks he's found. It's not an original manuscript."

"So you say." When Ira didn't respond, Wendell pressed on. "Just think it over. Imagine what you could do with an undiluted *Sefer Yetzirah*. The knowledge contained in it could be put to use for the advancement of all mankind. He wants nothing less than to cure the incurable diseases of the world, bring peace—"

Having heard enough, Ira stood up and walked to the bookcase. He returned the book to its place.

"You're skeptical," Wendell continued. "Who wouldn't be? But if anyone can appreciate the importance of this matter, it's you."

Ira's next stop was the door. He gestured into the hallway. "I'm not trying to be rude, Mr. Wendell, but as I said, I only had a few minutes. Time's up."

"Just give it some thought," Wendell said as he exited the office.

"I don't see how it's possible such an original document could exist," Ira said, walking the man to the side door. "Where did Lagati find it?"

"You'd have to ask him. He hasn't shared with me the details."

Ira merely shook his head as he opened the side door. He squinted at the sunlight brightening up the entrance.

Before leaving, Wendell reached into his pocket and pulled out a white business card. He pressed it into the rabbi's open palm.

"He looks forward to hearing from you." Wendell flashed one final smile, then walked away.

Once Wendell had turned the corner, Ira looked down at the card. The only writing was a small phone number printed in the top right-hand corner of plain white cardstock.

Ira let the door close behind him.

TWO

Zurich, Switzerland

SEPTEMBER 4

Emery Wörtlich was disappointed. At this point in his career, he would have expected more than a half-empty lecture hall. And if this class went anything like the ones preceding it, the numbers would dwindle to a mere handful by the time he presented his more controversial theories. If he had learned anything as a professor, it was that students couldn't be bothered to think for themselves anymore.

If I change even one mind, it will be worth it. Of course, he would have preferred to change several hundred at a time.

"Good evening," Wörtlich said, a slight German accent clipping the edges of his words. He unzipped his bag and pulled out a laptop, placing it softly on the lectern. He double-clicked on his presentation file and turned back to the class as the screen lit up.

Sadness once again took hold as he counted the number of empty seats between filled ones.

"Today we look at the Giza pyramids," he said. "You are all graduate students, so you think you know everything there is to know, but there is probably a lot you do not... things other instructors will not tell you because they do not think they are important. But they are. Vastly important."

He opened the first slide, an overhead view of the pyramids. "But before we get to that, I want you to pay particular attention to the Queen's Pyramids. These smaller structures surrounding the Pyramid of Khufu are like remoras on sharks. In and of themselves they are nothing special, at least not in comparison to the pyramids, and yet their proximity alone makes them worthy of study."

He brought up a view that accentuated the difference in size between the Queen's Pyramids and the Great Pyramid. "As you can see, these were not built by the same people, certainly not contemporaries of each other. The construction of the Queen's Pyramids is so shoddy that it requires a staggering absence of intelligence to make such a leap. No joke, you must have borderline dementia to accept such a ridiculous hypothesis."

Already three people in the back were gathering their stuff. Wörtlich wasn't going to stop them. If their minds couldn't take such a basic challenge, they weren't worth his time.

"These minor pyramids all contain mummies—or rather, they did before grave robbers got to them. What I find most interesting, though, is that the main pyramids did not. Contain mummies, that is. There is very little evidence to suggest that."

He changed slides again, but before he could return to his notes, he heard a voice from the front row.

"But isn't that why the Egyptians built the pyramids in the first place? For burial?"

Surprised, Wörtlich glanced over the lectern and eyed the few students staring back at him. One of them raised her hand. She was an American; her look and accent was unmistakable.

"For one thing," Wörtlich mused, "I do not accept the premise of your question."

"That the pyramids were intended for burial?"

"Obviously. But what I mean is, the Egyptians did not build the pyramids."

Skepticism blanketed the room in an uncomfortable silence, but it was nothing he hadn't experienced a hundred times before.

Once again, the student put in her two cents. "Forgive me, sir, but that's… well, that's preposterous."

"You are forgiven."

"What he means," said another student, a man, "is that the Egyptians made the Jews build them."

Wörtlich furrowed his brow. "No, that is not what I mean, but I appreciate you putting words in my mouth. Now, I am sorry to contradict your eighth grade history textbooks, but this is a center for higher learning. If you want me to stand here and contribute to one of the longest lasting and most ridiculous lies perpetrated by modern academia—well, I regret you will have to go somewhere else for that. I hear Professor Gingrich hosts an excellent class on Fridays. If, however, you are interested in expanding your minds and hearing what I have to say, then by all means, pay attention."

He replaced the slide with a profile shot of the Great Pyramid. In the margins, he had scribbled dimensions and proportions.

"In case none of you have seen it for yourselves—and I suggest you get around to it—the Great Pyramid is monstrous. Its base alone covers thirteen acres. It contains 2.3 million stone blocks, each weighing about two and a half tons. In fact, there are a few granite blocks higher in the pyramid structure that weigh over a hundred tons. Do not ask me how they got them up there; that is a question for much later. In any event, it is a hell of a lot of stone."

He looked squarely at the American student. "If you need a point of reference, that's enough stone to build a six-foot wall all the way from New York to Los Angeles."

The student shrugged. "Couldn't they have built ramps to get the blocks up?"

"Or a pulley system," another suggested. "One of our professors even theorized that they might have built it from the inside out."

Wörtlich nodded to the second student for at least doing her homework. "Well, certainly. I suppose those theories might be possible. But what traditional sources do not often admit is that for the Great Pyramid to have been built and completed during the timeframe suggested, the reign of Pharaoh Khufu, workers would have had to move one and half stone blocks into place every hour for twenty-three years, without stopping for nights, weekends, or bathroom breaks. And remember just how heavy they were. Still are, actually."

"It could have happened. There were thousands of slaves."

"Sure! Absolutely it could have happened. Let us consider for a moment that you are right. Also consider that the pyramids embody such a wealth of mathematical know-how and precision that its builders would have needed wisdom akin to the knowledge we have today."

"The Egyptians of that period operated at the height of ancient civilization, didn't they?" someone asked.

"That is highly arguable. But it is good of you to give them the benefit of the doubt. Let us look at some specifics now, so that you, all of you, can judge for yourselves. Begin with the impressive fact that the pyramid's base is a perfect square with right angles accurate to one-twentieth of a degree. That is very precise. Also bear in mind that the sides of the pyramid, perfect equilateral triangles, face exactly north, south, east, and west. And I mean *exactly*. Now, if we take the Hebrew cubit to be 25.025 inches, then astonishingly we find that the length of each side of the base is 365.2422 cubits. Does that number sound familiar to anyone?"

Wörtlich gave them a chance to weigh in. Truth be told, he was delighted that this group at least had the gumption to speak up.

"That's about the same number of days in a year," someone answered.

"No," Wörtlich said forcefully. "It is the *precise* number of days in a year, including the fraction that accounts for leap years. These builders placed a premium on precision, no? Is any of this starting to sound unlikely? In case there are any skeptics left in the room, and there always are, the numbers get even more interesting. Very juicy. If we multiply twice the length of a side, at the base, by the total height, at the apex—which is 232.52 cubits—we get pi. To within five decimal places! I must say, that is not bad for six-thousand-year-old Egyptians."

"Okay, I get it," the first student admitted. "It's weird."

Wörtlich rubbed his hands together excitedly. "And just to, how do you say, 'make the deal sweet,' bear in mind that the Great Pyramid stands at the precise center of the world, longitudinally between the west coast of Mexico and the east coast of China, and latitudinally between the northernmost coast of Norway and the Cape of Good Hope in South Africa. The Egyptians could not possibly have made such a calculation, what with not having discovered the existence of the Far East or the Americas. You cannot make this stuff up. If the

Egyptians were so damned precise, why did the Queen's Pyramids cave in on themselves after a few centuries while the greater pyramids continue to stand after several millennia?

"Now, Professor Gingrich and most of his peers would chalk all this up to coincidence, one piled upon another. But since I actually understand a thing or two about math, I know better. The odds of that happening are astronomical. I mean, truly and unfathomably massive."

When he paused, the class was silent. Wörtlich was pleased to note that he hadn't lost any more people since the beginning of his tirade. He couldn't help but smile. He hid it by looking down and changing the slide again.

"So, to summarize what you have just heard, these builders had access to knowledge beyond the scope of their worldview. They somehow intuited that the planet was a globe, flattened at the poles, and also seemed to know its rate of rotation, not to mention the 23.5 degree tilt of its axis. And of course, they knew the precise number of days required for the Earth to orbit the sun. But I am sure all that is *coincidental*. After all, the Egyptians just barely had a firm grasp on the wheel."

He returned the slide to the opening photo and waited for the inevitable response. Sure enough, they didn't disappoint.

"So who *did* build the pyramids?"

Wörtlich smiled crookedly and closed the lid of his laptop.

"Finally, a good question."

*   *   *

Outside the university, the jagged peaks of the Alps stood silhouetted against the night sky between an array of dancing stars and the Zurich skyline. Wörtlich didn't have time to admire the view, though. He let the door close behind him and crossed the walkway from the faculty entrance to the parking lot, pausing only to answer his phone.

"Yes?"

"You need to come out of retirement," a man's voice announced.

Wörtlich narrowed his eyes and stole a look back toward the faculty building. There was nobody there, and a quick scan of the windows didn't reveal any peeping Toms. "Who is this?"

"You don't recognize my voice?"

"I do not care for guessing games." And then it came to him. "Noam Sheply?"

Sheply laughed on the other end. "Of course! Sorry for the late hour, Emery, but I just got back to Cairo."

"Sounds like you are in a good mood. Got back from where?"

"Italy," Sheply said. "Are you sitting down?"

Wörtlich unlocked his car and swung open the driver's side door. "No, should I be?"

"I really think you should."

The German man sighed and lowered the phone just long enough to toss his things onto the passenger seat. He sat down with his legs still swung out the side. "Okay, what is this great news big enough to bring me out of retirement?"

Across the lot, a couple walked toward their car, the only other vehicle left in the lot.

"Emery, they've found the index to the Library of Alexandria."

Wörtlich peered once more at the passing couple, then closed his door for privacy. He instinctively looked into his rearview mirror to make sure there was nobody else nearby. He leaned back in the seat and let out a long whistle.

"They're busy confirming the dates of the scrolls now," Sheply went on, "but so far it looks like mid to late 40s B.C."

Wörtlich nodded to himself. "The Caesar conquests."

"Exactly."

"Where were they found?"

"The Villa of the Papyri in Herculaneum. I just got back from the site."

"You are certain this is authentic?"

"Absolutely certain," Sheply confirmed. "There's no way this could be faked. The room where it was found has been sealed shut since the time of Christ."

Wörtlich shifted the phone to his other ear while he fished through his bag for a pad of paper. Pulling a pen out of his shirt pocket, he jotted down the details of the discovery. *Herculaneum. Caesar conquests. Late 40s B.C.*

"Emery, they're just starting to open the index scrolls. There's more than three dozen of them so far. Three dozen!"

Wörtlich's pen hovered over the top of the paper, his eyes still focused on the couple getting into their car. The woman laughed while the man opened the door for her.

"Are there any new clues about the pyramid builders?" he asked.

Sheply hesitated. "I don't know, yet."

Wörtlich turned the key in the ignition and capped his pen. Dropping the pad next to him, he flicked off the overhead light.

"I need you in Cairo," Sheply said. "I realize you're in mid-session at the university, but I could really use your expertise."

Wörtlich allowed himself a smile just thinking about it. "A lot of people at the Institute would not be happy to see me back."

"You've earned a place at this table a hundred times over."

And then some. "I have no classes until Monday. I can be on a plane first thing in the morning."

Wörtlich took a deep breath as he closed the phone. His heart raced. His first instinct was to drive straight to the airport, but logic told him to play it cool. But the index! If it was true, it would provide a more comprehensive picture of the Ptolemaic period than anyone had dared hope for. He thought he had given up Egypt for good, but now…

Maybe I walked away too quickly.

Of course, this wouldn't be the first time he was guilty of that.

THREE

Washington, D.C.
SEPTEMBER 4

A subway car pulled into the crowded metro platform. Its doors slid open, making room for people to get on and off under the white and gray tiled concrete of the station's arched ceiling. Sherwood Brighton slung a computer bag over his shoulder and stepped through the automatic sliding doors. He took the escalator stairs two at a time to find the sun pounding down on the National Mall. He dug a hand into the front pocket of his bag and pulled out a pair of sunglasses as he took a right toward Jefferson Drive.

Brighton broke into a jog, sidestepping pedestrians as he came to the rectangular lawn separating the Museum of Natural History from the Smithsonian Building—or "the Castle," as it was affectionately known. The Castle's red sandstone, thirteenth-century European design stood out from the surrounding architecture. Its two crimson turrets punctured the blue sky like devil's horns.

He hurried up the front steps, passing under the watchful stone eyes of former Secretary of the Smithsonian Joseph Henry. Brighton gave the statue a wink, invisible under his glasses, as he headed through the front doors, fastening an ID clip to the lapel of his jacket.

A minute later, Brighton steered straight down the middle of the basement bullpen. He was focused on his own cubicle when a strong hand grabbed him by the left shoulder. He spun around to find his friend, Alan, keeping pace beside him.

"Alan," Brighton said, not slowing down. "I'm late, so—"

"Haven't seen you in a while," Alan said.

Brighton shrugged, taking a turn and heading toward an elevator. "They kept me in New Mexico a few extra days to finish mapping the Sulaweyo dig."

"I thought you were in Utah. I was trying to figure out what you'd done to make them send you there." Alan pulled out his phone and checked the time. "You heading upstairs?"

Brighton patted his computer bag. "They're waiting for me."

"Better hurry the hell up!"

They arrived at the elevator. Brighton hit the button next to the arrow pointing up, and the doors slid apart.

"Hey, drop by again after your meeting," Alan said. "Something came in last week that I've been dying to show you."

Brighton flashed him a thumbs-up as the doors closed.

He got off on the fourth floor, a part of the building he rarely saw. A receptionist held court over an empty waiting room. He approached her desk, tapping his fingers anxiously on the raised wooden ledge, waiting for her to get off the phone. Behind her, a long hallway faded back toward a series of rooms he'd never been in before.

"You have an appointment?" the receptionist asked.

Brighton blinked. "I'm Sherwood Brighton."

She picked up the receiver again and held it to her ear.

"He's here," she said, then hung up and returned to work. She didn't spare him another glance. Confused, Brighton didn't know whether to take a seat or continue standing when a loud, familiar voice carried down the hallway.

"Mr. Brighton!"

Peering up, he found himself looking into the eyes of an elderly Japanese man who, if he remembered correctly, was about twenty years older than he looked.

"Professor Kannasaki?"

Kannasaki waved him back. "We're waiting for you. Come on."

Brighton stepped around the desk and followed his old college professor.

He saw at least ten or twelve offices on either side of the corridor as they headed for the one at the back.

"I haven't seen you since graduation," Brighton managed to say. "I guess that's three years now."

"Just because you haven't seen me doesn't mean I ceased to exist."

Brighton flushed. "Of course. I just meant that—"

"Every once in a while, these guys call me in to consult," Kannasaki said, shrugging. "You didn't think my professor's salary paid for that house in Pasadena, did you?"

The younger man smirked. "Chalk it up to that eternal optimism you always saw in me. I can't believe you've been working for the Smithsonian all this time and I didn't know it."

"The director and I go back a long way. Didn't you think it was a little strange when she hired you without a second interview?"

Brighton hesitated, not quite sure how to respond to that.

"Don't worry," Kannasaki said. "You still earned it. Sometimes these guys just need a little help recognizing a good thing."

Together, they turned and entered the last room on the hall. He found himself standing in the director's office. Doctor Regina Holloway, a tall woman with auburn hair and piercing blue eyes that exuded confidence, waited for them behind the desk.

As if the director wasn't imposing enough, the window behind her offered a spectacular southern view of the garden stretching toward Independence Avenue. Brighton shifted his weight under her penetrating stare.

"Take seats, gentlemen," Holloway said.

Only then did he notice the other men off to his left, also waiting for him to say or do something important. Brighton slipped into a chair near the door, hoping his presentation wasn't the first order of business.

It was.

"Mr. Brighton, you're the man of the hour." Holloway navigated around the desk and leaned against the wall. "You brought your work?"

"Yes, ma'am," he said, standing again but hanging back.

"Well, plug it up and let's take a look."

Brighton picked up his bag and carried it to the front. He connected his computer to the projector cable coiled up on one of Holloway's office chairs.

Before he began the presentation, Holloway said, "Doctor Sulaweyo had nothing but good things to say in his weekly logs—"

"Thank you, ma'am, I always appreciate a good word."

A short pause followed in which Brighton noticed Kannasaki

lowering his eyes to the floor. Doctor Holloway was smiling ironically. "I wasn't trying to flatter you, Mr. Brighton," she said in a deadpan. "If you'd have let me finish, I was going to say that Doctor Sulaweyo had nothing but good things to say about the progress of his excavation." She paused just long enough for Brighton to melt into his proverbial shoes.

"Of course," she went on, "I'm sure your personal contributions were exemplary as well. Even though he failed to single them out." By this time, Brighton was turning a discernible shade of red.

"Don't be embarrassed," she added. "Just show us what you came here for."

Brighton's eyes connected with Kannasaki's, which looked back encouragingly. Brighton popped open his mapping program.

"My task was to digitally map the position of artifacts against those reported three years ago, accounting for differing soil compositions. Using this data, we were able to accurately predict the location of two new burial sites just east of the main dig. Since these are untouched, we expect they'll yield a far better range of samples than anything we've found from this particular tribe before." He magnified a section of the screen displaying the new area. "The, uh—the full schematics are included in your briefing packs. So, I'll take any questions now, if you have them."

The group opened their folders to look through the material, and Brighton settled in for a protracted Q&A.

*   *   *

Three hours later, Brighton was back in the elevator, waiting for it to whisk him to the safe, welcoming anonymity of the bullpen.

"Room for one more?"

Kannasaki slipped inside just as the doors closed. The elevator gave a short jerk before descending.

Brighton hung his head. "I can't believe I did that."

"A healthy dose of ego helps you more than it hurts you in this business. You probably managed to endear yourself to them. Now, if the work had been subpar, that would be a different story. But seeing as you're completely brilliant—"

"Good to know."

"I'm glad I ran into you today. Have you heard anything about a Swiss company called Creation Tech?"

Brighton pondered the name for a few moments, drawing a blank. "Don't think so. Why?"

"They seem to have your Caltech records," Kannasaki said. "I'm not sure why they're interested in you specifically, but they are."

"Maybe it's a job offer?" Brighton asked hopefully.

"Could be. The man I spoke to said his name was Wendell. If they haven't talked to you yet, I'd be on the lookout."

The doors opened to the bullpen and Brighton disembarked.

"Thanks for the heads up, Professor."

"It's the least I could do. Let me know if you find out what kind of work they're doing."

Brighton nodded. "Of course."

The doors closed on the professor, taking him back upstairs.

Alan fell into step beside Brighton as he made his way into the heart of the cubicles.

"You said there's something you want to show me?" Brighton asked.

Alan's face brightened. "You're gonna love this. Follow me." He changed direction.

Feeling tired, Brighton waited a minute before heading after him. "Where are we going?"

"The archive room," Alan called over his shoulder.

When they got to the archive room, a young woman was at the computer controls with her back to them. Alan sat next to her.

"Hey, Sarah," Alan said. "Pull up that picture you sent me last Friday."

Sarah thought for a minute. "You mean the giant?"

"Yeah."

Sarah bit her lip and opened a search window, digital thumbnails flashing across the screen as she scrolled through the results. Brighton took the third chair and sat next to her. She noticed him out of the corner of her eye and trotted out a smile.

"Hey, Sherwood."

Brighton smiled halfheartedly. "What's this about, anyway?"

"Just… wait… one… second…" Sarah murmured.

"Seriously, man," Alan said. "It speaks for itself."

Finally finding what she was looking for, Sarah clicked on a file and waited for the photo to fill the screen. At first, Brighton didn't know what he was looking at. He leaned forward and narrowed his eyes.

"Holy mother of—" He glanced sidelong at Alan.

Alan merely threw him a look that said *I told you so.*

On the monitor was a picture of a full-grown, bearded man standing in what appeared to be a grassy meadow. Right next to him, leaning up against an earthen embankment, was a bone—a femur bone, by the looks of it. But the bone itself was about a foot and a half taller than the man next to it.

Brighton glanced at Alan. "You can't be serious."

"Nah," Alan said. "Apparently one of the photo guys on the third floor found some digital manipulation between the bearded man and the bone. The scale is all wrong."

"Hard to believe, though," Sarah said. "I'm pretty good at figuring out which ones are real and which ones aren't. This looks pretty real to me."

"Well, as far as hoaxes go, it's elaborate," Alan said. "I dunno, this is, like, art or something. Whoever did it should get an award. I mean, there's photoshopping, and then there's *this*."

Brighton turned back to the picture and continued studying it.

"No way, guys," he said quietly, leaning close enough that he could make out the individual pixels. "This is real."

Sarah laughed, giving his hair an affectionate tousle. "Haven't you been listening to a word—"

"No, seriously. I don't know who debunked this, but…"

Brighton reached for the keyboard and isolated a section of image where the edge of the bone overlapped with the man's shoulder.

"Look at where the layers would have to overlap," he said, pointing to the shoulder area. He scrolled down to the bottom of the photo, looking at another section. "Nobody's this good. I've seen my share of hoaxes, but this isn't one of them."

"I don't know what to tell you, man." Alan stood up and stretched. "You're wrong this time."

Sarah frowned. "Sherwood, think about it. If this femur bone was real, the person would have been over thirty feet tall."

"At first we thought maybe it was a dinosaur bone," Alan said, "some species we'd never heard of. But it looks human to me. If the photo's legit, maybe the bone itself is manufactured or something, made out of wood and sanded down. People get into all kinds of creative hokum for publicity."

"I just think—" Brighton stopped himself, then pushed his chair back and stood. He walked to the door. "Okay."

Alan peered at him quizzically. "Okay, what?"

"Okay, you're right." Brighton waved goodbye to Sarah, then made his way back out into the bullpen.

Alan hurried to catch up. "So, you're dropping this?"

"Yup."

"And that's it. You're just going to walk away."

"Sure am."

"You feeling all right? This isn't like you."

"Hmm?"

"The way you just stopped arguing with me, like I'd somehow convinced you. I've never managed to convince you of anything you hadn't already made up your mind about."

Brighton rounded a corner into his cubicle and put down his computer bag. "And that isn't going to change today."

Alan smacked him on the back and grinned from ear to ear. "I knew it."

Brighton lowered his voice and leaned in confidentially. "I want you to send me a copy of that picture. You can do that, right?"

"I think it may have already been leaked on the web."

Brighton shook his head. "I want the original. The high-res one."

"Okay. Uh, what for?"

He slipped his hand into the bag, pulled out the sunglasses again, and dropped them over his eyes. "Because it's cool. Isn't that reason enough?"

*   *   *

Sitting at an outdoor café overlooking Fourteenth Street, Brighton stared at his laptop screen. The more he studied the picture Alan had sent over, the more surprising it became.

"Hey, you looking at porn?"

Brighton's eyes shot up as his girlfriend, Rachel, walked around behind him and gave him a hug. "What? I—"

"Just never saw you look at anything on a computer screen with that much... intensity... that wasn't porn."

"It's not..." Brighton turned to give her a quick kiss. By moving his head, she was treated to a full-on view of the photo. She made a disgusted face.

"Good god! That's not porn."

"As I tried to tell you. Normally I'm not supposed to take stuff like this out of the office. I mean, they're pretty anal about security, but I had to show you..."

He looked up to see the waiter approaching. Rachel went around the table and pulled out the chair across from him, the sun catching her long blond hair. She picked up the drink menu, then discarded it.

"We'll need a few minutes," Brighton told the waiter. "Thanks."

He eyed the waiter until he was out of earshot, then picked up the computer and adjusted the screen so Rachel could see, too.

"You gotta check this out," he told her. "It's just nuts."

"Sherwood, that's disgusting."

"Well, yeah, it's probably a few thousand years old."

"That bone is freaking massive." She was unable to take her eyes off it. "It's not real, is it? I mean, it's not human."

"Alan showed it to me this morning. Supposedly it came in last week but the photo analysts debunked it." Then with a scoff, he added, "Said it was a fake."

"You don't think it is?"

"Because it isn't. The only person good enough to make something like this... well, baby, you're looking at him."

"That's my boy, so modest." Rachel pursed her lips into a cute smile and reached across to give him another kiss. "So, how do you explain it? I mean, you're the one who can do math in his head, but that guy would have been, like, I dunno—twenty feet tall!"

"More like thirty."

She nodded, giving the table a mild thump with her fist. "Yeah, so explain that."

"I can't. The guys threw this out way too fast. Don't you think it's a crime against archaeology not to investigate it?"

The waiter returned to take their lunch order. They again waited for him to leave before returning to the subject.

"I could make some extra cash off this," Brighton mused.

"Oh?"

"Sure. I could dig into it a little, get the real story. Publish it somewhere. I don't care what anyone says, there's something here. Something interesting."

"So you'd do it for the money?" Rachel asked.

Brighton tilted his head, twisting his mouth into a sneer. "No, I'd do it for the good of all humanity."

All he got out of her was a dramatic eye roll.

"Of course I'd do it for the money. I'd love to take a few months off, not work for a while. Or at least, only do the work I wanted to. You can't put a price on that."

"And yet isn't that exactly what you're trying to do?"

"Whatever."

Brighton looked off over her shoulder. A man across the street from them caught his eye. He didn't seem to be walking, didn't seem to be going anywhere. In fact, he was staring right at them.

A shiver ran through Brighton as he subtly gave Rachel's hand a little tap. "Don't look now, babe, but that guy down the street is totally stalking us."

Rachel swiveled to check it out. "What guy?"

He grabbed her hand to get her attention back. "Don't look!"

"How am I supposed to know who he is if I don't look?"

"I don't know," he said. "I guess it doesn't matter so long as he goes away and leaves us alone."

But the man didn't make any move to leave. His back was to the wall of a nearby building and he had a hand in his pocket. Before Brighton could react, the stranger started toward them, waiting for a lull in traffic to cross the street.

"Oh God, here he comes," Rachel moaned. "You know him or something?"

"Never seen him before in my life."

A minute later, the man approached them from the sidewalk. Rachel did her best to ignore him, but soon the man stood just a few feet away. He stopped outside the fence separating the patio from the sidewalk and cleared his throat.

"Sherwood Brighton?" he asked.

Brighton stiffened. "That's me."

The man held out his hand for Brighton to shake.

"I was hoping we could have a word?" His eyes darted to Rachel, who was watching him suspiciously. "Alone would be best."

"Listen, man," Brighton said, "I'm having lunch with my girlfriend. Who the hell are you?"

"The name's Wendell. I know about that picture you saw today, and I know where it came from."

Brighton's confusion intensified.

"Of course," Wendell added, "I might have the wrong man."

Wendell turned to go, but Brighton pushed back his chair.

"Just a minute," he said to Rachel before hopping over the fence and onto the sidewalk. Once he and Wendell had moved far enough that they wouldn't be overheard, they stopped.

"I'm the guy you're looking for," Brighton said. "Are you from Creation Tech? What do you know about that picture?"

Wendell slipped a business card out of his jacket pocket. "Call the number and we'll talk."

Brighton looked at the card. There was no name, no address; just a phone number. Before he could ask any more questions, Wendell disappeared into a group of tourists.

Lunch was waiting when he got back to the table.

"Well, that was creepy," Rachel said before taking a bite of her salad. "You're not going to call him, are you?"

Brighton's gaze shifted to the picture still on his laptop monitor. He tried in vain to make some connection between the bizarre image and the mystery man. He shrugged it off and picked up his sandwich.

"Of course not," he said. "You can't call every crazy guy who gives you a business card."

Satisfied, Rachel turned her attention back to her food, but Brighton couldn't help stealing a glance down the road where Wendell had disappeared.

FOUR

Fair Haven, Vermont
SEPTEMBER 4

I ra tried to shake the apprehension he felt every time his mind returned to his encounter with Wendell. As preposterous as the man's claim about Raff Lagati's discovery was, a part of him took it seriously. Wendell had known exactly what to say and hinted at just enough of Ira's private research to pique his curiosity. Still, he couldn't help feeling manipulated.

The day after Wendell's visit, Ira placed two calls. The first was to a close friend in New York City, Lawrence Hoffman. The second was to locate a colleague he hadn't spoken to in many years, a man who could hardly be called a friend. Yet Ira hoped there was still some vestige of respect between them.

Aaron Roth was an elderly man, well into his nineties by now. Even though they hadn't been in touch in nearly ten years, Ira knew Aaron still lived; he would have heard otherwise, such was Aaron's prominence in the rabbinical community. The man had been a force to be reckoned with, and Ira hoped that hadn't changed—some things never did.

The last time they'd seen each other, Ira had openly opposed Aaron's decision to remain in his teaching position at their seminary. After training under him for nearly twenty years, it had been a harsh parting gift, one Ira still regretted. Ira had thought he had done the old man a favor by making public Aaron's privately expressed desire to return to a life of pure research, but in truth it had been an act of betrayal. When Ira was offered Aaron's position the following semester, he felt too guilty to take it and instead left the school altogether.

Ira missed his former mentor. Nobody else possessed the old man's wisdom or judged a situation as objectively. Ira didn't know how to approach Aaron after all these years. But Ira needed him now, more than ever.

*　　*　　*

The two hundred mile drive to Fair Haven, Vermont took Ira a little over three hours, but it was time well-spent as long as he got the chance to speak with Aaron. Just past the Vermont state line, he pulled into a gas station parking lot to wait for Lawrence to arrive at their prearranged meeting point. According to Lawrence, Aaron had a house in the nearby countryside.

A half hour later, he and Lawrence wound their way up through the hills. Somehow it didn't surprise Ira that the old man had found such a remote spot in which to settle down; he had always seemed out of place in the city.

Aaron's house, when they found it, was large and whitewashed. A veranda enclosed the square, colonial-era home. The porch light illuminated a path that led from the driveway and up the wooden steps.

"What did you say when you called ahead?" Lawrence asked before getting out of the car.

Ira hesitated. "I didn't call."

Lawrence's shoulders dropped. Even into his sixties, his friend hadn't mastered the art of keeping his surprise in check. "Why not?"

"I couldn't risk him turning us away."

"You mean turning *you* away. I never did anything to the man."

Ira pushed open the car door and stepped outside. The night was cool for early September. A bite in the air portended the coming of winter.

"What are you going to say?" Lawrence asked, his eyes drilling into Ira. He could be intimidating when he chose. Ira had joked that if he hadn't become a rabbi, he would have made a great CIA interrogator.

"Something will come to me."

The wooden deck boards had a bit of bounce to them. They let out a tired groan each time Ira took a step.

A shadow passed momentarily over the white curtain covering the door's lone window, alerting them to the fact that someone waited on the other side. Before Ira could reach his hand up to knock, the door's hinges swung inward, revealing a young man in his thirties.

Ira marveled at how much the man looked like his grandfather. The eyes and nose were exactly as he remembered them, except on a different, younger face. Ira could imagine this was exactly what Aaron had looked like in his prime. He also felt a moment's pain that he would never have a grandchild of his own.

"David? David Roth?" Ira asked.

"You're here to see my grandfather." David held the door open for them. "He mentioned you were coming."

Lawrence glanced sidelong at Ira as they stepped into the front hall. Ira kept his eyes down as he slipped off his shoes. His friend shut the door behind them.

"Let me see if he's up," David said and bounded up a flight of stairs.

Once he was out of the room, Lawrence turned his piercing eyes back on Ira. "I thought you said you didn't call ahead."

"I didn't."

Ira's head swung back at the sound of descending footsteps. David was halfway down the stairs when he beckoned for them to follow.

They were taken to a square sitting room on the second floor, each of its walls sporting a door. The one to their left stood slightly ajar, and David gestured for them to go inside.

The first thing that struck Ira when he entered the room was the sheer volume of books. Dark wooden shelves covered three of the walls, each packed with books of all shapes and sizes. Most bore Hebrew lettering on their spines.

In the middle of the library sat an old man, hunched over with a book in his hands. His full gray beard softened his otherwise bony features, allowing him to come across as grandfatherly as opposed to merely stern. He looked up over half-moon reading glasses as the two men entered. If Ira had expected the man's eyes to be dimmed by age, he was surprised to see them as sharp and lively as he remembered from the old days.

The man's remarkably well-preserved, as though he hasn't aged a day. For all I know, maybe he hasn't.

"So, this is the meeting God told me about," Aaron said in a quiet yet commanding voice. Reacting to the surprised look on Lawrence's face, Aaron balked. "What, he doesn't talk to you?" He sighed, peering back at Ira. "You know, Ira, I would like to have heard from you sooner."

"I didn't know how you would receive me."

"Perhaps I was angry, once. I can hardly remember why. These last years have been good to me." Aaron gestured for them to take seats. Then the old man's eyes landed on Lawrence. "Who's this?"

"Lawrence Hoffman."

"I teach at Yeshiva University," Lawrence added. "But you... quite frankly, I've heard a lot about you."

Aaron cracked a smile. "That tends to happen when you're nearly a hundred years old. I hope my word of mouth is positive."

"It certainly is," Lawrence assured him. "I've read everything you ever wrote. Your name still carries a lot of weight, at least in the circles I run in."

"Then he's one of us," Aaron said softly, his glance falling warmly on Ira. "You trust this man?"

"I do."

"Then I do as well."

The old man reached for a glass of water on the lampstand next to his chair and took a long sip. He closed his book and set it aside.

"Why don't we get this council underway?" Aaron said. "You obviously have something on your mind, Ira. I'd like to know what it is."

"I had a visitor after service today," Ira said. "He was asking some suspicious questions."

"What do you mean, suspicious?"

"Questions about us. About what we used to be, about our old pursuits. He also asked about the *Sefer Yetzirah*. I wouldn't have thought much of that, but..." Ira paused, looking for the right word.

"The only word I can use is *heavy*. I've been feeling heavy all day, as though his very presence was somehow dangerous. I can't put my finger on it. In fact, he was entirely pleasant. But there was something underneath his smile. I would hesitate to call it darkness, but—"

"Surely this isn't the first time you've gotten questions about the *Sefer Yetzirah*," Lawrence remarked. "I've taught from it many times, though I don't think my students understand it any better now than they did before I opened my mouth on the subject."

Ira rubbed the bridge of his nose. "He knew things about what we tried to accomplish, Aaron. I don't know how. All of our old meetings were kept secret." He cleared his throat. "And then this man claimed to be visiting on behalf of Raff Lagati."

"I don't suppose there are two Raff Lagatis," Aaron mused, tapping his finger methodically on his leather armrest. There was no surprise in his voice. Perhaps weariness, but no surprise.

"Just the one." Ira took a long, deep breath. "The man who came to see me—his name was Wendell—told me something impossible. Apparently, Lagati has come into possession of an original copy of the *Sefer Yetzirah*. One written by Abraham himself."

Upon mention of Abraham, Aaron's tapping stopped and he furrowed his thick eyebrows.

"He also claims it's somehow different from the translations we have today," Ira added. "Undiluted, he called it."

When Aaron spoke, his voice was gravelly. "It's a lie, of course."

Ira nodded. "That was my first reaction, too. But I don't know why he would lie about this."

"He must want something from you," Lawrence surmised.

"He wants a meeting. He wants me to help translate his find." Ira paused again, his eyes resting on Aaron's glass. His mouth dried up. "I'm sorry, Aaron, but could I have something to drink?"

"Oh, of course! David!" After a moment, David appeared at the door. "Could you bring my guests something to drink? Water is fine."

His grandson nodded and ducked back out, later returning to hand both men a glass of their own.

"Thank you," Ira said, taking a few short sips.

Once David had left the room again, Aaron prodded, "Raff Lagati wants your help."

"Of course, I'm not going to do it." Ira expected some sort of reaction from the others, but they seemed content to sit in silence. "Even if his claim is true, the *Sefer Yetzirah* is one of the sacred texts! It would be anathema to everything we stand for to help an outsider get his hands on it—which is one of the reasons you and I started meeting fifteen years ago. Books like these must be protected from the wickedness of all men."

Lawrence nodded. "Indeed. You can't help him acquire or decode the book, assuming it exists at all. Which I doubt. No matter his motives, that information is too dangerous to fall into his hands."

"I'm glad we're in agreement," Ira said, relieved that at least one of them shared his conclusion.

Aaron grunted quietly. "I concur. And yet you must take the meeting."

"Surely I can't!"

"But you have to," the old man countered. "The only way to know that Lagati has nothing is to confirm it."

"And if it's real?"

Aaron raised his eyebrows as though the answer was obvious. "Then it's all the more important to be there and take appropriate action. I know this isn't what you wanted to hear, Ira, but it is the right thing to do."

Defeated, Ira couldn't argue. As much as he wished Aaron was wrong, his advice was, as usual, right on the money.

"Imagine the value of an original *Sefer Yetzirah*," Lawrence said. "It would be beyond anything we've ever hoped. It would be absolutely reliable."

"And absolutely dangerous!" Ira reminded them. "The trouble, if Mr. Wendell is any indication, is that Lagati seems to have a good idea of the power described in the book, and an accurate appreciation of what it could mean for him. It may only be a matter of time before he pursues it outright, for his own purposes—and those purposes aren't half as altruistic as he would claim. Whatever he's after, it's not the betterment of mankind."

Ira looked from one man to the other and found nothing but grim agreement. His heart sank, heaviness once again setting in.

Aaron leaned forward and placed his frail hand on top of Ira's arm. "There is only one thing we *can* do. In your heart, you know what it is."

He's right, just like I knew he would be. If he had said anything else, I would have been surprised. This is what I came to hear.

But was it? As Aaron withdrew his hand, Ira sank back into the chair, looking away. Of all the rabbis Lagati could have approached, it seemed both lucky and strangely unnerving that he'd chosen him.

An overwhelming sadness came over Ira as his eyes returned to Aaron. He couldn't believe he had waited such a long time to come back. If he had known there was no conflict left between them—

But I did know.

"I'm sorry," Ira whispered.

Aaron said nothing, tilting his head as though he hadn't quite heard correctly.

"I'm sorry," he repeated. "What I did ten years ago was wrong. I sacrificed a friend… I sacrificed you, Aaron, and for what? For nothing. Except here you are, behaving as though nothing amiss happened."

"As far as I'm concerned, nothing did," Aaron said, his smile like a warm embrace.

"I don't deserve your forgiveness."

"Perhaps not." The old man thumped his hand firmly on Ira's knee. "But from time to time we get better than we deserve. I wish you the best of luck, my friend, though I suspect luck has little to do with it."

Ira put his glass aside and stood. "I'll let you know what happens."

"Of course, I don't have to tell you to be careful."

Lawrence stood as well, shaking Aaron's hand as Ira walked to the door. Ira could sense the old man's gaze burning into his back.

With a newfound sense of resolve, Ira left the room with precisely the thing he had come for.

FIVE

Cairo, Egypt
SEPTEMBER 5

They've found the index to the Library of Alexandria.

The words echoed through Wörtlich's mind. The more he replayed them, the more indistinct they became, the syllables bleeding into each other and growing incoherent, like the way sound carries underwater, slow and protracted.

Another of Sheply's bombshells joined the chorus. *You need to come out of retirement.*

But his career was over, wasn't it?

As he sat on the plane, staring forlornly into the back of the seat in front of him, Wörtlich laughed, drawing the notice of the young man across the aisle. He couldn't help himself. The visual of his career somehow rising from the dead in the manner of a B-movie zombie was funny—and disconcertingly hard to shake.

"Sir, your seatbelt."

Wörtlich refocused on the orange and red seatbelt light glowing brightly on the bulkhead above. He managed a smile and waited for the attendant to move on.

Three years ago, he had been nominated to the European Council of Antiquities, which would have secured him a powerful voice at the Cairo Institute. The nomination was the most exciting development of his long career in archaeology, the culmination of years of tireless work to which he had lost two wives, a father, and a stepson. The sacrifice had always seemed worth it.

Wörtlich was a truth seeker, always had been and always would be. Unfortunately, the trail of facts had led him in a decidedly different direction than the rest of the pack. The deeper he dug, the more evidence he discovered to support an unpopular truth: the ancient Egyptians weren't the ingenious masterminds that modern archaeology gave them credit for being. Somewhere along the line, they'd received some outside assistance in building their society; they hadn't done it on their own.

The key to understanding the nature of this influence lay in discovering who had built the pyramids. Perhaps aliens? Wörtlich couldn't rule out the possibility, at least not scientifically, but certainly there was no reliable data to substantiate a claim apart from the inconclusive, vaguely UFO-shaped inscriptions on some monuments and temples.

Wörtlich had a better theory, one that had been balked at by each and every person he had shared it with.

Perhaps the source of the influence was nothing short of the Egyptian gods themselves. Perhaps they had been real, flesh and blood creatures who walked among the Egyptians, guiding their steps and building a religion that would endure for centuries. Perhaps the myths and stories were literal, and one could mine historical accuracies from the ancient books and writings. But if this was the case, where had these so-called gods come from? And where had they gone?

He realized with a start that the plane was in the air. How had he completely missed takeoff? He looked down through the window, where craggy mountains peeked snow-covered heads through the clouds that hugged and obscured them.

That damn paper, he recalled. Why had he had to publish that damn paper? To say it had become infamous would be a colossal understatement. The lightning speed at which his nomination had been yanked would have been something to marvel at had it not been so spiteful.

Looking back, maybe the whole ordeal shouldn't have caught him so flatfooted, but he hadn't taken into account how stodgy and immovable his colleagues had become. The facts didn't seem to matter; he had been laughed out of every meaningful project at the Institute within a month. So, while he'd technically taken an early retirement, for all intents and purposes he had been forced out. The treatment still made him angry.

But the index to the Great Library—that was easy to get excited about. The words alone sounded like something out of a fairy tale. The rational part of his mind assumed some mistake had been made, a phenomenal misunderstanding. In a few days, it would surely turn out to be a false alarm, the random misfiring of a computer algorithm.

Or it could be real. That was the scariest possibility. Throughout his career, he had looked for facts and followed them wherever they led, even to his own detriment. Especially there.

Why do I want to go back to the Institute?

He had promised himself not to return until he could prove once and for all that he'd been right all along, and not one day sooner. It occurred to him that the key was somewhere in the library index. He could hardly imagine the quantity of new information that would soon flow through the scientific community. He had to make sure nothing was missed, that every piece of evidence was carefully weighed. With a whole library of new material, there would be a strong temptation in the establishment to squelch anything that didn't line up with the accepted view of history.

He sat up straight, pulled down the tray, and accepted the styrofoam cup of coffee the attendant offered him.

Then there was the more terrifying possibility, that some new piece of evidence could concretely disprove what he had lost everything to bring to light. He couldn't bear to be wrong, not after all he'd gone through.

Wörtlich finished his coffee and stuffed a napkin into the empty cup. He reclined his chair as far as it would go and closed his eyes.

He was quite sure he wasn't wrong.

*   *   *

From the moment Noam Sheply returned to Cairo from Herculaneum, the Institute was abuzz with speculation about what had been discovered there. Researchers of all stripes jockeyed for positions on the translation teams or Sheply's Alexandria excavation. Sheply himself couldn't have been more thrilled. In addition to being associated with a find of such magnitude, he enjoyed having the upper hand at the Institute again.

The downside was having to attend so many meetings. How he

would have loved to gather all the texts, return to Alexandria, and just go to work.

He was in just such a meeting when Emery Wörtlich peered through the window. Sheply told the others to continue without him and stepped out into the hall.

"Emery!" he called, shutting the door. "It's good to see you. You have no idea."

The two men shared a quick hug.

"If you'd like, I can set you up with an office right away," Sheply said.

Wörtlich nodded and followed Sheply down the corridor.

"You know I am too old for wild goose chases, right?" Wörtlich asked.

"You think the index is a wild goose chase?"

"I am glad to be here, really. The question is, am I ready for a project that could take five or six years to resolve, if it ever gets resolved?"

Sheply chuckled. "So, now you're enjoying the lecture circuit?"

"No, definitely not."

"That's what I figured. Anyway, I can promise this won't be a waste of your time. You'll have a substantive role."

Sheply stopped, looking both ways down the corridor. A few people got off the elevator at the end of the hall, so he swung open the door of the nearest office and held it for Wörtlich. Once inside, Sheply pulled out a couple of chairs.

"I haven't spoken to any of the teams yet," Sheply said, "but I have the go-ahead from Doctor Menefee to offer you a real position: Assistant Site Director at Alexandria."

He watched Wörtlich's expression carefully, noting the surprise around his friend's eyes. Whatever Wörtlich had expected to come of this meeting, a job offer clearly wasn't it.

"You'd have complete control of your project load," Sheply said, "with a full team at your disposal, and your pick of site assignments. In short, everything you asked for before leaving the Institute."

"Do not remind me."

"They should never have forced you out."

Wörtlich shrugged. "But they did, and I moved on. And let us not forget the reason for my departure. What about my views on Egyptian history, Noam? I know you do not agree with me, and I have not changed my mind."

Sheply fell silent. Wörtlich was right. When he was forced to leave the Institute, Sheply hadn't so much as lifted a finger in his defense.

"I don't have to agree with you to respect you," Sheply finally said. "But I always thought the facts would change your mind."

"Nobody, including you, seems to understand that it is precisely the facts that I pay attention to. If anyone should have their minds changed, it's everyone else." Wörtlich's gaze wandered out the window where the skyscrapers of the western city stood against the morning sky. "As much as I would like it, I am not the man for the job."

"Nonsense," Sheply argued. "Theories and interpretations be damned. It's facts we're after. What you make of them is your own business. Please consider the offer. Just bear in mind that I'm going to need an answer soon. I'm returning to Alexandria in the morning and I'd like it if we could go together."

The uncertainty on Wörtlich's face spoke volumes.

"Look," Sheply said, "we're both pioneers in our field, which means we can't necessarily expect to be recognized right away. Maybe not even in our own lifetimes. Just because you haven't gotten your name in any textbooks yet doesn't mean it won't happen."

Wörtlich cracked a smile. "I do not care about textbooks, Noam."

"Of course you don't."

Sheply's phone rang, startling him. He put up a finger to say he'd be right back and stepped out into the corridor to take the call. The conversation was a short one; he barely needed to let the door close behind him before he poked his head back in.

"That was the first floor," he said. "There's a walk-in, some guy who's looking for you. Said his name was Wendell. You know him?"

"No."

"Anyway, he's waiting." Instead of sitting back down, Sheply looked down the hall. He had to get back to that awful meeting. "Think about what I said, Emery. Just don't take too long."

He smiled one last time, then hurried off.

*   *   *

Wörtlich left the room mulling the name of the man Sheply had mentioned. *Wendell, Wendell, Wendell...* At the very least, keeping his mind on the strange message prevented him from having to acknowledge the awkward glances being thrown his way from familiar faces as he passed.

Only one man sat in the waiting area, and he turned his head as Wörtlich's footsteps clipped across the tile floor. He seemed to recognize the archaeologist right away.

"You are Wendell?" Wörtlich asked.

Wendell reached out and shook his hand. "You want to take a walk?"

"Why not talk right here?"

"But it's such a nice day."

Wörtlich narrowed his eyes and inclined his head toward the door.

The two didn't walk far, just across the street into a small park that edged a nearby roundabout. Through a gap between buildings, Wörtlich could make out the Nile's reflective waters.

Wendell didn't take long to get to the point, explaining that his employer was anxious to make his acquaintance.

"Why does Raff Lagati want to meet with me and not one of the hundred other more prominent Egyptologists?" Wörtlich asked.

"Lagati doesn't want just anyone. He specifically requested you. Your literal interpretations of history are going to come in handy for what he has in mind."

"Which is?"

"I'll leave that for Mr. Lagati to explain."

"Surely you cannot expect me to head all the way to Switzerland to satisfy my curiosity," Wörtlich said.

"Don't you live in Switzerland?" When Wörtlich didn't respond, Wendell added, "I looked for you there first, at the university, but I was told you'd gone to Cairo. Took me by surprise, actually. My sources tell me you left here on a bad note."

Wörtlich snorted. "Your sources, your employer, your invitation... everything about this is very vague."

"But surely you're curious?" Wendell asked. "It's up to you, of course, but Lagati has the proof you're looking for. That's all I can tell you for now."

Wörtlich stopped him. "What kind of proof?"

"Proof that would convince anyone with half a brain that you've been speaking the truth all these years."

"I did not believe anyone was listening."

Wendell pulled out a business card. "Lagati hears everything. Call the number once you've had some time to consider his offer, and we'll set something up."

With that, Wendell started off in the opposite direction.

"Wait!" Wörtlich called after him. "I have questions!"

Wendell spun around just long enough to make eye contact. "And Lagati has the answers."

Wörtlich looked down at the card and cursed loudly. The last thing he needed was another difficult decision to make.

SIX

Zurich, Switzerland
SEPTEMBER 7

Brighton snatched up his suitcase from the carousel outside the security checkpoint at Zurich Airport. He was gratified to find English on most of the signs leading out of the terminal. Getting turned around in foreign airports was something he always feared, even though it never happened. In fact, he didn't need the signs; the bulk of the passengers corralled him in the right direction.

Light poured into the Arrivals Lounge through a long bank of windows reflecting the blue-screened arrival and departure monitors. Six concrete columns lofted toward the room's gray ceiling.

Brighton shuffled over to the nearest column and put down his suitcase, checking the time. The flight had arrived on schedule, but he

had no idea who was picking him up or where they were going. Once
again, it occurred to him how stupid it was to fly halfway around the
world with so little to go on. For all he knew, this Wendell fellow was
some sort of international serial killer.

"Mr. Brighton?"

Brighton turned to find a short, round man with a mop of brown
hair. He wore a uniform which Brighton couldn't identify, though he
guessed the man was a chauffeur.

"Did Wendell send you?"

The man nodded enthusiastically, pointing toward the row of
glass doors beyond the columns. "This way, sir."

Feeling a bit adventurous, Brighton slipped his computer bag
over his shoulder. He reached down to grab the suitcase, but the man
intervened and picked it up himself. Brighton got off a quick thanks
and trailed him outside.

The driver opened the rear door of a gleaming diamond black
Bentley. Brighton let out a low whistle, signaling the driver to wait
while he took an admiring stroll around the front of the car where four
signature headlights provided bookends to a stainless steel grille. The
car was a sight to behold, a relic from another time, a symbol of old
world extravagance.

"So, you're really taking me to see Raff Lagati."

The driver continued to hold the door open, sun glinting off the
car's chromed panels. "You were told this, yes?"

"I didn't entirely believe it," Brighton murmured, coming back
around and ducking into the car. He heard the driver unlatch the
trunk and slide his suitcase inside.

As the Bentley pulled away from the curb, Brighton realized that
the back seat of Lagati's car was better furnished than his entire
apartment back home. The forty-inch LCD screen, attached to the

partition separating the rear compartment from the driver, was impossible to ignore.

"The ride is an hour and a half," the driver's voice told him through a speaker. "There is a remote in the center console. You can hit the red button to talk to me."

Like the rest of the interior, the center console was topped with a burnt oak finish. The circular bulge in its center betrayed a hidden compartment. He pressed it with his elbow, pulling it back as a serving tray lifted into view. Two bottles waited beneath the umbrella-shaped lid. Brighton uncapped one and wafted it under his nose. He allowed himself a thin smile. Bourbon. A pair of crystal shot glasses sat next to the bottles. He closed the compartment; whatever happened next, he would need a clear head.

His eyes roamed across the back of the seats in front of him. A cabinet directly behind the driver's seat held a stock of champagne and various cheeses. To his right, where he would have expected nothing more complicated than an automatic window opener, he found buttons that blacked out the windows, reclined the seats, and activated massage rollers in the leather upholstery.

The remote the driver had told him about not only controlled the TV, but also a satellite navigation system that allowed him to chart their route. According to the map, Lagati's estate was quite far south of the city, in the mountains near the town of Linthal.

He glanced up at the large television and yawned. Thinking better of it, he blacked out the windows and closed his eyes as the daylight receded. Surrounded by all the luxuries money could buy, all he really wanted was sleep.

*   *   *

When Brighton peered out the window sometime later, he let out a gasp. The Bentley raced along a narrow road that twisted up through the mountains, taking one hairpin turn after another. Whereas Zurich had been lush and green, the peaks south of Linthal were covered in snow. They were skirting the edge of a sheer cliff, about three hundred feet above a green valley where a clear mountain stream rushed north.

He picked up the remote and pressed the red button. "How far away are we?"

"Just a few minutes, sir," the driver said.

Brighton reclined as the car took a sharp turn. They left the main road behind and climbed onto an even narrower private drive. The screen in front of him folded up into the ceiling, opening up a panoramic view out the front.

Brighton's mouth hung open as he was treated to his first view of Lagati's estate. Through some incredible feat of modern engineering, the three-story castle had been built into a cliff face. The small road leading up to its portico had been blasted from the rock of the mountain, creating a slim ledge of real estate where none had existed before. It was a modern-day Petra, its designer having obviously taken a few cues from the ancient Jordanian city.

Brighton had to catch his breath when he exited the car. An instinctive fear of heights compelled him to remain as close to the front doors as possible, as though the slim roadway could sheer itself off the mountain at any moment.

The peaks around them were jagged and treacherous while the green valley below was so distant it appeared teal, a result of hazy blue atmosphere getting in the way. His mind reeling, Brighton stumbled backward up the steps to the double doors where the driver had already left his suitcase. Still dizzy, Brighton picked it up and turned to face the door.

I guess I'm supposed to go inside?

He gave the handle a pull.

The cavernous entrance hall was wide, deep, and surrounded by open archways on either side. A mezzanine overlooked the entrance, accessible by a pair of curved staircases deeper down the hall.

I'm inside a mountain, Brighton reminded himself as he ventured further. Below him, above him, somewhere beyond the floors and limestone moldings, was rock. For a home that for all intents and purposes should have felt more like a tomb than a residence, it was surprisingly airy.

Hearing the soft sound of padded footsteps crossing hardwood, Brighton turned to find someone approaching—the mysterious Mr. Wendell.

"Welcome, Mr. Brighton. I trust you had a pleasant drive."

Wendell put out his hand to take Brighton's coat. Slipping it off, Brighton took note of the wall behind him, a dramatic stretch of stonework that rose no less than forty feet.

"There are some inspiring views in the south country," Wendell added. His voice and personality seemed somehow bland against the awesomeness of their surroundings.

"Very, uh… inspiring, yes." No words could adequately do this place justice.

"I realize much of this day must seem surreal."

"You could say that."

Wendell patted the coat, which he folded neatly over his arm. "I'll take care of this. You're free to have a look around. Your host will be with you shortly." He turned to walk away, then paused as though having forgotten something. "You may find the drawing room more comfortable. Up the stairs, to the left."

The first thing that caught Brighton's eye in the drawing room was a vast Botticelli triptych depicting an underwater scene. A woman with long, flowing blond hair was pictured in the center emerging from a seashell on the ocean floor while a man, woman, and child in loose clothing looked on. Something about the painting made him uncomfortable, though he couldn't say what.

A dozen pedestals of varying heights were positioned around the room's periphery. On the nearest he found a collection of old coins—though the word *old* hardly sufficed; a few hadn't been circulated in over a thousand years. His hand hovered nervously over them as he fought the urge to pick one up.

"Take care," a voice intoned. "Those are two thousand years old. They date back to Egypt's Ptolemaic dynasty."

Letting his hand drop, Brighton turned to find a middle-aged man walking toward him from the steps. From his accent, he guessed the man was German.

"I didn't notice you when I came up."

"I have always been a bit easy to miss." An uncomfortable pause followed. "Emery Wörtlich, another of Lagati's guests."

Brighton's eyes lit up. "How many more are there?"

"I do not know," Wörtlich acknowledged. "So far just the two of us. Any idea what this is about?"

"I was contacted by the man who met me downstairs. Wendell. My guess is that he's the front man for a group called Creation Tech. I don't know who they are, but they've been asking after me for several months."

"I had a similar experience," Wörtlich said, "though I know nothing of Creation Tech. Wendell told me his employer, Raff Lagati, has been following my career and that I would be perfect for... well, that is a little up in the air."

Wendell never said anything about inviting others. I wonder how many—

"Oh, sorry! Sherwood Brighton," he said, remembering himself. "It's good to meet you."

*   *   *

Wörtlich continued his circuit of the drawing room, examining the rest of the pedestals. The young man, Brighton, didn't make further conversation, which suited him well enough.

While standing over a marble bust of one of the late Roman emperors—*perhaps the first Theodosius?*—he caught a glimpse of a second entrance to the drawing room, this one located rather discreetly in the furthest corner. Its arch was at least two feet narrower than all the other doors along the mezzanine, and the room behind it was dark and windowless. As far as he could tell, it was one of the deepest rooms in the house, positioned in a recessed wing where natural light had no hope of reaching.

Wörtlich approached the arch, half-expecting Wendell to reappear at any moment to turn him around. The dark room had an air of secrecy, and yet there was no door shutting it off from prying eyes.

He stopped before entering. Ahead of him was another pedestal, this one more ornate than the others. He forced his legs to continue moving, his eyes widening as he got his first look at the incredible artifact perched upon it.

It cannot be.

What he was looking at was impossible. That was all there was to it. It shouldn't exist in the physical world, and yet…

And yet it does.

Overwhelmed with a combination of terror and reverence, his legs stopped working altogether as his eyes settled on the hollow, empty sockets of a petrified bird's skull. The skull appeared quite fragile, prompting the archaeologist to keep his hands firmly at his sides; he worried that even the slightest touch would cause it to crumble.

But this certainly hadn't been just any bird. Wörtlich couldn't imagine a species that would have possessed a skeletal structure large enough to support the weight of the cranial load. The size of the creature's brain, if the skull's capacity was any indication, would have been ten times larger than the biggest avian brain he was familiar with. He wasn't a biologist by any stretch, but the bone structure around the cheeks seemed almost human.

Hearing footsteps behind him, he turned to see a tall, slim Frenchman stride into the room like he owned the place. Wörtlich realized at once that he did.

Raff Lagati was one of the richest men in the world, and he looked the part. Everything about him was slick, from his choice of clothing—a black silk waistcoat over a light blue dress shirt—to his square jaw and steely blue eyes. Once you glanced at him, it was hard to look away. He had a way of holding people's attention even when they were reluctant to give it.

"I thought you might find this of particular interest, Doctor," Lagati said, patting Wörtlich on the back as though they were old friends. "Truthfully, I put it on display for your benefit."

"Then you know what it is." Wörtlich tried to mask his amazement. And then, almost in a whisper, he added, "And what it means."

"Well, of course I do. I went to a lot of trouble acquiring it." Lagati turned back to the archway, where Brighton hung back, silently watching the two men's interaction. Lagati waved him in. "Please, don't be shy. It's a pleasure to finally meet you both in person. I've been meaning to contact you for a long while."

"I still do not understand why," Wörtlich said as Brighton joined them.

"The *why* is not important for now," Lagati said. "Besides, I thought perhaps this artifact might begin to answer that."

Wörtlich nodded. "This is a beginning, yes, if an enigmatic one."

"Yes, well, we'll get to your questions. Patience is a virtue. Step closer, Mr. Brighton, and have a look for yourself. There are no secrets between friends." With a flourish, Lagati stuck out his hand toward the strange-looking skull. He let out a sudden burst of excited laughter. "This is the remains of a human/avian hybrid, from ancient times. Geneticists were particularly clever back then. Far more so than today."

The peculiar explanation hung in the room like a nuclear cloud until Brighton spoke up. "Forgive me if this is a stupid question, but… genetic engineering?"

"Yes, of course," Lagati said plainly, as though it was, indeed, a stupid question. "Six, maybe seven thousand years ago."

The young man stared back with a blank expression. Wörtlich could hardly blame him.

"I suppose it's hard to believe at first," Lagati said.

"Hard to believe what?" the young man asked. "I scarcely know where to begin. That we were genetically crossing people with animals before the time of Christ? What's hard to believe about that?"

"Don't be ludicrous!" Lagati laughed loudly again. "*We* did no such thing, I assure you. It was the Egyptian gods who did it."

Brighton looked longingly toward the drawing room. "You know, I think I may have walked into something a little over my head. Excuse me."

He barely cleared the arch before Lagati asked, "Mr. Brighton, where are you going?"

"Away from the crazy people. No offence, but… Egyptian gods?

You can't be serious."

Brighton continued walking.

"Mr. Brighton!"

Brighton stopped again, but this time he didn't turn, instead holding his back to the two men.

"You can walk away if you like," Lagati called. "I certainly won't keep you here against your will. But I do at least hope you stay long enough to hear what I have to say."

Brighton made his way back. His eyes flicked to Wörtlich as if hoping the archaeologist would be as baffled as he by all this business with gods and genetics. But to Wörtlich, it was anything but baffling.

"If nothing else, it'll make for an interesting story," Brighton mused.

Lagati wagged a disapproving finger. "I'm afraid you won't be allowed to share what I'm about to reveal. I'll have to insist on that, if you choose to stay."

Brighton gave that a moment's thought. "You were saying?"

Clearly pleased and unsurprised, Lagati's attention fell on Wörtlich. "I think I'll let the doctor do the talking."

Wörtlich sighed. "This is what Wendell meant when he told me that my literal interpretations would come in handy."

"Literal interpretations?" Brighton asked.

Lagati beamed at the young man. "You're not familiar with them? A pity. They're so very interesting."

"Egyptian monuments are covered in hieroglyphics and scenes portraying larger than life pharaohs and gods, fierce-looking animal/human hybrids, and giants sometimes two to four times the size of regular people," Wörtlich explained. "Most historians and archaeologists have tacitly agreed to work from the assumption that those drawings are figurative. For instance, the pharaohs were drawn of greater stature because they were of greater social importance and yielded influence with the gods. Very few people believe they actually *were* taller. I am one of those few. Those scenes could reflect literal events." He paused, his hand gesturing to the skull. "Even so, I have never beheld such obvious proof of my claims."

Wörtlich took a step past Lagati to get a different angle on the skull. No matter the perspective, it was impossible to believe.

"There were giants in the earth in those days," a voice intoned. Each of the three men turned as a new arrival swept into the room, his timing dramatic. "And also after that, when the sons of God came in unto the daughters of men, and they bare children to them, the same became mighty men which were of old, men of renown."

Lagati was positively radiant, his face aglow like a child's at Christmas. "At last, a spiritual perspective. Thank you! Doctor Wörtlich, Mr. Brighton, meet Rabbi Ira Binyamin, the final guest at our little dinner party."

"Was that a quote?" Brighton asked the rabbi.

"The Torah," Ira answered. "More correctly, the King James Version of the Book of Genesis. You can be forgiven for not recognizing it. It's a passage often left out of Sunday school lessons."

Wörtlich glanced back and forth from Brighton to Ira. The look on Brighton's face confirmed his mere passing familiarity with Sunday school lessons of any stripe. That confusion soon morphed into something else—insight.

"Wait," Brighton said. "You both spoke of giants."

"Is that so?" Ira asked. "The giants are no myth. They are real."

Ira appraised Wörtlich for a moment, then took a few steps closer to the skull. Instead of showing surprise, he seemed to immediately recognize it for what it was. He circled the pedestal, eyeing Lagati warily.

"So this is one of them?" Ira asked. "Where did you find it? I wasn't sure such evidence still existed from those times."

"Evidence of just about everything exists somewhere," Lagati replied. "If you know where to look."

"Hold on," Brighton interrupted. "I don't mean to repeat myself, but just to clarify, there were giants in ancient Egypt?"

Lagati shrugged. "Not *just* in Egypt."

Brighton leaned up against one of the walls, apparently still trying to sort out everything. "And they existed simultaneously with the beings we now know as the Egyptian gods, who weren't mythical either?"

"Quite so," Lagati said.

"They were not *gods*, per se," Wörtlich said. "At least, not in the way we might understand that term today. Their technology caused them to be perceived as such. Genetic engineering is just one example of what they could do. I can think of a few others."

"Like what?" Brighton asked.

"For one, they seem to have had flight capability. Surviving records report the existence of ancient flying machines we would probably describe now as UFOs."

The young man let out a noise. Disbelief. "Yeah, right."

Wörtlich shrugged. "There is plenty of evidence to suggest—"

"I challenge you to show me some," Brighton said defiantly.

Lagati laughed again, as pleased as could be. "Gentlemen, please. You have no idea how excited I am to have all three of you in one place at the same time. But save the fireworks for a few more minutes, if you will."

As the guests glanced at each other guardedly, Lagati clapped his hands together. "Why don't we check on dinner?"

*   *   *

Dinner passed with a surprising lack of conversation. Ira noted that Lagati didn't enjoy mixing food with business, but as soon as the plates were cleared away, the Frenchman explained himself.

"A year ago, I formed a small research group called Creation Tech." Lagati took a sip of wine while a steward filled his guests' glasses. "I've been using that corporation to gather artifacts and intelligence from around the world to support some of these unorthodox approaches to science and history I'm so fond of."

Wörtlich glowered at that revelation. "Then you are a creationist."

"Evolution, creation, I try not to get bogged down in terminology. I don't find those distinctions to be especially useful. I'm not out to push any particular agenda. The reference is to the sort of scientifically-created beings you've just seen upstairs. Manmade creations, just like we build cars today. It's all science."

That is a lie, Ira thought. *He is a creationist.*

"Trust me, I'm not being deliberately mysterious," Lagati continued. "Once you hear my proposal, you'll understand why I've had to keep this meeting so secretive."

Ira put down his wine. "What proposal?"

Lagati crossed his legs, getting comfortable. "First of all, I must regretfully admit that I had to operate under false pretenses in order to lure you all here. I apologize for that and hope you can see the greater good in my plan."

He turned first to Brighton. "For instance, I know nothing specific about the photo you saw, though I made sure your friend came across it before your presentation in Washington. Don't be disappointed, though. I can help you, in time, to understand its true nature."

Lagati looked down the length of the black-topped table toward the rabbi. "To you, Rabbi, I am most sorry. I don't actually have an original *Sefer Yetzirah*, as you were led to believe. I have my own copy, of course, but it's no more special than your own. You see, I had to get you here, and it seems to have done the trick."

Ira expertly disguised the wave of relief that passed over him.

"You see, the *Sefer Yetzirah* is at the heart of my pursuit," Lagati concluded. "As it is with yours."

"What is the *Se*—" Brighton began, unable to quite master the Hebrew title.

Lagati smiled. "The *Sefer Yetzirah*. It's an ancient Hebrew text. According to the Jews, it provides a demonstrative account of the methods God used to create the universe."

Brighton grinned. "No kidding. There's a user's guide for that?"

"Essentially, yes," Lagati replied. "At least, for those who come to grasp its full implications. Unfortunately, nobody really does. Not yet."

"What a religious load of crap."

Three pairs of eyes turned in unison to Wörtlich. Ira bristled at the remark.

"Please, Doctor," Lagati cautioned. "While I understand your skepticism, I do believe in the book's divine origins. I'm not asking you to share that belief, in the same way that I'm not asking Mr. Brighton to convert to Judaism or the rabbi to deny the existence of God. In the grand scheme of things, our differences are small—very small—and we must not let them interfere with bringing our unique contributions to the table."

Ira's guard came up again. "What are we contributing to?"

"I'm glad you asked. For years, I've done my part to relieve suffering around the world. I cannot physically build a house, knit a sweater, or conduct life-saving medical research, but I can contribute financially to all these pursuits and more. And yet, if I've learned anything, it's that there's no amount of money I can throw at a problem to make it disappear. Wealth alone is not a solution. After so many years of accumulating it, that's a humbling admission, but there it is—money can't change the world. It's just not enough."

Lagati took a deep breath as the steward reappeared to fill his wineglass. "Thanks to Kaballah, I've learned a host of new truths and discovered a greater purpose for myself. It's revolutionized the way I look at problems. Again, I don't require you all to accept what I'm about to say, only to listen and consider.

"It was Rabbi Binyamin who first introduced me to the law of attraction, a subject on which he speaks both passionately and eloquently. Not to mention persuasively! Whatever beliefs we hold in our hearts and in our heads, we constantly attract people and situations that contribute to the furthering of those beliefs, consciously or otherwise. Even if those beliefs are false."

"Especially in those times, I have found," Ira commented.

"Here's an example. I'm a very wealthy man, but it wasn't mere luck that got me here. I didn't just win the lottery one day. I've used this law continuously for most of my adult life to get where I am. It sounds crazy, but—" Lagati gestured widely, taking in the scope of his magnificent home. "—as they say, the proof is in the pudding. I can't count the number of times I would meditate on a business deal and within minutes be contacted about a new, lucrative opportunity."

"Instant wish fulfillment?" Brighton asked.

"Oh no, not at all," Lagati said. "The results of my meditations are never predictable, and that's the problem. I can't close my eyes and think about a new Mercedes, then watch as it materializes on my driveway. Rather I meditate on success and financial freedom, all of which are natural desires. As natural as breathing. I don't always get what I want, hope, or expect, but one thing's for sure—the end result is usually something I could not have come up with on my own."

Lagati gestured toward Ira. "But this is no different than the rabbi's sermon this week. What he held back, however, was the more profound truth, which is that if I suddenly became overwhelmed with the desire for, say, ice cream, I should be able to manifest an ice cream cone in my very hand. It *should* be predictable."

"Well," Ira warned, "that's a very simple example."

"True enough," the Frenchman said. "You have me there."

Wörtlich groaned. "Preposterous! You are describing physical transmutation and telekinesis. Nothing but bedtime stories, and not even good ones."

Lagati frowned sympathetically. "It *is* physical transmutation, Doctor. Imagine the implications for peace and prosperity in the world today if we were all putting these principles to altruistic uses."

"But we are nowhere near understanding how these things could work, if they work at all," the archaeologist challenged.

Brighton leaned back in his chair, open-faced. "I don't know about physical transmutation, but I do believe in the paranormal."

Lagati snapped his fingers, causing Ira to sit up straight. "That's the first step, isn't it? But we're getting away from the point, I think."

"I'm still not certain just what that point is, Mr. Lagati," Ira pointed out.

In the pause that followed, Lagati stood up and approached the window. He shifted his weight from foot to foot, betraying his agitation; perhaps he was frustrated by his inability to articulate himself.

"I know it sounds too good to be true. As I've said, the problem with the *Sefer Yetzirah* is that nobody understands it." Lagati turned back to the table, making eye contact with Ira. "Rabbi, you've spent a lifetime studying these teachings, and even you are fundamentally at a dead end."

Ira acknowledged this with a slight nod.

"I propose that the reason for this confusion is that we no longer have a definitive version of the *Sefer Yetzirah*," Lagati said. "But this was not always the case. What we need to find is the original Book of Creation."

"I thought you said you were not a creationist," Wörtlich observed.

"Like most scientists, I've come to the conclusion that there was, at minimum, a beginning to the universe. Cosmologically, I cannot dismiss intelligent design without some thoughtful soul-searching."

Wörtlich grunted and pushed his chair away from the table. "You, sir, are not a scientist."

Throwing his napkin down, Wörtlich got up and stalked out of the room.

SEVEN

Linthal, Switzerland
SEPTEMBER 7

S ilence fell over the dining room. Ira also stood, somewhat more gracefully than Wörtlich before him, and said his goodnights.

Lagati let him go without protest as he leaned resignedly on the back of Wörtlich's vacated seat and ran a hand through his now-unkempt brown hair. "I'll level with you, Mr. Brighton. You're one of the best analysts at the Smithsonian. But you're young."

Brighton took a deep breath and blew it back out. "What does that have to do with anything?"

"That's what I say," the Frenchman said. "But there's seniority to think about. A pecking order. Unfortunately, you're on the bottom working your way up. Now, you did great work at Caltech. I've been paying attention for quite some time." He took a breath. "I also know what it's like to struggle to make ends meet."

Brighton rolled his eyes, looking around. "Yeah, I can see that."

"I got past it. You can, too. I won't try selling you on idealism and changing the world, because we both know that isn't going to help you make up your mind. Am I right?"

Brighton didn't have to look deep into his own motivations to realize Lagati had read him like a book. He turned his eyes down, studying the carpet.

"Don't waste your time feeling embarrassed. And speaking of wasted time, the Smithsonian's not the place for you. You shouldn't be working entry level analysis. You're too talented for that, which is why I'm offering you a job."

Brighton's head shot up.

"In addition to an experience I can guarantee will blow your mind, I'll pay you a quarter million dollars for your first six months, upfront salary."

"A quarter million," Brighton repeated, having to say it out loud to believe it.

"You didn't think I wanted you to help me for free, did you?"

As a matter of fact, that's exactly what I thought.

"No," Brighton said instead, "but that's a hell of a lot more than I expected."

"You're worth it." Lagati stood, reflexively dusting off his pants even though there was nothing on them. "Think it over."

*   *   *

A stiff breeze rushed over Wörtlich, billowing his short, curly hair into a mass of tangles. The expanse of open air above, below, and in front of him took his breath away. The sun was setting in the western sky, tendrils of green, purple, and blue threading across the rugged horizon like an artist's brush strokes.

Wörtlich breathed deeply of the cold mountain air, trying to sort out his next move. Sheply's offer had come and gone, a missed opportunity he didn't know if he had even wanted in the first place.

But the index…

"I passed on a chance to join the dig in Alexandria," he spoke after a while, sensing the presence of someone approaching from behind. He didn't have to be a psychic to know it was Lagati.

Lagati stepped into view. "Yes, I heard. The discovery of the index has once again made the library a tantalizing prize."

"You know about the index?"

"Of course. They can keep it quiet from the public a little while longer, but not from me. I have sources everywhere."

Wörtlich allowed himself a tight smile.

"You find that funny?"

"I find it admirable, actually," Wörtlich said.

Looking out over the mountains made him feel lightheaded. He had grown up visiting these Alps, and yet something about the view on this particular night had a magical quality. "What I have seen tonight changes everything. That skull in your collection, I cannot describe… with the right words…" He gave up, frustrated. "I cannot describe how I am feeling."

"I understand," Lagati said softly.

"I do not see how you could."

"You've been discredited by your peers. That, I understand. You've taken a professional beating for your theories."

"Yes," Wörtlich acknowledged. "But what I saw tonight confirms everything I have been teaching. All I can think of is taking that skull

back with me to Cairo so that everyone can see the truth for themselves and wallow in their wrongness. Just once."

"You know I can't let you do that."

Wörtlich nodded. "And that is what I find so infuriating."

The two men stood in silence a while longer. Wörtlich didn't
know quite what to say. In the absence of words, silence was enough.

"Nobody is interested in historical truth anymore," Lagati said at
last. "You're unique in that respect. Most historians are more interested in maintaining what has already been established and written about
for centuries than in charting a new course. Can you imagine, for instance, how much it's going to cost to republish all those textbooks
after we expose what was really going on in ancient Egypt?"

Wörtlich couldn't help but be amused at that. After clearing his
name and reputation, what did it matter about the textbooks?

Lagati studied him carefully. "How about the truth of the pyramid
builders?"

Those words practically seared through Wörtlich's soul. "What
do you know?"

"Right now, I could only speculate. But together, we'll find out."

"And what about this crazy talk about gods and Judaism and ice
cream?"

Lagati chuckled. "We all have to pursue this for our own reasons.
I'm not asking you to believe all that. Come to your own conclusions."

"You say that now, but how do I go about helping you without
accepting even your most basic premise? You want to find the Book of
Creation, but I do not believe such a thing exists. How do I reconcile
that?"

"You don't have to believe something exists to find it," Lagati
noted. "Consider it. If whoever is responsible for our world left us a
note about how he did it, wouldn't that be a note worth tracking

down? You need to trust me. The Book of Creation is probably in Egypt, sitting right there under our noses for millennia, waiting for people like us to dig it up."

Wörtlich turned his head absently. The sun had sunk below the horizon.

"Over time, you'll have the opportunity to share your findings with the world," Lagati said. "They can't close their eyes and plug their ears forever. Now, we could get into a debate over spiritualism versus secularism, faith versus science, but where would it get us? Still, I suppose I was asking for it by pairing you with Ira Binyamin. But those questions are immaterial. I need your help and can't trust anyone else." As that sank in, he added, "And when you think about it, you need me as well."

Wörtlich was quiet as Lagati gave him a gentle pat on the back.

Lagati turned and walked back into the house.

*　　*　　*

A wedge of moonlight streamed into Ira's bedroom, lighting up half the room and leaving the other in shadow. He pulled a book out of the side pocket of his suitcase, sat in a comfy chair next to the bed, and switched on the reading lamp. He tried reading, but every few minutes he looked up distractedly. Frustrated, he shut the book.

He slipped on an evening coat he found hanging on the bathroom hook and peered out into the hall. Seeing no one, he decided to take a walk.

The guest wing ended where the hall met the main stairway. From this perch, he could see down to the darkened mezzanine and the crisscrossing tile pattern on the entrance hall floor. He grasped the railing and started down.

Ira turned left at the bottom of the stairs. Through the glass door at the far end of the mezzanine he saw windows facing out the front of the mansion. Inside was a library. Intrigued, he tried the door and found it unlocked.

Stacks surrounded the room, shelves of books climbing one atop the other to the ceiling where only a sliding ladder could reach. Four large, overstuffed chairs faced the center, creating a sitting area.

Ira walked past the shelves, staring intently at the titles printed on worn spines. He stopped now and then to pull a book out and check its cover.

When he got to the end of the row, he caught sight of a second glass door from the corner of his eye. This door led out onto a flat terrace jutting out from the cliff on a wide shelf of rock.

Ira stepped closer, then stopped in his tracks. Lagati sat in the middle of the terrace in a meditative position. Giving in to his inner voyeur, Ira watched for a few moments longer than necessary.

Lagati stirred. He opened his dark eyes and stared forward. Even though he faced away from Ira and the library door, it was clear that he had somehow sensed the rabbi's presence. Like a coiled snake, he swiveled his head, spotting Ira inside.

Ira looked down at the book in his hands and hastily returned it to its place as Lagati stepped into the library.

"What were you doing?" Ira asked. He realized it might not have been the most tactful question, seeing as he was the one caught spying.

"Meditating. Just as you do, I'm sure."

The rabbi nodded, though inside he wasn't so sure the two men shared a definition of meditation.

"I'm sorry," Ira blurted. "I didn't mean to disturb you. It's very late, and this is your private—"

Lagati waved off the apology, using his other hand to flatten his windswept hair. "No, no. Don't apologize. I hoped you would make yourself at home."

Ira inclined his head. "From the looks of it, you're incredibly well-read."

"If anyone could appreciate that, it would be you," Lagati remarked. "Feel free to borrow anything you like. Just leave it in your room when you leave."

"Thank you. I might do that." Ira looked back at the books, already identifying a few titles he wouldn't mind taking a further look at. But he didn't anticipate staying long enough to take advantage of the offer.

Lagati pointed to the sitting area. "Have a seat with me?"

The chairs turned out to be as comfortable as they looked. Ira didn't know what material they were made from, but he knew he didn't want to get up again for quite a while.

"Rabbi, I—" Lagati stopped himself, drawing a deep breath. "Once again, it's me who should apologize. I haven't been entirely forthright with the others."

"I could sense that."

"You're very intuitive. That must be a useful skill in your line of work." Lagati offered up a thin smile and clasped his hands together in front of him. "At dinner, I downplayed my spiritual views, for Doctor Wörtlich's sake. I didn't want to scare him off. My personal beliefs do nothing to help convince the others to join our cause. The Book of Creation is a lot to take in even for believers, never mind skeptics."

Our cause. Either Lagati assumed Ira would agree to help, or it was a subtle manipulative tool to drive him toward a favorable decision. One way or the other, the implication disturbed Ira.

"What's on your mind?" Ira asked.

Lagati's eyes met Ira's dead on, as though gripping them. "We have to go back to the source."

"You mean, of course, that we must seek God."

The Frenchman wavered. "In a sense, that is true. But the source I have in mind is a bit more tangible than all that. I assume you're familiar with the Book of Enoch?"

"Intimately."

"It's an incredible story, one that plugs a lot of holes in the historical record. Enoch describes in great length the Watchers, the fallen angels of heaven, and their achievements on this earth after their expulsion."

Ira reclined, feigning comfort when inside he was growing increasingly troubled with the direction of the conversation.

"These Watchers are the sons of God you mentioned earlier when you quoted from Genesis," Lagati murmured. "They came to the earth to mate with women, siring children that were both angelic and human at the same time. These hybrid children—"

"They were the giants that once roamed the earth," Ira finished.

Lagati furrowed his brow. "It's written in Enoch that they stole the mysteries of heaven when they fell from grace. These mysteries of heaven, stolen from God, and taught to mankind..."

"That's the Book of Creation you seek to discover," the rabbi whispered. "You believe information from that stolen book has since been incorporated into our modern *Sefer Yetzirah*."

"With all my heart I believe it."

Lagati seemed so profoundly moved by the grandeur of the revelation, so taken up in the moment, that his eyes lost focus and he seemed to forget where he was. Before he could say anything, Lagati returned from his state.

"The Book of Creation still exists on earth," Lagati said, "a book written in Jehovah's own penmanship. Not just the message of God, but his very *handwriting*. Rabbi, this is a phenomenon not witnessed since the fall of Babylon! The others would never understand it. I hate to keep it from them, but I fear the meaning would escape them entirely. For that reason, I leave this secret in your hands."

Ira struggled to maintain his composure over the underlying terror mounting in his heart. "And you know where to look?"

"Oh yes," Lagati said. "The Book remains in the Watchers' ancient seat of power—Egypt."

Ira lowered his eyes, worried that the fear inside would show itself there. He did not know how long he could keep the mask in place.

Saying goodnight, he returned to his room, quickening his pace the closer he got. His heart pounded. His breathing echoed loudly in his ears.

He had to get back, as quickly as possible.

EIGHT

Fair Haven, Vermont
SEPTEMBER 8

Rain poured and lightning lit up the sky as dark clouds seethed over the rolling hills north of Fair Haven. The trees on Aaron Roth's property swayed in the wind as the headlights of Ira's car illuminated them.

The rabbi jumped out of the car and released an umbrella. Slamming the door behind him, he hurried up the walk, veering occasionally to the left or right to avoid puddles.

Moments after answering the door, David led him up to Aaron's study. The old man was looking out one of the windows, supporting himself against a bookshelf. Ira was too anxious to sit, and yet by standing in place he let water drip into pools around his feet.

"He's going after it," Ira announced.

Aaron shuffled toward his chair. He didn't say anything for a while. Instead he merely sat, his eyes focused on a point on the wall just left of where Ira stood.

"Did you hear me, Aaron?"

His eyes shifted to Ira. "Yes, I heard you."

"You don't seem surprised."

"I am not surprised." He was as unflappable as the last time Ira had seen him. "Ira, sit. You're getting the floor wet."

Ira shed his jacket, draping it over the doorknob. He fell into the chair, haggard and worn out. *Strange that the old man probably looks younger than I do right now.*

"Tell me everything," Aaron said.

Starting with his arrival in Switzerland, Ira spilled every detail of his evening with Raff Lagati. Despite being out of sorts, he managed to get through the story in a matter of minutes without leaving anything out.

"So, he's after the stolen Book of Creation," Aaron said in summation. "And if what you say is true, he is determined to find it."

"Very much so, and he has put together just the team to do it. That said, I suppose we don't know for sure that the book still exists. His quest could be an empty one."

"And if it's not?" Aaron asked.

Ira nodded slowly. "It's just as the Torah tells us of the corrupted men of old, that when they were of one mind, nothing they purposed could be withheld from them. Raff Lagati is a madman! He says he would use the power of creation for the betterment of mankind, but—"

"But in the hands of a man, it could not be so," Aaron said. "He is too eager to possess this knowledge."

"He must be watched and monitored. We must keep him under constant scrutiny."

Aaron looked at him in astonishment. "We must do more than that, Ira. Surely you see that you have no further choice in this matter."

"No further choice?"

"I am sorry," the old man continued. "I don't know why you were chosen for this, but I'm grateful that Lagati came to you and not someone with fewer scruples. The results could have been disastrous."

"They still could be!" Ira insisted. "All my instincts cry out that this can have no good end."

"Lagati cannot be permitted to acquire the Book. But the only way to make certain it doesn't happen is for you to find out where it is yourself. You must join him and gain his confidence."

Ira stared at him in shock.

"If you find it, you will have the opportunity to destroy it," Aaron rasped. "That is our only hope. Entire civilizations have been destroyed from mishandling the true creation science. We must not allow history to repeat itself." He sighed heavily. "As ever, the writings must be kept hidden… and safe."

"You're right," Ira managed, gaining confidence from forcing himself to repeat it. "You're right."

Aaron reached out his frail hand and grasped Ira's, holding it firmly and with greater strength than Ira had thought he possessed.

"*Go your way, Daniel,*" Aaron quoted somberly, "*and seal up the books until the last days, lest many shall go to and fro and knowledge shall increase.*"

Ira lowered his head.

"Ira, do you see?" Aaron whispered. "It's as though the prophet was speaking to you directly. You know what must be done."

After a long moment, Ira raised his head, but instead of fear and uncertainty, his eyes shone with calm resolve. Looking into Aaron's old, fading eyes, he made a silent promise to complete the task they had set out to do so many years ago, to protect the ancient secrets or die trying.

NINE

Alexandria, Egypt
SEPTEMBER 15

From the moment Pompey's Pillar became visible over the crest of the hill, Wörtlich dreaded his upcoming reunion with Noam Sheply. For one thing, there was the embarrassment of having to appear as though he'd changed his mind. Making firm decisions was a point of personal pride, so begging to be given a second chance at the Alexandria job hadn't been his proudest moment.

However, the subterfuge was worse. If scouring the index hadn't been so important to him, he wouldn't have considered helping Lagati; indeed, what Lagati planned went against everything he stood for. It was almost unthinkable to steal such a priceless discovery, as Lagati now demanded of them, but Sheply had the access they need-

ed, and that necessitated taking advantage of their career-long friendship.

That is all, he told himself mockingly. *Nothing much.*

At this point in his life, he probably wouldn't get another chance
to look for real answers—at least, not with any realistic chance of success. Some of the world's greatest secrets almost certainly resided in
the pages of the index, and those were secrets he couldn't rely on the
Institute, or even Sheply himself, to straightforwardly release to the
general public. He and Lagati agreed on that much.

Once Wörtlich's arrival was radioed in, the guard at the security
checkpoint let him through. He was given a pass to clip to his breast
pocket. Security here was tight in the wake of anti-Western protests in
recent weeks.

Built from polished red granite, Pompey's Pillar was nearly a
hundred feet tall and had once been part of a temple colonnade. Two
thousand years later, it stood alone, one of the few remnants left over
from the city's glory days.

One of Alexandria's few sites of interest that hadn't been built
over by modern neighborhoods was the land around the pillar. It
stood atop the city's ancient Greek acropolis, beneath which the real
history could be found. Subterranean ruins of the Serapeum, a temple
revered by the Egyptians for thousands of years, were still largely un-
explored. One of the few things they knew for certain was that several
vaults had been used to provide overflow storage space for the library
when the city was in its prime.

Wörtlich walked to the edge of the excavation and looked down.
A metal staircase had been constructed to provide access to the temple ruins. The sound of boots on steel ten feet below barely preceded
the appearance of a man climbing up.

"Emery!" Sheply grinned as he clambered up onto solid ground.

His face glistened with sweat. "I can't tell you how glad I am you decided to join us after all."

"How could I stay away?"

"The thought of you missing out on this, well, it nearly broke my heart. As soon as we got off the phone last week, I shook my head and said to myself, 'He'll be back. He'll change his mind.' And here you are."

"How about a look around?"

The Englishman shrugged. "Do you even need to ask?"

Wörtlich's tour of the site was short, on account of there not being much to see. The only notable difference between this and his last visit several years before was a pair of freshly unearthed but otherwise empty vaults.

Fifteen minutes later, they were back out of the hole. Sheply led the way to a line of parked trailers which were just a stone's throw from the checkpoint. His friend's cramped office was set up in the trailer on the end. A couch, presumably the site of more than a few afternoon naps, was sandwiched between a filing cabinet and a mini-fridge. That left a tiny area for the desk and a pair of foldable metal chairs.

Sheply pulled a couple of bottled waters from the fridge and tossed one to Wörtlich.

"I saw that look on your face earlier, and I know what it means," Sheply said. "Don't worry. I didn't entice you back just to put you in charge of the Serapeum."

"The thought had crossed my mind."

Sheply settled down into the couch. "The index has already led us to discover a new lecture hall that was probably part of the original library complex. It was a good deal further south than we ever thought to look. We're hoping to find books buried there."

"I would like to take a look at that as soon as possible."

"We'll head out tomorrow at first light. They've found a series of inscriptions I'd like you to see."

Wörtlich took a sip of water, hoping the action would override any involuntary physical tell that might betray the hidden agenda behind his next question. "Where is the index being kept?"

His heart skipped a beat as Sheply hesitated.

"The original scrolls have been sent to Brigham Young to be digitized," Sheply said.

"I assume then that a digital copy exists."

"Yes. At the Institute in Cairo."

"You know, I would like to examine it for myself," Wörtlich finally admitted. "If it is authentic, I may never see anything else like it in my lifetime."

Sheply let out a low whistle. "Trust me, it's authentic. I've seen some of the originals." He paused again, this time taking a little longer to get going. "Even I'm not being allowed access to the index, Emery. So far, my information comes straight from BYU, because I know some of the researchers there."

"Like Elisabeth?" Wörtlich felt a pang of jealousy at the mention of her name. He had a complicated past with Elisabeth Macfarlane. They might have been together, in another life, if Wörtlich hadn't been married to someone else at the time, if he hadn't been obsessed with his work. Irrational though it was, the notion of Sheply spending time with her turned his stomach.

"Yes, she's in charge of the papyri project," Sheply said, almost offhandedly. "If it wasn't for her, I wouldn't have seen a word of it. The Antiquities Council is restricting access to an unusual degree. Even for them."

Wörtlich didn't bother trying to disguise his disappointment.

This reaction, at least, fit his story like a glove. "So, it is true."

Sheply drained the rest of his water, giving the bottle a final squeeze. He stood up and carried it to the trash can by his desk. Instead of coming back, though, he peered out the window. Pompey's Pillar stuck out of the ground like a sore thumb.

"Listen, I want you to forget everything I just told you," Sheply managed through a long sigh.

"Excuse me?"

The Englishman turned around. "I said exactly what they told me to say. The truth is, I have a digital copy of the index with me right now."

Wörtlich didn't dare react, though he found himself sitting up a bit straighter.

"I'm sick of all this cloak and dagger, conspiracy theory rubbish," Sheply said. "I'm a scientist. An archaeologist. Who cares about who knows what and when and how they find out? The Institute is so concerned with restricting information, keeping it proprietary, that they've lost perspective on what we're here to do in the first place. Which is to find out where we come from, learn about the past, and share it with the world. We've forgotten what we're all about, haven't we?"

Wörtlich's mind raced. "You *do* have the index—"

"I couldn't lie to you. I need it to do my job, and it's becoming clear that you'll need it to do yours."

Wörtlich stood, running a hand through his hair. *What on earth am I doing here? I'm not sure I can go through with this. Perhaps if I stay on board, work with Sheply, I'll get all the access to the index I need.*

But Lagati would have something to say about that.

You're not in it for yourself anymore, he reminded himself. *Lagati needs you to steal the index, and you need him to find the proof—*

"You're upset," Sheply observed.

"No," Wörtlich lied. In fact, he didn't know what he was feeling. His stomach lurched, his head spun, his throat was dry as particle board. He wasn't nervous. He was relieved.

"Good. The two of us are going to unveil this thing together. We'll release our findings, the Institute be damned. We'll talk about it. We'll explain what it means. Of all the men I could have found myself with today, I'm so pleased it's you."

"So am I," Wörtlich agreed, feeling guiltier than ever. Under any other circumstances, he would have leapt at such an opportunity. But Lagati had something Sheply would never be able to offer—unlimited resources.

Sheply opened the bottom drawer of his filing cabinet. He took out a mass of files and placed them on the floor of the trailer. Once he had a good stack going, he pulled out a hard disk.

"What is it?"

"The digital index," Sheply said. "We can't see the big picture yet, but we're learning more every day. The library was larger than first imagined. The references, Emery, identify thousands of historical texts we've never even heard of before."

Sheply snatched back the disk when Wörtlich was finished running his hands over it and returned it to the filing cabinet. "The index is proving to be the most efficient validation tool we've ever had for judging the authenticity of ancient texts. A single mention of a book in the index is enough to prove its relative importance two thousand years ago."

His eyes grazed over to the clock mounted behind the desk.

"We're out of time, I'm afraid." Sheply stood and headed back for the door. "We can catch up more tomorrow, but in the meantime I've scheduled a meeting with the members of your new team. You have a lot of people to meet."

Wörtlich joined him by the door, relieved that even if he met a few dozen new faces that night, he wouldn't have to remember any of the names that went along with them. It was a small comfort, one that barely scratched the surface of his overwhelming shame.

*   *   *

After the rest of the crew left the site, Wörtlich remained behind. He'd told Sheply he wanted to get up to speed on recent developments and plan out everything he wanted to accomplish in the upcoming weeks. Sheply had given him a key and free rein over one of the unoccupied trailer offices.

At precisely 10:30, he stepped out of the trailer and looked down the road toward the checkpoint. Nothing moved across the dark landscape, so he sat down on the steps to wait.

Ten minutes later, a car approached the checkpoint, its headlights catching him directly in the eyes, blinding him for a moment. He jogged over to the gate, where a guard was shining a flashlight into the driver's side window.

"He is with me." Wörtlich flashed his site pass. The guard stepped back, waving the car through.

The car pulled forward to the first dirt road intersection and stopped. Wörtlich strolled up to the window and knocked on it lightly.

"You are ten minutes late," he told Brighton when the window rolled down.

"I took a few wrong turns," Brighton explained. "The streets aren't very well marked, at least half of the traffic lights don't work, and most drivers don't use headlights. It's amazing I made it here in one piece!"

"Welcome to Egypt," Wörtlich said ruefully. He pointed out Sheply's office ahead. "Pull up to the trailer over there, the last one in the row."

Brighton drove up to the trailer and got out of the car while Wörtlich caught up. The men walked up the steps to the front door.

"How are we getting in?" Brighton asked.

Wörtlich gave his eyes a tired rub. "Is that not your department?"

"Sorry, I didn't realize…" The young man returned to the car and fished through the glove compartment. He came back with a thin length of metal just small enough at the tip to fit through the keyhole. Wörtlich knew better than to ask questions.

"Are any of these trailers alarmed?" Brighton asked before pushing the door open.

"I do not believe so," Wörtlich murmured. The last thing they needed was a swarm of security types converging on them.

Wörtlich proceeded into the office first. Halfway through the open door, he hesitated as if expecting an alarm to go off anyway. When none did, he motioned for Brighton to come the rest of the way in.

Inside, the office was dark. Wörtlich stood in place, not wanting to accidentally trip over anything. The goal was to copy the disk and leave without anyone being the wiser. If anything was out of place, Sheply would know.

Wörtlich heard a soft click followed by the pale glow of a desk lamp. Brighton stood behind the desk, pulling his hand back from the lamp.

Wörtlich again shoved aside his rising guilt. He needed the index, but he couldn't betray a friend. The cognitive dissonance was enough to make a man's head explode. This was no time to have a crisis of conscience.

"You remember where he kept it?" Brighton asked.

Wörtlich cut him off with a stern glare. He reached down and gave the bottom drawer of the filing cabinet a tug. It was locked. He frowned, rubbing his lightly bearded chin.

"It was not locked before." Wörtlich glanced up. "A little assistance would be appreciated."

Wasting no time, Brighton got down on his knees so that he was at eye level with the lock. Wörtlich stepped away to give him some space, and within a few minutes the drawer popped open obligingly.

Wörtlich reached forward and shuffled through the contents. When he extracted his hand, it was holding the hard disk.

"This is it," he said, turning it over. "Now, just copy the disk so we can get out of here."

"Fine," the young man said. "Here goes nothing."

Brighton removed a laptop from his bag, then gently placed it on the floor and connected the hard disk. He licked his lower lip as a sea of windows started opening one after another across the screen.

Wörtlich had no idea what Brighton was doing, but he did his best to follow along. *I guess this is the difference almost forty years makes,* he mused as Brighton jumped from window to window, his fingers moving across the keyboard like a concert pianist's.

"Damn it."

Wörtlich leaned forward in an effort to seem as though he'd been paying closer attention than he was. "What is it?"

"This thing has some serious encryption. I won't be able to copy the data without digging into the code manually."

"Find a way around it."

Brighton shook his head in frustration. "It's not that simple. Whoever encrypted these files knew what he was doing."

"Did we not see this coming? Is this not why Lagati sent you along?"

"I *can* break through, but time is a factor."

"How long?"

Brighton shrugged. "Five or six hours, I think, but I haven't seen all the layers of code yet. It could take longer."

"Obviously, we do not have that kind of time."

Wörtlich considered the options. If they stayed too long, the guard at the checkpoint would eventually get suspicious. It was still an hour before midnight, but if they remained well into the morning, Sheply might come back. He'd intimated getting an early start. On the other hand, if they took the disk with them, the police would be after them by mid-morning. But at least they would have a head start.

"We have to take the disk with us," Wörtlich finally decided.

"I thought we were supposed to cover our tracks. Don't you think he'll notice when the index turns up missing?"

"At this point, I cannot see any way around it," Wörtlich said. "We just have to ensure we get far enough away by the time he does."

"You're sure?"

"Unless you are holding out on me … "

Brighton ejected the disk and stuffed it into his bag with the computer. Wörtlich took one last look around the place to make sure they hadn't disturbed too much, and flicked off the light.

Brighton was already halfway to the car.

TEN

Tanta, Egypt

SEPTEMBER 16

We should avoid Cairo," Wörtlich said, looking over a map he'd found in the car's center console.

Brighton kept his eyes straight ahead. Egyptian roads were especially treacherous at nighttime.

"Sheply will be expecting us to go there. In fact, we should find a place to stop as soon as possible."

Brighton raised an eyebrow. "Stop? I thought we needed to get as much distance from Alexandria as possible."

"We are already a hundred kilometers away. The authorities will be looking for us all over Cairo and Alexandria, but we can buy ourselves time by finding someplace in the middle."

This sound suggestion landed them at a motel ten miles southeast of Tanta, several blocks off the main thoroughfare. Brighton removed the car's license plate before going inside, working on the assumption that their rental car was being targeted by the authorities. There were enough unregistered vehicles on the road; one more wouldn't be suspicious.

The first thing he did when they got a room was check his e-mail. Wörtlich would be a prime suspect in the theft of the index, but it was unclear to Brighton whether or not he himself would be classified a fugitive as well. If anyone had seen them together these past few days, they might connect him with the archaeologist.

Alan had sent him a message asking if he'd found out anything regarding the debunked photo. He answered in the negative, also letting his friend know that he was in Canada visiting relatives. The lie would ring true; he went to see his cousins in Winnipeg a few weeks every year around Thanksgiving.

The only other message was from an e-mail account he hadn't seen before, but a little bit of research showed that the sender's IP originated in Zurich. He was almost positive it was from Lagati, but the message didn't make a lick of sense:

> *Barren behavioristic air*
> *ate the megahertz lie.*
> *Irk us at Faddy.*
> −CT

The "CT" seemed to stand for Creation Tech, but the rest was gibberish. And what, or who, was Faddy?

"An anagram, clearly," Wörtlich noted when he saw it. "Lagati is trying to get in touch, but he cannot afford to be obvious about it in case anyone hacks into your account. Anyone looking for clues to your whereabouts might just think this is junk mail."

"What does it mean?"

The German sat down on the bed. To Brighton's ears, the archaeologist's accent sounded more pronounced than usual. "I am not very good with English word games."

Brighton tried puzzling it out for a few minutes, the mathematical part of his brain working out an algorithm. The word *barren* seemed to suggest the existence of *rabbi* somewhere in the first phrase, which made sense if the message was about Ira Binyamin. Instinct told him these were instructions for locating the rabbi, who had yet to join their little adventure. Ira's most obvious point of arrival would be Cairo, and if he took those letters out he was left with *rrenehaviist*. By identifying *arrives*, he postulated a solution, at least for the first line: *The rabbi arrives in Cairo*. It fit their circumstances too well to be coincidence.

He plugged the last two lines into a piece of anagram-solving software. *Friday* kept appearing in the last phrase, making it a likely arrival date. The rest was easy: *at dusk*. Friday at dusk.

"So, you know he is arriving in Cairo tonight," Wörtlich said. "Whatever the middle line is, it must be a meeting place."

"It's not the airport," Brighton pointed out.

"Lagati would not be so bold."

Brighton nodded in agreement. "Perhaps a public place?"

Wörtlich thought about it for a minute. "Or it could be where he is staying. Customs would flag him if he did not have a hotel reservation or someone meeting him. Chances are he booked a hotel."

"In that case, the *z* seems like a giveaway. There can't be many local hotels with *z*'s in the name." He opened another search window. A travel agency might have a list of popular destinations.

The list proved to be much more extensive than he'd have guessed, but there weren't many that fit. There was a Four Seasons at the Nile Plaza, but there weren't enough corresponding letters for that to work. The Zayed was similarly no good.

Then, he found it.

"The El Gezirah," he announced, raising his head.

Wörtlich seemed surprised. "That is a five-star hotel, one of the best in the country. Why would Lagati put him up there?"

"Why not? It's not like money's an issue."

"True," the archaeologist allowed. "And here we are staying in a cheap motel. It hardly seems fair."

Is it just me, or is Wörtlich's hair getting grayer by the minute?

"We're trying to maintain a low profile," Brighton reminded him. "Until we pick him up, there's no reason for Ira to do the same. And where else would a well-to-do American Jew stay on a trip to Cairo?"

"Point taken."

*   *   *

Built on the site of an Egyptian royal palace, the cylindrical El Gezirah high-rise towered over the Nile waterfront. But Wörtlich hadn't come to sightsee, and Cairo's urban landscape had long since passed from the exotic to the familiar.

Wörtlich had chuckled at Brighton's wide-eyed reactions to their surroundings since arriving in Egypt. The young man had a lot of acclimating to do. They had only known each other for a few days, and in that time they had conspired to steal one of the most precious treasure troves of knowledge in the history of the world. They should have bonded to some degree by now, at least on a professional level if not on a personal one. It didn't seem possible that more than half the time he struggled to remember the young man's first name. Maybe it was the generational gap. Maybe it was the cultural one.

The hotel's front traffic loop was busy. As cars pulled up, valet drivers stood ready to drive them away again. A line of black limousines was parked across from the main loading zone, their chauffeurs standing around a copse of palm trees, cigarettes hanging out of their mouths.

Between the valets, chauffeurs, and guests coming and going, there were far too many eyes on hand for Wörtlich's comfort. Under no circumstance would he risk going inside.

Pulling out the phone Lagati had given him, he dialed information, asking in Arabic for the El Gezirah. He was quickly connected to the hotel lobby.

"I am looking for one of your guests," he said. "Ira Binyamin. Please call up and let him know his car has arrived."

"Yes, sir," a thickly-accented man answered.

Instinctively, he whipped his head around to look out the driver's side window. Perhaps he had imagined it, but he felt as though someone was watching him. Darting his eyes to the rearview mirror, he spotted a figure standing about twenty feet behind his car. It was a woman, her eyes shielded behind a pair of dark sunglasses. The rest of her was hidden by a beige headscarf. She was light-skinned, but that was as much as he could determine from this distance.

He turned his attention back to the front doors just as Ira stepped out of the hotel, dressed in jeans and a t-shirt, looking every bit like a man on vacation. He certainly didn't look like a rabbi, though he supposed that was something one didn't want to look like while walking the streets of Cairo.

He rolled down the window so Ira would be able to see him. Sure enough, the rabbi steered toward him. He pulled the car forward to make sure none of the building's surveillance cameras would catch Ira getting into the car. Perhaps he was being paranoid, but he didn't want them to meet in plain sight.

"Well, here you are, just as planned. I guess that means we're actually doing this," Ira noted as he buckled his seatbelt. "I half expected no one to show up. Truth be told, I was sort of hoping for it."

"I thought you would be more excited."

Ira blinked in surprise. "I have too good an idea of what we're getting ourselves into."

Wörtlich shifted the car into gear, his eyes going back to the rearview mirror. The woman was gone. Had she been watching him? He chastened himself for not being more vigilant. He couldn't afford to be so careless.

A few moments passed in silence as Wörtlich charted a more circuitous route out of the city than he had planned, just in case they were being followed.

"Where are we going?" Ira asked when it became clear their destination was somewhere outside the city. "And where's Mr. Brighton?"

"Back at the motel, working on the index. We are flying under the radar, about an hour and a half north of here."

"The index? What on earth is that?"

He suddenly realized Ira didn't have a clue about the index. *Damn you, Lagati, for not telling him the whole truth.*

Wörtlich cleared his throat. "Have you heard of the Library of Alexandria, Rabbi?"

"By answering my question with another question, I surmise it has something to do with this hunt of ours," Ira said. "I also surmise you'll fill me in on the salient details."

"A document has been discovered that offers us glimpses into the contents of the library. It is also potentially invaluable for our 'hunt,'

EVAN BRAUN & CLINT BYARS

as you call it. The Book of Creation seems to be connected to ancient Egypt in some way. Unfortunately, our knowledge of that period of history is somewhat scattered and poorly understood. Perhaps the Alexandrians knew of the Book, and if so, the index could offer us important clues as to its location. Perhaps it was even in the library at some point."

Ira sighed. "It wasn't. It could not have been. The *Sefer Yetzirah*, certainly, but not the Book." Pausing, he stroked his chin. "Lagati has been given access to the index, you say?"

Wörtlich hesitated. Every indication was that Ira would not respond favorably to their methods, yet there wasn't much point in avoiding the truth. They were going to be spending a lot of time together; a lie would start them off on a sour note.

"No," he answered. "Not given."

Ira frowned, and that frown deepened with every passing moment. "I see. You took matters into your own hands. We're staying outside the city because you're concerned—and rightfully so—about being apprehended. Who did you steal it from?"

The corners of Wörtlich's mouth lifted in a smile at that bit of reasoning. "It came from the Archaeological Institute in Cairo, but we only took a copy of the index. There is no reason we cannot all share the information."

"There must be a reason they didn't want to share."

"I suppose that is true." He glanced over at Ira and found the rabbi calmly staring out the window, watching the buildings pass. "I thought you would be more upset."

"Don't mistake my composure for acceptance. I am extremely upset. One thing I am not, however, is surprised. Not remotely. It would be naïve of me, after our meeting with Lagati, not to entertain the likelihood of us being asked to engage in criminal activity. But I certainly didn't think we would cross that line so soon."

Ira closed his eyes for a moment. Wörtlich didn't know what he was thinking, but whatever it was had Ira feeling torn.

"I have resolved to temporarily look to the larger purpose in this," Ira said. "I believe our objective could be worth breaking a few laws for. Mind you, there are some lines I will not cross."

*   *   *

Ira wasn't one for creature comforts, but the stark contrast between this motel and the one he had just left gave him a sinking feeling.

Inside, they found Brighton sitting cross-legged on the bed, his computer on his lap. A small box was hooked up to it by a cable, its external light blinking furiously. No doubt that was the "index" Wörtlich had told him about.

Brighton and Wörtlich caught him up with their efforts to access the information on the hard disk. Ira didn't know the first thing about decryption, so he had to rely heavily on Brighton's explanations.

Essentially Brighton had to solve two puzzles, both of which were further complicated by the fact that for whatever reason the index had been split into seventy-two different files. The first thing Brighton needed to figure out was what algorithm, or cipher, had been used to encrypt the files. The cipher was the mathematical formula needed by the computer to correctly transform the garbled text into a readable form. But even if he were to identity the correct algorithm, Brighton wouldn't be able to open any of the files until he obtained the correct passwords—and each of the files had unique protection. Whoever had encrypted the information on the hard disk had left it dauntingly secure.

Brighton sighed, putting the computer aside and getting a glass of water from the bathroom sink. He perched himself on the edge of the bed.

"There's good news and bad news," Brighton said. "The good news is that I think I've cracked the cipher. There's an algorithm called Medusa-6 that a few of my friends from Caltech worked on last year. It's not a very common algorithm, but it's highly secure. As far as I know, the only people who are aware it's been solved are me and three other guys I went to school with."

"It seems a bit lucky that the one code you broke is the one they used," Wörtlich said.

"Well, it's not the only code we broke, but it's definitely the most complicated one mathematically," Brighton said. "It's just about as perfect a cipher as there is. I might have used it myself if I didn't know it had already been compromised."

Ira smiled to himself. "Then I guess it's a good thing we have you on our side."

"And the bad news?" Wörtlich asked.

"Assuming Medusa-6 cracks all seventy-two files, I'm still left with having to find seventy-two unique passwords. The first thing I tried was a dictionary attack."

Ira felt a headache coming on. This was such a young man's game...

"Basically, my computer tried every dictionary word in ten languages. There weren't any matches. Next, I put together combinations of multiple words, but that didn't work, either. If the Institute was smart, they would have created passwords from completely random characters. Those would be impossible to guess, short of trying every combination of letters, numbers, and symbols—which would take forever. We don't have that kind of time and my computer couldn't handle the processing load."

"Then we are at a dead end," Wörtlich concluded.

Brighton sighed. "Nearly. From what I can tell, the passwords are long. Extremely long. They could be a hundred thousand characters or more, containing more than ten thousand bits of information. There's no limit. I've never seen anything like it."

"It seems excessive," Wörtlich said. "If a few dozen random characters would be too difficult for a computer to sort out, why go to the trouble to include a hundred thousand of them? Is that not overkill?"

"Definitely," Brighton agreed. "The passwords could easily be longer than the documents they're protecting. It doesn't make any sense."

Unless the length of the passwords is in itself a clue, Ira thought.

"Perhaps they're books themselves," the rabbi suggested.

"Excuse me?" Brighton asked.

"The passwords could be complete texts, couldn't they? If that were the case, they wouldn't be needlessly random."

Brighton put aside his computer and threw his weight against the backboard. It bounced against the wall with a loud clack. "Okay, sure. But which texts did they use?"

"I have a guess," Ira said. The other two men looked at him in surprise. "If you assume the passwords are books, and that the books are more likely than not to be related to the subject matter, then there is only one probable guess. You said the index was split into seventy-two pieces. That is a clue, I think. The passwords you're looking for come from the Septuagint."

Brighton stared at the rabbi blankly. It took a few moments for Ira to realize that his deduction wasn't self-explanatory.

"The word Septuagint means *the translation of seventy men,*" he continued. "The story dates back to the court of Ptolemy II in old Alexandria. As he was assembling the Great Library, Ptolemy sent a letter to the high priest at Jerusalem, requesting that the seventy-two most knowledgeable Hebrew scholars be sent to Alexandria to create a Greek translation of the Torah."

"Why seventy-two?" Brighton asked.

"It was the result of requesting six men from each of the twelve tribes of Israel. When the men arrived, Ptolemy sequestered them on the island of Pharos, just off the coast. With no contact with each other or the outside world, they proceeded to develop seventy-two unique translations, which would be helpful for canonization. But when the men emerged, it was found that every one of the translations was identical, to the very letter. And from that remarkable occurrence, we have the Septuagint."

Wörtlich shook his head. "Clearly a legend, Rabbi. I would not put faith in it."

"I doubt you put faith in much of anything. Mr. Brighton—can I call you Sherwood?" When Brighton nodded, Ira went on. "Sherwood, do you have any other ideas for getting into the index?"

The young man picked up his computer again. "No, your Septuagint theory is the best we've got."

He got to work immediately as Ira and Wörtlich waited.

"What are you doing?" Wörtlich asked.

"Looking for digital copies of the Septuagint," Brighton responded without looking up. "I'm going to try splitting it into seventy-two equal parts. Keep your fingers crossed."

The puzzle only looked insurmountable, Ira concluded as Brighton got back to work and Wörtlich vanished into the bathroom. The coincidence of Brighton knowing about the Medusa-6 cipher didn't escape him. And how easy would it have been to secure the index with smaller, randomly generated keys? Seventy-two separate files, indeed. With a rabbi close at hand, the solution had been as obvious as a trail of breadcrumbs.

From start to finish, the encryption puzzle seemed to have been custom tailored for them, as though someone was gauging their ability to problem solve and work as a team. The only someone who made sense was Raff Lagati, except that he had been the one to send Wörtlich and Brighton after the index in the first place. Was it possible he'd had access all along?

This was a test. If Lagati was behind it, he's gone out of his way to give us the illusion of control. He's not a trusting man, is he?

Ira didn't like being manipulated. He had to fight the impulse not to air his concerns. As long as Lagati felt he was in control, Ira had to keep quiet. He had to play along.

ELEVEN

Tanta, Egypt

SEPTEMBER 17

Brighton fell asleep on the floor. He woke once during the night to go to the bathroom only to find Wörtlich hadn't moved an inch. The archaeologist hovered over the portable printer, snatching one sheet of paper after the next from its thin metallic lips. His eyes were wide and full of childlike excitement. It was a side of the man Brighton hadn't seen yet. The hour was late, or early, depending on how you looked at it, and they were all tired, which made the force driving him all the more unmistakable. Passion.

When he woke again in the morning, Ira was gone and Wörtlich had shifted some of his paperwork over to the bed where he had more room to spread out. He wore his glasses, and his fingers were paging through his notebook.

"Where's Ira?" Brighton scratched a sudden itch on the side of his cheek and wondered if there were bugs in the carpet.

He couldn't be sure Wörtlich had heard him. Finally, the archaeologist looked up, his expression vacant. "Hmm?"

"Did Ira leave?"

"He is getting something to eat," Wörtlich said. "He should be back soon."

Brighton stood, rubbing his eyes. He went into the washroom to run some cold water over his face. It was only midmorning and already the heat was radiating through the front window faster than the tiny air conditioner could keep up.

I can only imagine what it must be like in August, he mused before getting into the shower.

Ira soon returned with coffee and a loaf of bread. Ira wasted no time eating, his eyes flitting back and forth as Wörtlich paced the front of the room. Looking disheveled and overtired, the archaeologist stood back from his research clutter. When Ira offered him some coffee, Wörtlich took the cup and drank deeply.

"You found something?" Brighton asked.

Wörtlich sat down heavily, wiping sweat off his forehead. He looked feverish. "I just need a minute to sort it all out."

"Maybe you should take a break," Ira remarked. "Take a walk, clear your head."

It didn't take a moment for Wörtlich to be out the door and halfway down the parking lot.

*   *   *

With the sun almost directly overhead, the heat was oppressive, and it was only going to get worse. Wörtlich belatedly thought of his hat, which he'd left on top of his bag so he wouldn't forget it the next time he went out. Sweat was already gathering in hot, sticky patches around his temples.

The feeling of being watched returned. This time, he didn't have far to look. A woman was approaching him from the street. He was almost certain it was the same woman who had seen him at the El Gezirah. She wasn't Egyptian; even with her eyes covered, he could tell she was staring right at him. Egyptian women were rarely so forward. Eye contact was considered flirtatious.

Her hand came up to peel off her sunglasses, and Wörtlich's breath caught in his throat. That face was unmistakable.

"What on earth are you doing here?"

Elisabeth Macfarlane finally reached him. Now that she'd been recognized, she slipped the glasses back over her eyes. "I should ask you the same thing, Emery."

Wörtlich steadied himself by putting a hand against the trunk of a nearby palm tree. The bark was rough and shingled, pressing painfully against his palm until he released it.

"How did you find me?" he asked.

"Believe it or not, it's partly luck. You've covered your trail well." She paused, checking the time on her wristwatch. "I wouldn't stay in one place too long, though. The Institute's after you."

"After what I did, that is their right."

Looking at her, he had to give himself a mental pinch to make sure this wasn't a dream. Her brown hair was mostly pulled back beneath her headscarf, but the light breeze teased a few stray curls. God, she was beautiful. He wanted to gently remove the sunglasses and get a good look at those green eyes he could never get enough of.

Even so, she was just about the last person he had expected to run into. "You still have not told me what you are doing here."

"I came to see you," Elisabeth said. "I was staying at the El Gezirah. A taxi had just dropped me off when I spotted you, waiting for that man to arrive. Who was he? What's going on, Emery? Why are you doing this?"

He wanted to tell her everything, the explanation traveling right to the tip of his tongue before being forced back down. He wasn't in this alone; he had a responsibility to the others.

"I cannot tell you. For that matter, you cannot tell anyone you saw me here. If I am caught, I will go to prison. Why did you have to come looking for me?" He took a deep breath as he automatically glanced around to see if anyone could hear them. "We cannot talk here, not out in the open."

"How about in your room?"

"No, not there," he said. She didn't know any specifics about his two companions and as far as he was concerned it should stay that way; it was bad enough that she'd seen Ira.

Over her shoulder, he spotted a small park. There wasn't much cover between the trees, but at least there wouldn't be any people around.

The only place to sit without resorting to the ground was a wooden bench situated beneath a cluster of date trees. The bench was covered in splotches of purple, discolored from where mushy dates had fallen from the branches above.

"Emery, there's something very serious going on at the Institute," Elisabeth said. "Someone has removed pages from the index. What the Institute is distributing is not the same version I digitized at the university. The copy you stole is missing an entire scroll."

"Are you certain?"

"Yes," she said firmly. "I oversee the spectral imaging department.

I saw the originals with my own eyes. There's no mistake."

Wörtlich frowned. "I do not understand. Who would do that?"

"Of all people, you shouldn't have to ask. Not everyone who works at the Institute shares our agenda of getting to the truth. Someone must not have liked what they found on that scroll. At times like this, I really wish I read Greek."

His mind raced as she reached into her purse and pulled out a disk.

"You brought the missing scroll with you?" he asked incredulously.

"Of course I did. The whole point of coming was to get this into your hands. I don't know what you'll do with it, but you should have all the information." She took his hand and squeezed it affectionately. "Emery, I trust you. I always have, even when I had no reason to, and you've never given me reason to regret that. You must have a good reason for what you're doing. Why won't you tell me what it is?"

He reached up and tenderly pulled the glasses from her eyes, which looked back at him longingly. She was such a beautiful woman. If it hadn't been for his wife at the time, who knew what might have happened? The year Elisabeth had lived in Cairo had been the best year of his life.

"I am looking for something," he admitted quietly.

"You're always looking for something."

Wörtlich bit his lip and looked away, an act that brought pangs to his stomach. "This is different. My hope is to find clues in the index, but so far…" He turned back, and his butterflies-in-the-stomach feelings subsided. "There are some amazing discoveries in there, to be sure, but none of them have anything to do with my search."

"Does what you're looking for concern the Hall of Records?"

He stared at her in surprise. Mainstream Egyptologists didn't talk much about the Hall of Records in professional company. If it existed, it would necessarily have to have been far older than even the oldest artifacts and sites attributed to the ancient Egyptians. It was mythical. Apocryphal. Actually locating it was not a serious pursuit.

"Why?" he wondered.

"There are mentions of it on the missing pages," Elisabeth said. "At least, I think so."

"I thought you said you cannot read Greek."

"I can't read *much* Greek," she amended. "Alexandria seemed to have at least one book dedicated to something called 'the repository of knowledge.' I put two and two together. It's got to be the Hall of Records, right?"

Wörtlich stood up, distracted. He couldn't involve her in this. "I have to go."

"Emery, please. Talk to me."

He eyed the disk still clutched in her left hand. As much as he wanted to spend more time with her, to catch up and chat about all the mundane things that would have occupied them for hours had these been normal circumstances, he didn't have that luxury. If they were ever going to be together—and for the first time in years, that seemed a possibility—he had to figure this out. Fast. Before the authorities caught up with them.

"At least contact me from time to time so I'll know you're safe," she said.

Wörtlich avoided her eyes. If he looked at her even one more time he would want to go back with her. Could he trust himself to say no?

"I cannot promise that," he said.

She handed over the disk, her hand lingering for a moment on his fingers. The touch sent a chorus of tiny shivers running up from the point of contact to his shoulders. He couldn't avoid her any longer. He looked up just as she leaned in and gave him a light kiss. She had been aiming for his forehead, but instead her lips brushed against his.

"But I will try," he added, even though the truth was that, for her sake as much as anyone's, he probably wouldn't.

*   *   *

Brighton was astonished to learn of Wörtlich's encounter with Elisabeth and the disk she had given him. He wanted to talk about it, to get the details, but instead Wörtlich insisted on getting some sleep. By the looks of it, the man could hardly think straight.

He desperately wanted to get out of the motel, to explore, but Ira wouldn't let him leave. Without a doubt, the rabbi was spooked about Wörtlich's encounter with his colleague. If one person had spotted them, who else might be lurking in the shadows?

They reconvened that evening, after Wörtlich had an opportunity to look over the new index pages. Brighton had also gone through the pages, but without a better understanding of Greek he couldn't glean much from them.

Wörtlich sat on the floor, his papers all around him. He looked bone-tired. "I have been trying to find a way to explain everything, to communicate all the things that are running through my mind. It is very difficult."

Brighton spread out across the bed where he had cleared away some of Wörtlich's things. "Tell us what you found."

Wörtlich glanced up at him. "You worked at the Smithsonian, did you not?"

"Yes."

"In that case, what do you know about the Hall of Records? Anything?"

Brighton rolled his eyes. "Oh God, not another library..."

"So, you do know something."

"Not really," Brighton said. "Just that it may have been a really old library. Perhaps the very oldest."

Wörtlich nodded. "If it existed, no question it was the oldest. Even when the pyramids were new, the Hall was unspeakably old."

"But it's a legend," Ira remarked ironically. His eyes twinkled as Wörtlich caught the inherent joke.

"Touché," Wörtlich said.

The rabbi bore a wide smile. "Actually, I think we'd all be surprised at how many supposed legends are true."

"You mean how many legends have their basis in truth," Brighton corrected.

"No," Ira said. "I mean actually true. As in factual."

Brighton shrugged. He'd held his tongue this long; why not a little longer?

"The missing pages of the scroll are dedicated to any and all books pertaining to the Hall of Records." Wörtlich paused to rub sleep out of his eyes. "It even implies that some of Alexandria's books originated there."

"What about the *Sefer Yetzirah*?" Ira asked.

Wörtlich stabbed a finger at Ira excitedly. "Exactly! What about it? I was troubled to find that it was not listed in the original index copy we stole. If Alexandria's collection was so all-encompassing, how could such an obvious volume be left out? As one of the very oldest Hebrew texts, it must have been there." He ran a finger through his hair, gearing himself up for a major revelation. "It is, however, listed in the missing scroll."

Brighton found the reference on the index file and enlarged it for

Ira, who pulled his chair closer.

"There's a small Greek inscription next to it," Ira said.

"What does it say?" Wörtlich asked.

Ira scrunched up his forehead, performing a loose translation in his head. "I think it says *House of Draco*, but I don't know what that means."

"Perhaps that's the family name of the household that donated the book to the library," Brighton suggested.

"Books were not donated," Wörtlich said. "Usually they were seized from people entering or exiting the city. How did you think the library got to be so big?"

Draco... Smiling, Brighton snapped his fingers. "Wait, isn't Draco the name of a star constellation?"

Wörtlich inclined his head, giving that some thought. "I think it is a mythological creature. A dragon, as I recall."

The professor of archaeology stood up, and suddenly Brighton felt a lecture coming on.

"Through the index, the ancients are directing us," Wörtlich said. "It is like a map, and if we know how to read it, it will tell us exactly where to go next. Every book listed in the missing scroll has some connection to the Hall, which means that the *Sefer Yetzirah* must also. We need to go to the Hall. Unfortunately, there is no consensus on its location. Archaeologists cannot even agree that it exists."

"The Smithsonian would call it pseudoarchaeology, chasing something that doesn't exist," Brighton put in.

Wörtlich reached down and picked up his notebook from the floor. "One of the Alexandrian books was dedicated to the study of the Hall of Records, calling it 'the repository of knowledge.' The book's title, strangely enough, is *Beneath the Strangler*."

"What does that mean?" Brighton wondered.

"The strangler was a female monster in Greek mythology," the archaeologist explained. "It is also what the ancient Greeks called the Sphinx—the strangler. It seems clear to me that the Greeks believed the Hall of Records was located beneath it, on the Giza plateau, near the pyramids."

Brighton shook his head. "But why under the Sphinx and not under the older pyramids?"

"You have it backwards," Wörtlich replied. "The Sphinx is a great deal older than the pyramids. The pyramids are about six thousand years old, but the Sphinx could easily be ten thousand. According to legend, the Sphinx was built at a time when the constellation of Leo was perfectly aligned between its front paws. If that is true, we can date it."

Brighton turned his head to Ira, who was awfully quiet. The old man was paying attention, though, despite appearing at times like he was about to nod off. It was a decent trick to pull off false indifference so well.

The rabbi stirred. "You're planning to go down there, beneath the Sphinx?"

"*We* are, actually," Wörtlich corrected. "Lagati wants us to work together. We do complement each other, do we not?"

Ira looked about to argue when Brighton interrupted. "I hate to throw a wrench in this plan of yours, if you could even call it that, but how do you suppose we access the site? It's not like we can just walk up to the Sphinx, pull out a shovel, and start digging. There are people everywhere."

Wörtlich looked ponderous, though by no means dissuaded.

"Often people with guns," Brighton added. "If we were to ask permission, the Egyptian government would never go for it, not in a million years. Plus we're fugitives!"

Wörtlich managed a nod. "You are right, of course."

Brighton smiled in smug satisfaction.

"Then how do we get there?" Ira asked.

The archaeologist shrugged. "The ancients have already done the digging for us. All we need to do is find the door."

Brighton closed his eyes and let his head hit the pillow. A sticky pool of sweat gained critical mass on his forehead and rolled down his cheek. God, it was hot! They'd only been talking for ten or fifteen minutes, but his armpits were soaked through just from lying on the bed. How hard could it have been to find a room with better air conditioning? He excused himself and went into the bathroom to splash some water on his face.

By the time he came back, Wörtlich had a plan.

TWELVE

Giza Plateau, Egypt
SEPTEMBER 17

S unset had come and gone by the time the trio left the motel. It would have done no good to show up before dark; the last thing they needed was an employee getting a good look at them.

Brighton first spotted the unmistakable shapes of the pyramids several miles distant, their tips thrusting up over the purpling horizon. He fought the urge to pull out his camera and start snapping away. If everything went according to plan, he'd get a much better view in just a few minutes.

The guardhouse was deserted. Just like Lagati had promised over the phone.

The roving beam of a flashlight cut through the air just ahead—someone in the middle of the road, waving them down.

Was it a guard? Or perhaps someone a bit more friendly? Wörtlich was the picture of tranquility as he stopped the car on the side of the pavement.

As Brighton climbed out of the car, he was struck by how unnaturally dark it was in the shadow of the massive pyramid. The monument blotted out a full third of the night sky, making it difficult to even distinguish his feet beneath him, never mind the face of the silhouetted man now approaching them.

Brighton stuck close to the car in case they had to jump back in. As far as Arab countries went, Egypt's justice system was more progressive than most, but he didn't have any intention of putting it to the test.

"Doctor Wörtlich?" the silhouetted man called softly. "Rabbi Binyamin, is this you?"

Beside him, Brighton saw Ira stiffen at the sound of his name. After all, who would want to be identified by name while committing a crime?

Wörtlich reached for the flashlight clipped to his belt and flicked it on. A young Egyptian man squinted back at them.

"Doctor Wörtlich?" the man asked again.

"Yes," Wörtlich answered, frowning. "You are not Zahi Menefee."

Doctor Menefee, Wörtlich had explained on the way over, was on the Institute's board of directors—and apparently in Lagati's pocket. Brighton's heart beat faster and he stifled the urge to leap back toward the car. This wasn't the man Lagati had sent?

The young man bowed shallowly. "Many sorries. Menefee cannot come, busy with council matters." He paused, his white teeth flashing in a smile that caught the moonlight. "Very important man, Menefee!"

Wörtlich nodded. "All right, then. Who are you?"

"Najja," the man said. "My name is Najja Fadil."

Satisfied, Wörtlich gestured to the others. "This is the rabbi and Mr. Brighton."

Najja nodded, giving each man a half-bow. Wörtlich pointed his flashlight to the ground, then returned it to his belt.

"Come, this way." Najja pointed to a stone causeway leading around to the pyramid's north face.

They reached the entrance after two hundred paces, which turned out to be little more than a roughhewn hole a few feet up the base. Brighton was almost disappointed; somehow he had imagined there would be a grand gate of some kind. He exchanged a quick glance with Ira, but the rabbi's face gave away nothing. It was though he had been here a hundred times before.

"Thousands of years ago, the pyramid was covered with limestone," Wörtlich said. "Without an obvious entrance, the looters broke through right here."

"I leave you now," Najja told the archaeologist. "You know the way?"

"I do."

Najja withdrew a cell phone from his pocket and placed it in Wörtlich's hand. "Only one number programmed. Call if you must, but once you are down, you will lose... what is the word?"

"Signal," Brighton put in.

"Yes, signal," Najja finished. "You have five hours."

Wörtlich turned his flashlight back on and took a few steps into the passage, rough on both sides and angled sharply downward.

Brighton watched Najja disappear down the causeway. A few moments later he heard the sound of a car engine.

When he turned back, Wörtlich and Ira had already vanished into the dark, the faint glow of the archaeologist's flashlight the only evidence anyone had been there at all.

Brighton spared one more glance up at the pyramid's towering exterior. *It's so big. Everyone I've known who came here told me so, but it's so damn big.*

"You coming, Sherwood?" Ira's voice called from inside.

Brighton gripped the metal handrail that followed the length of the passage and ventured into the dark.

They soon came to a set of recently installed metallic steps, which eased the visitors' descent into a hole where Wörtlich stood waiting. A halogen lamp, hooked to an electrical line that ran along the ceiling, lit the space bright yellow.

"The descending passage continues in a southerly direction," Wörtlich said as Brighton caught up.

A huge granite slab blocked the northern passage. Wörtlich knocked it with his fist. "Rocks like these were placed to seal off the upper chambers. They have not been moved in six thousand years."

"Why were the chambers sealed off?" Ira wondered.

"A security feature, to keep out looters." Wörtlich looked further down the passage. "Watch your heads. The ceiling is only four feet high in places, so you will have to bend over."

Brighton hunched down as best he could, trying to make himself as short as possible. After just a few steps, his shins strained from the difficulty of maintaining the position while shuffling forward. To make matters worse, with both Wörtlich and Ira ahead of him, he couldn't see a thing except the rabbi's backside, which didn't make for the most picturesque of views.

"Breathe slowly and regularly," Wörtlich cautioned, his voice sounding muffled. "These lower passages tend to be a bit oxygen-deprived."

As if on cue, a cloud of dust wafted up into Brighton's open mouth and he coughed fitfully. He managed to recover by wetting his lips, but the air was increasingly dry.

They continued on for what seemed like hours, even though he knew it was only a matter of minutes. He wondered how Ira was holding up… if he was having trouble. Surely a man three times his age would have three times the challenge. But when he asked, Ira insisted he was fine.

The floor leveled off, signaling their proximity to the bottom.

We must be nearly to the subterranean chamber. That meant they'd travelled about four hundred feet underground. Brighton shivered, feeling a wave of cold envelop him.

To his relief, a moment later they emerged into a cramped chamber carved out of the bedrock. The room had just enough room for him to stand to his full height. Ahead, a metal railing enclosed a dark shaft. He braced himself against the railing and leaned over the edge, straining to see the bottom. There wasn't one.

"How deep is it, do you think?" Brighton asked.

Wörtlich came to stand beside him. "Sixty feet, I am told. I have only been here once before, years ago. Only researchers with special permits are allowed this far."

"It's cold," Ira remarked.

Brighton felt another shiver coming on and tried not to think about the five million tons of stone piled above their heads.

Wörtlich pressed his fingers up along the north wall of the tomb-like chamber. "The bedrock does not retain heat."

Because the room had been carved out of bedrock, everything was unnaturally smooth. No creases marred the transitions where the walls met floor or ceiling. Behind them, a series of rough steps led up onto a second, unfinished level. Whatever the builders had intended for this space had been abandoned, a mystery that might never be solved.

"No artifacts of any kind," Brighton said. "No pottery, no signs of burial, nothing." The Sulaweyo dig in New Mexico had been overflowing with such artifacts.

Wörtlich let out a little snort. "The official story is that the Egyptians intended this as an alternate burial chamber. Alternate burial chamber, indeed! I find it highly improbable that the pyramid builders would have gone to such trouble to include any spare rooms considering the effort required."

Brighton raised an eyebrow. "But if there's nothing here—"

"Far from nothing, Mr. Brighton," Wörtlich said. He peered into the darkest corner of the room. "This is the door I told you about, the one the ancients dug for us."

Leaning over, the archaeologist ran his hand along the edge of a metal grate blocking access to another passageway, this one hardly larger than a heating duct.

"This is called the Dead End Passage," Wörtlich explained. "No one has ever explored it to the end, but robotics has shown it to end fifty-three feet in." He paused for effect. "Except it does not end there."

"What's on the other side?" Brighton asked.

Ira's hand clapped him on the shoulder, causing him to nearly jump. "Why, the Hall of Records, of course."

Brighton moaned as he looked at the small passageway. "Looks like a tight squeeze."

"We will have to crawl," Wörtlich admitted, inspecting the edges of the grate. "Mr. Brighton, could you look in my pack for the crowbar?"

Brighton fished in the bag, finding the tool. He handed it to

Wörtlich, who exchanged it for the flashlight. Without missing a beat, Wörtlich plunged the tip of the crowbar into the space between the grate and the stone wall. He pulled back, testing the metal's durability. Satisfied, the archaeologist gritted his teeth and then put all his weight behind the effort of prying the screws loose one by one.

Brighton flinched at the screams of metallic protest as Wörtlich worked free each screw. With each flinch, the flashlight's beam wavered against the wall where he pointed it. He felt Ira's hand settle on his shoulder, settling him.

When the last screw dropped to the ground with a high-pitched *ping,* Wörtlich removed the grate and tossed it aside.

Brighton got down on his knees and peered into the opening. A lightless abyss peered back. Centuries had probably passed since anyone had crawled inside.

*   *   *

"Will we fit?" Brighton asked.

Wörtlich would have confidently said yes if Brighton had asked from the luxury of their motel room, but now that he stared into the confined space, he wasn't so sure. Mathematically, he knew the dimensions were large enough, but he could imagine getting trapped inside, suffocating—

"We will fit," Wörtlich said. "Of course we will fit."

He stretched his arms into the opening. About a centimeter of dust had accumulated on the bottom, which he'd be breathing in for the first few minutes of the crawl.

He slid his head in, forcing himself to remember there was another chamber at the end of this tunnel. There had to be. But if they were wrong…

"Let me go alone," Wörtlich said. "To make sure. If there is nothing there and I have to crawl back, you will not be in the way. If I find something at the end, I will call for you."

"Sounds good," Brighton said.

Of course it sounded good to Brighton. He wasn't the one putting himself on the line.

Wörtlich's knuckles whitened as he pulled himself the rest of the way into the hole, his fingernails scraping against the rough surface of the rock. The passage was such a tight squeeze that his shoulder blades grinded occasionally against the top of the passage. He constantly fought the urge to panic. If he went back or called for help now, he wouldn't have the courage to try again.

Dust billowed up in front of him. He tried to regulate his breathing, but it was difficult; deep breaths caused his lungs to expand, which in turn pushed his ribcage into the unyielding rock beneath him. Grunting, he clawed himself forward by his fingertips, one steady hand length at a time. He could feel sharp stones cutting into the skin of his hands and lower arms, but he ignored the pain.

Damn, I should have taken back the flashlight!

It was too late now. He kept looking ahead, hoping to see something, anything, in the pitch black space ahead of him.

Lagati had assured him this tunnel extended fifty-three feet, but Wörtlich felt like he'd already traveled sixty or more. He tried not to dwell on it, but his mind kept flashing to the possibility that there really was just a dead end coming up. He could not possibly be wrong, though; all the evidence pointed to the Hall being here.

At first, he thought he was imagining that the tunnel constricted further, but after a few meters the ceiling steadily pushed against his back, unyielding. The top of the tunnel lowered, tightened. It was like being buried alive in a sarcophagus, the air running out. He would have laughed if he could, so apt was the analogy to his predicament.

He reached, searching for purchase in the rough stone floor, but unexpectedly—impossibly—he found only empty space.

Wörtlich let out an involuntary gasp, then felt for the edges of the opening. Finding them, he leveraged his full weight against the rock and heaved his torso out of the hole. He took a deep breath and just about collapsed from the relief of it.

Holding himself up by the sides of the opening with his legs still within the tunnel, Wörtlich realized he didn't know what was below him. For all he knew, he knelt above a gaping, sixty-foot shaft like the one in the chamber behind him. He stopped pulling himself out of the tunnel and straightened his arms. Straining, he finally felt ground below. Pressing both palms flat against that unknown surface, he freed his legs until he stood on his hands.

Wörtlich closed his eyes, said a little prayer to a god he didn't believe in, then tumbled forward.

His feet hit ground and he let out a victory shout. He stood, clapping off the mixture of sweat, blood, and dust that had accumulated on his hands.

"You okay in there?" Brighton called from the other side of the tunnel.

"Yes!" Wörtlich turned from the passageway and squinted into the darkness. "I am standing in a chamber on the other side."

Except it wasn't quite darkness that greeted him. Somewhere further on, around a bend where the cavern curved to the left, soft light glowed. But what could be emitting it?

He waited for the others, helping to pull them through, first Ira and then Brighton. The rabbi looked a little winded but otherwise no worse for wear.

"So much for the dead end," Ira muttered.

But Wörtlich wasn't listening. He snatched the flashlight from Brighton and shone it toward the mysterious light.

"Do you see that?" He drew an excited breath. "Light!"

All three men walked toward the glow. When they came around the corner, they found a row of large, glowing rocks lining the cavern's walls, held in place by short metallic bars. They almost looked like streetlamps, as ridiculous as that sounded in Wörtlich's mind.

Investigating one up close, Wörtlich found no source for the light apart from the rock itself, which shouldn't have been possible in the absence of extreme radioactive heat. At least, not by the physical laws he knew.

Wörtlich reached out toward one of the rocks, half expecting it to burn him. Instead, it was barely even warm to the touch.

"Where's the light coming from?" Brighton wondered.

"The hell if I know," Wörtlich said.

When he looked to the side, he realized that Ira's eyes weren't on the strange, glowing rocks. The old man's attention was directed at the end of the passage, where the walls, floor, and ceiling converged toward a sheer metallic barrier as reflective as a mirror.

The rabbi approached the barrier warily, reaching out and grazing it with his hand.

"Is that metal?" Wörtlich asked, astonished.

Ira nodded.

"But that could not be. It is not right for the period. They could not have refined such—" Wörtlich came to stand next to Ira, staring straight into the eyes of his own reflection. He placed his hand flat against the barrier.

"You feel how smooth it is?" Ira asked.

Wörtlich regarded him quizzically. "It makes no sense. It is inconsistent with—"

"Of course it's inconsistent with the period," Ira interrupted. "Remember, you said it yourself. The Egyptians didn't build any of this."

"Yes, but even I did not imagine this degree of sophistication," Wörtlich acknowledged. He brushed his hand along the nearly invisible seam where the rock wall met the metal barrier's periphery. He had no explanation for it.

Brighton joined them at the barrier. "What do you think is behind it?"

"We will probably never know." Wörtlich let fly a series of curses under his breath, giving the metal a swift kick with his boot. He turned away from the barrier and ran a hand through his hair in frustration.

Brighton's mouth hung open. "You mean we came all this way only to meet a—"

"A dead end!" the archaeologist cried bitterly.

* * *

Ira slowly tuned out the others' voices, drawing into himself as he focused instead on the barrier itself. He stared into his reflection's eyes, but the more he concentrated, the more he was drawn to the reflected glow of the rocks.

That's when he saw the movement.

Faint markings, seemingly etched into the metal's impossibly smooth surface, were visible near the reflection of the lights, moving, elongating. When he felt for them, he detected nothing, yet he saw them clearly.

Lines extended from those first crude markings, stretching and lengthening until they crossed the full width of the barrier. As they traced their way from one edge to the other, he stepped back to see the larger picture developing.

He gasped. The image was wide and circular, without any of the common trappings to betray its presence. It was unmistakable.

"It's a door," he whispered.

Wörtlich and Brighton studied him carefully, as if they hadn't heard him correctly.

Brighton was the first to speak. "A door?"

"Yes," Ira said. "I can see it, clear as day."

He put his index finger along the circular outline and traced its edge for the others to see, from one side of the barrier to the other.

Wörtlich treated him to a blank stare. "I do not see anything. Ira, the surface is perfectly smooth. There is nothing there."

"It's smooth, yes, but I can see it. Oh yes, there's definitely something."

"How come only you can see it?" The question had come from Brighton, a fair question even if there was no fair answer. "Where does it lead? If it's a door, it has to lead someplace."

"I don't know," Ira said. "Yet."

Wörtlich leaned again the rock wall. Ira could imagine cogs turning inside the man's head, all sorts of synaptic processes working overtime to discover some reasonable, sensible solution that wouldn't violate his basic understanding of nature.

"A lot of the ancient texts talk about doors," Wörtlich finally said. "Not all of them are described as having physical form. For instance, the Door of Enlightenment or the Door of Awareness. The Emerald Tablets of Thoth are full of such philosophical references. Even so, I cannot bring myself to believe they are real."

Brighton flashed an ironic smile. "Do any of the Emerald Tablets mention anything about a key to these mystical doors?"

Wörtlich's eyes snapped to Brighton. "Actually, they do. Thoth wrote about sonic keys, doors that could be opened with specific sounds and tones. I do not know very much on the subject. I have always thought it a bit ridiculous ... "

Ira zoned off again, his eyes fixed on an invisible point in the center of the door only he could see.

"Rabbi?" one of the men prodded, his voice coming to him as though from a great distance.

In response, Ira began to sing.

He started soft at first, the melody slow and cautious, the Hebrew lyrics overflowing with weight, dripping with history and age. As he continued, his voice grew louder, strengthening with every note.

Abruptly, he hit a tone and stuck with it, stretching it, growing it, until it resonated, the pitch so perfect that it filled the space around them, reverberating effortlessly, rhythmically, vibrating at just the right frequency. He should have needed to take a breath, but instead he sustained the note for an impossibly long time. The entire cavern vibrated from the subtle power of the tone, but Ira remained steady, planted in place as though he was a part of the earth itself.

Then Ira moved, as if pulled forward by an invisible force. He smiled, stepped—

—and passed straight through the barrier.

THIRTEEN

Giza Plateau, Egypt
SEPTEMBER 17

The tone stopped as soon as Ira disappeared into the barrier. Brighton didn't know how to respond. It had to be a trick, though he couldn't guess its purpose. He wasn't still back at the motel sleeping, was he? Everything was so real—

"Where'd he go?" Brighton finally asked.

"Give me a second," Wörtlich said, stunned. "Let me think this through."

"He just walked through the wall!"

Wörtlich closed his eyes and rubbed his temples. "Just one second."

"He walked through the *wall*, Wörtlich! He's gone!"

"Not gone," Ira's voice said. His arm snaked its way out of the wall, its palm upturned and waiting. "I'm just on the other side of the door."

Wörtlich's face darkened. "There is no door."

"Take my hand," Ira insisted.

Neither man moved a muscle.

"I said, take my hand."

Brighton reluctantly reached for the hand, but Wörtlich shoved him back. "Do not touch it!"

The young man looked at him in open-faced amazement. "What?"

"Who knows what that is? It sounds like him, yes, but that does not mean it *is* him. For all we know, he is gone."

Brighton lifted his arm again, weighing his next decision.

"Think it through, Brighton," Wörtlich said. "Do not do it. It does not make sense. It cannot be real."

But even if it was a trick, even if it was dangerous, even if walking through walls was impossible—a basic scientific precept he was no longer sure of—the rabbi didn't have any malice toward them.

"No, it's him," Brighton said finally. "It must be. Can't you hear his breathing? It's like he's standing right next to us."

"Take my hand," Ira said again.

Making his decision, Brighton took hold of the hand and held on tightly.

"What are you doing?" Wörtlich asked.

Slowly, the hand pulled Brighton effortlessly into the barrier. The barrier gave no resistance as the tips of his fingers slid through, and it felt no different than the air in the passage. If his eyes weren't telling him there was an obstacle, he could have walked straight through it without a second thought.

Gaining courage, he advanced further, his arm vanishing up to the elbow, then to the shoulder. Losing first his right, then his left foot, he passed through altogether.

*   *   *

Wörtlich made his hand into a fist and hit the barrier as hard as he could. Bone collided with metal and he recoiled at the pain. His knuckles reddened and he felt like he'd maybe broken something.

"What the hell is going on here?" he cried out at the top of his lungs.

Ira's hand reappeared.

"It's all right, Doctor," Ira said calmly. "Take my hand."

"I cannot." Wörtlich shook his head obstinately, cradling his hand. "It just does not—I need to think it through."

"This doesn't require a great deal of thought."

Wörtlich edged closer until the toes of his shoes pressed against the barrier. He tested the wall again with his uninjured hand. Solid as the stone around him.

"I cannot believe it," he whispered, his conviction slipping. He had to say it again, perhaps to convince himself. "I cannot believe it."

"Then I'll believe enough for both of us."

He gave in. Drawing a long, deep breath and taking the hand, Wörtlich clamped his eyes shut and crossed through the barrier.

He half expected to break his nose, or worse, but when he felt nothing, absolutely nothing, he wondered whether or not anything had happened at all.

"You can open your eyes, Doctor," Ira told him. "I assure you, you're still in one piece."

His eyes fluttered open. The rabbi stood directly in front of him.

Wörtlich whirled around to see the glowing rock-lined passage. He blinked. The barrier was nowhere in sight.

"There is no wall," he breathed. "I do not understand."

"What kind of technology is this?" Brighton asked.

"Whatever it is, it is very advanced," Wörtlich noted. "Much more advanced than we have today. There must be some explanation for it."

Ira sighed loudly. "I suppose it's meant to stop those who aren't ready to see what lies beyond it."

Wörtlich examined the rabbi expectantly. "I guess Lagati was right about you. I will admit I had my doubts, but you seem to know what is going on here. What's next?"

"I have no better idea than you, Doctor."

"I think we both know that is not true."

"Have it your way," Ira said. "Aren't you the least bit curious to find out where you are?"

Remembering himself, Wörtlich turned again. In that moment, his breath escaped him more surely than if he'd been punched in the gut.

A wide gallery stretched out ahead of them. Colossal stone columns bore the weight of the ceiling some thirty feet over their heads, and between each column, about ten feet apart, stood life-sized stone figures of men with the heads of animals, graceful birds, reptiles, and terrible beasts, presiding over the long-abandoned chamber like gods—and perhaps they had been once, long ago. With their outstretched arms, each figure held in its cupped palm a bright stone globe.

"The Hall of Records!" Wörtlich exclaimed. "It *is* real."

Wörtlich took the first tentative steps, feeling stone eyes follow his every movement.

"Maybe we shouldn't—" Brighton faltered. "Maybe we don't belong here."

"You're right about that," the rabbi agreed in a heavy tone.

"But this is what we came for!" Wörtlich charged forward, surprise and confusion taking a back seat to exhilaration. "Surely we are not going to stop until we find what we came for."

*   *   *

They passed silently under those sightless stone eyes, the sounds of their footsteps echoing from one end of that cavernous gallery to the other. Ira hung back as Wörtlich hurried forward, pointing his flashlight into the eerie half-light at the chamber's end.

"There is another room here," Wörtlich called. "Another door."

The ceiling gradually sloped downward to accommodate a rectangular entryway, beckoning them to enter. Inside was a humble room, at least by the gallery's grandiose standards. Its walls, however, boasted an impressive treasure. Hand-carved into the rock from floor to ceiling, covering all four walls, was line after line of hieroglyphics.

"Just incredible, there is no other way to describe it. There is so much to read and translate…" Wörtlich's voice was filled with wonder. He studied the etchings carved at eye-level. "These characters are familiar."

"You mean you can read it?" Brighton asked.

"Somewhat," Wörtlich said. "There are extra characters I have never seen before, and the way they are combined—well, it is quite unusual. It does not correspond to anything I know of from the Old Kingdom."

Ira sat down to rest for a few moments, putting his back up against one of the walls. He wanted to close his eyes and catch his breath, but he couldn't; the air was too heavy, the feeling similar to what he had felt just before meeting Mr. Wendell the first time. He couldn't rest, not down here.

Instead, he stared at the hieroglyphics. No part of the wall in front of him was empty of text. It must have taken months to carve it all. It was excellently preserved, a side effect of not being exposed to fresh air in a few thousand years.

The shadows cast by the flashlight moved erratically, making certain sections of the wall difficult to see. As Wörtlich and Brighton busied themselves taking pictures, Ira honed in on the furthest corner of the room, where the shadows were deepest. Every once in a while, Brighton's camera's flash went off, temporarily banishing the shadows. But on one particular flash, he noticed a large shadow remain undisturbed, as though light had no effect on it.

And it was moving.

With each successive flash, it shifted further away from the working men. At first Ira thought it was a product of his overactive imagination, but then he spotted it again and knew he wasn't seeing things. It felt... alive. A chill ran up his spine.

"Rabbi?" Brighton had stopped his work and turned to him, holding his camera loosely at his side. "What are you seeing? What's there?"

Ira peered back into the depths, but now that the flashes had stopped there was nothing to see.

It's still there, whatever it is, he told himself. *Hiding in darkness.*

"Tell me what you see," Brighton repeated.

Ira pretended to be distracted. "I'm sorry?"

"That wall," Wörtlich said, pointing to almost the exact spot where Ira had been looking. "Was there something there?"

"No," Ira lied. "For a moment, I thought I could read it, that's all." He sighed audibly. "But I guess that's your area of expertise, no?"

The archaeologist nodded, seeming to accept that explanation. Both men returned to work, and in a moment Brighton was snapping pictures again. Ira settled back to listen in on their conversation.

"Be sure to get a photo of every part of the wall," Wörtlich was saying. "We can study these films later."

"It feels strange in this room," Brighton said, the statement coming out of the blue. "Do you feel it, too?"

Wörtlich didn't answer right away. Then, dismissively, he said, "No."

"I've done a lot of traveling, been to a lot of countries, but this doesn't feel like any other place on earth I've been."

"Perhaps you are not as well-traveled as you think," Wörtlich said. "I assure you, Mr. Brighton, we have not left Egypt."

"I know, but that's not—" Brighton seemed to have more to say, but Wörtlich was preoccupied.

Ira's head snapped to the side. Movement again!

There's something behind you! he wanted to shout to Brighton.

Acting on pure instinct, Ira jumped to his feet. Paying no mind to the strange looks from the other two men, he raised a hand to point at the wall behind Brighton. It had been right there!

Taking deep, calming breaths, Ira gathered himself again.

"Are you okay?" Brighton asked. He turned to look where Ira had pointed, but there was nothing there now. "You look shaken up."

"I'm fine," Ira replied, the second lie in as many minutes. "What time is it, anyway?"

"Huh?"

"We shouldn't stay too long," he reminded them. "We don't have much time."

Wörtlich glanced down at his watch. "A shame, too. I could spend a lifetime down here. The world needs to know about this place."

Ira shot him a look that could have shattered glass. "A little knowledge can do a lot of harm."

Wörtlich didn't say anything, instead returning to the task at hand.

"You two finish up in here," Ira said. "I'll head back up and try calling Najja."

He took the phone from Wörtlich and stepped out of the room.

The gallery was completely still, a remnant of another time and place. The architecture reflected a different interpretation of thought and expression than was evidenced in other old world cultures, like the Romans and Greeks. It was much older, for one thing, and its style was bleak and simple. Minimalistic. Imposing. The stonework was round and unbroken, its lines straight as arrows.

Ira had just about reached the midpoint between the hieroglyphics room and the barrier when he heard quiet rustling. He stopped and turned, unable to decide which direction the sound had come from. There was certainly no one around to have made the noise.

He continued the way they had entered, trying to ignore the sound, but it grew ever more insistent, at times resembling a footstep or the clearing of a throat. At one point, he even thought he could make out a distant peel of laughter. Indeed, there were voices mixed in, perhaps dozens of different ones, some shouting, some whispering, but all fighting for his attention. He attempted to shut them out by quickening his pace, but it did no good.

He stopped abruptly, and the noise died away.

"Is anybody there?" he called.

In response, a throaty laugh sounded very near to him.

A chill again ran down Ira's spine as he looked across the faces of the gargoyle-like figures framed by stone columns. His eyes were drawn to one particular statue depicting a man with the head of a crocodile. Its eyes were cool, unseeing, and its jaws turned up at the corner in a pitiless smile, as though it were about to inflict some great cruelty.

"Who are you?" he demanded, not addressing the crocodile in particular. The silence that greeted him was almost as deafening as the cacophony of noise that had come just before. Even after repeating the question, he was uncertain whether or not he expected someone, or something, to answer.

Out of the corner of his eye, he saw the dark spot again, now approaching from the hieroglyphics room entryway. He remained rooted to the spot as it came closer, but the clearer his angle became the less certain he was that it was there at all. It was more like the silhouette of a man, the shadow cast by a person standing on the other side of the stone wall.

"Who are you?" he asked again, softer this time.

The same soft laughter echoed in his ears. When he looked down, he found goose bumps pebbling the skin of his forearm.

The whispers started speaking to him again, the voices crowding each other out. Whatever they were saying, the words were in a language he couldn't understand. A language he didn't *want* to understand.

"Leave us!" he shouted, his eyes burning with intensity.

I wonder if the others can see and hear this, he thought. *We're not alone down here, not for a moment—*

As he continued on, he noticed a feature of the room he hadn't seen before. One of the spaces where a stone figure should have stood was empty. On closer inspection, he saw that there had likely never been a statue here. Indeed, the gallery wall between these columns wasn't cut from stone like the rest of the chamber; this wall was constructed of the same metallic substance as the barrier.

This was another door.

Without overthinking the decision, he pivoted and walked straight through it.

*   *   *

They continued on quietly after Ira departed with the phone, Wörtlich working on translating a part of the inscription important enough to have been placed in a central location.

"This is interesting," he murmured after a while, drawing Brighton back over.

"You recognize those characters?" Brighton asked.

"Yes. Right there, in the middle." Wörtlich pointed out the glyphs in question. He tapped the figure at the end. "This is an island, except an island submerged. If I did not know better, I might surmise the writer was talking about Atlantis."

"The myth of the lost continent? Maybe you should take another look."

Wörtlich scratched his head. "Indeed."

"What else does it say?"

Moving left, he circled another glyph with his finger. "This indicates an exodus of some kind, a mass departure. Perhaps it was from a natural disaster." To its right was another glyph. "This character is very similar to one used for water in Khufu's era, but it could also mean a number of other things. There are variations."

"Who was departing? The Egyptians?"

"No, I do not believe so. Possibly the Atlanteans." He snapped his fingers in a moment of inspiration. "Or the pyramid builders!"

Moving down, Wörtlich pointed to another character surrounded by smaller glyphs. "Here, this is knowledge, and the act of migration.

These people took their knowledge with them. Of course, they moved the books!" He turned to Brighton excitedly. "If this is the Hall of Records, I kept wondering, where are the books? If I read this right, then the builders of this place might have taken them to a safer location. Except this character, knowledge, is singular."

"So?"

"According to this, there was only ever one book here."

*   *   *

Ira found himself standing in darkness, but from the moment he thought of pulling out his flashlight, a row of light globes illuminated. At first, all he could make out was the immensity of this room. It was shaped like an inside-out pyramid, the walls sweeping in from the edges and tapering to a point in the center. Without measuring them, he felt certain the dimensions would reflect those of the Great Pyramid, though on a much smaller scale.

He looked behind him and saw the gallery through the barrier clear as a bell, but the gallery no longer interested him. In the middle of this room was a raised platform, and atop it stood a shining podium that seemed to reflect light rather than absorb it. The podium was blinding, and yet he stepped closer, drawn to it.

Ira climbed the platform and surveyed the room. He placed his hands on the podium, realizing as soon as he did so that it was gilded, perhaps even solid gold. He drew in a deep breath. The pyramid looters had never discovered this place, or they would have absconded with its treasure.

As he stood, perfectly still, the voices returned. They weren't speaking to him, as he had thought; it was more like he was overhearing something, something he couldn't wrap his mind around.

Sensing movement, his eyes snapped to the left in time to catch a stirring in the air. Ordinarily, he would have thought it strange to be able to *see* the air in any capacity, but the very fabric of the empty space in front of him rippled and fluctuated, almost like waves of heat over concrete on a summer day—and the effect was spreading. As he gazed at the phenomenon, he realized that it wasn't the air at all but the beings in the room with him. They weren't corporeal, not yet anyway, and they hovered above the floor like disembodied spirits. The vague outlines of faces became visible and the voices emanated from them. He could even hear their unseen feet shuffling on the ground.

This was a vision, he realized. These spiritual creatures weren't physically present with him. They had been here long ago and now went about their business without paying him any mind.

The light from the podium pulsed. He slammed his eyelids shut but couldn't keep it out. A gleaming scroll now sat where his hands had rested on the podium, its brilliance forcing him to avert his eyes.

The Book of Creation!

His heart pounded. He tried reaching down to touch it, to unroll it, but before his hand came into contact, it vanished.

Along with the mysterious beings.

Plunged into silence, he hurried from the platform and back through the barrier. Once in the gallery, he hurdled toward the hieroglyphics room as fast as his legs could carry him.

A low voice stopped him in his tracks, the sound carrying down the length of the gallery. Ira froze, his eyes catching the sight of two men standing near the entrance. They were speaking in Arabic.

Ira's first instinct was to make a run for it, but then he understood. *They can't see me! They're on the other side of the barrier.*

He smiled to himself, turned his back on them, and jogged in the opposite direction.

Ira was out of breath when he returned to find Brighton and Wörtlich very much as he had left them, except now occupying the far side of the hieroglyphics room.

"There are men looking for us," he reported.

Wörtlich spun around. "Who are they?"

"Possibly the authorities."

The archaeologist cursed. "I take it you did not talk to Najja."

Ira shook his head, remembering that the phone was still in his pocket. He handed it back.

"Something must have gone wrong," Ira said. "Perhaps Lagati gave us away."

"No, I refuse to believe that," Wörtlich said.

Ira debated whether to tell them about his own discovery but decided against it. He needed an opportunity to reflect on what he'd seen. Was there a chance he had misunderstood the vision? No. The Book of Creation had once resided here, long ago.

Brighton took a step toward him. "Rabbi—"

"I think it's time you started calling me Ira."

"Okay, Ira," the young man said, testing it out. "The Book of Creation… it was here. Wörtlich read about it on the wall."

Ira raised an eyebrow. That confirmation had come quicker than expected. "Do you know where it was taken?"

"Only that the inhabitants of this place took it somewhere to keep it safe," Wörtlich explained. "I will have more answers once I have time to study these inscriptions more closely."

"Anyway, the authorities will be waiting for us to make our escape," the rabbi said. "Fortunately, I don't think they know these rooms even exist. We may be able to wait them out."

Wörtlich once again consulted his watch. "The sun comes up in an hour."

Brighton sagged. "By which time the pyramids will be swarming with people."

"The way I see it, we have no choice but to wait until tomorrow before trying to leave," Wörtlich decided. He glanced over at the wall where they were still working. "At least it will give me more time."

Ira hung back as the two continued their work. As Brighton's flash went off, he watched the dark spot once again roam along the walls, unseen by the others.

It's only a vision, he thought, willing himself to believe it was so.

"I suppose you're right," he agreed, his voice raspy. He lowered himself to the ground. "We must wait."

Though how long he could stave off sleep, he wasn't certain.

FOURTEEN

Somewhere Else

I t wasn't a dream. Not exactly.

No other explanation could account for why Brighton found himself standing at the bottom of a rocky slope. Boulders the size of full-grown men protruded from the ground at haphazard angles. A few of the boulders looked too heavy to bear their own weight, like they might succumb to gravity, snap off from the bedrock at any moment, and careen down the slope. Of course, they'd probably formed over hundreds, if not thousands, of years. On such a timescale, it seemed unlikely any of them would pick this particular moment to make their move, and yet he couldn't help feeling wary.

Brighton didn't have any idea where he was, which was one of the reasons he was certain it wasn't a dream. He'd had lucid dreams on rare occasions, but in each of them he had gone someplace recognizable—like the gym or his girlfriend's living room—or somewhere he'd at least heard of or seen on television—like the surface of Mars or the Great Wall of China.

This barren slope was wholly foreign. Aspects of it bore a casual resemblance to certain parts of southern Utah, but the horizon was all wrong. Like the dessert, though, it was so dry that his lips cracked. He tasted blood.

The landscape was dreary, the sky clouded, and loose rocks ground beneath Brighton's shoes, but there was one thing to recommend the place: the air was sweet-smelling. Arid, yes, but unpolluted, such as he imagined only existed in the most remote corners of the world where modern civilization had yet to lay down roads and build smelting plants.

He stood on the edge of a shallow valley, the slope part of a series of low-lying hills that stretched on for quite some distance before giving way to mountains. A hill crested about fifty feet further up the slope. He trotted up to see if he could get a clearer picture of his surroundings.

Brighton shielded his eyes as a brilliant light ignited the sky in the direction of the mountains. A low, rhythmic pulse repeated itself over and over, its rumbling bass shaking the ground.

The light finally dimmed, though it didn't fade entirely. Instead of one large light ensconcing the mountains, there were now a hundred glimmering points above the tallest peak. They twinkled like stars.

It sparked a memory.

Brighton paused, frowned, then searched his memory again. Something wasn't right. A picture in a book, perhaps? A painting? He couldn't put his finger on it, but... a painting, yes, of a mountain surrounded by hundreds of twinkling stars.

Where did that come from? Brighton thought. The memory hadn't seemed to be his at all, as though it had leapt out of the ether.

He tried focusing on the non-memory, but it was gone now.

Looking behind him, he spotted the hill where he'd started out almost a mile back, yet he couldn't remember crossing the distance. Had he walked? Why didn't he remember it? Perhaps time was somehow out of sync; after all, the normal laws of physics often didn't apply in dreams—

He began walking and the miles passed quickly. He learned to ignore the time lapses. It felt as though he were skipping across the landscape like a needle over a record.

The rocks here grew more rugged than the ones in the valley behind him. Sharp ridges, most shallow enough to climb or hop down from, zigzagged across his path. They should have slowed him down more, but he didn't let up his pace.

The mountains grew closer—he was drawn to them—and the pinpoints of light became less indistinct. They didn't even look like stars anymore and they hovered closer to the ground than he'd originally thought.

Then they disappeared.

He blinked, wondering if the lights had been an optical illusion. After the barrier they'd encountered under the pyramid, anything was possible.

Brighton whirled at the sound of footsteps on gravel.

"Barakel, is that you?" a voice asked.

A tall man with severe features and brown hair stood not twenty paces back, unmoving, and staring straight at him. Was this man addressing him? What name had he used?

Barakel… he thinks my name is Barakel.

The tall man closed the distance between them. "Good, it's you. The others are waiting. I won't be the only one to approach from the north."

The man's features were smooth like glass, yet strong as steel. His eyes bore the same strength; he was not to be trifled with.

Before Brighton could respond, or even think up what he might venture to say, the tall man was already several feet ahead, a small cloud of dust billowing along the ground behind him.

"Is something wrong, Barakel?" the man asked, turning around. "We should hurry."

"You said they're waiting?" Brighton asked. At least that question was safe. The longer he stalled, the more information he could gather. If he was being mistaken for someone else, the last thing he wanted was to run into the real Barakel.

Brighton was about to catch up when the man's brown curls caught the sunlight. Another memory flashed before his eyes—a woman, a beautiful woman, with curly brown hair and the sharpest green eyes he had ever—

It's not my memory. I've never seen that woman in my life.

"What are you waiting for?" the man asked, not quite angry but impatient.

Brighton looked up as the memory fell away. This was no time for mental slips. He could feel the danger in his bones.

"I'm sorry," Brighton managed. He started walking again. "You're right. We should hurry."

"I see you are as hesitant as I. Azazel will love that, won't he?"

Azazel? Brighton searched his memory for some reference to the name. He came up blank.

It sounds Arabic.

The moment the thought occurred to him, Brighton knew it had come from somewhere outside himself, like another man's thoughts were intruding on his own.

An alarming prospect, to say the least.

"We will have to hurry," the tall man continued. "The others will have already arrived."

Without knowing where they were going, Brighton had no choice but to follow. Turning and running wasn't an option, not without somewhere to run to.

The path wended upward at a steep enough slope to make him stop occasionally to catch his breath, but the tall man's pace didn't lag. By the way the man continued without looking back, it was clear he fully expected him to be perfectly capable of keeping up.

The path leveled off before taking a sharp turn into a natural amphitheater. Ominous cliffs sprouted up in a circle around them, their heights coming to sharp pinnacles that must have been the tops of the mountains. He felt very much like he was standing in the bowels of a volcano, the ground below him potentially just minutes away from eruption.

The only thing more menacing than the cliff walls was the group of men gathered in the center of the amphitheater. At least a hundred of them, though more were still arriving, some of them in flashes of light. They all dressed similarly, in low-hanging white robes, though their hems never came into contact with the ground.

"Barakel!"

It took Brighton a moment to realize it wasn't the tall man who'd spoken, but another man approaching them from the pack. This second man had almost identical features, except for the angles of his face, which were as sharp and hard as diamonds, and the eyes—they pierced him with a sheer, crisp blue that shone like the edge of a steel blade.

"I expected you sooner, Barakel." The newcomer's lips twisted into a sneer. Those dangerous eyes swung briskly to the tall man. "And you, Semyaza. Is there something I don't know about?"

"No." Semyaza paused to clear his throat. "Is it time, Azazel?"

So this was the man Semyaza had mentioned. One look at his frightening visage filled Brighton with dread.

Azazel made his way back into the crush of new arrivals, where the numbers seemed to have doubled.

Brighton listened as Azazel launched into a rousing speech, but it was almost impossible for him to follow what was going on. From time to time, Semyaza made contributions, as did a few others, but there were a dozen or so attendees who were more invested in what was going on than the rest. Barakel, by all appearances, was one of them, given the frequency with which Azazel gestured in his direction.

Just what it was he was supposed to be invested in, however, was far trickier to determine. Two things he could hardly have missed were the words *Jehovah* and *Shamballa*, the first being a reference to a person and the second being a city taken straight from legend. The way they spoke of it, Shamballa was a physical place, though Brighton still hadn't discounted the possibility that this whole event had somehow been imagined by his subconscious, though what could have triggered it he had no idea.

Startled, he realized Semyaza was standing directly in front of him.

"Barakel, you are the ninth," Semyaza said. "You must have some thoughts."

The ninth what? Brighton wanted to ask, but he didn't dare. Before he could decide between agreeing and shaking his head, Azazel interrupted, putting a hand on Semyaza's shoulder. By the look on Semyaza's face, this was neither a welcome gesture nor a common occurrence.

"It doesn't matter," Azazel said. "I have already come to a decision."

"Not for all of us," Semyaza put in. The two men locked eyes, a silent battle waging between them. "Azazel, I fear you may not wish this deed to be done, should you alone pay for it."

"I, alone?" Azazel let out a peel of laughter as a murmur passed among the others. He walked in a circle that brought him inches from the men standing nearest. He met each man's gaze and exchanged a few words.

Brighton braced himself when his turn came. Azazel looked up at him with terrible resolve.

"Barakel, I know your heart."

If that's true, does he know it's about to hammer itself right out of my chest?

Azazel's expression said he didn't know.

"You are unusually quiet," Azazel said. "Share your thoughts."

He's looking for support, Brighton realized. *Whatever he's planning, he doesn't want to do it alone.*

"I have not decided," Brighton said at last.

Azazel's face turned angry. "I expect more of you."

Without saying another word, Azazel brushed past him, on to the next man.

Brighton breathed a sigh of relief. To his amazement, Azazel continued until he accounted for every last individual in the amphitheater. Time was not a factor; the sun had barely moved since the start of the meeting.

"So let us all swear an oath," Azazel crowed once he had returned to the center of the group, "and bind one another with curses so as not to alter this plan. We will—all of us—carry it to conclusion."

Azazel outstretched his arm toward the man nearest him and waited for the other to clasp it. The exchange took only a moment, and appeared to signify agreement with whatever plan Azazel had hatched. Within a few minutes, virtually everyone had joined in the display of solidarity, though a few chose instead to depart the mountain.

Semyaza was one of the last to stretch out his arm, and Azazel's eyes lit up with pleasure when he did so.

"It is our time! We are coming!" Azazel's fearsome glare then turned in Brighton's direction—

Brighton closed his eyes tight, as if the mere act of shutting them would somehow avoid the inevitable confrontation.

When he opened them, he was thankfully no longer on the mountain.

Dust lifted off a lonely road as his feet traveled over it, the brisk wind wafting it into clouds that trailed behind him in long, ponderous strands. Ahead of him was a cabin. Its leaning stone walls barely seemed able to hold its thatched roof.

The creaking of wagon wheels made Brighton turn in time to see a cloaked figure leap off the wagon's perch and circumnavigate the vehicle, giving it a thorough inspection. One of the cloaked man's hands clasped the front of his hood as the cloth billowed out behind him, the wind catching the fabric like a sail. A strong gust tore the fabric from his grip and flung the hood back to reveal a man with worn features and graying hair. The pupils of his eyes were milky with age.

"Lord Barakel," the old man rasped. "This is a rare honor."

If Barakel keeps company with the likes of those men from the mountaintop, it seems a very small honor indeed.

"My wife has not finished absorbing your last lessons. We have not memorized the position of the evening stars." He hesitantly pulled back the flap on his wagon and dug around for something. When his hands reappeared, they clutched a small box of tools. "Nor has my granddaughter."

Not wanting to give away his obliviousness, Brighton offered what little he could conjure up on the fly: "I am sorry to hear that."

Apparently that was the wrong thing to say. The old man dropped a hammer, spilling the tool into a patch of tall grass. He fell to his knees, his head bowed, and his body shook with sobs.

"Have mercy, my lord," the old man whispered, the wind nearly stealing the words from his mouth. "We have done our best. Please, we need more time."

Brighton grasped the old man by the shoulder, pulling him to his feet. But the man refused to meet his gaze, his shoulders convulsing uncontrollably.

"I am not angry," Brighton assured him.

But the man shook his head. "I know what you seek, Lord Barakel, and I will not keep it from you. Your friends... they have their eyes on my granddaughter, but I have saved her for you. She's as chaste as the day she came from her mother's womb, I assure you."

Nothing could have prepared Brighton for these bizarre words, yet the meaning was unmistakable. The old man's arm stretched toward the cabin, his index finger pointing.

A young woman stood in the doorway, her simple grey dress spilling around her legs, dancing in the swirls of dust that collected on the steps. Though streaked from head to toe with dried mud, probably from digging through crops on her hands and knees, her beauty was breathtaking. The soft lines of her face were punctuated with full lips and pear-shaped eyes, opened wide—perhaps a sign of fear. After all, her grandfather was clearly giving her away. And against her will.

Was this the brown-haired, green-eyed woman whose face had appeared to him earlier? Brighton looked closer at the girl, but no, she was too young. Twelve, maybe thirteen years old.

"Take her, my lord," the old man pleaded, leaning heavily against the wooden hitch of his wagon.

"Take her where?"

The old man sputtered, his mouth opening and closing of its own volition. "Would you make me to say it, my lord? Would you not spare me the decency to go in ignorance of what you shall do to her? Make her your wife and be done with it."

My wife. Brighton continued to watch the girl. How old was she? Certainly not old enough to marry, not by a wide margin.

"She will not want it," the old man continued, his voice shaking, "but you may override her wishes." He began to weep again. "Apologies, my lord. You do not need permission. Take what is yours and go, and do not subject me to this heartache any longer. If I look into her eyes even once more, I could not..." He composed himself. "My remembrance of your wrath is strong. You need not remind me of it."

Brighton had so many questions. He longed to ease the man's terror and assure him he had no lascivious intentions toward the girl. Having felt sexual urges for only three women in his life, the thought of taking someone against their will angered him—

Three women! He shook his head at the faulty memory. *That isn't right. There has been three hundred, at least.*

And yet the thought of raping an innocent girl turned his stomach.

He could not bring himself to speak. To his surprise, his mouth was dry, dry as bone, caked with dust.

More memories swirled around him—faces he didn't recognize, places he had never been to—and he just about lost his footing. He steadied himself against the frail man, except as quickly as the thought occurred to him, the man vanished into thin air.

Brighton's arms fell forward through the air as he tumbled. Instead of the ground meeting him, however, his fall stretched on, the morning sky diffusing into blackness as all detail leeched out of the world, its vibrancies fading into an expanse of uniform darkness.

FIFTEEN

Giza Plateau, Egypt
SEPTEMBER 18

Wörtlich's eyes snapped open and he coughed. A thin layer of dust had settled along the edges of his mouth; he spat it out and forced himself into a sitting position. He swallowed, attempting to work moisture back down his throat. His hand came up to ensure his glasses were still on his nose. Stumbling out of this place without his glasses would have been quite a trick.

Ira and Brighton leaned against their respective walls within the hieroglyphics room, just where they'd been when Wörtlich drifted off to sleep. Brighton had found a relatively smooth section of stone in the furthest corner—not that the young man looked comfortable; they were surrounded by one hard edge after another in this tomb-like room. He wanted nothing more than to escape and get some fresh air.

Ira stirred. The rabbi looked disoriented, as though trying to re-member where he was and how he'd gotten there. Wörtlich could hardly fault him; his own dreams had taken him to strange places.

Wörtlich got to his feet and shivered involuntarily, surprised again at how cold it was. The rock seemed to press into his skin like ice.

Brighton was awake soon as well, looking groggy. Wörtlich took a small measure of satisfaction knowing that a man half his age had no easier time adapting to these cruel conditions.

They emerged from the room a short ten minutes later and crossed through the columned gallery. Wörtlich couldn't keep his eyes off the stone faces lining either wall. One part of him wanted to escape them as soon as humanly possible; another wanted to stay be-hind forever.

He glanced toward the camera bag slung over Brighton's shoul-der. At least they had evidence. The pictures they'd taken would fuel Wörtlich's scientific curiosity for the rest of his life. Perhaps he was old-school, but he couldn't wait to print them off. He wouldn't feel secure so long as something as banal as an unexpected power outage could wipe out all the digital proof they'd gained.

Wörtlich stopped, turning his back to the others.

"Doctor Wörtlich?" Brighton called, but Wörtlich hardly heard him.

He sighed and threw Brighton a lopsided smile. "I wanted to get one last look at the place, in case I never see anything like it again."

"You will," Ira said.

Wörtlich swung to look the rabbi over, caked with dust and look-ing older and more worn than just a few hours ago. "What do you mean?"

"Simple. We haven't found the Book yet. I have a feeling wherever it is now will be at least as revealing."

Holding onto that faint hope, Wörtlich turned and followed the others out of the gallery.

Najja Fadil was waiting for them in the subterranean chamber.

"Where have you been? What has took you?" the Egyptian demanded. "You had five hours! Five!" He felt up five fingers.

Wörtlich brushed off the cobwebs clinging to his clothes from squeezing through the narrow tunnel. He leveled his gaze at Najja. "We were betrayed," he said. "A search party was loosed into the pyramid to track us down. Either you or someone you told gave us away."

The young man's eyes widened. "Not me!"

Wörtlich detected no indignation in Najja, only fear.

Ira put his hand on the Egyptian's shoulders. "We are not accusing you, Najja. However, we must have proof that it's safe to go with you."

"I am your only hope," Najja insisted. "Someone in the Ministry knows about you. You must hurry, you must follow."

Najja walked around the dark pit in the side of the chamber, his hand grazing the metal railing as he passed it.

"What time is it?" Brighton asked just as they entered the next passage.

"You mean, what day!" Najja said.

Wörtlich gave his eyes a rub. "Indeed, Mr. Brighton, it appears we slept nearly twenty hours—"

He stopped cold, his eyes fixed on Najja's backside and the holster resting on his hip.

"Excuse me, but why are you wearing a gun?"

Najja looked back at Wörtlich, anxiety written on his face. "Silly question. For protection."

His reaction struck Wörtlich as sincere.

"There is waiting car," Najja urged.

The passage felt less oppressive the closer they got to the surface. As they neared the pyramid entrance, Wörtlich heard Brighton still mumbling about the hour. Apparently, the young man hadn't slept twenty hours since infancy.

Before exiting, Ira leaned in close to his ear and whispered, "It was Menefee, wasn't it?"

Wörtlich nodded, having already come to the same conclusion. According to Elisabeth, someone at the Institute was censoring information about the index, and while Menefee purported to help Lagati, he was the logical candidate. Very little happened in Cairo that Zahi Menefee did not know about, and if he felt Raff Lagati or anyone else was encroaching on his territory…

Ira murmured, "He's the only one except us and Lagati who knew we were in the pyramid. And something makes me doubt Lagati called the authorities."

"Agreed," Wörtlich said. "If so, I doubt Najja is in on it."

Wörtlich wanted to double over and rest his weary bones at his first taste of fresh air. But there was no time. He squinted against the full moon's glare. Just as Najja had said, a car waited for them.

Menefee's car.

"Quick, quick!" Najja said, hurrying down the causeway, kicking loose stones as he rounded the edge of the pyramid. "We must go. Quick now!"

"Where are we going?" Ira asked.

Najja rapped on the window and whispered something to the car's driver. He looked back toward the men. "Away from here. No talk. No time."

Ira stopped. "I'm not getting into that car until you tell me where it's taking us."

A bewildered Brighton watched the exchange, his mouth slightly open.

"Get in," Wörtlich urged them. "Whatever is going on, we will be captured if we wait too long. Najja is right to hurry."

Reluctantly, Ira walked around the car to take the seat behind the driver.

"No, Ira, sit in the front," Wörtlich said.

Wörtlich and Najja piled into the back seat, Brighton sandwiched between them.

An awkward silence settled over the car as the driver navigated the lonely path toward the highway. Brighton's head swiveled around, taking in a last view of the receding pyramids.

Once they were on the main stretch of road, traveling north toward Cairo, Wörtlich decided it was time to make a move.

"Take the gun," he whispered into Brighton's ear. Wörtlich watched as Brighton absorbed his meaning. To his mild surprise, the young man gave nothing away.

Brighton's hand slid down, steady as a rock, inching closer to Najja's holster. Then, in a fluid motion, Brighton flipped open the catch and drew the weapon. The gun's black steel glinted eerily in the darkness of the rear compartment.

Najja murmured something in Arabic. Wörtlich couldn't make out the words, but they were almost certainly expletives. Najja's mouth clapped shut as soon as Brighton pressed the barrel to the side of his head.

"What's going on back there?" the driver asked in Arabic.

Najja swallowed nervously, his eyes locked straight ahead.

Brighton's arm shook. This was most likely the first time he'd held a gun in his life. Wörtlich placed his arm on the young man's shoulder, steadying him.

"Everything is fine," Wörtlich called to the driver. "But you might as well pull over for a minute."

The driver paused uncertainly. "Najja?"

"My friend has a gun pointed at his head," Wörtlich explained. "Just take the curb and everything will be fine.

The driver swallowed. "How I know you will not shoot?"

"You don't," Brighton said.

Wörtlich glanced at Ira, but the rabbi ignored them. Who could say what he was thinking? If Menefee was playing dirty, they wouldn't get far keeping their hands clean. Besides, they were working for Lagati now—and there was no doubt in Wörtlich's mind what the Frenchman would want them to do in this situation.

Wörtlich felt the car slow, jostling as they dropped off the pavement and onto the rocky shoulder.

"Now open the door and get out," Wörtlich instructed the driver.

The driver reached for the keys, but Ira's hand intervened.

Wörtlich still couldn't see Ira's face, but he could imagine the rabbi would be furious with them when this was all said and done. Wörtlich could live with that.

The driver stepped out, leaving his door open. Once he had taken a few steps away from the car, Wörtlich got out and started around the front of the car.

"Where you take us?" the driver asked.

"We are not taking you anywhere. You can stay here."

The driver's eyes pleaded with him, but Wörtlich hardened himself. "Walk away from the car. Ten feet should do it."

"Don't forget his phone!" Brighton called.

"Yes, good thinking, Mr. Brighton." Wörtlich smiled at the young man's forethought. To the driver, he said, "Take out your phone."

"I be stranded!"

"There will be other cars. Hurry!"

The driver took a phone from his pocket and tossed it at Wörtlich, who handed it to Ira through the open door.

"I am sorry," Wörtlich said as he backed into the car. "I really am."

He didn't know what would happen to the driver, and a part of him didn't want to give the matter any thought. At least the man was a local and could find his way back. He wasn't sure that was sufficient justification, but Ira would be glad to know he still had some scruples... even if he was choosing to ignore them.

"What you want from me?" Najja asked once they were underway again.

Wörtlich struggled to pay attention to the road. Driving at night was dangerous; most of the other vehicles didn't have running lights, and it wasn't uncommon for cars to be stopped in the open roadway.

"What you want?" Najja demanded again.

"Where were you going to take us?" Brighton asked.

"I do not know plan!" The Egyptian was shaking.

Wörtlich sympathized, and yet they needed to figure out their next move. He had counted on Najja being able to tell them what was going on. If he was as much in the dark as they were—

Ira let out a long sigh. "What have you gotten us into, Doctor?"

"We should keep driving," Wörtlich said. "Get some distance."

"Face it," Ira said. "The kid doesn't know anything. He probably had nothing to do with this."

Wörtlich kept his eyes focused on the road.

"Maybe we should get off the main highway," Brighton suggested.

Wörtlich waited for the next turnoff, then took a sharp right. He didn't know where the road led. The upside to getting lost was that they would be less likely to be found.

"It all started with the index," Ira muttered to himself. "If you hadn't stolen it, we wouldn't be here now."

Wörtlich drummed his fingers on the steering wheel. The remark had been just loud enough to ensure they all heard it. The rabbi was trying to bait him—and it worked. As the quiet seconds turned to minutes, he only grew more furious at the man beside him.

"Did you even think about the consequences—" But Ira didn't have time to finish.

"Lagati needed the index," Wörtlich snapped. "More importantly, *we* needed it. Without the index, we never would have found the Hall of Records. We would not even have known to look for it!"

"And you, Sherwood," Ira continued. "You just went along with it?"

The silence from the rear compartment was palpable, but Wörtlich knew he didn't need Brighton to jump to his defense. Going after the index hadn't been Brighton's idea.

"The discoveries we have made justify our actions," Wörtlich finally said. "It is a simple matter."

"No discovery justifies what you did."

Wörtlich shook his head in astonishment. "No discovery, you say?" He gestured to the back, where the camera case rested on the seat next to Brighton. "Back there is evidence that completely contradicts our current view of world history, and you would tell me it was not worth the effort? Then why the hell did you come along? I have not the words to describe what we saw down there. You will have to excuse me. From where you sit, I must seem contemptible."

"Not contemptible."

"No?"

Ira turned to him, the heat draining from his voice. "Knowledge isn't really the Holy Grail you seek. I'm sure that's a difficult truth for you to accept."

"Knowledge has done more for humanity in the last hundred years than anything else I can think of," Wörtlich said. He paused, fighting to keep his temper in check. "Certainly it has done more than your God has! When is the last time God did something to make the world a better place? It has been a while, if he even exists at all, which I doubt. Medicine, on the other hand, has saved millions of lives. Mine included, on at least two occasions. Where was God then? Agriculture, computer science, land reclamation—these are sciences that make a difference in peoples' lives."

Ira took the bait. "Where did knowledge get you when you were standing on the wrong side of that metallic wall?"

"Well, you knew how to get through. Fortunately for us, you had the piece of knowledge we needed."

"It wasn't knowledge in the way you understand it. The knowledge you seek leads to chaos and self-destruction. You don't understand that now, but you will once you find what you're looking for."

The rabbi didn't make a lick of sense. His argument wasn't just flawed; it was borderline insane.

"Where are we going?" Brighton asked.

"We cannot return to the motel," Wörtlich said. "The authorities may know by now where we were staying."

"Then I suppose the same goes for the airport," Brighton said. "In fact, we shouldn't go back to Cairo at all."

Wörtlich agreed, but where did agreement get them? All the major cities were to the north, and there was nothing of importance in any other direction. All he knew about the desert region was the location of certain digs, and those were few and far between.

A part of him, a strong part, wanted to throw Ira bodily from the moving vehicle, but as capably as he had threatened that driver, he was no murderer, and a tumble across the pavement would probably kill Ira. Besides, he was a clergyman. Despite Wörtlich's beliefs, he had been raised to respect men and women of the cloth, regardless of circumstance or personal feelings. That respect was one of the only things left over from his Catholic education. Of course, Ira wasn't Catholic—

"There is one place we can go," Najja volunteered, his white smile gleaming beneath the short hairs of his upper lip.

Wörtlich had an inherent distrust of people who smiled, even nervously, in crisis situations. His experience with Egyptians was that they smiled altogether too much. There was something to be said, after all, for the dour solemnity of his German brethren.

"Where?" he asked.

"South." Najja paused, trying to find the words, but his inadequate English brought him up short. Then, in a burst, he said in Arabic. "I have a cousin who lives south of here, in Al Bawiti. He won't be expecting visitors, but he would not object to seeing me. If he knew I was in trouble, he would want to help."

Al Bawiti. The name barely registered, but Wörtlich had heard of it. A small oasis town. There was not much there.

That might work to our advantage.

"What's he saying?" Brighton said.

Wörtlich translated for them, then glanced over at Ira. The rabbi's eyes were focused out the side window, even though there was nothing to see but passing darkness. There was no telling what thoughts ran through his head.

"What makes you think we can trust him?" Brighton asked.

"I do not know if we can, except that we may not have a choice."

"Couldn't we just go to this town ourselves? Why do we need

Najja?"

"Because we are not in Cairo anymore," Wörtlich reminded him. "Three white men would draw a lot of attention in a desert town— unwanted attention. This is not friendly territory, so it will be to our advantage to have a guide and someplace safe to stay."

Brighton leaned back, disappearing from view again.

"What do you think, Ira?" Wörtlich asked.

"I concur," Ira said, his voice more strained than usual. He glanced at Najja. "He may legitimately desire to help us. Who knows? He might be in as much trouble as we are at this point."

"All right, Najja. How do we get to your cousin's?" Wörtlich asked.

"Keep this way," Najja said.

Wörtlich turned his sights back on the highway, once again watching for road debris and stopped cars. When he took a moment to peer through the rearview mirror, all he could see were those bright teeth smiling back at him.

SIXTEEN

Al Bawiti, Egypt
SEPTEMBER 18

Most of the day passed before they reached the eastern edge of the oasis. Exhaustion pulled at Brighton. He could see the same exhaustion reflected in the other three men by the time the first trees came into view, distorted by extreme heat and the setting sun, a giant red orb sliced in two by the distant horizon. The wave-like dunes gave way to a sea of green. The landscape looked almost like an ocean covered in algae.

It was a shock to find real trees, rooted in topsoil that didn't whip up and blow away at the slightest gust of wind. For the first time, Brighton understood the tales of Bedouins who bypassed places like this, mistaking them for desert mirages. There was something unnatural about an oasis, and this one, several miles wide, seemed nothing short of impossible.

The town was more substantial than Najja had led them to believe. The sun's dying rays glinted off the golden domes of a half-dozen mosques, around which the town's other buildings revolved. The buildings sprawled on into the canopy of trees, and there appeared to be homes for tens of thousands of people.

Maybe we'll sleep in real beds tonight, Brighton thought wistfully. The motel in Tanta seemed a lifetime away.

Najja guided them down a couple of streets until they hurtled down an avenue bordered by the battened down shops of daytime street merchants. A few turban-clad men on bicycles rode down the middle of the thoroughfare, oblivious to the odd vehicle trying to get through.

"They will not move for you," Najja mumbled. "Use the horn."

"Won't that be seen as rude?"

Najja offered a smile. "Only if they see you are white."

Suddenly, Najja began tapping against the window. He shouted excitedly in Arabic and pointed to a two-story building on the right. Its uneven walls, built from large rectangular bricks held together with grey mortar, looked to have been crumbling for several decades. Corrugated tin sheeting served as a roof, supported on the sides by turret-shaped white columns that lent it the appearance of a gap-toothed smile.

"This is it?" Brighton asked.

Wörtlich nodded, listening as Najja continued to chatter animatedly. "He says his cousin owns this shop."

Brighton stopped the car. When they got out, he couldn't help but notice the people staring at them. Walking alone through a darkened street in the heart of Islamic territory was this American's worst nightmare, so he was grateful when Najja beckoned them around the side of the building where they would be out of sight.

They climbed a steep embankment to reach the back door. Beyond a line of towering palms, a brown concrete wall formed a barricade between the street and a modest field of grain. Strange to think the ground just another mile east wasn't suitable for so much as a cactus, yet here...

The door opened, and Najja spoke to someone just inside. Brighton craned his neck, trying to get a look, but Najja was in the way. The Egyptian then waved Wörtlich over, probably to explain what they were doing there.

Brighton wondered what kind of lie Wörtlich would concoct. Surely he wouldn't tell these strangers the truth!

"Would you look at that," Ira said beside him. The rabbi gazed up at the sky, a look of awe on his face.

Brighton looked up and saw what Ira was so transfixed by. Night had come and the sky blazed with a million stars. Most of the constellations were the same ones he could have seen on a clear night in New Mexico, but none were in the right places. Piscis Austrinus was swimming through foreign waters. Andromeda struggled to break her chains. Cassiopeia used her mirror to check for strangers creeping up from behind.

He knew how they felt.

"There's so much to see way out here," Brighton said.

Ira didn't say anything. The rabbi was such a strange man. Brighton couldn't gauge his moods, his temperament. Sometimes he was passionate and involved in what was going on, but other times he became distant and reflective—like now.

Footsteps alerted them to Wörtlich's approach.

"Najja has arranged for us to spend the night here," the archaeologist explained.

Brighton breathed a sigh of relief. "What did you tell them?"

"We are visiting professors at Cairo University, where Najja is a teaching assistant. Our story is that he offered to show us some of the desert sites."

Brighton eyed the door. "You're sure it's safe?"

"It's safe," Ira said, sounding confident.

Wörtlich inclined his head in agreement. "I would still watch myself if I were you, and try to remember not to refer to Ira as 'Rabbi.' I do not know how open-minded Najja's cousin is, but I would not want to find out the hard way."

Ira pursed his lips. "Don't worry about me. I won't pretend. If it comes up, I am who I am."

*   *   *

Ira stood by as Najja and Brighton retrieved their bags from the car. They didn't have much with them. Only what they had carried into the pyramid. The rest of their luggage was still at the motel in Tanta, though by now it would have already been taken into custody. The authorities wouldn't find any trace of his ever having been there, however; his bags were still safe and sound at the El Gezirah. His reservation wouldn't run out for another week. Najja was the only one who could connect him to the other two.

Well, and the driver they had abandoned on the road. Ira said a silent prayer for the man's safety, even if he put them all at risk of discovery.

"Remarkable, is it not?" Wörtlich said, startling Ira as he joined him at the top of the embankment. "There is nothing quite like a desert sky. Without all the humidity, you can see with great clarity."

"Yes," Ira agreed. "Almost as good as having a telescope."

Wörtlich let out a soft chuckle, though for the life of him Ira couldn't figure what the man was laughing at. Wörtlich didn't have a zen bone in his body, Ira was certain.

"You know, the Egyptians had great reverence for the stars," Wörtlich said. "A lot of ancient civilizations did. In fact, they marked their seasons by the appearance and disappearance of the main constellations of the ecliptic: Taurus, Leo, Scorpio… I suppose all this talk of stars and the zodiac must sound very New Age to a Jew."

"Hardly. Our Kabalistic traditions place much significance on the zodiac. Many Jews are interested in astrological consequence."

"And you are one of them?"

"I suppose so, but I have a few convictions most modern-day Jewish thinkers wouldn't ascribe to."

"Such as?"

"Well, you would probably say that the stars were named for gods and other mythical creatures. I would add that each star, each and every one, represents one of the multitudes of angels in heaven—and even those angels who are no longer in heaven."

"No longer in heaven?"

Ira sighed. There were some things hardly worth explaining.

"Have you gotten any further with your translation of the hieroglyphics?" Ira asked, changing the subject. Wörtlich looked relieved to have avoided the subject of spirituality.

"A little," Wörtlich said. "I had about an hour to look through the photos before the camera died. I will work on it through the night. I doubt I will get much sleep."

The thought triggered a yawn.

"Well, I can't say the same. I predict a sound sleep for myself." Ira walked toward the door, surprised that the archaeologist wasn't following right behind him.

"There must be quite a few of them," Wörtlich said just before Ira reached the door.

"Of what?"

"Of angels, watching over us."

Ira didn't have to turn to sense the smirk on Wörtlich's face.

Inside, a woman sat at a round table, a small girl beside her. Mother and daughter, and they were whispering to each other. Voices came from an adjoining room, Najja and his cousin. They weren't shouting, but neither were they peaceable. Apparently, showing up unannounced with three Westerners stretched family obligation.

Not for the first time, Ira wished he understood the language. When he looked back to the mother, she glowered at him. At least he didn't need to know Arabic to translate *that*.

Najja's cousin stalked out of the adjoining room. He stopped a few feet short of Ira and pointed toward an arched doorway and a set of narrow stairs. Taking the cue, Ira hastened up to the second level.

Brighton sat on the top step, waiting.

"Eavesdropping?" Ira asked.

"For all the good it does me... I don't understand a word of it. Where's Wörtlich?"

"Still outside."

"Anyway, there's a room for us," Brighton said. "So we're not being kicked out. Not yet."

Najja appeared at the bottom of the stairs. "My cousin is very angry," he said. "But we stay."

Ira nodded. "Tell him we will leave first thing tomorrow. We don't want to impose."

Najja inclined his head before returning to the family. As uncomfortable as it was being unwanted house guests, worse still was being the one responsible for bringing them. Still, Ira was grateful for a place to spend the night. God always provided.

"Where will we go in the morning?" Brighton asked.

"We have an entire night to figure that out."

The room had one bed and no other furnishings. A small window looked out over the neighboring rooftops.

It's not much, Ira thought, looking over the room. *But it's enough.*

He offered to sleep on the floor, but Ira insisted the bed was large enough for both of them. The young man seemed somewhat uneasy with this arrangement, but the floors were hard and the hour late.

Almost an hour passed before Wörtlich joined them, by which time Brighton had fallen asleep. Ira suggested they take shifts in the bed, but the archaeologist insisted he'd had enough sleep in the car, so the rabbi let him be.

His thoughts turned dark as he hovered on the edge of sleep, and he wondered if he was about to have another dream…

A knock on the door roused him. Ira realized with a start that he had drifted off to sleep. Wörtlich was hunched over on the floor, scribbling something. He didn't seem to have heard the knocking.

When the second knock came, Wörtlich's eyes darted to the door, but he didn't say anything until the third knock.

"Yes?" Wörtlich asked.

On the other side of the door, a throat cleared.

Ira sat up and watched Wörtlich cross the room. He opened the door cautiously, affording Ira a direct line of sight into the hallway.

The young girl stood there, balancing three steaming cups of tea on a flimsy plastic tray. She wore a plain robe-like garment similar to the white *gallibiyas* he had seen worn on the streets. The robe looked secondhand; the far too long sleeves pushed up at the wrists to allow her small hands to jut out from them.

"*Sahlab?*" Her voice was soft. Terrified. "To help you sleep."

Ira assumed the unfamiliar term was a reference to the tea, which swirled around the rims of the cups when she extended the tray.

The German offered a shallow, respectful bow as he took the tray. The little girl scampered out of sight, and Wörtlich closed the door.

He offered Ira one of the cups, but he declined and lay back down. He managed to fall back asleep in minutes.

When he opened his eyes again, dim light was visible through the window, marking his favorite time of day—that serene half-hour of morning twilight before the sun poked up over the eastern horizon. Brighton still slept soundly, like only a young man could.

Ira swung his legs over the side of the bed and felt his feet crunch on flattened sheets of paper. Paper covered the entire square footage of the room, except for a narrow strip of worn carpet along the wall where Wörtlich lay, his chest rising and falling to the rhythmic timbres of soft snores. The sheets of paper had been ripped from the archaeologist's notebook and were covered in illegible scrawls. As he looked closer, Ira recognized many of the symbols and characters from the walls in the Hall of Records, copied from the digital pictures they'd taken.

The snoring stopped and Wörtlich cracked an eyelid open. "Apologies for the mess."

"Have you made any progress?" Ira asked.

Wörtlich grunted. "These writings describe a mass exodus of the pyramid builders from the Mediterranean region, and it can be inferred by some of the passages that they took the Book with them. Unfortunately, I still do not know the nature of the disaster. At least, not yet." He paused. "I also do not know where they escaped *to*, which is what we need to find out."

Wörtlich continued speaking, but Ira's mind wandered as his eyes scanned the characters, line by line, column by column, stopping periodically to investigate something that looked—

That one.

Ira walked over and knelt down to take a closer look.

By now, Wörtlich had stopped talking.

"This one here," Ira said. "Something about it reminds me of…"

It didn't seem possible to see that character here, of all places.

Wörtlich reached for the camera and found the frame in question. He handed it off to Ira, who sat down on the edge of the bed and studied it.

"I don't know the first thing about Egyptian writing," Ira admitted, "but I do know a thing or two about Ancient Hebrew, and this—" He turned the camera around so Wörtlich could share his view of the screen. "—bears some resemblance to something I've seen before. Slightly modified, this character means 'Son of Man.' In fact, the only pronounced difference is the slight curvature of the lines, which are straighter in the Hebrew."

"The Son of Man?"

"Traditionally, it would be a reference to the Messiah, appearing in only the oldest Messianic prophecies."

Wörtlich's eyes wore disinterest like a shroud.

"That was one of the passages I could not translate," Wörtlich said, "but you should not read anything into it. What would a reference to the Hebrew Messiah be doing here? The time periods do not line up, either. These inscriptions predate the Hebrew scriptures by several millennia."

Ira doubted the connection was a coincidence, but he thought it wise to avoid an argument. He wanted to start this day off fresh.

SEVENTEEN

Al Bawiti, Egypt
SEPTEMBER 19

The first words out of Brighton's mouth were, "So, where are we going?"

Those words rankled. On the one hand, Wörtlich was annoyed that the young man somehow presumed that he and Ira would solve the problem without him. On the other hand, he was annoyed that he hadn't managed it. He *had* spent the whole night trying, but the inscriptions hadn't offered many clues. Archaeological mystery aside, their first concern should have been getting out of the country, period.

Najja peeked his head in shortly after sunrise and invited them down for breakfast. Ira had promised they wouldn't impose longer than the night, which also annoyed Wörtlich, though he recognized that as irrational. They couldn't very well stay where they weren't wanted. They had to keep moving.

Hence, Brighton's question. A sensible one, if not annoying.

Najja's cousin—whose name was Omar—sat in a small outdoor courtyard. A sheet of brown canvas was stretched over the dining area, its edges held up by a pair of pillars marked by patches of stripped plaster, revealing bricks underneath. The sun was already warm, even low in the sky, and Wörtlich could feel the morning dew evaporating. Even in the oasis, the daytime temperatures exceeded thirty-five degrees—and sometimes peaked a good deal higher.

Despite the heat, Omar was sipping hot tea and smoking a thick, pungent Jose Bartolo cigar.

"What do you teach?" Omar asked, tendrils of smoke curling up from the tip of his cigar. Wörtlich was surprised by the man's near perfect English.

"Archaeology," Wörtlich said. Why tell a lie when the truth would do?

Brighton emerged from the back of the building with their bags. Ira wasn't far behind.

Omar's wife and daughter came outside for a few minutes at a time, but they never sat down. The girl brought them a plate of bean cakes and refreshed their tea when it got low. The girl's mother hovered just inside the door, her eyes darting from one man to the next, keeping them all in her sights.

Once they had their fill, they thanked Omar for his hospitality. The man only grumbled in response. It was clear he was anxious to have them out of his hair—and perhaps Najja as well, though Wörtlich had no intention of taking the young Egyptian any further.

Brighton stood first and carried the bags to the car. He wasn't gone long before the sound of a woman's shouts, so loud as to be incoherent, reached them from the street. Wörtlich laid down his cup and ran around the side of the building at full tilt, Ira and Najja on his heels.

His fears were confirmed when he saw a group of onlookers standing a few meters from the car. Several bicycles lay on their sides, discarded as their riders hurried to see what all the fuss was about.

Omar's wife stood at the foot of the stairs, her eyes bulging as curses flew out of her mouth.

Dumbfounded, Brighton had backed against the driver's side door, seemingly torn between driving off and making a run for it on his own two feet.

She wailed the same words over and over again in Arabic, and two of them were unmistakable to his ears: "Thief! Infidel!"

What had Brighton done?

"Thief! It is not for you! Not for you! You must leave it alone. Go back! Allah will not let you disturb it!"

After that, the words poured out in a rush, and Wörtlich only caught a few of them. *Death… pain… wrath…*

Ira placed his hand on his shoulder. "We must do something, Emery. She's drawing a crowd."

Wörtlich brushed past a couple of bystanders. Brighton's frightened eyes softened in relief as he saw the archaeologist coming toward him.

"What did you do?" Wörtlich demanded. "Did you take something?"

"Take something?" Brighton's face registered confusion.

"She is calling you a thief."

"I didn't take anything, I swear! I didn't even *say* anything. She just appeared on the steps and started screaming."

Wörtlich was conscious of all the eyes on them. "We have to go. Now. Before someone tries to stop us."

"But we haven't done anything wrong," Brighton insisted.

"It does not matter. These people are naturally suspicious of Westerners. Are the bags in the car?"

The young man nodded.

"Good. I'll drive."

Ira and Brighton piled into the backseat as Wörtlich slammed the door shut and started the engine.

"But we don't know where we're going!" Brighton said.

Wörtlich didn't have time to think about a destination. He honked the horn three times, signaling the people in front of the car to move, but they just stared at him with blank expressions.

"Move!" he shouted in Arabic. "Move! Move!"

After gunning the engine and honking a few times, the vehicle lurched forward and people finally dove out of the way. He could still hear the woman's cries fading behind them as they picked up speed. Their departure only made her scream louder. A few boys on bicycles rode after them, though they weren't nearly fast enough to keep up.

Stunned silence settled over them as they hurdled out of town. The main road took them south and within a few minutes the oasis was gone, replaced by dismal white sand and craggy outcroppings stretching into the vast distance.

Other than a single sign indicating the many hundreds of miles to a place called Mut, there was nothing to draw the eye. The horizon blurred and danced where the clear blue sky mingled with the beige expanse of desert. High winds blew sand across the road, and in many places dunes encroached far beyond the shoulder, covering whole lanes.

Wörtlich needed to think, but there was no time. They had a little over half a tank of gas and no direction. No direction at all.

The more he stewed on the problem, the worse it got, and before he knew it, anger seeped into the nest egg of resentment he'd been nursing for the last couple of years. His ex-wives, losing Elisabeth, the paper that had got him sent into academic exile… The anger ignited like a stick of dynamite. He slammed his hand into the steering wheel and accidentally sent the car into a lurch.

Ira's head snapped to stare at him, his eyes saying it as well as words ever could: *Pull over.*

Wörtlich put foot to brake and steered the car onto a clear patch of crushed rock. Ira kept silent, thankfully. Wörtlich would have come to regret anything that came out of his mouth. Brighton, too, seemed to sense his emotional state and sat back, waiting to see what would happen next.

Wise beyond his years, Wörtlich thought sourly.

He pushed open the door and a wall of heat pushed back, taking his breath away. The blast felt remarkably like his second wife's right hook. She had always said he would come to laugh at that one day, and perhaps now, in the direst of circumstances…

He did laugh. The wind blew out of his anger as quickly as it had blown in. He couldn't help himself, not really. It was all so funny. So *ridiculous.*

The tension abandoned him and his shoulders slumped forward.

"A direction," Wörtlich murmured, his chest still heaving from the laughter. He flung open the back door, startling Brighton, and reached for his bag. He heaved himself onto the seat and dug out the stack of papers he had scrawled on the night before, looking for something… looking for… *that…*

"A direction," he said again. He held up one sheet for the others to see, but they just stared back. "It is not a place, not exactly. It is a direction."

"You know where they took the Book?" Brighton asked.

"I might." Wörtlich tapped the paper with his index finger. "Look at this. A pyramid. But it is not really a pyramid at all, but a symbol for a geographic point of reference. You could think of it as a sort of compass representing the four corners of the earth—the four faces of a pyramid align north, south, east, and west. Therefore, this symbol pertains to a direction, not a physical location, as I initially supposed. You see this star positioned above its peak? It signifies north. We have to go north."

"No ... " Brighton said, the thought trailing off. "We can't go back. We'll be caught."

"You are missing the point," Wörtlich said. "I do not mean North Egypt. The star in the symbol represents the polestar. We must not just go north. We must go True North."

"Like the North Pole?"

Wörtlich's hand slipped as he gave Brighton's question some consideration. "Perhaps. The syntax here goes out of its way to emphasize *True* North."

"What's the difference?" Brighton asked.

"Well, the North Pole today is in a different position than it was six thousand years ago, when these inscriptions were made. Nothing on the Earth is static, understand. Everything moves. The planet's axis wobbles, the crust shifts over time ... Six thousand years is a relatively short time, mind you, on a geological timescale, but we must calculate this precisely."

A sudden blast of heat reminded him to shut the doors and turn up the air conditioner. The heat would distract him, and he needed to have a clear head.

"Now, one thing we do know is that the Great Pyramid was

aligned to the polestar at the time of its construction," Wörtlich continued. "Today's polestar is Polaris, but back then, it was Draco."

Brighton's eyes widened excitedly. "The House of Draco! That was the notation in the index next to the *Sefer Yetzirah* entry. Surely that's no coincidence."

Ira cleared his throat to call their attention and said, "If the *Sefer Yetzirah* was derived from the Book of Creation, the index may have been telling us where that information originated in the first place— the House of Draco, or the pyramids, which were aligned to Draco. And the pyramids, of course, mark the entrance to the Hall of Records."

Wörtlich's mind raced as he tried to fit all the puzzle pieces together. He reached back into his bag and pulled out the cell phone Najja had given them the day before.

Brighton snatched it away. "You can't use that! That phone belongs to Menefee. If we make a call from it, they'll trace it back to our location. We may as well go right back to Cairo."

"We can take precautions," Wörtlich assured him. "We can make the call here, then drive back to town, or perhaps back toward Cairo. That might throw them off. We will make ourselves a moving target. What choice do we have? Lagati is a powerful man. If anyone can get us out of here, it is him."

Wörtlich grabbed the phone back, and this time Brighton didn't stop him. "He will also have the resources to help us find True North. I am afraid a simple compass will not do the trick."

He flipped open the screen and waited for the signal bars to appear.

They never did.

"There is no signal out here," he announced at last.

"How far is the nearest town?" Ira asked.

Wörtlich looked up. "Mut is hours away. Maybe a day. And we do not have enough fuel to make the trip."

"So we return to Al Bawiti," Ira said. "At least it's nearby, and we know we'll be able to make a call."

"Did you see a cell phone tower there?" Brighton asked. "I didn't."

"The town is off the beaten track, but surely they have phones," Wörtlich insisted.

One can only hope, he added to himself.

*   *   *

They had invaded its lands, plundered its secrets, broken its laws, and Brighton couldn't help but think that Egypt was now fighting back. The air was hot, dry, and unfriendly. They'd already gotten what they came for and outstayed their welcome, for which the country was now making them pay dearly.

Every few minutes the car slowed, losing traction as its wheels churned through a drift of sand that had swept across both lanes. Each time Brighton was reminded that they were that much closer to town. He should have felt relief—the oasis meant civilization—but instead his apprehension only increased. The desert was a hellhole, but at least he didn't have to deal with that woman, who now personified every fear he suffered over being an American in the wrong part of the world. The desert was dangerous but not scary. Al Bawiti was both.

Brighton shoved his cultural fear aside as the town crept back over the horizon. Wörtlich turned off onto a street skirting the western edge of the oasis, keeping them off any roads where they would be recognized. After a few minutes, Wörtlich stopped the car and tried the phone again.

"It is ringing!" Wörtlich jumped out of the car and paced between a copse of towering emperor palms.

Brighton felt a headache coming on. Wherever Menefee was, this call would undoubtedly be traced, and chances were all three of them would be rotting in an Egyptian jail before the day was out. A quarter of a million dollars no longer seemed worth the trouble.

He glanced at his watch—12:32. Rachel was back home, in bed, sound asleep—either that or just getting up—unaware of the fact that his greed had led him to what could possibly be the defining moment of his life.

Wörtlich jogged back after a few minutes and swung himself into the driver's seat. "Lagati does not think we should stay in town."

"Then what are we supposed to do?" Ira asked.

Wörtlich smiled. "He is sending his plane to pick us up."

He's sending his plane? Brighton wondered, and then, *Of course he is. And I'm sure getting in and out of Egyptian airspace won't be an issue either…*

The scratching sound of pen on paper caught Brighton's attention. Wörtlich was scribbling something in his notebook.

"What's that?" Brighton asked.

"Coordinates. Where we wait." Without further discussion, the archaeologist restarted the engine and drove north.

They soon reached an airfield on the edge of the oasis. The airfield was a short stretch of concrete, far too short for a plane of even moderate size.

Wörtlich stopped the car and pulled out his notebook. Ira moved to the back seat and closed his eyes, meditating—damn the man and his ability to disappear into himself. Brighton got out of the car and walked up and down the abandoned airfield, kicking little piles of sand as he went.

The sun hung directly above them, crawling across the sky. The heat had a way of slowing everything down. Noon seemed to stretch for hours. They didn't know when Lagati's plane was coming, but Switzerland wasn't that far by air.

Brighton glanced up to the sky, where the sun had finally budged into its downward arc. How many hours had it been since Wörtlich's call? Four? Five?

Where are they?

Not Lagati; the plane was on its way, no doubt. But the authorities should have overtaken them by now. If Menefee had given Najja that phone, he must have expected them to use it at some point. It had been hours since they'd used it.

It didn't make sense.

Before he could give it more thought, a mechanical thrum filled his ears. Shielding his eyes from the sun, he spotted a small plane flying low, headed straight for them.

He ran back to the car.

"Take everything," Wörtlich said, already stuffing his notebook into his bag. "Leave nothing behind that will lead them to us."

If they're even looking, Brighton added silently.

A wave of heat distorted the air, obscuring the small plane's nose, making it twist in odd ways as it descended. It bounced a couple of times before the wheels grabbed the concrete, racing toward the end of the short runway.

When it came to a stop, it immediately reversed and turned itself around. Once it was pointed in the right direction for takeoff, the door swung open and a familiar face leaned out. Wendell's.

"Come on!" Wendell shouted as he lowered the steps, his voice almost drowned out by the roaring of engines.

Wörtlich was the first to the plane, but he waited to help Ira up the steep steps. Brighton climbed up after them, hands gripping the railing until his knuckles turned white. He spared one last glance out the door before Wendell slammed it shut, saying a brief farewell to the dismal landscape and blistering heat.

The plane reminded him of Lagati's Bentley. It had the same plush furniture and cabinets in the bulkhead which probably contained refrigerators and hidden television screens. After a week of cheap motels and dusty underground caverns, the plane was a welcome change.

Wendell had already disappeared into the cockpit by the time Brighton settled himself into one of the chairs. Out of the corner of his eye, he caught a glimpse of Wörtlich, eyes closed and leaning all the way back. He looked asleep, and Ira in much the same state.

Old men, he mused. *Globetrotting's a young man's game.*

Perhaps it was just that he'd gotten more sleep than the others, but Brighton was wide awake as the plane picked up speed.

The ground receded below, the oasis dropping until it became a splash of green paint on a huge beige canvas. This was one place he wouldn't miss.

EIGHTEEN

Malta

SEPTEMBER 19

W e're starting our descent."

Ira barely registered the voice. His bones ached, his muscles strained, his skin burned, his breathing labored. He didn't see anything wrong with sleeping through the landing. He would sleep through a lot more given half a chance.

"Where are we?" Brighton asked.

"Lagati has a private estate in Malta," Wendell said, raising his voice to be heard over the whine of engines. "You'll be safe there."

Safe from whom, exactly?

Ira opened his eyes, squinting against the afternoon sun. The beauty beneath him dazzled; whitecaps broke against the precipitous cliffs that wreathed Malta's southern shore. Verdant, rolling hills divided into farms edged by narrow gravel tracks and small cottages. The view reminded him of Fair Haven. He could imagine Aaron on one of the porches below, peering up at the sound of a passing aircraft.

Aaron. Did you know what you were sending me into?

The plane jolted as it touched down, screaming across a private airfield.

Once off the plane, Wendell directed them off the airfield toward a line of trees where a wooden staircase, sandwiched between two wide cedars, descended a cliff face. The descent was long. Ira normally would have had no trouble navigating the stairs, but today he leaned heavily on the railing.

Brighton kept twisting his head around to make sure Ira wasn't about to tumble forward. Ira wasn't as frail and doddering as Brighton probably assumed, but at least the young man's heart was in the right place.

Ira heard the crashing waves before he saw them. A final turn in the staircase brought the coast into view. Ivy-covered cliffs curved away to the north and south. A small natural harbor faced west, at the head of which waited a boathouse, the only building in sight. Six broad columns supported the triangular roof in the classical style of Ancient Greece: a mini-Parthenon by the seaside.

"Welcome to Malta," Wendell proclaimed as he led the way toward a set of double doors.

Ira felt dwarfed as he passed between the columns, and the feeling didn't fade once they went inside.

The ceilings hovered upwards of fifteen feet above his head. Intricate moldings lined white walls that housed several Picassos and at least one van Gogh in ornate frames.

Before Ira knew it, Wendell left him alone in a bedroom with a southern view. He opened a window to let in the cool breeze, then closed his eyes, sat on the edge of the bed, and fell back onto the soft blankets. The fresh air and crashing waves lulled him to sleep.

A knock woke him sometime later. His eyes peeked slowly and he realized he had fallen asleep with his clothes and shoes on. Clouds had rolled in while he slept, covering the blue sky, and the wind had picked up, tapping the shutters against the window frame.

Another knock.

"Mr. Lagati is waiting to meet you on the terrace," Wendell called through the door.

Ira sat up. "I'll be down in a few minutes."

After showering and changing, he stepped out into the hall and took a left, heading toward the side of the house that faced the waterfront. He walked through the large living room filled with comfortable couches. His slippered feet hardly made a sound on the smooth marble tiles, which alternated black and white squares like a giant chessboard.

On the terrace, Brighton and Lagati faced the railing, overlooking the water.

"This place is fantastic," Brighton said to their host. "Is it authentic?"

"It's a Greek boathouse, in the Athenian style," Lagati said. "The foundation is nearly three thousand years old, as are a few of the columns. Most of the building itself had to be reconstructed, but I insisted on using as much of the original material as possible."

"I'm impressed."

Lagati laughed. "Well, I've added a few modern conveniences, but the essential layout is the same as it was. It's not as large as my Swiss home, but it's—warmer, somehow. In Switzerland, I live entombed in a mountainside; here, I live in a wide open space. My tastes are quite varied."

Ira cleared his throat.

"Ah, Rabbi, good evening," Lagati said. "I trust you are feeling refreshed. Mr. Brighton has been telling me of your ordeals in the desert. Very dramatic."

"To put it mildly."

"A shame you would not let us archaeologists take a good poke around ruins like these before adding carpet and indoor plumbing," Wörtlich's voice boomed behind them. The archeologist approached, holding a glass of water. "After so many days in the desert, I will be parched for a week."

"You'll be leaving long before then, I'm sure," Lagati said. He clapped his hands in quick succession. "If everyone's well-rested, I've had my cook prepare dinner. The local cuisine is astonishingly good."

That much was true. After three courses of bread, fish, and pastizzi stuffed with ricotta cheese, Ira was ready to turn in again. But Lagati had other things in mind. Their host led them into the living room, where one of his household staff served drinks. Brighton and Wörtlich each accepted a glass of red wine, but Ira opted instead for a strong cup of coffee.

"So, you're trying to figure out where the pyramid builders took the Book," Lagati summarized once they had finished outlining the events of the last few days. A large world map rested on the round coffee table in front of him, the corners held down by various hardcovers from the shelves in Lagati's study.

"Yes. To do so, we must pinpoint the location of True North." Wörtlich used his finger to draw an imaginary line north from Egypt, right to the top of the map. "Of course, that could refer to more than one physical location. There is the geographic North Pole, but there is also magnetic north—where compasses point."

Lagati frowned. "If I'm not mistaken, the magnetic poles will be trickier to nail down."

Ira leaned back into the couch and took a long swallow of coffee. The hot beverage slid down his throat, warming his chest.

"That is correct," Wörtlich said. "They shift as much as fifteen kilometers per year, and the two poles do not move relative to each other, making them hard to calculate and predict. Which is why the location is more likely to be geographic."

Brighton studied the map. "If you're right, Doctor, getting to it will be almost impossible."

Ira narrowed his eyes. "Why's that?"

"The geographic North Pole is in the middle of a permanently frozen expanse of the Arctic Ocean," Brighton said. "The seabed is beneath five thousand feet of water and ice, and I wouldn't know where else to look but the seabed."

"And I suppose it's heavily monitored," Ira said.

Brighton nodded. "By the United States and the Russians."

For a few moments, everyone was silent.

"*Almost* impossible, you said," Lagati said, smiling. "Nothing is impossible."

"Personally," Brighton said through a stifled a yawn, "I think the magnetic poles constitute a more plausible scientific definition for True North."

Wörtlich put down his wineglass. "Mr. Brighton makes a good point. It would take months to mount an Arctic seabed expedition."

The archaeologist stood up and walked toward the door.

"Are you going to bed, Doctor?" Lagati asked. "We have much more to discuss. This mystery refuses to wait."

"I need time to think," Wörtlich said over his shoulder, a hint of irritation edging his tone.

Lagati didn't argue with him. Indeed, the billionaire withdrew a short time later, clearly disappointed that his think tank hadn't yielded any immediate answers. But maybe Wörtlich was right to take a break; it had been a long twenty-four hours, and the nap Ira had taken barely covered his exhaustion.

The rhythmic crash of waves did nothing to relax him when he got back to his room. Ira closed his eyes, but his mind wouldn't succumb. All he could think about was his vision of the Book resting atop the podium in the Hall of Records. He had to be the first to get to it— Lagati was right. This mystery refused to wait.

Ira found Brighton in the living room, legs tucked under him. The world map lay in front of him, lit by the soft glow of a lonely lamp, its darkened shade casting strange, shifting shadows across the continents. A square calculator hid the middle of the South Pacific and the western coast of South America.

Ira hung back for a few minutes, watching. "Not tired?"

Brighton sighed as the rabbi walked in and took a seat across from him. "Very tired. Can't sleep, though."

"I know what you mean."

Brighton picked up the calculator. "I guess there's nothing like a little math to wile away the hours."

Brighton was about to press a few buttons, then changed his mind and set it down on the table.

"What are you thinking?" Ira asked.

"The same thing you are."

Ira smiled, but doubted that was true, unless Brighton harbored anxieties about destroying the object of their search.

"Using 4600 B.C. as a reference point for the construction of the pyramids," Brighton said, "which is approximately when Wörtlich thinks those inscriptions were made, we can calculate the general location of magnetic north. But there's a problem."

Ira lay down on the couch, resting his head on a throw pillow. The ceiling was far enough above him that the lone light couldn't penetrate its heights. Disquieted, he lowered his eyes to the end table beyond his feet. An old, sepia-tinted globe sat there.

He turned back toward Brighton. The young man's lips were pressed tight, his eyes focused on the map's northern hemisphere.

"You can't find it," Ira said.

"Pardon?"

"There's a problem with the math. You can't find magnetic north."

Brighton's brows clenched into straight, horizontal worry lines. "My calculations should be simple, based on the constants. Instead of jumping around the geographic north pole, as it should, my numbers place it over Central Europe. Too south, much too far south."

Ira pushed himself up and reached for the globe. He carefully removed it from its wooden stand and turned it in his hands. Smiling, he made brief eye contact with Brighton, then tossed the globe across the room. Startled, Brighton reached out and snatched it.

"What was that for?"

Brighton instinctively adjusted the globe so that north pointed up. "Try turning it upside-down," Ira suggested.

Brighton flipped the globe. "Now what?"

"I know you've heard of polar reversals."

Brighton's frown lines deepened. "You can't be serious."

"I'm deadly serious."

The young man put the globe down on the table, taking a moment to ensure it didn't roll away.

"No offense, Rabbi," Brighton said, "but you're out of your depth. The last such event was almost eight hundred thousand years ago. As a Jew, you don't even believe the earth has been around that long, right?"

Ira fought back a grin. "You must have a very low opinion of me."

"No, not low. In some areas, though, I think you're unenlightened."

He chuckled out loud. "Unenlightened? Well, I appreciate your honesty. Friends are honest with each other." Brighton raised his eyebrow at the word 'friend,' but Ira pressed on. "The reason your calculations are off is that there was a much more recent pole reversal."

"Who's the guy with the degree from Caltech?" Brighton said. "I think I would have heard about something that big."

"You have heard of it," Ira said. "But this, my friend, has nothing to do with Caltech. Your education may have been the best money can buy, but there are many things even your professors didn't know. Why is it that people today only believe what they can read in a textbook? You've heard of the Flood, I take it?"

Brighton reached for the calculator and absently played with its buttons. "You mean from the Bible."

"That's the one."

Brighton sighed loudly. "I don't want to debate with you."

"Why? You don't think I can hold my own?"

"No, but I like you too much to try. The Flood didn't happen."

Ira's eyes danced playfully. He was fully awake now. "All right, except I know you're not that stupid."

Brighton's face blanched. "Stupid?"

"What I said is, I know you're *not* that stupid."

Ira put his feet up on the coffee table. His slippers nudged the edge of the map. "Let's think about this rationally. Objectively. After all, that's the goal of a good scientist, yes?"

Brighton shrugged and allowed a curt nod.

"The truth is, there's a multitude of facts supporting the Flood, not the least of which is that pesky fossil record."

"I thought you religious types didn't believe the fossil record," Brighton said.

"Then maybe I'm not the staid religious type you think I am. Anyway, we'll leave that discussion for another day. Hopefully, we have many other days." Ira lifted his head to look Brighton in the eye. "But nearly every religion agrees about the basic facts of a global flood. Not just Christianity and Judaism, but also Hinduism, the Greeks, the Ancient Chinese, the Mayans, the Incas... Everyone's on the same page if you look back far enough. Considering some ninety percent of the world's population belong to or affiliate with those religions, you're contending with a lot of people."

Brighton clasped his hands together. "Let me stop you there, Rabbi. In science, we don't make decisions by consensus. If nine out of ten people told you the earth was flat, would you believe them?"

The sound of a door opening made both men turn their heads. Wörtlich stepped out onto the terrace, the outdoor lights catching his back as he disappeared into the night.

Ira turned his attention back to Brighton. "Just because the Torah documents the Flood, the scientific community feels it's their special responsibility to dismiss it. And I can understand why that is: if they authenticated the Flood, they'd have to consider all the other scriptural events they don't like. People like you wouldn't be able to poke fun at us religious quacks anymore."

"I'm not saying you're right, but for the sake of argument, let's run with your theory. For a moment."

"Try plugging in the numbers, accounting for the possibility of a pole reversal around 2500 B.C.," Ira said. "I bet you end up with a more logical outcome."

Brighton's head was down, hitting buttons. After a while, his head came up. "This is going to take a while, Rabbi."

Ira lowered his feet from the coffee table and looked toward the terrace door, which was still partway open. He slipped through the door and peered into the darkness.

"You still out here?" Ira called, keeping his voice low.

He made out the figure of a man leaning against the railing. Wörtlich stared out at the water as the stiff evening breeze swept his hair up.

"I guess nobody feels like sleeping," Wörtlich murmured.

Ira joined him, resting his hands on the railing. "The sea breeze has a calming effect, doesn't it?"

"That it does."

Wörtlich turned away from the water and gazed thoughtfully at Ira. "I could not help but overhear the tail end of your conversation inside. The atheist in me was shouting in protest, but the scientist was ready to jump to your defense."

"Hopefully the scientist won," Ira said.

"He usually does. The pyramids are littered with fossilized remains of sea creatures, did you know that? At some point in its history, Giza was underwater. An Egyptologist, however, would get laughed out of a room by saying that. I would know."

The archaeologist rubbed his eyes and then turned them back toward the open water.

"Your religious beliefs are rubbish," Wörtlich said. "Forgive me for being blunt. The notion of eternal salvation is just a means of reconciling our feelings of universal emptiness. Even if there is a god, by no means does it follow that he is a benevolent one. Why should God care about us one way or the other, never mind love us? Your religion has constructed a complicated fantasy to avoid facing the fact that our world does not reflect the reality of a personal God. Deep down, we all know how the world works."

"Which is how?"

"Things do not get better. Technology improves, but not people," Wörtlich said. "I lost faith in the inherent goodness of people a *long* time ago. There cannot be a god looking out for us. It just cannot be."

Wörtlich turned to look Ira straight in the eyes. "An American friend of mine published an article a couple of years ago in a major scientific journal. He was writing about evolution's so-called missing links. He speculated that human life was perhaps a more recent development than previously thought, maybe as recent as twenty thousand years ago. He was surprised when the article was celebrated by prominent evangelical leaders as proof-positive that science was starting to change its tune. When he tried to clarify his statements, he was denounced and condemned by those same people. They were calling for him to step down from his position at the university.

"What is my point? Religious people only appreciate science when it suits them. Even when religious groups *are* right, they can represent such a sinkhole of human character that people like me are happy to fight them solely on principle. The fact is, science and religion do not go well together. They flirt with each other from time to time, but they always go their separate ways."

Silence reigned as Wörtlich stepped away and walked along the edge of the terrace.

Ira did not follow.

*   *   *

Wörtlich woke to the sound of people repeatedly walking past his bedroom window. He stayed in bed a few extra minutes, resting his eyes. He couldn't remember the last time he had indulged himself with such laziness.

The smell of fresh coffee finally convinced him to slide out of bed. The clinking of cutlery on a glass table presaged breakfast on the terrace. He slipped on the terrycloth robe hanging on the hook next to the bed and ventured into the bathroom.

After getting dressed, Wörtlich stepped outside and took in the scenery. He had spent several hours on the terrace the night before, but the darkness made it easy to forget the beauty of the coast. Gulls flew in languid circles far above his head, soaring out into the bay and perching on sharp rocks that protruded from jagged cliffs.

A servant approached with a tray holding a carafe and three downturned china cups. The blue floral pattern along their edges reminded him of his mother's dinnerware, which had only been used for extra special occasions. For Lagati, he supposed, every morning was a special occasion.

"Good morning, Doctor," Lagati said, emerging from the house. He wore white from top to bottom, perhaps in anticipation of a hot day. "Do you read Maltese?" He offered Wörtlich the newspaper he had tucked under his arm.

Wörtlich shook his head.

"A pity," the Frenchman said, sounding genuinely disappointed. "It's such a rich language."

Lagati gestured toward the table.

"I hear you had an opportunity to tackle our little dilemma last night," Lagati said.

Wörtlich put down his coffee cup and stretched his arms behind his back. "In a manner of speaking. We still do not know where to go next."

"Oh? I spoke to Mr. Brighton before he went for his morning run.

Apparently he had a very productive night."

Lagati shielded his eyes and peered down the coast where Wörtlich noticed for the first time a walking trail that disappeared around the cove.

"He should be back any minute now."

Ira soon joined them and they engaged in small talk. Lagati had more questions about Egypt, particularly the subterranean chambers they had discovered below the pyramids.

Wörtlich contributed as little as possible. A part of him felt uncomfortable around the rabbi this morning. He had said more than he intended last night, and he hadn't given Ira an opportunity to respond. Nonetheless, everything he'd said was true. Ira was an intelligent man, but there were areas where his faith blinded him.

"Good morning!" Brighton called, forcing Wörtlich to look up from the spot on the table he had been caught staring at.

Brighton trotted up to them in shorts and a brightly-colored t-shirt. He looked every bit the part of an American college student on vacation.

Breakfast featured more traditional fare than dinner had the night before. Lagati's table offered several loaves of fresh bread to choose from, along with a plate of sausage links, jams, and a serving of crepes, which Wörtlich declined. Brighton, however, shoveled two table spoons of confectioners' sugar onto his portion. The young man had earned the indulgence, having worked up quite a sweat from his morning run.

Once breakfast was cleared away, Lagati turned to Brighton. "Mr. Brighton, perhaps you could share with the others what you told me this morning?"

Brighton finished off his glass of orange juice and announced, smiling, "I have pinpointed the location of magnetic north."

"You have?" Wörtlich asked.

The young man regarded him with a look of youthful enthusiasm. "Indeed. And interestingly enough, the north magnetic pole back then turns out to be the *south* magnetic pole now."

Wörtlich's eyes widened in surprise as a satisfied look passed from Ira to Brighton.

"So, you're going to Antarctica," Lagati said.

"I would not say we have settled on it," Wörtlich said. "Aside from Mr. Brighton's assertions, we have no way of knowing that this is the True North the pyramid builders had in mind."

"The math makes more sense if you account for a magnetic pole reversal," Brighton said.

Of course. The Flood. Brighton's math must have substantiated Ira's theories.

"You were right, Ira," Brighton added as an aside. "I had a feeling last night you might be right, but I ignored it."

Ira shrugged. "Learn to trust that feeling. It comes from a far deeper and personal place than you realize."

Wörtlich cleared his throat and tried to steer the conversation back to the matter at hand. "We should not rule out simple geography. Even if you are right about the magnetic switch, the pyramid builders could have been referring to the Arctic."

Lagati smiled. The Frenchman seemed to get off on their collective curiosity. "I see you still have a big decision to make."

"Either way," Ira said, "if we're wrong, we'll have missed the target by some twenty thousand kilometers."

Lagati pushed back his chair and stood. "Then you'd better make sure you're right. As it happens, I think I can shed some light on the problem. Follow me."

Lagati led the way into the house. They passed through the living room, turned left up a flight of stairs, and came to a mezzanine level that had been appended to the north-facing side of the house. Lagati pulled open a pair of tall wooden doors and held them open as the others filed inside.

So much natural light poured into Lagati's private study through the enormous windows and skylights that Wörtlich almost felt like he had stepped back outside. The desk in the center of the room faced north, affording a spectacular view of the rocky coastline.

Lagati approached a cabinet along the far wall and removed a blue capsule. He brought it to the desk and put it down, clearing away several objects cluttering the workspace. He then popped open the plastic cap and removed a roll of paper. Once unfurled, Wörtlich found himself looking at a very old map, a throwback to the days of "Here There Be Dragons" cartography. Large portions of this hand-drawn world, such as the western coasts of the Americas, remained conspicuously absent.

"What are we looking at?" he asked, fascinated.

"A map," Lagati said in a reverential tone. He smoothed the creases in the paper. "This is not just any map, Doctor. It's a copy of the Piri Reis map. Have you heard of it?"

Wörtlich shook his head, continuing to survey for clues of what made the map so special. Certainly the original would have been very old. Sixteenth century most likely, after the discovery of the Americas but before their frontiers were explored.

"Piri Reis was an admiral in the Turkish navy and an avid cartographer," Lagati said. "He created a large number of maps during his career, but in 1513 he published this one, which was unique in many respects. Just twenty years after Columbus' discovery of the New World, he somehow managed to provide an astonishingly detailed representation of it. Much of the geography can be attributed to the explorations of Columbus and Vespucci, but even so, the detail of the Americas is exquisite."

"Not just the Americas from the looks of it." Wörtlich frowned, leaning in for a closer look. He pointed to the tip of South America, except instead of the coastline curving west around Cape Horn, making way for the Drake Passage, the coast continued south and east—

"Antarctica!" Brighton blurted. "Impossible. The coast of Antarctica wasn't sighted until the nineteenth century."

"Don't get ahead of me," Lagati cautioned. He pointed to the top of the map. "Here, Piri Reis wrote, 'In all the world there is no other map like this map.' That was no overstatement. As Mr. Brighton has so enthusiastically pointed out, this depiction of the Antarctic coastline came more than three hundred years before the continent's official discovery. But while that in itself offers a tantalizing puzzle, the story grows stranger. You see, this map provides the *actual* coastline. What I mean by that is that the data used to create this map reflects accurate knowledge of what the land looks like beneath two hundred feet of glacial ice. These coastlines cannot be glimpsed with the naked eye."

"What are you getting at?" Wörtlich asked.

"In the last few decades, with infrared mapping technology and the help of satellites, we've been able to get a look at this hidden coastline," Lagati said. "We're now able to confirm that Piri Reis' accomplishment was precise—and impossible. Most authorities on the subject assume that the similarities between this map and the real thing are strictly coincidental, that when making the map, Reis shifted the South American coastline to the east to avoid running out of parchment."

Lagati chuckled softly. "But that's not a very satisfying explanation. Fortunately, as you can see by this reproduction, Reis included some handwritten notes. He points out here that his information wasn't gathered firsthand, but rather was taken from a number of source maps, perhaps dating back to antiquity."

Wörtlich leaned forward, investigating the curvature of the alleged representation of Antarctica. "Actually, I have heard of this. Something about crustal displacement, unless I miss my guess."

"You do not," Lagati said. "Charles Hapgood, an American scholar, put forward the idea that an ancient and sophisticated race of mariners was busy exploring the earth, including the southern seas, during a period much earlier than mainstream history thinks is possible. In fact, Hapgood provides compelling evidence in his research that Reis' oldest source material came from Egypt, perhaps from the Library of Alexandria. The library's founder, Ptolemy II, is noted for having collected maps in large numbers. It was one of his greatest obsessions."

"Could the map be a hoax?" Brighton wondered.

Lagati waved his hand dismissively. "Even the Smithsonian released a statement authenticating it."

Wörtlich took a step back, allowing for Brighton a closer look, and wandered toward the windows.

If Piri Reis had discovered source maps of Antarctica, and they had originally come from the Alexandria, then they must surely have predated Ptolemy. Ptolemy's world maps hadn't mentioned a word about Antarctica, and his mapping of longitude and latitude had set the standard for several hundred years of cartographical advances. If source maps depicting Antarctica had cropped up in Alexandria, they would have originated somewhere else. Somewhere much older.

"This could be further evidence of the pyramid builders," Wörtlich said. "If those source maps came from Egypt, they almost certainly came out of the Hall of Records."

Lagati turned to regard him. "I reached the same conclusion. The pyramid builders had to have been the ancient mariners Hapgood describes. They charted the entire world and poured that knowledge into the construction of the pyramids, which explains its geographical significance."

Brighton let out a sudden gasp.

Wörtlich turned back. "What is it?"

The young man's eyes glazed over in that characteristic manner he had when he started doing math in his head.

"When's the last time Antarctica's coastline was ice-free?" Brighton asked. "When's the last time it could have been charted without the use of infrared technology?"

Wörtlich could practically see the equations flowing right to left across Brighton's eyes.

Brighton snapped his fingers as the answer came to him. "Just over six thousand years ago."

Ira sat wearily in Lagati's office chair. "The timeframe lines up with the building of the pyramids."

Wörtlich returned to the group, his heart pounding. "The pyramid builders mapped Antarctica because that was where they were going."

"That's our connection, boys," Lagati said. "Antarctica awaits!"

NINETEEN

Over the Antarctic Circle
SEPTEMBER 22

The waters below the plane were nothing like the clear blue Mediterranean. The southern ocean was grey and choppy— and frigid. For the last hour, Brighton had noticed floating ice bergs. Sometimes they were almost indistinguishable from the grey water around them, but when the sunlight hit them just so, they gleamed like diamonds.

He took a break from staring out the window and opened his laptop, but after a few minutes the screen made his eyes hurt.

"Having some trouble?" Ira asked, swiveling his chair to face Brighton's.

"Yeah. I can't seem to triangulate the exact spot of the magnetic pole. Too much time has passed to be accurate about it. The best I can do is narrow it down to a region. Even then, we're going to have a lot of ground to cover."

A door clicked at the back of the plane and Wörtlich emerged from the lavatory.

"That is the biggest airplane bathroom I have ever been in," the archaeologist remarked.

Brighton flashed a grin. "Spent a lot of time in airplane bathrooms, have you?"

Wörtlich frowned rather than dignify the joke with a response.

"Has the pilot found us a place to land yet?" Wörtlich asked.

"Yes," Ira said. "There's an airstrip in Queen Maud Land, at a Norwegian environmental outpost."

"It's close to our search area," Brighton said. "I'm going to try contacting Lagati for some satellite imagery. It might help us focus our search."

*　　*　　*

A wide glacier sloped upward into the heights of the Antarctic mainland, forming a panoramic expanse of glassy ice that stretched out in all directions. A foreboding layer of dense, fast-moving clouds indicated bad weather. Whatever storms threatened, Brighton doubted conditions could get any more bone-chilling. Wind whipped at his face. He pulled his parka tight and braced himself as he and the others trudged away from the airstrip, but there was no escaping the cold.

And this is supposed to be spring, he reminded himself.

Brighton had often visited family in Canada, and on one occasion an early blizzard had swept across the prairies in late November, snowing them in for several days. Antarctic spring made that weekend almost paradisiacal by comparison. For the first time since leaving Egypt, he longed for the desert heat.

A bunker door loomed ahead of them, blurred by snow flurries. Was that the outpost? Just a solitary bunker on the edge of a runway? He started at the growl of the plane's engines heating up behind him, already prepping to leave them behind in this desolate wasteland.

The door to the bunker opened and two parka-clad figures emerged. All those layers made it difficult to determine much about their shape apart from the fact that they each seemed to have two arms and two legs.

One of them extended a gloved hand to Wörtlich.

"My name's Doctor Faust!" the man said in a thick Norwegian accent. "You are right on time."

"It is so bright out," Wörtlich grumbled.

Faust shrugged. Or at least, Brighton thought it was a shrug. These parkas didn't allow for much freedom of movement.

"Yes, it stays daytime very late in the spring and summer months," Faust said. "You get used to it. It's much worse in the winter!" He gave his companion a pat on the arm. "This is Anders."

They all shook hands.

"Come inside where it's warm," Anders invited.

Behind them, the plane lifted off and soared into the swirling cloud cover, pulling behind it long, billowy fingers of icy vapor. Brighton resisted the urge to run after it.

The bunker was larger on the inside than it looked from the airstrip. The entrance was a small closet to store boots and winter wear, beyond which the floor sloped down to a combined living area and kitchen. Along two walls, banks of computer equipment and gauges monitored… well, whatever this station was built to monitor. Brighton would have to ask Faust about that later.

Faust pulled off his hood, revealing a shock of blond hair and a shaggy beard somehow appropriate for a man living in a bunker on the bottom of the world. The Norwegian rubbed his hands together and adjusted the needle on the thermostat.

Anders walked past them into the kitchen and poured himself a cup of hot water.

A sneeze drew Brighton's attention to two dark-haired women who appeared at the entrance to a short hall. They both wore brightly colored sweaters. The shorter of the two had a round face and kind eyes and smiled at the sight of the newcomers.

They probably don't get many visitors, Brighton mused. *If any at all.*

"I'm Anna," the shorter woman said.

Brighton had to look twice as she came closer. She bore a striking resemblance to his girlfriend, Rachel. They had the same long brown hair, the same blue eyes. They were even the same height.

God, I miss her.

Intellectually, he knew they had been apart less than three weeks. But it felt like a year. In that time, he had travelled more than halfway around the world.

The second woman sat in a patched-up living room chair that had seen better days.

"Bergitta," she said as introduction.

"Sit down," Faust invited, gesturing toward the other chairs huddled around the living area. "There isn't much room, but there's enough. Hot tea?"

"Yes, please," Ira said after hanging up his coat. The rabbi's short grey hair stuck up in disheveled clumps, making him look like an eccentric old man. His nose glowed red from the cold.

"We share three small bedrooms and a bathroom, and this," Anders said, gesturing to the humble quarters. "It's cozy. We can make space in the equipment room if you don't mind some noise at night. The gear doesn't run quietly."

"Good enough for me," Wörtlich volunteered. He took a seat and Ira dropped down beside him.

Not wanting to be the last left standing, Brighton took the only seat left, next to the woman who had called herself Bergitta. Anna was on the floor, leaning up against the wall while Faust and Anders remained in the kitchen.

"How long have you been here?" Brighton asked.

"Nine months," Anna said with the strongest accent Brighton had ever heard.

"But our assignment is a year," Bergitta finished.

Brighton coughed into his hand. "That's a long time to live in such close quarters. I'd feel a little claustrophobic."

"Claustrophobic?" Anna asked.

Bergitta explained the term to her in Norwegian, then said, "Yes, claustrophobic. We undergo a psych exam before coming here. This is the highlight of my career, though. I would stay longer if I could."

Anders walked out of the kitchen, balancing three mugs of steaming hot tea. Each of the visitors took one and thanked him.

"I see you conduct environmental research," Wörtlich noted.

"We measure climate change," Faust said. "With the glaciers melting, we're seeing new fresh water lakes form on the surface of the ice."

Bergitta sat straighter. "The glaciers dump a lot of fresh water into the southern basins, and the shifting balance is changing the ocean currents."

The Norwegians continued the shop talk, occasionally slipping back into their own language. When this happened, Brighton kept out of it and simply tried his best to follow.

Wörtlich at least knew a small amount of Norwegian, so from

time to time he offered a few words, which were greeted with smiles and comments about how strong his accent was. If nothing else, his attempts entertained them.

The conversation eventually hit a lull, with the Norwegians all exchanging furtive glances.

"It's very strange for you to be here," Faust finally said. "The NPI—uh, the Polar Institute—only told us you were coming this morning, but they didn't explain." Wörtlich opened his mouth to say something, but Faust waved him off. "Don't worry, you need not tell us. We were told not to ask questions."

"Whatever you are studying, it must be very important," Bergitta said. "By law, all visitors must post notice with the government a year ahead of time."

The wind howled over the roof, causing the light's pull rope to sway. The light flickered, then surged brightly before returning to normal.

"You've come at a bad time," Faust said as he grabbed the rope to steady it. "A storm system is brewing over the Weddell Sea. We are well-equipped to wait it out, but our calculations show it's going to track overtop us. Whatever outdoor activities you are planning will have to wait a few days."

"Could the storm miss us?" Brighton asked.

"I wouldn't get my hopes up. We've had bad luck with storms this season, and even if it does miss us, it's going to dump a lot of snow. We could be buried here for a while."

Flashbacks to his snowed-in November weekend returned as Brighton finished off the last of his tea and set the empty cup on the floor.

They made room for two people to sleep in the equipment room, so Brighton agreed to squeeze in with Wörtlich and leave the more comfortable couch to Ira. He wouldn't have been able to sleep knowing the poor old rabbi was sandwiched between a snoring German and a bank of bright, noisy equipment. Brighton wasn't looking forward to it, but after sleeping in Lagati's dreamy, pillow-ridden guest suite, he could live with the reality of a cement floor.

The low hum of equipment wasn't nearly as bad as Faust had made it out to be; it was more the alternating blue, green, and red lights that kept him awake.

Brighton braced his pillow against the wall and tried to stretch his legs out, but the space was too small. He bent his knees and tried to get comfortable, but his desire to stretch became so strong that it was all he could think of. Wörtlich, he noticed, didn't have the same problem, being a half-foot shorter.

"I noticed you looking at that woman," Wörtlich said, his voice muffled slightly by the pillow he was speaking into.

"Which woman?"

"The shorter one. Anna."

Brighton closed his eyes, but doing so made it no easier to get comfortable.

"She's cute, I guess." Brighton didn't need to see the archaeologist to know Wörtlich was smiling. "She reminds me of my girlfriend."

"You have a girlfriend?"

"Don't sound so surprised."

Wörtlich grunted in the darkness. "Hardly surprised. You have not mentioned this girl before."

"What do you want to know?" The question was met with silence, but Brighton decided to answer his own question. "Her name is Rachel. We met at a technology convention about a year ago in San Francisco."

"Does she also work for the Smithsonian?"

"She's a waitress, actually. How about you?"

"How about me, what?"

"Are you married?"

"No."

When Wörtlich didn't elaborate, Brighton decided not to press. What started as a short pause soon lengthened into several minutes, and Brighton assumed the German man had gone to sleep.

"I have been married twice," Wörtlich finally said. "Once when I was your age, which I do not recommend. It only lasted two years. I worked too much and travelled too often. I was employed by an oil company in the Middle East that needed somebody to inspect drilling sites to make sure they were not destroying anything of a historical nature. The money was very good."

Brighton heard him yawn.

"I got married again ten years later, to a colleague. It is a bad idea to get involved with colleagues, Mr. Brighton. Your girlfriend is a waitress, you say? That is a good sign. It will keep you from getting bored with each other so fast." Another yawn, followed by a drawn-out sigh. "And then there was Elisabeth…"

Brighton shifted onto his back and clasped his hands over his stomach as Wörtlich's voice trailed off. Positioned this way, his knees stuck straight up into the air.

He couldn't believe Wörtlich was being so forthright. Despite everything they had been through in the past two weeks, he hardly knew more than the man's name!

But we stole the index together and fled a country as fugitives, Brighton reminded himself. *Maybe it's time we get to know each other.*

"Who's Elisabeth?" he asked.

But his only answer was a series of soft snores.

*   *   *

Anders was cooking eggs and something that smelled suspiciously like canned salmon. It wasn't the most appetizing breakfast Ira had encountered, but he was a guest and would try to eat whatever was served.

After breakfast, he watched Wörtlich pull up a chair to the small kitchen table with three of the Norwegians—Bergitta had disappeared into the equipment room to make some calibrations—and asked to be dealt into the card game they had going. Ira did his best to ignore the occasional shouts and groans that came from their direction. Wörtlich was trying to use as much Norwegian as possible, to the others' delight.

Outside, the wind howled and whistled. Ira had to look away from the whiteout conditions; the light glared off the glass, making it painful to even glance in the window's direction. He thought about picking up the book he had started the night before, a compilation of six Shakespearean tragedies. It was one of only two English language books he had found in the bookshelf, with English in one column and the Norwegian translation in the other.

Instead, he sat next to Brighton and tried to follow what the young man was working on. He was scouring high-resolution satellite imagery. So much snow clouded the frame that it seemed almost as blinding as the window.

"Making any headway?"

Brighton blinked and rubbed the back of his neck. "The more I look over the area, the more discouraged I become. There's nothing out there. It's worse than the desert, which at least had roads."

Brighton twisted the screen around so Ira could get a better look, and indeed the young man was right. These satellite photos weren't going to be much use.

"It would help if we actually knew what we were looking for." Brighton bit his lip. "So far, all we have to go on is that the pyramid builders came to this area. But they would have been here long before the ice, so anything they built has been covered by hundreds of feet of glacier. It seems hopeless."

"I see what you mean."

The volume of the card game rose unexpectedly. Wörtlich and Faust seemed to be losing an exciting hand.

Ira kept his attention on the computer, scrolling horizontally through the imagery, frame by frame.

"I don't know what I was hoping to find. Just—" Brighton hesitated, his face screwing up in frustration. "I was so certain the answer would be in these pictures. If we can't figure out where to go next, we're lost. Needle-in-a-haystack lost."

Brighton ran a hand through his hair. A few strands at the back stood straight up. "What are we doing here? We should have done more research before coming all this way. Maybe we jumped the gun."

Ira sat back, gazing at the sullen young man. Brighton had so much potential, so much capability. Sometimes his youth and inexperience made him too prone to emotional highs and lows. This was one of those times. They had felt lost back in Egypt, too, but they had found their breakthroughs.

"Remember what you said about 'trusting a feeling'?" Brighton asked, shutting the laptop and sitting back.

Ira's eyes widened. "Yes."

Brighton crossed his legs and gazed absently across the room, but he was listening.

"You must trust that feeling when you're otherwise at a loss," Ira continued. "When you don't know what to do next."

A pregnant pause passed between the two men.

"Do you trust me?" Ira asked.

Brighton hesitated, then leveled his eyes on Ira, making a decision, focusing.

"Yes."

Ira reached forward and took one of his hands.

Brighton's arm stiffened self-consciously, and he peered over at the card game.

To make sure nobody's watching us.

Brighton jerked his hand back. "We aren't praying, are we?"

"Why? Does that make you uncomfortable?"

"You bet your ass it does."

Ira raised his eyebrows. "Think of it as a meditation."

Brighton considered that, his eyes shifting around the room as if unable to settle. After another moment, he nodded and closed his eyes.

Ira took his hand again. "Now, try to relax."

"This is weird. I can't believe I'm doing this."

Ira smiled inwardly but kept his face neutral. "You're very tense, Sherwood. It's important that you loosen up a bit."

"But they're going to stare at us."

Ira turned back to the others, who were oblivious to what they were doing. "Don't worry about them."

Brighton took a series of deep breaths and his grip on Ira's hand loosened.

"Now, form a mental picture of a river. This river is like the universe. Everything that exists is made up of streams of possibilities, and all those streams are caught up in the current of the river. People get caught up in the current, too, and they are swept downstream."

Ira paused, feeling Brighton's grip loosen a little more.

"Imagine yourself standing in the shallow riverbank. As you wade out, you feel the water coursing around you, pulling at you. Now, swim out into the middle of it. Let go."

Brighton's fingers tensed and his fingers again tightened their grasp.

"You're in control," Ira said. "Picture yourself reaching your feet down and touching the bottom, anchoring yourself. You are choosing not to be swept away. You are choosing your own possibilities. From here, you can see how the river branches and flows in all different directions." He paused, waiting for the young man to relax again, a signal that he was giving in to the experience. It didn't take long for him to get to that place. "Feel confident. Harness the flow of the stream. Relax and make your choice—"

A sudden pounding snapped them both out of the meditation. Their eyes flew open as the door crashed in and a figure plunged into the room, a wild flurry of wind and snow right on his heels.

At first, Ira thought it might be Bergitta—she was the only one not accounted for—but he soon realized this figure was much too tall. And a man.

Faust jumped up from the table and rushed over to push the door closed. Keeping the weather out was of primary concern. As soon as peace was restored, all eyes turned to the intruder.

We're in the middle of nowhere! Ira thought. *Where did this man come from? Was he wandering out in the wilderness?*

The newcomer dropped his backpack and began to unwrap the seemingly endless layers of scarves covering his face. The Norwegians crowded around. As the layers came off, Ira caught a glimpse of the man's eyes peeking out, and soon after, his face.

"Poulson!" Anders exclaimed, shock evident on his face.

Ira turned in surprise.

They know him.

TWENTY

Queen Maud Land

SEPTEMBER 23

Anna, be careful," Anders said.

Brighton watched as Anna took slow, deliberate steps toward Poulson, her eyes fixated on him. It was like watching a scene in slow motion. Anders grabbed her arm, but she pulled free and walked up to the newcomer. Her mouth was open.

"Anna!" called Bergitta, who had emerged from the equipment room upon hearing the commotion. She stood behind Faust, watching Poulson with wary eyes. "Anna, he may not be well."

When still Anna didn't stop, Bergitta let out a flurry of Norwegian.

Anna ignored those words as well. She reached up and brushed her hand along Poulson's unshaven cheek.

For the first time, Brighton found his attention drawn to Poulson's face. He frowned, searching the man's dark eyes and scruffy blond hair, his high cheekbones, his lips thin and pressed together until they were white.

I've seen him somewhere before.

Before Brighton could place him, Poulson took Anna's hand in his, forcing it down. He wasn't violent about it. The man had a wild look in his eyes, but it was hard to say if he was dangerous. The other Norwegians certainly thought he could be.

Poulson kept his grip on Anna's hand, and she didn't seem upset about it.

"Let her go, Poulson," Faust demanded.

Neither Anna nor Poulson reacted to Faust's command. Confusion and joy crossed Anna's face, and Brighton got the distinct impression that the two of them had been involved in the past. They cared for each other, and more than just as colleagues.

"You're alive," Anna whispered, warmly, tenderly. "How are you alive, Olaf?"

Poulson let go of her hand and his eyes hardened. "Yes, of course I am! Can't you think of something useful to say?"

Anna clamped her mouth shut at the outburst.

Anders reached for her a second time and pulled her toward him protectively. This time, she didn't resist.

"Why are you yelling at her?" Anders asked, his voice low and threatening.

Poulson turned to regard him. "I did not mean to yell. I—" An emotion crossed over his eyes. Anger? Fear? Relief? It could have been any or all of them. "I have not been around people in some time."

"Don't blame us for being surprised," Faust said and stepped closer. Poulson took a step back, maintaining the distance between them. "We searched for a week. A whole week! We didn't think you survived. Once the storms came, there was no reason to hold out hope."

Poulson's gaze landed on Brighton next. His eyebrows furrowed and he said something in Norwegian. Brighton didn't understand the language, but from the context he guessed it was something like, *"Who are these people?"*

Faust gestured to Brighton and toward where Ira and Wörtlich hung back, watching in amazement. "These are scientists, Poulson. They are here for a short time, conducting research."

"Would somebody mind explaining what's going on here?" Brighton interrupted.

Wörtlich half-turned to the young man and allowed a small smile. Perhaps he had been about to ask the same thing.

Bergitta and Faust helped Poulson sit down, then gathered some blankets to throw on him. Despite being well-dressed for the Antarctic cold, the storm had caused snow to rush up into every nook and cranny of Poulson's clothing, packing into solid, irregularly shaped blocks. He shivered when his coat came off, slowly at first but faster as each successive layer peeled away.

Anders hurried to the kitchen to get Poulson something hot to drink. When he returned with tea, Poulson merely cradled it in his hands, as though his fingers had fused to the side of the cup. His eyes kept closing, as though they hurt to stay open. The man's cheeks, red when he'd first come in, had faded to a pale white. Brighton didn't remember enough about cold weather to gauge whether that was a good or bad sign, but Faust ran into the supply closet, returning with a small area heater. He plugged it into the wall and pointed at Poulson's convulsing toes.

Anna sat close to him, her head rested on Poulson's shoulder, and she clutched his arm. They had definitely been lovers, Brighton decided, and she'd thought him dead.

"Poulson was with us when we first arrived," Faust explained once they had Poulson situated.

"What happened to him?" Brighton asked.

Faust glanced to Poulson, checking to see if he was well enough to take up the story. But he was in no condition to talk. "We were conducting a survey up on the southern glacier a few weeks after we got here," Faust said. "Water was beginning to pool in one of the new ice basins and a few of us volunteered to hike up and see if a new fresh water lake was forming."

Anna shifted, her eyes losing focus. She wiped a tear from her cheek.

"I went with Poulson and Anders, and we brought back pictures," Faust said. "It was the largest melt lake we had detected so far, but we hadn't thought to bring any sample containers with us. The next morning, Poulson asked to go back."

"I found something incredible," Poulson said quietly. His teeth had stopped chattering, and his cheeks had regained a trace of color.

"You *thought* you found something incredible," Bergitta said. She looked about to go on, but Faust silenced her with a hard glance.

"Damn it, I am not losing my mind!" Poulson insisted.

Anders crossed his legs. "Maybe if you hadn't run off in the middle of the night with half our supplies, we wouldn't think that."

Brighton looked from Anders to Poulson in confusion. Run off in the middle of the night?

"It doesn't matter if you believe me or not. I saw what I saw," Poulson said with a glare at Anders. Reining himself in, he instead focused his explanation on Wörtlich, Brighton, and Ira. "The water was gone the next day, which was impossible. There had been more than twenty cubic kilometers of water in that lake. It had to have gone somewhere. Then, in the middle of the basin, I saw a dark crack in the ice. Getting to it was tricky, because the ice was slick and the wind was picking up, but after a couple of hours I got to the edge of what appeared to be a ten-foot fissure. When I looked down, I saw what was unmistakably grass. Bright green grass."

"There wasn't any grass!" Anders maintained.

Poulson ignored him. "It was late, so I decided to head back to camp to share my findings. When it came down to it, though, nobody believed me. Faust and Anders at last agreed to see it for themselves. But when we hiked up the next day, they couldn't see the bottom of the fissure like I could."

"It was sheer ice all the way down," Faust said.

"Everybody thought I was crazy." There was a sharp, bitter edge in Poulson's voice, and the looks he threw toward Anders and Faust might have melted steel under different circumstances. "When we trained for this assignment, we were warned that some people aren't suited for isolation. We all heard the stories about those who were sent back. So, it didn't matter what I said. The others came to believe I was out of my mind. Faust even sent off a request to have me sent home."

Noticing Poulson's empty cup, Anders grabbed it and carried it back to the kitchen to fill. He returned and sat back down. "Why don't you get to the part where you stole from us and took off into the wilderness?" he asked.

"I couldn't stop thinking about the fissure," Poulson admitted. "I was obsessed with it. I couldn't let the others send me home before I had the chance to get a better look. It had been cloudy the day Anders and Faust walked up the glacier with me; I thought maybe the light had been better the first day. I told the others I wanted to go back."

Anna's mouth tightened. "We said no."

"Why?" Ira asked.

"A storm was on the way," Faust said. "But Poulson was insistent. He wanted to take more pictures, prove to us that there was something at the bottom of the fissure."

Poulson's features clouded over. "They said we would go after the storm, but I knew the storm could change the conditions."

Faust let out a long sigh. "Perhaps."

"So, you went anyway," Ira surmised.

"Yes. I waited until everyone else had gone to sleep, then snuck out with two backpacks' worth of supplies." He glanced down at Anna, whose head still rested on his shoulder. "But I couldn't leave without telling Anna. We were in bed and she tried convincing me to stay."

Anna's face grew despondent again, her eyes misting with the pain of memory.

Brighton glanced toward Wörtlich by instinct, recalling their conversation from the night before, and wished at the last moment that he hadn't. The archaeologist caught the look and scowled. Wörtlich seemed to have some experience with romance between colleagues— and whatever it was, it wasn't good experience.

"She let him go," Anders filled in, having missed the two men's awkward exchange. "We waited out the storm, and it was the longest two days of our lives. We figured that if Poulson had somehow found shelter, he might have survived. The snow was safe to eat, and he had extensive training."

"We went out as soon as the storm passed, making our way up to the lake. We looked for three more days." Faust paused. "We assumed he had died. The way that wind had been blowing, he could have been kilometers away and buried in a drift somewhere."

Bergitta took a deep breath. "The temperature dropped to forty below, Olaf. What were we supposed to do?"

Faust looked at Poulson incredulously. "How *did* you survive?"

"I used my ice pick to climb down into the fissure." Poulson stopped to appreciate the amazed looks on everyone's faces. "It may seem crazy, but I *knew* there was a bottom, remember? There was a habitat down there and everything. You would have found it, too, if you'd trusted me."

"A habitat." Faust exchanged a look with Anders. He walked to one of the equipment walls, put a set of headphones to his left ear, and turned a radial dial, listening.

"Stop it!" Poulson was already half out of his seat.

Anna tried holding him back, but she wasn't strong enough.

Anders, however, overpowered him, throwing him into the wall and holding him there.

"Stop it, stop it," Poulson raged. "Stop it!"

"Relax, Poulson." Faust took the headset off. "I can't get a message out until the storm passes. But we'll need to tell someone you're alive. You were reported dead back home."

Poulson strained against Anders' hold and finally broke free, pivoting away. He lost his balance, smashed into the card table, and fell to the ground in a tangle of folding chairs. Cards fluttered to the floor like so many snowflakes.

"You don't understand," he said, propping himself up on his elbows. "I didn't come back to rejoin you."

Anders took a few steps closer to him, but Poulson grabbed a broken table leg and brandished it.

"Then why are you here?" Anna asked, her eyes wide with confusion.

Poulson scrambled away until his back pressed against the door of the supply closet. He reached for his backpack, lying within arm's reach. He unzipped one of its folds and pulled out a pistol.

"Isn't it obvious?" he asked, dropping the table leg and pointing the gun at Anders. "I need more supplies."

*   *   *

Wörtlich stepped away with Brighton and Ira, pressing his back to the wall as Poulson herded the Norwegians into their bedrooms and then wedged kitchen chairs under the knobs to lock them in. He left Anna for last, nudging her back into the living area where she sat in a corner chair, timid and still.

"Let us out!" Faust shouted, but Poulson ignored him and kept his gun trained on Anna.

"Why are you pointing that gun at her?" Ira asked in a calming tone. Poulson swept the gun toward him, but the rabbi didn't blink. "She has feelings for you, can't you see that?"

Poulson was sweating. "I just want to get my supplies and leave."

"She is not going to hurt you," Wörtlich said. "And neither are we. Just put the gun down."

The steady keening of the wind rose in volume and intensity, and they waited for it to die down again.

"Poulson!" Faust called. "This isn't going to get you what you want!"

"We won't tell the NPI," Anders chimed in. "After you tell them what you told us, everything's going to change."

Poulson shut his eyes tight, but it was clear to Wörtlich that what he was really trying to do was shut out their voices. When his eyes opened again, Poulson trained his gaze on Anna's lowered face. She was shuddering.

"Are you just going to take your supplies and leave again, Olaf?" Wörtlich said. "Can you not see how much she misses you?"

Poulson's eyes darted to him. "Leave her out of it. She has nothing to do with this."

"Is that true?" he asked. "It looks to me like she loves you."

"What do you know of it?"

Wörtlich took a step forward, not flinching as the aim of Poulson's gun panned toward him.

"I know a lot about it, I think," Wörtlich said. "I once walked away from someone I loved, Olaf, and I always regretted it." He paused, glancing over at Brighton, who met his gaze straight on. Brighton thought he knew what this was about, but he didn't.

Elisabeth, Wörtlich thought. *Forgive me, Elisabeth. I always make the same mistakes. Please do not let me end up like this man.*

Anna looked up, listening to the exchange. "Please don't hurt them, Olaf."

That did it. Poulson lowered the gun halfway.

"Poulson!" Faust called a third time. "Poulson, are you listening to me?"

The gun shot back up.

Wörtlich cursed under his breath, considered the situation, then decided on a different approach.

"I believe you."

Instead of showing relief, Poulson's face twisted into a sneer. "I doubt that, stranger."

"Believe me, I do," Wörtlich insisted. "The truth is, Faust and the others do not know what we came here for, but that fissure you described might be just the thing."

Doubt broke out on Poulson's face. His jaw twitched, and

Wörtlich knew he was thinking it over.

"I am an archaeologist," Wörtlich continued, pressing his advantage. "Our information tells us that there is evidence of an ancient civilization somewhere in this region. They may have built a structure here, thousands of years ago. Have you seen anything like that?"

Poulson eyed them suspiciously. "An ancient civilization?"

"Highly advanced people who were related to the Egyptians. Possibly they are the ones who built the pyramids."

"Or maybe you were sent by my government to collect me."

Wörtlich smiled. "You should hear how bad my Norwegian is. Just ask your friends. Why would your government send someone who does not even speak the language?" Poulson's gun dipped again. "We knew nothing about you. Your friends said not a word about a fifth member of their team. You surprised us as much as you did them."

Poulson finally lowered the gun until it hung limply at his side. "There is some writing down there that could be Egyptian."

"In the fissure?" Brighton asked.

"In the habitat," Poulson said.

Wörtlich's mouth fell open. He could hardly believe their good fortune. Assuming, of course, that Poulson wasn't the unhinged man the other Norwegians thought he was…

Poulson frowned. "Who *are* you people?"

"Scientists," Wörtlich said. He gestured toward Ira and Brighton. "And investigators. Just like you."

"You won't try to stop me?"

Ira stepped forward again. "Stop you? No. We want to help you."

Poulson's entire demeanor slackened. He returned the pistol to his backpack. He walked into the kitchen and opened a few of the cupboards, pulling out cans of food and stacking them on the counter.

"I'll take you with me," he said at last. "I'll show you what I found. On one condition."

"Name it," Wörtlich said.

Poulson inclined his head toward the bedroom doors. "They can't come—and you can't come back and show them. It's not for them. It's not for them to find."

The words hit Wörtlich like a brick wall, and a memory of Omar's wife shouting at Brighton as they left Al Bawiti flooded back over him.

"It is not for you! Not for you! You must leave it alone."

The similarities were eerie.

"Promise me you will not show them," Poulson said, more adamant.

Wörtlich shook off his unease. "We would not dream of it." Out of the corner of his eye, he saw Anna watching them closely. "What about Anna? Can she come?"

Poulson looked across the room at her, conflicted. "No. She must stay. This life isn't for her, either. She should be free of me."

Poulson's words again brought up a surge of memory; Wörtlich had said nearly the same ones three years ago. Wörtlich steadied himself against the back of the couch as Poulson continued gathering supplies.

"You better get dressed," Poulson said, closing one cupboard door and opening another. "We've got a long way to go, and it's damned cold."

TWENTY-ONE

Queen Maud Land
SEPTEMBER 23

Brighton bared his teeth and pushed himself forward, straining every muscle to fight the storm raging around them. His boots weighed him down. Wind swirled around his face, whipping up against the cold-weather goggles strapped to his head; the goggles kept his eyes from freezing, but he couldn't see much out of them. The rest of him was covered head to toe in layers of sweaters, jackets, scarves, hoods, boots, socks, and long underwear, but after ten minutes he couldn't feel much below the knees and past the elbows. The gradual numbness made every step a little easier than the one before, but he knew it was a bad sign. He imagined this was how a leper felt, unable to tell if one of his extremities was damaged to the point of serious injury. From time to time, he looked down to make sure he hadn't lost anything.

They struggled up a steep path away from the bunker and trudged through drifts that were up to three feet deep in places. The snow had hardened enough that they could walk atop it without sinking, but every once in a while the snow gave out beneath one of them and they had to fight their way through a trench. While these trenches proved difficult to move through, at least they provided some shelter from the wind.

Poulson took the brunt of the weather. Brighton and the others followed in the path he made. Several times, Brighton felt the urge to sit down and rest, to gain back his energy, but the wiser part of his mind knew that was certain death. He wouldn't take long to freeze in this storm, and he doubted any of the Norwegians would come to their rescue.

Brighton had opted to walk last, to make sure Ira kept up and didn't fall behind. Watching the old man's humped shoulders tacking into the wind reminded Brighton that as tired as he was, Ira was much worse off. If a man in his sixties could make the journey, he had no excuse for falling behind.

They soon came to a rocky overhang, which blocked the chilliest gusts from the south. Despite the welcome shelter, it wasn't a good idea to stop for too long. Ahead of him, Ira slumped to his knees, wheezing heavily.

"How far are we from camp?" Brighton shouted over the howling wind.

"About a mile," Poulson shouted back.

That far? We've gone further than I thought.

Wörtlich positioned his body between Ira and the cold wind still whistling around the edges of the rock. "Are we close?"

"Yes," Poulson said. "It's just a little further, but it's uphill."

Brighton put his hand on Ira's shoulder and leaned in so that Ira would be able to hear him. "Ira, can you make it?"

Ira seemed exhausted, but his eyes showed steely resolve; he wasn't going to give up.

Brighton helped steady him as Poulson trudged around the outcropping and continued against the wind.

The second leg of the hike was worse than the first. They headed straight uphill, and at times it took everything Brighton had just to stay upright. But somehow they all kept marching. Brighton's right arm rested on Ira's shoulder, and Ira's arm disappeared into the white maelstrom beyond, presumably holding onto Wörtlich. The physical contact kept them from getting disoriented in the terrible, featureless white that churned around them.

"I hope you know where you are going!" someone called up ahead. The voice was too faint for him to tell who had spoken.

A blast of wind struck Brighton full in the chest and he stumbled backward, losing his hold on Ira. He hit the snow and felt it collapse under his weight.

His arms pinwheeled and he swam toward the surface in a blind panic. Unexpectedly, his hand struck something hard above him, and he opened his eyes to pitch blackness.

His panic doubled. He had lost his grasp on up and down.

The "something hard" was the ground, or what passed for ground here—the top of a glacier, most likely. He closed his eyes again and forced himself to calm down.

The first thing he noticed when he stopped fighting was the almost complete absence of sound. There was a hollow rustling in the distance, the sound of the wind shrieking across the surface of the snow, but down here the only noise was the beating of his own heart.

Once his head was clear, he pushed himself backwards.

A hand gripped him by the forearm and yanked him to the side. His eyes flew open and he gasped for breath. The wind once again pulsed in his ears.

Wörtlich let go, and Brighton struggled to stand on his own two feet.

"We cannot fall behind," Wörtlich said. "Poulson is not slowing down."

"Where's Ira?"

Wörtlich turned to look the way Poulson had gone. There was no sign of either man.

"Poulson! Ira!" Brighton shouted.

"They are too far ahead," Wörtlich grunted, continuing forward through a trench the men had left behind; presumably Brighton hadn't been the only one to break through the snow.

Brighton started moving, but he couldn't feel anything from the waist down. "Emery, we're going to die out here."

Wörtlich said nothing, and Brighton focused on keeping his feet under him.

Suddenly, Poulson's face appeared out of the white haze in front of them. His blue lips turned up in a smile.

"We are there!" he bellowed.

Wörtlich looked around him. "There is nothing here."

Poulson turned into the storm again.

"Wait!" Wörtlich called. "I cannot see anything!"

Brighton found a last bit of strength and took another step, brushing past the archaeologist. And then another step. And then another.

The wind stopped.

Silence roared for a moment as he blinked. He looked around, orienting himself. Snow crunched beneath his boots.

Impenetrable white still surrounded him, but the snow wasn't blowing, and the cold—the cold was gone, replaced with a sudden burning sensation on his cheeks and forehead.

Brighton tore off his goggles.

Ira was there, looking around in awe, his hood pulled back and a grin on his face.

"What the bloody hell—" Wörtlich said.

Brighton turned to see the archaeologist standing right behind him, in the same state of shock as the rabbi.

They stood in a "bubble" of sorts. The storm still raged, but around them the air was warm and still. The instant the wind hit the bubble of warm air, it died, and the snow turned to mist. Brighton could see nothing to warrant such a phenomenon, but there was no denying it.

The sound of gagging brought Brighton's attention back to Wörtlich, who was hunched over, emptying the contents of his stomach.

Wörtlich groaned and straightened up, looking as weak as Brighton had ever seen him.

"What is this place?" he asked.

"Whatever it is, it isn't natural," Brighton said.

Poulson barked a laugh. "It's a shelter."

Wörtlich didn't look convinced. "What kind of shelter?"

"I don't know," Poulson said with a shrug. "But it's always warm and clear around the fissure." He pointed ahead. "There! Can you see it?"

All Brighton could see was the edge of the supposed "shelter," where the storm raged on.

"We cannot go that way!" Wörtlich said. He gestured to Poulson, but spoke to Ira. "We were wrong about him. He is not well. We have to rest here, then go back."

Ira looked back at him incredulously. "Look around you, Doctor. This is not a natural phenomenon. Poulson was right about what he saw, or this place wouldn't exist."

Wörtlich fell silent. Had the cold affected his judgment?

In the meantime, Poulson began walking in the direction he'd pointed, toward the center of the bubble of warm air.

Brighton narrowed his eyes, then made out a thin black line stretching across the horizon. The closer they got, the thicker and wider the line became, until they approached a chasm in the ground.

The fissure!

Brighton stopped just short of the edge and gaped into a bottomless pit. They might have walked right into it without Poulson to guide them.

Brighton got down to his knees and leaned further over the drop. Nothing but blackness down there.

"How far down does it go?" Wörtlich asked.

"About two thousand feet," Poulson said.

Brighton sensed Wörtlich, turned to see the archaeologist kneeling next to him, and asked, "What could have caused this?"

Wörtlich shifted his goggles onto his forehead to get a better look. "Perhaps an explosion of gas beneath the surface? Whatever it was, it swallowed up the fresh water lake we were told about."

"It's beautiful," Ira intoned.

Brighton regarded the old man with amusement. Typical Ira. When everyone else was confused, he was reverent.

"I see nothing." Wörtlich took a step back from the edge of the fissure. "I do not understand. There cannot be anything down there."

Poulson licked his lips. "That's what the others said. I thought you believed me."

Ira rested a gentle hand on Brighton's back and asked, "Do you see?"

Brighton stared harder.

"Open your eyes," Ira urged. "Remember the river."

Brighton blinked, then closed his eyes tight and tried to relax, taking a deep breath.

Relaxing doesn't come easy when you're perched on the edge of a two thousand foot drop.

Brighton exhaled and opened his eyes again. He leaned forward, his fingers gripping the edge where the ice fell away into darkness.

There was... something.

"Is that...?" He focused on a tiny glimmer of non-blackness, a sliver of—

A sliver of something green.

"My God, you were right!" He staggered back from the opening. "Ira, he was right!"

Ira remained calm as ever—maddeningly calm.

"Help me with the harness," Poulson said and unslung the largest pack. "We'll have to go down one at a time."

"You cannot be serious," Wörtlich protested. "We are not going down there."

Poulson eyed him. "What do you think we came here for?"

*   *   *

It took each man five minutes to repel to the bottom and hoist the harness back up, which gave Brighton a long time to stare down into the hole and anticipate his descent. But whatever anticipation he felt, he knew Wörtlich felt more.

Wörtlich watched uncertainly as they lowered themselves down.

From time to time, he glanced back at the storm around them, as if considering whether or not to venture back into it.

Ira went down second, after Poulson. As the rabbi disappeared over the edge, his feet scraping along the fissure wall, Brighton's eyes remained fastened on the mysterious green glimmer.

When the harness hoisted up for Brighton, he stepped into it, locked the waist strap in place, and double-checked to make sure it was secure. He settled his body on the edge, rocking back and forth on the balls of his feet.

"See you in a few minutes," he told Wörtlich.

Brighton counted silently to three, then pushed off. His body fell backward.

He gripped the rope and flew back toward the ice wall before pushing off again. He fell into a comfortable rhythm and continued downward.

The further into darkness he repelled, the brighter the green light grew. Soon, he saw the two men standing below him, seemingly in midair. He gripped the rope harder, but then neither man showed any sign of unease.

He slowed the speed of his descent, taking shorter jumps, until he landed on something like ground. The surface had the slick feel of ice, but its thick translucence reminded him more of glass, allowing a warped hint of green to shine from someplace below.

"What is it?" he asked.

Poulson tapped it with his foot. "The ice dome."

"How do we get inside?" Ira asked.

"There's a way in." Poulson tilted his head further down the wide fissure where the walls narrowed and the dome gently sloped away.

Once Wörtlich neared the bottom, he clutched the rope as though it was the only thing preventing him from plunging into an abyss. When he ran out of rope, instead of dropping to the dome like the rest of them, he clung to it, hovering a few inches above the glassy surface.

"How are you doing that?" he demanded.

Brighton was confused. "Doing what?"

Wörtlich bumped off the wall, then used a free hand to gain purchase on a sharp protruding rock. His fingers whitened on the rope. "What are you standing on?"

"You still can't see, can you?" Ira said, as serene as ever. "Doctor, it's just like the barrier underneath the pyramid. From one side, it was invisible, but from the other it was solid. What we're standing on now is quite solid. Take my hand."

Ira offered his arm.

Brighton stared at the rabbi. Was it possible Ira was right? If this was just as it had been in Egypt, why was he himself able to see through the illusion while Wörtlich remained blinded?

The rabbi's logic made no more sense to Wörtlich, who continued to hold onto the rope.

After a few long moments, Wörtlich extended a shaking hand, took Ira's steady arm, and allowed himself to drop the remaining few inches. His eyes widened in surprise when his feet hit the surface. He was utterly speechless as he looked down and finally perceived the same thing the others had been able to see all along.

"There *is* something green down there," Wörtlich said and turned to Brighton. "Why could you see it? Do you understand—"

"This way," Poulson said.

Poulson picked his way down the dome's slope, pausing every once in a while to make sure his feet had a solid hold.

Wörtlich followed but continued to question. "What will we find down there?"

Poulson looked back. "You'll see."

"How thick is the ice?" Wörtlich asked, his eyes glued to the translucent dome beneath his feet.

"Thick enough," Poulson assured him.

Up ahead, Brighton saw a green light emanating from a hole just wide enough for a person to slip through. That there could be grass on the bottom of a glacier didn't seem possible, but it also didn't seem possible that there could be a habitat beneath one, either, so all bets were off.

As they gathered around the hole, Poulson grabbed a rope that was knotted to a rock in the ice wall. The rope dangled into the dome, but it didn't look like it dangled far; it hovered a few feet over the top of a grassy hill.

It's really true.

Poulson slid down. When the rope slackened, Brighton took hold of it and followed Poulson.

Alice's Wonderland had nothing on this place.

TWENTY-TWO

Queen Maud Land
SEPTEMBER 23

When his feet hit the soft clay, Ira let go of the rope and turned in a circle to better appreciate the panoramic vista before him. The first thing he noticed was how bright the light was inside the habitat—or "ice dome," as Poulson called it. The second was the green—the color was everywhere.

The dome was more than a mile in diameter, and six or seven hundred feet high at its apex. The ground was mounded with low-rising hills covered in tall prairie grasses and shrubs and dotted with trees.

The view took Ira's breath away. The only word Ira could think of to properly describe the scope of the subglacial enclosure was *monu-*

mental.

After gawking for a few moments, the men unzipped their coats. Once down to a t-shirt and single pair of pants, Ira walked down the hill's gentle incline, intending to explore.

Up ahead, between the tall grasses, he saw something white and irregularly shaped.

"Ira!" Wörtlich called. "Maybe we should not just go walking around."

Then the archeologist's eyes caught on the same strange, white shape and jogged to catch up.

"Is that a bone?" Brighton asked, taking a more leisurely pace down the hill.

Ira pushed aside long stems of grass and got a good look at it. Indeed, it certainly looked like a bone, though it was much larger than any bone he had ever seen before.

It *was* a bone, and it had belonged to a giant.

"A hip bone," Poulson said. "There are bones littered everywhere down here. Part of the mystery."

After a few minutes of walking along a well-worn path through the grass, and coming across other large bone fragments, they reached one of the highest points in the dome habitat. From this hill, they could see hundreds of bones strewn across the ground, each partially obscured by thick overgrowth.

"Look at them…" Wörtlich trailed off, the impossibility of the find surely threatening to short-circuit his brain. He grinned at Poulson. "Skeletal remains. And I thought Lagati's bird skull provided the best proof of the real pyramid builders. There can be no denying the existence of giants now!"

Ira sighed at Wörtlich's naiveté. Men denied self-evident truth all the time; they would deny this as well, given the chance.

Brighton turned away from them, his eyes fixed on a large femur bone on the ground nearby. He knelt next to it, touching it with his forefinger.

"This is the bone from the picture," he spoke softly.

"What picture?" Ira asked.

Poulson turned, overhearing them. His face showed open amazement. "You saw my pictures?"

"*Your* pictures?" Brighton's eyes widened in recognition. "Yes, that's where I've seen you before. You're in the picture."

Brighton pulled off his backpack and searched inside it for his laptop. He pulled up the picture in question.

Ira squinted to get a closer look. It was a man standing next to a bone, and not just any man—it was Poulson, though he was standing far enough away that it was hard to make out his features. The green hill in the background of the photo matched the hill they were standing on now.

"I was shown this picture at the Smithsonian," Brighton explained. "It was debunked, but aside from the unusual subject matter, I determined it had all the markings of an authentic shot. It's the main reason I came. Lagati promised to help me get to the bottom of it."

"Looks like he kept his word," Ira said.

"I took that picture as proof of my discovery," Poulson said. "I tried transmitting a number of pictures via the NPI satellite link, but I didn't think it worked. But if you saw them, everyone must know the truth now."

Brighton rested his elbows on his knees. "I wouldn't count on it. The others back at the base believed you were dead, remember?"

"Then someone at the NPI intercepted them," Poulson concluded.

For men who claimed to trust their senses more than their feelings, Brighton and Wörtlich took a long time grasping what their eyes were telling them. It was just as hard for them to accept the unexplainable when it was right in front of their eyes as when it remained an idea, a figment of someone's distorted imagination.

"What I'm having trouble accepting," Brighton said at last, "is that everything we've seen so far adds up to a single truth."

Wörtlich leaned over, running his fingers through the grass at his feet, as though to confirm it was real. "The pyramid builders." His voice had a faraway quality.

Brighton's eyes lit up. "Yes. It's clear they must have built this dome, but what about the other ancient monuments we haven't been able to understand. Stonehenge? The Nazca lines? Easter Island? Is it all the same people, an ancient race?"

"*There were giants in the earth in those days,*" Ira quoted. "*And also after that, when the sons of God came in unto the daughters of men, and they bare children to them, the same became mighty men which were of old, men of renown.*"

The rabbi sighed, long and hard. He'd known about this civilization ever since Aaron had taken him under his wing, but reading it in books was one thing; seeing it for himself was quite another.

The genie couldn't be put back in the bottle. Wörtlich would want to shout this from the rooftops, and despite how much he had come to love the man, Ira couldn't allow that.

"You have been studying these bones?" Wörtlich asked Poulson.

"For many months," Poulson said. "Even so, you seem to understand more about all this than I do. Do you want to see more?"

Brighton was the first to jump up and follow as Poulson crossed over the crest of the hill toward another path of trampled grass. Hundreds of such paths cut through the landscape and intersected each other. Ira felt like they were wandering through a hedge maze.

"I've been mapping the bones, trying to identify them," Poulson explained. "I have concluded that while the bones do not belong to a human, they correspond to a similar skeleton. I was also amazed to discover that no bone is duplicated."

"What does that mean?" Ira asked.

"All these bones belonged to one being," the Norwegian answered. "The only bone I haven't been able to locate is the one that should be the most conspicuous—the skull."

"Indeed, you'd think it was here somewhere," Brighton said.

They rounded a bend in the path, which brushed up against the largest bone yet. Ira recognized it as a spinal column, marked every foot by a pair of monstrous vertebrae.

"By measuring the pieces, like the spine, I've been able to determine that this being would have stood twenty-eight feet erect," Poulson said, then watched the others for a reaction.

Wörtlich didn't disappoint. His eyes widened and he sputtered, "Twenty-eight feet!"

"I hope he tried out for varsity," Brighton quipped.

Poulson ignored the joke—or, more likely, he didn't understand it. "I have not found any significance in the way they're arranged."

When they came to the end of the spinal column, the path shifted to the left and wended around the trunks of two trees.

"How wide is the diameter of this dome?" Wörtlich asked.

"Almost exactly two kilometers. I have measured it."

Wörtlich turned to Brighton. "Can you do the math? If a cubit is twenty-five inches, how many cubits would fit across this dome at its widest point?"

Brighton took a moment, most likely moving numbers around in his head. Ira marveled at his facility for mathematics.

"Hold on," Brighton said. His eyes shot upward, then drifted off to the left before centering again. "3141, I think."

Wörtlich laughed out loud.

Ira frowned. "What is it?"

"Do you not notice anything special about that number?" the archaeologist asked.

"No," Ira admitted.

But Brighton did. "3141 ... the first four digits of pi. That can't be a coincidence."

As he said that, they emerged from the brush to find a squat, circular tower built from meticulously hewn blocks of stone. It was very old. As old as the pyramids, maybe, if it had been built by the same people. If they could be called *people*.

Poulson walked up to the doorless entryway. He disappeared inside, then came back with fragments of broken stone tablets. He put the largest piece down and pointed to the markings on them.

"These are the Egyptian markings I told you about."

Wörtlich sat on the ground as Poulson put them down. The archaeologist picked up a few of the fragments to inspect under the light. "Where did you find them?"

"Scattered around the bone field," Poulson said.

"Unfortunate. They will be difficult to reassemble."

Poulson went back in and brought out more fragments. He showed the archaeologist how a few of them pieced together. Most of the fragments, however, didn't fit the puzzle in any obvious way.

"Thank you," Wörtlich said. "Are these all of them?"

Poulson shook his head. "I know where there are more."

Without another word, Poulson ventured back into the underbrush.

Ira watched him go, then sat down on a stone step.

"Where is the Book, guys?" Brighton asked. "Wasn't the Book

supposed to be here?"

Ira closed his eyes tiredly. A part of him had wished neither man would bring up that accursed Book again.

"Perhaps it's hidden," Ira said. "There's a lot of ground to cover."

He glanced at Wörtlich, who was uncharacteristically silent. Something was bothering him, and it was more than the impossibility of the ice dome's existence; no, he had already accepted that and moved on.

A long time passed before anyone spoke.

"There is something here that Poulson is missing," Wörtlich finally said. "Just because he cannot see a pattern to the bones does not mean there is none. I find it difficult to accept that whoever designed and measured this dome so meticulously would scatter the bones in a random fashion. I think this enclosure was constructed specifically to house these bones, and by studying them we can determine their purpose."

"What do you suggest?" Brighton asked.

"We need Poulson to share his mapping information. We can use your computer to analyze it."

Ira lay back on the grass and stared up at the dome ceiling. If it wasn't made of ice, what was it made of? And what made it glow? Whatever it was, it simulated sunlight well enough to produce a veritable jungle of growth.

"I'm sure he'll offer to show us that information if we ask," Ira drawled lazily, arching back to relieve the tension he had built up over the last few days. "He seems mostly concerned with being believed. Any opportunity for validation should satisfy him. He probably *wants* us to look at his data."

Wörtlich leaned back as well. "I hope you are right."

*   *   *

Indeed, Ira had been right, Wörtlich noted. When he asked for the data, Poulson eagerly raced into the tower to retrieve a pack of supplies. "I keep most of my work here so I don't misplace it." Poulson pulled out a notebook. "One time I took my notebook with me into the bone field and left it on the ground somewhere. It took me two days to find it again."

Wörtlich opened the cover and flipped through the opening pages.

"I haven't looked at it for a few weeks. I thought the answer might come to me if I took a break." Poulson paused to scratch an itch on his nose. "So far, nothing."

"An answer to what?" Brighton asked.

Poulson looked at the young man as if he'd asked why the grass was green. He threw open his arms in a wide, all-encompassing gesture. "An answer to *this.* The bones are the key. They will talk to us if we're quiet enough. If we listen to what they have to say."

The man's unstable, Wörtlich reminded himself. *But he is also right. The bones are the key.*

Wörtlich looked back down at the notebook. Poulson had covered its pages in numbers, formulas, and drawings showing the size of particular bones in relation to each other. His maps showed that he had triangulated every bone, creating a natural grid on which to plot. Without a computer, however, there was bound to be imprecision.

He flipped over to a full-page aerial representation of the dome's interior. Grid lines intersected at regular intervals with simple dots to represent the locations of bones, with coordinates and measurements sketched into the margins.

"Can you set up a grid that looks like this?" Wörtlich asked Brighton.

Brighton nodded. "I'll need a few hours to input the data."

Leaving the young man to his work, Wörtlich went in search of Ira.

About an hour later, he spotted the rabbi on a smooth, flat patch of grass at least three hills away. Ira sat cross-legged on the ground and had his eyes closed.

Wörtlich had intended to just walk up and begin speaking, but he hung back, realizing Ira was in the middle of some sort of meditation. He stood there a good few minutes, waffling between interrupting Ira and respecting his privacy.

Wörtlich's impatience won out.

"Ira, did you know this dome was going to be here?" he asked.

Ira's eyes flew open, but his face registered no surprise. "No."

Wörtlich leaned his weight against a wedge of rock. "I notice you never seem surprised. Frankly, this has got to be one of the strangest things I have ever seen."

"It's not a matter of having foreknowledge, Doctor," Ira told him. "It's a matter of expectation."

"Do you mean to say you expected the dome to be here, even though you did not know it existed? If so, you are splitting hairs."

The rabbi extended his arms in front of him and held the stretch. "Words sort of get in the way sometimes."

"But you cannot have seen this coming."

Ira lowered both arms and turned to Wörtlich, his gaze as thoughtful as ever. "There are things I believe, things that I have never seen with my own eyes, things that I have very little, if any, direct evidence to support. But I still believe in them. I have my convictions."

"I suppose your faith lets you do that."

"Skeptics have a way of lumping everything that can't be explained or understood into this broad, amorphous category called 'faith.' Or 'paranormal.' The thing is, everything we've encountered so far is very normal. No laws of physics have been broken, or even bent. Just used in ways we haven't seen before." Ira paused and took a deep breath. "Let me put it this way. Faith isn't just about believing in something that can't be seen, even though that's often the result. You see, truth doesn't necessarily come through physical observation. I experience spiritual truth all the time. Everyday."

Typical religious doublespeak, Wörtlich thought. He opened his mouth to reply but realized he had nothing to say. Getting into an argument with the rabbi was a waste of time. Ira wasn't going to change his mind.

But there was one thing they did agree on. There had to be a natural explanation for everything they'd seen. Rocks that glowed, metal you could walk through, invisible domes you could stand on...

Wörtlich looked up and frowned. Was it just him or was it getting darker?

He added another item to the list: Domes that gave off light and simulated the circadian cycle.

"It is getting dark," Wörtlich said. "What do you suppose the scientific explanation is for that?"

Ira smiled. "You're far more qualified to answer that question than I, Doctor."

Wörtlich looked off into the distance and saw Poulson standing on the grass outside the tower. "We should get back."

"You go on ahead. I'm going to stay a few more minutes."

Wörtlich nodded and returned the way he came, leaving Ira to his meditations.

Back at the tower, Brighton was exactly where Wörtlich had left

him, leaning up against the stone wall and staring at his screen.
Poulson lay flat on the grass, gazing up at the darkening sky. "The level light changes throughout the day," he said reverently. "I have studied the dome up close, but I have not been able to learn how it works."

"It is incredible," Wörtlich agreed.

Ira returned in time for them to eat. By then, the dome had darkened altogether and the only source of light was the dancing flames of the cook fire. Whoever had created this place had left out the stars, which lent the evening an ominous atmosphere.

Ira and Poulson gathered up the remains of dinner and took it away as Wörtlich and Brighton returned to work.

"I think I've found something," Brighton said as he pulled up a window showing the new aerial perspective of the bone field. "This is a much more sophisticated representation of the dome floor than what Poulson had to work with. Each bone is drawn to scale. I think maybe it's a map. But without any shared points or known landmarks, it's next to useless. At first I thought maybe it was a rendering of the Antarctic Circle, or perhaps the entire southern hemisphere. But I got stuck. I tried superimposing other maps of the southern regions overtop, but the locations of the bones don't seem to align with any significant landmasses, ancient monuments, or bodies of water."

Wörtlich narrowed his eyes. "It is a good theory—but the wrong one."

"You have a better idea?"

"I think so." Wörtlich stood and fetched his backpack from the tower, all the while fishing around inside. At last, he pulled out the sketches he had made of the Hall of Records hieroglyphics. "I believe it is a message of some kind. The bones are arranged to form a hieroglyph. If so, we just have to figure out which Egyptian character it is, and what it means."

"Are we supposed to go through all those sketches?" Brighton asked. "It could take hours."

"Yes. It could."

Brighton blew a stream of air out through his teeth, then took a pile of sketch pages and began sifting through them, one by one.

*   *   *

"It's a message?" Ira asked. "What does it say?"

Brighton clicked his tongue against his teeth and leaned back, waiting to see how Wörtlich would answer. The archaeologist was the only one among them in a position to translate an Egyptian hieroglyph, and yet so far he had remained coy.

"He doesn't know," Brighton said when Wörtlich continued to sit in silence, pondering the problem.

Wörtlich pulled up grass by the handful, making a small but mounting pile between his legs. "I cannot translate it here. I need help."

"What kind of help?" Ira asked.

"I have a friend at the University of Sydney who specializes in Egyptian writing. We have worked together on many projects over the years. He is probably the only person who knows more about hieroglyphics than I do."

Brighton smiled and coughed into his hand.

Wörtlich shot him a withering look. "I am not being immodest, Mr. Brighton. Just stating a fact."

"Can you trust this friend of yours?" Brighton asked.

"Yes," Wörtlich said after thinking about it. "Anyway, what choice do we have? We need to understand what this symbol means, and we cannot do it on our own."

Perhaps he's right about that.

"One more thing," Wörtlich added, glancing around the tower to where the Norwegian lay sleeping on the hillside. "We cannot take Poulson with us."

Wörtlich was right, Brighton realized. Adding a fourth man to their team, and an unhinged man at that, would only draw attention. And if Lagati found out—*when* Lagati found out—he wouldn't be happy.

Brighton watched for Ira's response, and was unsurprised to see Wörtlich doing the same.

"I agree," Ira said, having given it proper consideration.

Brighton was startled. "What? I thought you were our moral center!"

"Wörtlich is correct," Ira said. "It's hard enough for three people to work together, never mind four."

Wörtlich smiled in smug self-satisfaction. "Good."

"Also," Ira continued, "we have no reason to believe Poulson would want to join us. He has been living in this dome for a long time and seems to enjoy it. As long as he has access to supplies, I see no reason to trouble him. He's able to take care of himself well enough."

"Access to supplies?" Brighton asked. "By stealing them from his countrymen at gunpoint, you mean."

Ira was very quiet for a few moments. When he spoke, his tone was clear: he would brook no further argument. "We are not responsible for his methods, Sherwood. Poulson could return to the Norwegian base at any time. His choices are his own."

Still, something felt wrong about taking off in the middle of the night without even waking the man.

"On the other hand," Brighton pointed out, "he's been so open with us. Perhaps we should pay him back for his trust."

Wörtlich stopped pulling grass and pushed the pile away with his foot. "Even Ira is on my side this time."

"This isn't about friendship or hospitality," Ira said. "The fact that he's been open with us tells us that he will probably be just as open with others. We've been called to a higher level of discretion."

"In other words," Brighton said, "he's a security risk."

"Precisely."

"We will leave tomorrow night," Wörtlich said. "I do not plan to climb that fissure without a good night's sleep. The extra day will give me a chance to study the tablets Poulson unearthed. We cannot take those with us."

After their conference, Brighton looked around for a comfortable spot to lie down. He didn't like sleeping on the ground, but at least the earth was soft. It was a honeymoon suite compared to the Norwegians' equipment room.

He stretched out on his back and folded his arms above his head. Except for the occasional snores from Poulson, the dome was deathly silent. Nothing stirred. In the darkness, there wasn't so much as a rustling breeze.

It was too quiet.

He wanted to sleep, but a feeling of dread pitted his stomach, preventing him from closing his eyes.

This was not a good place to rest.

TWENTY-THREE

Somewhere Else

B righton peered into the depths of a crackling fire but couldn't remember how he had gotten there. The sound of snapping bark and the dry, almost sweet smell of roasting logs hit him hard, the senses stronger and more provocative than they should have been.

He stood next to a hearth, the sickly yellow flames casting strange, alien shapes on the stone fireplace. He shifted his feet, his shoes grinding pebbles into the grooves of the stone floor.

Apart from the fire, the room was pitch dark and silent. Brighton narrowed his eyes, trying to pierce the blackness through sheer force of will, but he saw nothing beyond the flickering fire. The room was achingly cold and empty, making him cling to the fireside all the more.

Door hinges creaked nearby. For an instant, he glimpsed a bright starry sky before a massive, hulking figure blotted out his view. The door slammed closed with another moan of protest.

Moments later, a light was struck. An enormous hand carried a swinging lantern, and it crept toward him. With every step, the floor shuddered, paralyzing him with fear.

A giant!

The thought unlocked a host of memories—some of them his, others wholly foreign. Bones scattered across a field of grass and low-lying hills. A cook fire. A tower of stone, not unlike the stonework on the fireplace behind him.

Brighton put his hand against that stonework to steady himself as the giant loomed over him, its grotesque face leaning into view.

He had nowhere to run, no safety to find from which the giant wouldn't be able to reach out and snatch him back.

By good fortune, the giant looked almost... friendly. Unhappy, but friendly. Its eyes pinched together in concern.

A name floated across his memory, and Brighton latched onto it.

Barakel. They thought my name was Barakel.

The giant's massive shoulders slumped and it swung its lumbering body around, grabbing the arm of a wooden chair and pulling it roughly toward the fire. The giant sat.

"Father," the giant said in a low, gravelly voice.

Father? Brighton looked down at his own diminutive body. How could it be that he was this creature's father? He remained pinned in place, confused and terrified.

"Father, you must hide. If the others see you here, they will be displeased." The giant paused and pointed to the darkest corners where the firelight failed to penetrate. "Hide. And listen."

The sound of the door creaking open stole the giant's attention for a moment, then its eyes flashed back.

"Hurry!" it whispered.

Brighton backed into the darkness and crouched, waiting. The floor vibrated again as two more creatures—giants—tromped toward them. One carried a torch.

He pushed himself as tightly to the stone wall as possible. What if that torch swung in the wrong direction and revealed him? How would these creatures demonstrate their "displeasure"?

"Greetings, Mahaway," the first of the newcomers growled.

Brighton listened closely to the introductions. Mahaway was the giant he had spoken to—his own son? No, Barakel's son. The first newcomer was Nariman, but the second, the one with the torch, did not identify himself.

All three sunk into the oversized chairs by the fireside. Their conversation was difficult to make out, and even more difficult to understand; he felt certain he was missing important details.

"The secrets were theirs to conceal," Mahaway was saying.

Nariman spat venomously, and considerable globs of saliva hit the floor in a thick stream. "Theirs to exploit, you mean! You have but to look at yourself to see *that*."

Mahaway turned to look at the unidentified giant.

It was difficult to tell for sure in the dark, but he thought this second giant was the largest of the three.

"You've hardly said a word, Master Gilgamesh," Mahaway rumbled.

Gilgamesh. The name sounded familiar, but he couldn't quite place it.

"Did you have another dream last night?" Master Gilgamesh asked.

"Yes," Mahaway replied. "A vision came to me."

Nariman leaned forward. "What did you see?"

"It concerned a stone tablet," Mahaway said.

Master Gilgamesh's torch swung slightly, its circle of light brushing close to Brighton's hiding place.

Brighton inched his way back, and in so doing heard a soft splash of water. He nearly gasped, but then clamped a hand over his mouth. Looking down, he found himself standing in a pool. Water was bubbling up through the floorboards.

His eyes leaped back to the three chairs where the giants were conversing, but none of them seemed to notice the disturbance.

"And upon that tablet were names," Mahaway continued. "Perhaps every name, of every man who lives, and every woman, and every child."

Brighton felt his panic rising in concert with the water. Already it was lapping at his ankles. How could the giants not notice it?

"And the tablet was drenched in water."

Surprise shot through him when the water tickled the tips of his fingers. Water had filled the lower portions of the room by now, and lapped against the giants' legs. Yet they were oblivious, blissful, unconcerned.

What's happening? Brighton couldn't move. His breath came in short, anxious bursts.

No longer concerned with discovery—if anything, maybe Mahaway could help him—he cried out.

The water rose to his elbows, then he felt his body lift, his feet losing touch with the stone floor.

"And the water rose around it, and then up over it."

He tried to remain afloat as long as possible, kicking his legs to keep from being pulled under, but the water only rose more quickly. It had come up to the giants' shoulders, their necks, their ears, the tops of their heads, and then there was no trace of them at all.

His eyes searched the surface of the water, desperate for something to stand on, for some escape. He pressed himself up into the corner of the room, bracing his palms against the ceiling.

Realizing he had only seconds of air left, he opened wide and drew the longest and deepest breath he could. Holding it, he plunged into the water.

Brighton swam across the room, hoping to find the door, but the fire of Master Gilgamesh's torch had gone out. The water was black as pitch. He groped blindly, hoping to find something. Anything.

At last, he found a raised column of stonework on the far wall, and beside it the narrowest crack.

The door!

He searching for the doorknob—and found it. Mustering his remaining strength, Brighton tugged with all his might, straining hard.

It wouldn't budge.

He planted his feet against the doorframe and pulled again, this time using his weight to add the necessary leverage, but no matter how hard he pulled, nothing happened.

He couldn't hold his breath any longer. He was drowning! Fighting to the last, he finally had no choice but to let out his breath, and in so doing take in a lungful of water. The water felt heavy, burning as it filled his mouth and throat.

Brighton's eyes bulged with fatal realization. He tried to let out a scream, but the muffled sound was swallowed up by the darkness.

As he sank to the floor, losing control of first his arms, then his legs, he remained conscious. The last thing he saw before the end was a heap of bones settled on the chairs where the giants had sat.

Brighton gasped and his eyes fluttered open.

Mahaway's eyes shifted slightly to the dark corner in which Brighton hid, a warning glance as though to say, *Be quiet!*

Brighton took slow, steadying breaths as he oriented himself. He was still in the stone room, completely dry. The fire crackled, Master Gilgamesh's torch flickered, and the three giants' low voices carried through the darkness.

Brighton pressed a hand to his chest and felt his heart beat madly within. He still felt the burning sensation of water pouring down his throat, thick and viscous.

He gasped a second time, but more quietly. The water had been a figment of his imagination. Hadn't it?

"Who showed you this vision?" Nariman asked.

Mahaway's eyes again flicked in his direction, but the giant masked it by looking the opposite direction as well.

"Barakel, my father, was with me," Mahaway said.

"The dreams are for cursing and sorrow," Gilgamesh said with anger in his voice. "The spirits of the slain call out, complaining of their injustices, their killers walking free of penalty. They cry out that we shall die and be made examples."

A spine-chilling scream filled the room, snapping Brighton's attention away from the giants.

Long, elongated shadows played against the far wall, products of the fire in the hearth. Within those shadows, a woman lay prostrate, helpless as a dark figure loomed over her. She screamed again, and the figure laughed, a course and wicked sound that made Brighton's blood curdle.

He wanted to close his eyes, to shut out the struggle, but he could not look away.

The young woman was familiar to him. Where had he seen her before?

—a woman, a beautiful woman, with curly brown hair and the sharpest green eyes—

No. Someone else.

A dusty road. A thatched roof.

Her pear-shaped eyes were wide with terror. Her simple grey dress was hiked up to her waist, revealing silky white thighs gripped by her assailant's long, smooth-skinned fingers. His nails bit viciously into her flesh, drawing bright red blood which rolled down the sides of her legs.

She fought and kicked, but the man had her pinned. And he continued to laugh.

Once again, the giants ignored the commotion, and in a moment the scene ended. All signs of the struggle vanished as though it had never happened.

Another figment of his imagination? That woman... that *girl*... he had seen her before, framed in a doorway, her face streaked with mud...

"This penalty is too severe!" Nariman thundered. "It is not for us! We have done nothing. It was Azazel! We are but the children, the byproducts, neglected and forgotten."

Azazel.

A mountaintop flashed through his memory, and hundreds of others were present, each of them tall and imperious, smooth-skinned and powerful. Azazel was one, Semyaza another.

And Barakel. Myself?

"You!"

Brighton's eyes shot up to find Azazel towering over him, as though summoned from memory to this spot. His heart pounded relentlessly. The being's eyebrows rose to points, his features severe.

Azazel's mouth twisted into a cruel smile, and then he leaned forward, his words invoking terror: "We will make our escape!"

Fear overtook Brighton and he turned to run, even knowing there was no escape.

Azazel's mocking laugh followed him as he fled for the stone room's door, finding that unyielding handle again and pulling for all he was worth.

But this time it gave way, and the door creaked open on its rusty hinges. Relieved, Brighton fled into the night—

—only to find himself running along a riverbed in broad daylight. The noonday sun beat down and lines of sweat formed on his skin.

The ground was green and lush, and the river's course was edged with reeds. He had lived long enough along the banks of the Nile to recognize its muddy and fast-flowing waters as it stretch north and south as far as the eye could see.

I never lived along the Nile, Brighton reminded himself. He focused on his own memories, his own thoughts, terrified of losing himself.

To the west rose the Great Pyramid, in mid-construction, but he did not have time to gawk at it.

He was not alone. A tall, smooth-featured man stood next to him, staring out into the distance, his eyes flicking across the width of the valley.

Semyaza. A friend?

Semyaza pointed.

Brighton's eyes followed the extended hand until he saw a short, bearded man approaching from further upstream.

"Look, Barakel," Semyaza said to Brighton. "It is Enoch, the scribe!"

Enoch's walk was labored, but he strode toward them with purpose and determination. When Enoch arrived in front of him, Semyaza scowled. "Azazel has been waiting for you. You bring news?"

"I know you have awaited my report," Enoch said. The bearded man's gaze strayed toward the pyramid. "I see you have not waited patiently, however."

Semyaza looked at Enoch with contempt. "We could wait no longer. We were forced to act."

Barely containing his disdain, Semyaza turned on his heel and led Enoch and Brighton toward the pyramid.

The Giza plateau was flat and barren, strong gusts of wind blowing sand across the land in sheets. The smooth eyes of the Sphinx followed their progress. Brighton tried to ignore the stone beast's unflinching gaze.

They arrived at the pyramid in minutes even though it looked to Brighton to be an hour's walk.

Brighton trailed behind as Semyaza took them down a wide passage that sloped into a gallery, bordered on either side by colossal stone columns holding up a lofty ceiling.

This, too, was familiar. The Hall of Records.

Other beings like Semyaza walked back and forth through the crowded gallery, and between them scurried a host of bizarre creatures, strange and unnatural hybrids of humans and animals. Eagles and crocodiles, snakes and jackals. They were hard at work, carving stone figures in their own likenesses. Giants like those in the stone-walled room towered above them; the hybrid creatures weaved paths between the giants' enormous feet.

The crowd parted for them. Whoever these creatures were, they feared Semyaza.

They stopped halfway through the gallery and turned into an adjoining room. This room, shaped like an inverted pyramid, featured a raised platform in the center, and upon that platform stood Azazel.

"He has returned to us!" Azazel crowed, taking slow, plodding steps down the platform toward Enoch. "And what news do you bring of our petition?"

A few other tall, proud beings like him and Semyaza drifted in from the gallery and took up positions around Enoch, who now found himself surrounded.

Enoch raised his head. "Your petition cannot be granted, for all the days of eternity." Azazel drew himself up, but Enoch pressed on. "You shall have no peace. You shall not ascend. It has been decreed that you be bound to the earth. You shall witness the utter destruction of your beloved sons, and you shall not enjoy them."

Azazel's eyes flashed fire as he let out a cry of rage that echoed off the walls.

The room grew dark, but Azazel's cry went on and on, the sound burrowing into Brighton's ears. He pressed his hands to the sides of his head, but the protective measure did nothing to dispel the pain. When he pulled his hands back, he found them splattered in blood. His only relief was the increasing darkness, for the darker it became, the more the pain receded, until it was but a distant memory and he was surrounded by a formless, featureless, colorless void—

TWENTY-FOUR

Queen Maud Land
SEPTEMBER 24

Wörtlich awoke. He had a crick in his back from having slept awkwardly and the glowing light from the dome made his head ache. His head felt full, sluggish, teeming with memories not his own. He had dreamed the night before, but like most dreams, the more he chased the details, the faster they darted off into his subconscious mind.

There had been water. He swallowed hard at a strong sense memory of choking, gulping water down by the lungful.

He sat up and rubbed his chest, easing the dull pain that lingered there. His throat felt raspy, sore.

Ira, already awake, sat cross-legged, arms folded and eyes closed.

"Is he asleep?" Brighton's voice whispered. Wörtlich craned his head to see the young man still on his back, his eyes blinking open.

"I think he is meditating."

Brighton shook his head. "No. I mean Poulson."

Both men looked toward Poulson, who was curled up with his back to them, snoring softly.

"We should leave now," Ira said, coming out of his trance.

Wörtlich stood and walked closer to the rabbi so that he wouldn't have to raise his voice. "Tomorrow would be better. Plus, I would like another day to look at that broken tablet—"

His voice broke off as another memory rose from its watery grave. Something about a tablet.

"It isn't safe here," Ira said.

Wörtlich looked back toward the tower, where their packs rested, propped against the stone base. The headache worsened, the pain growing sharp. He winced.

Ira was right. It was time to go.

He looked steadily at Brighton. "All right. Gather your things. And be quiet about it."

They only took a few minutes to get dressed for the cold again. Their packs were much lighter for the return voyage as they weren't weighed down by supplies. Wörtlich had considered taking the rock fragments, but he didn't want to hoist them up to the surface. He decided instead to settle for pictures snapped with Brighton's camera.

Travelling back up the single rope that led topside took some effort, but they all managed the ascent—even Ira, who didn't looked like he had the upper body strength for such a climb.

Eventually, I will have to stop underestimating that man, Wörtlich thought with a smile as they picked their way up the slope of the dome.

Within minutes, they stood at the bottom of the fissure, the light of dawn pouring down the shaft toward them.

Wörtlich tested the waiting harness by giving the thick rope a tug. It was sound.

Ira went first, tightening the harness around his waist and starting up. He quickly assumed a smooth hand-over-hand motion, picking up speed.

Wörtlich and Brighton watched until he was nearly out of sight. The look on Brighton's face was one of awe.

"How does he do it?" Brighton asked.

Wörtlich touched his temples. The headache had eased since leaving the dome. He would have to ask Ira about the dome's artificial light; despite what the rabbi insisted, he knew more than he let on.

"I do not know, Mr. Brighton. But there is something about him, no?"

"Call me Sherwood. Don't you think it's time we used each other's first names?"

Sherwood. The name tasted funny on the tip of his tongue.

Wörtlich allowed himself a tight smile, but didn't say anything back. Did he *want* them to be on a first name basis? He wished he hadn't told Sherwood about Elisabeth. What had he been thinking?

Wörtlich's ascent took longer than expected, and his arm was sore by the time he arrived on the surface. He shook his hand and stretched the fingers out, working the blood back through them and loosening up the joints.

Ira rested nearby with his hands on his knees. The posture seemed to allow the rabbi to draw long, deep breaths. Wörtlich decided to do the same thing, and it worked. Within a few minutes, he felt much better. His heart rate lowered and he was able to breathe normally.

Brighton soon joined them and looked around in amazement. The storm had passed, leaving behind a breathtaking view from the top of the glacier. The sky was a crystal clear blue. In the distance, a line of weathered, snowcapped summits peeked out through the ice. Wörtlich squinted to keep from being blinded by the sun's reflection off the newly formed snowdrifts.

"If I never see another cube of ice, it'll be too soon," Brighton mumbled. The young man's face flushed and worry lines creased his forehead. "How are we going to get back to the Norwegian camp? I don't know about you guys, but I lost all sense of direction when we came in."

Wörtlich smiled and withdrew a crumpled piece of paper he had ripped out of Poulson's notebook.

"What is that?" Ira asked.

"Directions to the camp," Wörtlich said.

Brighton's worry lines faded and a smile took over. "So, which way?"

Wörtlich read the first few lines, then glanced up. Spotting the nearest landmark—those weathered peaks—he pointed off into the distance, where the glacier sloped downward almost imperceptibly.

"North," he indicated. From the South Pole just about *everything* was north. "As long as we keep those peaks behind us, we should come to that rocky overhang we saw on the way in."

Before moving off, Wörtlich remembered to lower the harness back to the bottom of the fissure. Stranding Poulson down there would have cost the Norwegian his life, eventually. What a terrifying thought that a small act of forgetfulness could doom a man to a slow and excruciating death.

TWENTY-FIVE

Sydney, Australia
SEPTEMBER 26

Wörtlich looked down at the paper and his heart lurched at the sight of his own handwriting. How long had it been since he'd written a letter, never mind by hand? An email would have been faster, but emails were professional and sterile; this was not a professional letter.

Elisabeth had asked him to keep in touch, so that she would know he was safe. He was no safer now than he'd been when they had that conversation, but he didn't want her to know that. He'd written the letter, careful to leave out the details—he hadn't even mentioned their adventure in Antarctica.

And yet their time there had changed his mind about sending the letter. When he went to sleep at night, visions of Anna plagued him. Her eyes had conveyed the depth of her feelings for Poulson. Even knowing she might never see him again, she hadn't been able to do anything to change his mind.

For years, Elisabeth hadn't been able to change Wörtlich's mind, either. How ironic that Anna, who he hardly knew, had done the trick. He just hoped he wasn't too late.

He folded the letter into thirds and slipped it into the blue envelope he had purchased at the postal kiosk in the University of Sydney's student center. He affixed four stamps, hoping it was enough. He then sealed the envelope and held it up to the mail slot.

He hesitated before dropping it in. He couldn't change his mind after this.

Wörtlich squeezed his eyes shut and conjured up his memory of Anna, then mentally replaced the image with Elisabeth's round face and curly brown hair.

The letter thumped softly as it slid to the bottom of the chute.

He walked out of the student center into the sunny Australian afternoon and hurried down a flight of concrete steps.

Whoever had designed the buildings of the main quadrangle had obviously been inspired by the sprawling grounds of Oxford University. Lazy plumes of drifting cloud showcased the dozens of brick chimneys poking up into the sky. The clock tower, braced by four octagonal brick columns, flew the Australian flag, its corner Union Jack keeping a watchful Commonwealth eye on this remote part of the world.

A burst of bright purple flowers drew Wörtlich's gaze to a large Jacaranda tree in full bloom, its petals glistening. This brought to mind something an Aussie professor had once told him about exam time in Queensland. The rumor was that if one of those petals fell on the head of a studying student, they would fail their exam; the bad luck could be broken by plucking a second bloom out of the air. The professor had laughingly referred to the superstition as "purple panic." Wörtlich smiled as he passed the tree.

Afternoon shadows were already lengthening as he crossed Eastern Avenue. A short walk took him past Victoria Park, and then a block later to the front doors of the towering Fisher Library. The building, constructed in the modern style, featured a third-story terrace from which several onlookers gazed down at the street.

Inside, behind a long black-lacquered desk, sat a formidable old librarian, exemplifying the stereotypes of her occupation, and a pretty young girl who was no doubt a first- or second-year student.

He approached the younger woman. "Excuse me. I am looking for Room C12."

The older woman slid her chair over to him.

"Third floor," she said, her voice deep hoarse from too many years of cigarettes—or so Wörtlich liked to imagine. "But it's occupied at the moment."

"Thank you, I know."

The elevator deposited him on the top floor, at the start of a corridor lined with small study rooms. A set of larger doors was closed at the end of the hall, and as he walked toward it he confirmed that the doorplate read "C12." He looked through the narrow window to the right of the door at a group of men clustered around a conference table.

He knocked.

One of the men turned at the interruption, then gestured for him to come inside. Wörtlich stepped in, his eyes dancing from one man to the next until he found the person he was looking for.

Max Holden sat at the end of the table, chairing the meeting. Thin wisps of almost entirely white hair were combed over a pronounced bald spot.

When did he get so old? Wörtlich asked himself. *It has not been that long, has it?*

"This is good work," Max was saying gruffly to those around the table. "We'll reconvene at four o'clock to go over your suggestions, Greg. I want to see a final schedule before I sign off."

The men stood and gathered their papers.

Wörtlich stepped out of the way as they converged on the door. Once the room was clear except for Max, Wörtlich approached.

Max had a huge grin on his face. "Come in, come in!"

Max came around the table and gave Wörtlich a hug. "Emery, it's been at least four years. What happened to that trip you promised me two summers ago? Well, you're a little late, but better late than never."

Wörtlich lowered himself into one of the seats and gazed across the conference table at his old friend. He felt a surge of fondness and appreciation for Max, one of his oldest and dearest friends. Max had only worked at the Cairo Institute for a couple of years, but he had been one of the Institute's most frequent visitors ever since.

Wörtlich clasped his hands in his lap. "I have been reading your articles about the work in Queensland. From what I hear, you have overseen some interesting developments."

"To put it mildly! I'm glad to hear you're still keeping up with me, Emery. Like you, I spent too much of my career digging around in Egypt. I'm convinced now we were looking in the wrong place! All the answers are here, I swear it, in this part of the world." Max narrowed his eyes. "I heard you retired."

"I did," Wörtlich admitted. "Two years ago. Although I seem to have been pulled back in."

Max smiled again. That smile was infectious. "It's hard to stay gone, isn't it? The work pulls on you like a magnet. Still, I was surprised to get your call."

"By all accounts, you are the best translator of Egyptian hiero-glyphics alive today. I need your help with something. Something you will be very interested in, I promise you."

"You think too highly of me."

"No, just high enough." Wörtlich looked toward the door as though expecting one of the men from earlier to burst back in at any moment. He forced himself to relax. "Max, I can number the people I trust right now on two fingers. And one of them is me. The other is you."

Max leaned forward, his curiosity piqued. "Tell me about it."

Wörtlich settled his attaché case on the table in front of him and popped open the lid. He pulled out a hard copy of the bone field rendering taken from Brighton's computer.

Wörtlich remained quiet for a moment as Max slid on a pair of reading glasses to inspect the rendering.

After a moment, Max's eyes shot up. "Are you going to explain this?"

"I just got back from a site in Antarctica that was—well, *astonishing* hardly does it justice. You would not believe what I uncovered there."

"Give me the benefit of the doubt, Emery. Go on."

"I stumbled across a field scattered with massive bones belonging to a creature of generally human anatomy but who would have been nearly thirty feet tall. The field was approximately three square kilometers and was spread out across natural grassland."

"Grassland? In Antarctica?" The white-haired man wagged a finger at him. "You're pulling my leg."

"Hardly. This bone field was located a mile beneath a glacier in the Norwegian territory."

Max took that in and held his breath. After a few long moments, he let it out. "Emery... it may take a few moments to determine which of my fifty questions to ask first."

"Take your time."

"Aside from the obvious ones then, like how you found this place and how you got to it, I'm left with an underlying feeling of, well, I don't know...let's call it 'unsurprise.'"

"You are not surprised?"

"Don't get me wrong. This is extraordinary. But we should be honest, you and I." He tapped his fingers on the edge of the conference table, the rhythm slowing down and speeding up irregularly. "This is a confirmation of something I've already uncovered for myself—that we were not the first advanced civilization on this planet. I've become more and more convinced that this race of ancients, whoever they were, circumnavigated the globe and colonized all the continents, to varying degrees. This process would have started some ten thousand years ago, but I'm not sure when it ended."

Wörtlich almost gaped, but he kept his surprise in check. "I take it there is evidence of this in Australia."

"Loads!" Max said. "But Emery, the Australian government, not to mention scientific circles, isn't exactly jumping up and down for joy. You have to be very careful who you talk to. This work is bound to be unpopular. But tell me more about Antarctica."

Wörtlich cleared his throat. "The bones we found were not scattered randomly, which is where this picture comes in." He tapped the edge of the paper between them. "When we transferred the—"

"We?"

"I have a team," Wörtlich said, hoping Max wouldn't ask more questions. "When we transferred the positions and dimensions of the bones onto a grid, this is the image we ended up with."

Max turned the paper ninety degrees to face him. "It's a hiero-glyph of some kind. Very antiquated."

"I believe whoever preserved the bone field left this as a message."

Max nodded, rubbing his chin. "You could be right, you could be right. In Queensland, we found a series of tablets containing an interesting story that might be related to your find."

"Oh?"

Max heaved a breath. "It has to do with the Epic of Gilgamesh."

Gilgamesh.

Wörtlich put his hand to his temples, feeling a headache coming on.

Master Gilgamesh.

He looked up tiredly, meeting Max's gaze. "I am familiar with it, of course."

"Emery, you don't look so good."

Wörtlich waved him off. "I am fine, Max. You were saying something about Gilgamesh."

"Yes," Max drawled, not buying Wörtlich's protestations of well-being. "The story of Gilgamesh, the hero-king of ancient Babylon, was found chronicled on clay tablets—twelve of which are still known to exist, though it has always been believed the epic was incomplete." Max smiled. "No longer. The tablets we found in Queensland extend the story and depict Gilgamesh in an attempt to save his kingdom from an environmental disaster. Our research indicates this might be a reference to the 'Great Deluge.'"

"Noah's Flood?"

"Indeed. These new tablets include the story of Gilgamesh's flight out of Mesopotamia toward the 'southern continent.' Or at least, that's as close as we can translate it. There's great debate raging among my team about what it means." Max pointed to the map. "This may shed some light on the question. In any event, Gilgamesh fled to this southern continent, seeking protection from the flood. Funny thing is, all accounts of Gilgamesh depict him as being a giant, or two-thirds god. Now you come telling me that there are remains of a giant on the southern continent, in an enclosure preserved for millennia." The old man cracked a smile. "You can't deny the striking resemblance between the two stories."

"It demands further investigation. That much is certain."

"Yes, it does." Max folded up the bone field image. "Do you mind if I hold onto this for a while?"

"Of course not," Wörtlich said. "That is why I brought it to you."

Max slid the paper into a carrying case on the floor. "Good. I'll look at it later today."

Wörtlich stood. "I apologize for not having a number you can reach me at. How about we meet tomorrow. Same place, same time?"

"Count on it." Max headed for the door. There was a slight limp to his walk, Wörtlich noticed. Age had taken a toll on his friend. In another few years, it would take its toll on him as well.

"Listen, Emery," Max said as they walked toward the elevator at the end of the hall. "I'm holding a lecture tonight. You should come."

"What kind of lecture?"

"On the Alexandrian index."

Wörtlich grew very quiet. Did Max suspect his involvement in the theft? Did he even know about that?

Max is trustworthy, he reminded himself, perhaps more to clear away the cobwebs of doubt. *I have to trust somebody!*

"I will try to attend," Wörtlich assured him, trying to sound casual about it. "Always a pleasure, Max. Thank you for your time."

*   *   *

Max's lecture was held at the five-star Sheraton on the Park in downtown Sydney. The drive from the modest motel Brighton had picked out for them would have been short, but Wörtlich chose to walk. A beautiful spring evening had set in, and he'd always found large cities easier to navigate on foot. Besides, he didn't have the patience to contend with parking garages and one-way streets.

The hotel towered between two neighboring high-rises. As he approached it, Wörtlich spotted a row of limousines pulling up to the front curb, dropping off passengers more appropriately dressed for the ballet than a scientific lecture. Somehow the discovery of the index had achieved that rare feat of making science sexy. Trendy. This was more than a scientific lecture; it was a gala.

Ferns and plush furniture were positioned around the edges of the tall-ceilinged lobby, and in the center bubbled an ornate fountain. Pennies littered the tiled floor of the pool, their images dancing and distorting in the water. One of the largest crystal chandeliers he had ever seen hung twenty feet above the fountain, outshone only by a half-circle window that arched across the back of the room, showing off a magnificent view of downtown. He didn't stop to look; he had seen that view many times before.

He dodged bellhops and hotel guests as he came to a folding sign placed in the center of the lobby:

THE LIVING LIBRARY

Join Archaeologist Max Holden

on a virtual tour of the newly re-envisioned

Library of Alexandria!

An arrow pointed to the left, down a corridor toward the auditorium.

Wörtlich's shoes squeaked across the marble floor as he came to a short staircase rising between black stone columns. Opposing flights of stairs led both right and left from the landing. He chose left.

A long line of guests streamed through the open doors to the auditorium. He took his place in the line, feeling conspicuously underdressed.

The auditorium was set up with round tables. He selected a spot near the back wall where he could remain out of sight, in case anyone recognized him. The last thing he wanted was to fall into a long conversation with an old colleague. As far as most of the world knew, he wasn't in Australia, and he wanted to keep it that way as long as possible.

The lights soon dimmed. As the noise of the crowd dissipated, a short video was projected onto a large screen. As the sign in the lobby had stated, the video featured an animated mockup of the Great Library's original layout, taking the viewer on a tour through the major lecture halls and depositories. The voice of the English narrator reminded him sharply of Noam Sheply, even though he knew that wasn't the case. It was almost certainly some famous actor he was unfamiliar with. Brighton would have known who it was.

When the video concluded, the screen rose, revealing in dramatic fashion Max standing behind the lectern. The video screen stopped a few feet above his head and displayed a prepared slideshow.

Wörtlich only half-listened to the actual lecture; there was nothing to be revealed here that Wörtlich didn't already know from having browsed the index firsthand. The rest of the room, however, seemed to live and die on Max's every word.

Wörtlich couldn't help but feel a little envious; he had never lectured to a crowd so large or so interested in what he had to say.

"The discovery of the index to this great collection, perhaps the greatest collection of works ever amassed from the ancient world, provides astounding insight into the Greco-Roman period," Max said. He was an excellent speaker, a skill Wörtlich had never bothered to cultivate. Maybe that was the reason nobody cared what he had to say.

Max went on to describe an ambitious proposal to rebuild the library on its original site, a project which would involve reclaiming large portions of the seafloor directly off the modern-day coast.

The artist's renderings of the rebuilt library were extraordinary. Wörtlich had to admit it would be an impressive project if it ever got off the ground. If men like Lagati chose to back it, it probably would.

"Upon the completion of the library's reconstruction," Max spoke, "students from around the world will be able to travel to Egypt to study in the same manner as Aristotle and other great thinkers of the ancient era. With a firm grasp on the contents of Ptolemy's collection of scrolls, we can enter such an endeavor with greater conviction than ever before. Surely this will change the face of global scholarship in this new millennium."

As the presentation ended and the lights came up, the guests mingled amongst each other, filling the room with a low, reverent murmur.

Wörtlich stood as well, looking over the crowd to chart the best route through it. He stuck close to the walls, where the people were fewer and farther between, and picked his way to the front of the auditorium where Max had stepped offstage and disappeared into a back room.

He quickened his pace... and then stopped. Ahead of him, engaged in conversation at one of the front tables, was a man who looked extremely familiar. As that man turned, revealing his profile, Wörtlich did a double take.

Noam Sheply.

Panic overwhelming him, Wörtlich immediately turned and headed back the other direction. What was Sheply doing in Australia, at Max's lecture? Was it a coincidence? Not likely. If so, it was a coincidence Max had failed to mention. And if Max had been in contact with Sheply, then it strained credibility to think Max didn't know of Wörtlich's fugitive status. But if so, why hadn't Max turned him in? Was his old friend playing an angle?

Once out of Sheply's line of sight, Wörtlich looked back.

The Englishman had vanished.

Wörtlich's heart beat faster as he made a line for the nearest exit and stepped through, closing the door firmly behind him.

He stopped with his back to the door and breathed heavily for a few moments, trying to understand what Sheply's presence meant. Coming to no conclusions, he looked around and saw that he stood in the backstage area.

Wörtlich was about to head toward the lobby when he heard voices behind him. As he listened, he determined one of them was Max. And the dulcet tones of that second voice were just as distinctive: Sheply.

Conflict raged within him as to what he should do: run and stay out of sight or try getting closer to hear what they were saying. His feet overruled his better instincts.

He slowed as he came to an intersection. The voices drifted toward him from about ten meters down the hall. He crept as close as he dared, then risked a short glimpse around the corner.

Sheply and Max stood with their backs turned and voices lowered. He strained to listen, but to no avail.

Just as Wörtlich was about to give up and hurry back, Max dug his hand into his carrying case and pulled out a couple of documents. On top was the folded map of the bone field Brighton had provided. A second document was attached to it, and although Wörtlich stood too far away to make out any details, he could see handwritten notes.

Max solved the mystery, Wörtlich thought. *And instead of giving the answer to me, he is passing it along to Sheply.*

Feeling betrayed, he stumbled through an emergency exit out into the chilly night air. He pulled his jacket around him a little tighter and broke into a jog.

By the time he crossed the street, he was running.

TWENTY-SIX

Sydney, Australia

SEPTEMBER 26

Wörtlich couldn't remember the last time he had run so hard. When he got to the motel and climbed the stairs to the second floor, he was bone tired. He slowed to a walk and crossed the balcony overlooking the parking lot, his hands sliding along the steel handrail. He got to the room they were staying in and knocked lightly.

The door opened a crack and Brighton's eyes peered out at him. The young man closed the door again and slid the locking chain free.

Once inside, Wörtlich ripped the plastic off a disposable cup and filled it with water from the sink. He drained it in one swallow, then filled it a second time. He turned around and dropped himself into a low-riding easy chair. The cheap upholstery itched against the bottoms of his arms where they touched the armrests.

Wörtlich took another long drink of water and leaned his head back, looking up at the ceiling. He was still out of breath, but his news couldn't wait.

"You will not believe who I just saw," he managed. Neither Ira nor Brighton offered a guess, so Wörtlich answered the question himself. "Noam Sheply."

Brighton looked troubled. "He's here?"

"He was at Max Holden's lecture tonight."

"I was afraid something like this might happen," Brighton said. "Did Sheply see you?"

"I do not believe so. But Australia is an awfully long way for him to travel—especially since he was not doing any speaking himself…"

Wörtlich rubbed his temples. His headache was back.

"Are you all right?" Ira asked, concerned.

Wörtlich closed his eyes. "I just need to think."

He finished his glass of water. Brighton took it from him and refilled it in the bathroom sink.

"Do you think Sheply knows we're here?" Brighton asked, handing him the full cup.

"Maybe," Wörtlich said. He swallowed a gulp of water, feeling it travel coolly down the back of his throat. "But I do not believe so. The only person who knows where we are is Lagati, and Lagati went to a lot of trouble to rescue us from Egypt. Why would he turn against us now?"

Brighton sighed. "Actually, there is one other person who knows. Max Holden."

Wörtlich looked at the young man pointedly. "Max did not know we were coming until I arrived at the university at lunchtime today.

Even if he leaked the news to Sheply the moment I left, Sheply would not have had enough time to get here. As far as I know, Sheply and Max have only met a handful of times, and that was years ago. There is no connection there." His shoulders dropped in resignation. "At least, not until now."

"You think they are involved now?" Ira asked.

Wörtlich fondled the plastic cup in his fingers. "Max gave our hieroglyph to Sheply."

Brighton's eyes flared. "What?"

"Doctor," Ira said, "I thought you said you trusted this man."

"I did! I cannot think of any reason he would betray me."

Brighton stood up and walked to the door, then back again. His footsteps were muted by his woolen socks. It looked like he hadn't been the first person to pace there; the prickly carpet was well-worn in a long stretch from the door to the bathroom.

"Maybe Sheply's presence is a coincidence," Brighton said, thinking out loud. "Maybe he was already in town for the lecture."

Ira's eyes had a faraway look. Whatever he was thinking, he wasn't sharing. Which was typical.

"I cannot believe this is a coincidence, as much as I would like to." Wörtlich leaned forward, putting his hands on his knees. "We will have to be much more careful from here on out."

"But we were already being careful," Brighton insisted.

"Obviously not enough," Ira said, shifting toward Wörtlich. "Did you at least get some useful information from your meeting with Doctor Holden?"

"Yes. On that front there is some hopeful news. He said he needed some time to translate the hieroglyph. He sounded quite confident about it." He paused, and glowered. "Unfortunately, I never got it back. I think he did solve the problem, but he gave it to Sheply."

Brighton made a sour face. "I'm still waiting for that good news."

"Sorry. Max has discovered some stone tablets here in Australia that corroborate what we found in Antarctica."

"How so?" Ira asked.

Wörtlich tried to remember all the details. "These tablets contain a story attributed to Gilgamesh, the Babylonian king who was also a giant. Or so the legends claim. Apparently, Gilgamesh went to Antarctica seeking refuge from a flood."

Brighton looked thoughtful. "Gilgamesh. I feel like I read something about him recently."

"I had the same thought. It's been bothering me all day."

Master Gilgamesh, Master Gilgamesh, Master Gilgamesh—

Brighton snapped his fingers. "I had a dream the night we spent under the dome, and I think it had something to do with Gilgamesh."

"I had a similar dream." Wörtlich sat up straighter. His headache had gone. "There was a group of giants sitting around a fire, and one of them called himself Gilgamesh. I cannot remember what they were talking about, though—"

"Visions," Brighton said.

Wörtlich looked at him with blossoming curiosity. "Is it possible that we had the same dream?"

"One of the giants dreamt about a tablet."

"And water," Wörtlich added, his mouth running dry. He shook his head clear.

"There was also something about a mountaintop," the young man said. "But that was another time—when we were—"

"When we were under the pyramids," Wörtlich finished for him.

Both men turned to confront Ira.

"What about you?" Brighton asked.

Ira said nothing. He had withdrawn into himself. Whatever this business with the dreams meant, it had shaken him.

"Ira?"

The rabbi's soft gaze fell on Wörtlich. He looked more tired than Wörtlich had ever seen him before—more tired than he had been in the desert, or the trek over the glacier, or after pulling himself up the fissure. Whatever inexhaustible source of energy powered Ira had finally dried up.

When Ira spoke, his voice was tinged with regret. "You're starting to figure it out."

The words were so quiet at first that Wörtlich almost missed them. When he realized what the rabbi had said, his mood changed from excitement to frustration.

His face darkened. "What was that?"

Ira sighed. "I said, you're figuring it out."

"Just what I thought you said," Wörtlich said. "I am so tired of you sitting by and watching us grapple for answers. It was clear from the start, from the first time we met, that you know a lot more than you let on. All the way through Egypt, through Antarctica, everything we found you met with 'expectation.' We have labored and sweated and tried our damnedest to figure everything out, and this whole time you have *known* the answer. You hoped we would remain in the dark. All along, Ira! I have had it up to here with you. Why did you come along in the first place, if you had decided not to help?"

Ira maintained that damned serene expression of his. Wörtlich wanted to rip it off his face and trample on it.

"I get it," Brighton said softly.

Wörtlich whirled on him. "What do you get?"

"Ira didn't come along to help us find anything." He looked up, meeting Ira's gaze. "He doesn't need to locate the Book of Creation at all. He knows what we'll find in it. Don't you see? He came to hide the

Book, maybe even destroy it."

Understanding flooded Wörtlich, and his mind reeled. Everything Brighton said made sense with what he had observed of the rabbi. The man who had condemned them for stealing the index would blithely destroy or nullify the greatest archaeological discovery of all time. Such hypocrisy.

"Is that true?" Wörtlich asked, unable to contain his mounting rage.

"Yes."

Wörtlich leaped to his feet. "Damn it, Ira!"

The rabbi exhaled. He took a moment to look from one man to the other, gauging their reactions, and then said, "You're right. You do deserve an explanation."

*　　*　　*

As Ira looked back and forth between Wörtlich and Brighton, who knew nothing of the danger they intended to expose, Ira felt sympathy. But also, on a deeper level, revulsion. They were pursuing secrets they had no right to pursue, let alone obtain. They had to understand, and there was only one way to make them.

What he was about to attempt, he had only tried once before.

One evening, Aaron had invited him and a few other instructors to a dinner hosted by him and his wife, Madeline. The dinner had proceeded just as countless other dinners had during their years together at seminary, but this one ended differently. After Madeline served coffee, Aaron asked them to pull the sitting rooms chairs together so they all faced inward. He had closed his eyes and instructed them to do the same.

What happened next had been unlike anything else Ira had ever experienced. He had never shared it with anyone; not even Lawrence. That night, after the others left to return to their families, Aaron had initiated him into the council, and his life had never been the same. Aaron had shared with him the greatest burden of responsibility one could place on another, and Ira had accepted it with humility and a sense of destiny.

"The secrets of the ancients must be protected," his mentor had said. "The secrets of the deep, the secrets of Jehovah… no one must learn of them. There cannot be another Babel."

Nothing they purposed could be withheld from them, Ira thought grimly.

The ancient secrets had been exposed once before, and had led to knowledge of things mankind had no business knowing. Knowledge had corrupted the world, and only one solution could cleanse it.

The Flood had been an act of mercy. An act of necessity. An act that could never be repeated.

Ira took Brighton's hand, just as he had back at the Norwegians' camp, and the young man relaxed. Brighton was receptive. His breathing slowed in response to the touch, his heart rate stabilized, and the pent-up anger left him.

Ira smiled inwardly. Brighton was envisioning the river, the streams of possibilities, and he was lowering his feet to anchor himself against the quick-moving current. But Wörtlich—

His eyes turned to the archaeologist, whose eyes expressed nothing but wrath and distrust. He had to be made to see truth.

Ira extended his arm. "Take my hand."

Wörtlich merely stared at it for the longest time, but Ira would be patient. He had to choose.

"If you want to understand, Doctor, take my hand." Ira closed his eyes and waited.

Remember the other times, Doctor? Where would you be if you hadn't taken my hand? Lost. Confused. Directionless. Tormented.

Ira felt Wörtlich's hand curl around his. But through the touch, Ira could still feel Wörtlich's all-consuming anxiety. He was a vessel of pain and sorrow, of cynicism and suspicion, of rage and regret.

He had to choose.

"Now, close your eyes," Ira instructed. Through his palm, he felt Wörtlich's apprehension in his quickened pulse. Even though he took Ira's hand, a wall was in place, keeping him out. That wall had to come down.

"Once something is in your memory, it is possible to access it," Ira spoke. "It takes discipline and reflection. It takes patience. And you must open yourself to it. Most of all, it does not happen by accident. It happens through intention."

"What happens?" Brighton asked through even breaths.

Ira squeezed his hand, a gentle affirmation. "You will remember. Come along with me."

Ira reached back into his own memory and formed in his mind the image of a mountaintop. As he focused, details appeared: a winding path, ominous cliffs sprouting up in a circle, their heights coming to sharp pinnacles. Heat radiated from the ground.

Wholly within the memory, Ira opened his eyes and surveyed his surroundings. Before him stood a group of men; he was not a part of them, though he sensed he had been in the dream. Standing before him was a tall figure whose eyes he had once seen through.

Barakel.

As the man named Barakel approached the group and was joined by another—*Semyaza*—Ira looked over to find that Brighton had joined him.

"The mountaintop," Brighton whispered.

Ira felt the young man's mounting terror as he looked upon the meeting in progress.

"In the dream, I was that man." Brighton pointed toward the retreating form of Barakel. "The memories were his."

Ira paused, then looked to his other side, but there was only empty space there. He could still feel Wörtlich's hand gripping his, but the man had not followed them into the memory. It had to be a choice.

"Doctor, come along with us."

Wörtlich's disembodied voice was strained. "I cannot."

Ira squeezed his hand. "Patience, Doctor. Open yourself."

In front of them, the meeting revolved around a central figure, a man taller and colder than the others. The tall man's eyes burned with red flame and his jaw set in malicious intent. Despite this, his face, like those of all the other men meeting here, was beautiful and perfect, pure and clean, untouched by age.

Azazel.

"Where are we?" Wörtlich's voice asked.

Ira smiled and turned to the spot which had a moment before been empty. He was pleased to find Wörtlich occupying it.

"This place is called Mount Heron, but we haven't gone anywhere," Ira assured them. "We're still in the motel room. We have merely accessed a shared memory."

"We are asleep?" Wörtlich asked. The archaeologist's image brought up his hands and flexed the fingers. His face demonstrated awe.

"In a manner of speaking."

Ira smiled and squeezed both men's hands. Wörtlich looked startled for a moment, glancing down at one of his hands, no doubt trying to comprehend how he was able to feel Ira's grip without seeing it.

All three men took steps forward, intending to listen in on the meeting.

"Azazel," Semyaza said, addressing the being whose expression was tinged with bitterness, "I fear you may not wish this deed to be done should you alone pay for it."

"I, alone?" Azazel let out a peel of laughter.

A murmur passed among the others as Azazel paced in circles around them. He stopped in front of each individual and made eye contact. After some time, he even shared a private exchange with Barakel—an exchange Ira remembered well.

"Who are these men?" Wörtlich asked.

"The Book of Enoch refers to them as the Watchers," Ira said. "Today we would probably use the term 'angels.'"

Wörtlich looked at them more closely. "But they look like men."

Azazel returned to the center of the group. A number of them had gathered around him more tightly, as though a silent coalition had formed.

"So let us all swear an oath," Azazel said. His eyes rested securely on Barakel's, "and bind one another with curses so as not to alter this plan. We will—all of us—carry it to conclusion."

Barakel and Azazel outstretched their arms toward each other and locked them in place, a vicious sneer on both their faces.

"I don't understand," Brighton broke in. "This man," he pointed to Azazel, "is proposing a plan, and he wants to ensure that the others stick to it?"

"Yes, Sherwood," Ira said. "When the earth was first created, there was a rebellion in heaven, and many angels were cast out. Some of this may be familiar to you as folklore."

"This is where the devil comes from," Brighton said. "He was cast out of heaven."

"Right. But he was not the leader of this group."

Wörtlich wasn't buying it. "Cannot a dream just be a dream?"

Ira chose to be patient. *Choices, choices.*

"I assure you, this really happened," Ira said. "The man in the middle, Azazel, proposed a plan to meddle with creation, to defile what God had made and called perfect. He recruited these others to join him in taking human women as wives, impregnating them and creating sons of their own."

Brighton looked at them oddly. "But those sons wouldn't be—"

"Human?" Ira said. "Indeed, they wouldn't. Not entirely."

Ira blinked, and the three men stood in a dark room covered in stonework. A fire blazed in the hearth.

"This I remember too well," Brighton said, bringing a hand to his chest and resting it there. "This is where I drowned."

"Not you," Ira corrected. "You experienced a memory. Barakel's memory."

"Who was Barakel?"

"One of the Watchers who joined Azazel. He took a wife along with the others. Somehow, by walking where he walked, we have encountered his memories." He frowned. "I have not determined how it happened."

"So, you do not know everything, Rabbi," Wörtlich said.

"Of course not," Ira said. "I never claimed to have all the answers."

Brighton drew in a gasp. "Giants!"

Indeed, when Ira turned away from the fire, he found the three oversized wooden chairs occupied with three enormous creatures.

"Like the bones in Antarctica," Wörtlich breathed.

"Indeed," Ira said. "One of these men may have become that skeleton. We may never know for certain. In any event, these were the children of the Watchers. Part human, part anything but."

Wörtlich hesitated. "Can they see us?"

"Not in memory, no." Ira turned and peered into a dark corner. In the farthest recesses of the room, he could see the dim outline of a crouched man hiding there. "Barakel again, overhearing a secret meeting."

Ira turned away from the hiding man, father of the giant Mahaway, and returned his attention to the three giants in mid-conference.

Wörtlich had stepped closer to the giant known as Master Gilgamesh, inspecting him more closely.

"In the legends, Gilgamesh was two-thirds god," Wörtlich spoke over the creatures' low, sonorous voices. "Are you saying that was based in truth, Ira?"

"Every good lie is." Ira joined Wörtlich in the center of the three chairs, where he could practically feel the gazes of the giants passing over his head. These were dangerous creatures. His blood ran cold at the thought.

Mahaway was hunched forward, eyes on Gilgamesh. "You've hardly said a word, Master Gilgamesh."

"Did you have another dream last night?" Gilgamesh asked.

"Yes. A vision came to me." Mahaway looked tired, and for good reason.

Footsteps behind him alerted Ira to Brighton's approach.

"So the… men… on the mountaintop," the young man said, avoiding the term "angel." "Their plan succeeded? The Watchers defiled creation?"

"Oh yes. Scripture is clear that the wickedness following these events was great all over the planet. The Torah says that every imagination of the thoughts of man was evil continuously."

Wörtlich turned away from the giants, returning to the fireside.

"Here is where the religious argument goes off the rails for me. How could God allow this to happen? If there is a God, and he created the world, why would he allow everything to go so terribly wrong?"

"You ask an age-old question. Why do bad things happen if God is in control? You won't like the answer," Ira said, staring into the fire. "God may not be in control."

This revelation usually had more of an impact on his listeners, but Brighton and Wörtlich seemed to take it in stride, as though to say, *Of course he isn't!*

"How could we all be free to live and choose if he could just reach down and interfere whenever he wants?" Ira continued. "He may very well be God, but he created us to be free. That same freedom requires choice, and in order for us to make good choices, we must also be free to make bad ones. Of all the possibilities man can choose for himself, he usually chooses to live in the middle of whatever chaos he perceives around him, believing there to be no better way."

Ira felt the pool of water forming around his feet before he saw it. *This is just a dream,* he reminded himself. *None of this is real.*

Brighton stepped up onto the hearth to avoid the water, but in mere moments the water had risen past his ankles.

"I remember what comes next." Fear crept into Brighton's voice.

The water came up to their knees. Brighton's chest heaved in panic, but panicking would take him out of the memory. Ira squeezed Brighton's hands and the young man's eyes instantly met his.

"Don't be afraid, Sherwood. This isn't real. We are not here. We are not going to drown. We are safe and sound in the motel room. Remember that."

Still, Ira couldn't fight the instinct to take a deep breath before the water swelled over his head. Realizing the futility of that, he expelled the air from his chest and allowed himself to sink into the depths. He opened his mouth wide and inhaled a stream of water that burned going down, and his eyes bulged in pain.

There is no water. There is no water. There is no water.

He repeated the sentiment over in his mind, closing his eyes and relaxing, overcoming the vision.

He opened his eyes and found himself in the Nile valley. Barakel and Semyaza stood together, waiting for an approaching man.

It's Enoch, in the flesh!

"So the giants knew the Flood was coming," Brighton concluded.

Ira turned to find the young man standing next to him. He also spotted Wörtlich, a little further off.

Wörtlich wandered closer, the long grasses beneath his booted feet making swishing sounds as he walked through them. The sun beat down, its light reflecting off the river's swift waters.

"The rest of the story we know," Wörtlich said. "The giants were trying to escape. Part of their plan was to go to the True North."

Brighton nodded, putting the pieces together. "The magnetic pole."

"But then I was right!" Wörtlich said.

Ira looked at him, once again exuding patience. "What do you mean?"

"The Flood proves that God can do whatever he wants, that he can wipe everything out if the mood strikes."

Ira smiled. How could he make someone understand who was so determined to misunderstand? All he could do was present the information; what Wörtlich did with it was his own choice.

"You miss the point," Ira said. "What was on the earth at that time was no longer mankind, but a perversion of it. Azazel and the other Watchers succeeded. The only people who were untouched by this... let's call it genetic warfare... were Noah and his family."

"It is Enoch, the scribe!" Semyaza jeered.

Brighton tapped Ira on the shoulder. "Who's Enoch?"

"A scribe who lived before the Flood," Ira explained as the two waiting men encountered Enoch and exchanged words. The three of them turned and headed toward the pyramids in the distance. Ira gestured for Wörtlich and Brighton to follow along.

"Because of Enoch's close relationship with God, some of the Watchers went to him for help. They asked him to petition their cause to the Lord, in the hopes of gaining sanctuary from the coming disaster. But when Enoch came back with God's reply—as he is doing now—it wasn't the answer they hoped for."

Hardly any time passed to cover the vast distance to the pyramid. Time and distance didn't work the same way in memory as it did in the real world.

They followed Barakel, Semyaza, and Enoch down into the gallery. Ira expected what came next, but from the looks on the other two men's faces, he knew they were remembering for the first time the bizarre creatures that populated this underground chamber.

The Watchers roamed up and down the gallery, surrounded by giants—their sons and daughters—and a host of strange, created beings: living, breathing versions of the unnatural human-animal beasts the Egyptians had worshipped as deities.

Ira confronted the scene with disgust, then followed the action into the room of the inverted pyramid.

Azazel stood upon the raised platform. Ira remembered the podium he had found here during his visit to the Hall of Records, and on it the presence of the Book of Creation, its glowing parchment illuminating the air.

Enoch stood before the leader of these fallen angels, his head raised confidently.

"Your petition cannot be granted, for all the days of eternity," Enoch proclaimed. "You shall not have peace. You shall not ascend. It has been decreed that you be bound to the earth. You shall witness the utter destruction of your beloved sons, and you shall not enjoy them."

Ira turned away from the anguished cry that issued from Azazel's throat. Squeezing Brighton's and Wörtlich's hands in the real world, he opened his eyes and looked around the hotel room.

Brighton was the first to open his eyes, and in those eyes Ira saw torment. "It was a death sentence."

Ira laid a hand on his back. "But one of their own making."

Without saying a word, Wörtlich dusted himself off and stepped around Brighton and Ira.

The door slammed behind him as he left.

*　　　*　　　*

Brighton ran down the street, his eyes searching the darkened sidewalks. Nearly ten minutes had passed since Wörtlich disappeared from the motel room, and still he couldn't be found. He couldn't have gone far. The car was still in the lot, but there was a park nearby that took up an entire city block; the archaeologist might have gone there on foot.

At last, Brighton saw the short-sleeved man sitting on a bench, facing away from the street. Brighton approached, his shoes crunching on the gravel path to announce his presence. Wörtlich didn't turn.

Brighton walked around the bench and saw the older man holding his head in agony. "You don't look so good."

Wörtlich brought one of his hands down into his lap while the other continued to clutch the left side of his forehead. "It is nothing. A headache."

"You're upset."

"Of course I am. Everything Ira revealed to us... do you see that none of it matters if we cannot get that hieroglyph back from Sheply and find out what it says?" Wörtlich swallowed and clenched his lowered hand. "I should not have trusted Max Holden. I put my faith in him, and look where that got us."

Brighton said nothing. What was there to say?

"What do you suppose comes next?" Wörtlich asked. "The way this is going, I would not be surprised if Ira led us straight to the Holy Grail."

Brighton managed a laugh. "You can't be serious."

"I honestly do not know."

"What I know is that we have to get our hands on the hieroglyph," Brighton said. "But I wouldn't be so quick to give up on it. Remember when Lagati told us about the Book, over dinner? He described a world where we could use the principles of creation to make things happen, to bring about wealth."

"To bring about ice cream, you mean."

Brighton coughed into his hand and smiled. "Yes. That, too."

Wörtlich stuck his hands into his pockets and stood up. The confusion on his face said it all. Nothing he had ever believed was turning out as expected. Brighton had a hard enough time accepting the notion of angels and global floods, but what about for a man like Wörtlich, who had dedicated his life to learning and exposing such matters?

"Even if we found the Book, Ira would destroy it to prevent it from falling into unscrupulous hands." Wörtlich's mouth twisted on the word *unscrupulous*. "Into our hands, is what he means."

Brighton shrugged. "Who knows? Maybe that's the right thing to do."

"You are no different from the book-burning Nazis if you believe that. Progress never came from destroying knowledge."

They walked on for some time. When they came to the end of the park, Wörtlich looped around, taking the sidewalk that led back toward the motel.

"What about the hieroglyph?" Brighton asked.

Wörtlich quickened his pace. "That is what I am working on."

TWENTY-SEVEN

Sydney, Australia
SEPTEMBER 27

Brighton's hands were sweating as he watched the rental car pull away from the curb and disappear down the street. He stood in place, passersby flowing around him as though he were an island in a fast-flowing river. He stuffed his hands in his pockets and walked up the block, falling into the hurried pace of people heading off to work.

There was a chill in the air and dense cloud cover overhead. He forced his head to the side to avoid a gust of wind tunneling down the street, causing bits of trash to scatter across the chipped, sun-worn pavement.

He glanced at the hotel coming up on his right. A stream of cars poured in and out of the front loop, taking on passengers and merging back into traffic. As he got closer, he spotted what he was looking for: a line of waiting taxis. He made a beeline straight toward them, hoping Wörtlich was right about this.

Brighton walked up to the window of the taxi at the front of the line and knocked on the window.

"You got the time?" he asked the driver.

The driver, a tall man with dark hair and tanned features, stared at him in bewilderment, then stole a glance at the display on the car radio. "Nearly eight-thirty."

"How about taking a break?" Brighton asked.

The driver mumbled something inaudible and hit the button to roll up the window. Brighton reached into his pocket and pulled out a wad of hundred dollar bills. He counted out five and held them up. The driver lowered the window again.

"What's this?" the man asked.

Brighton shrugged. "Take a five-minute break."

"I'm waiting for a passenger." The driver shook his head and inched his finger back toward the button. "No thanks."

Brighton added two more bills. "I only need five minutes. Your car will be waiting when you come back."

Conflicted, the driver pulled back his hand and glanced at the time. He came to a quick decision, then pushed open the door. Brighton stepped out of his way, holding the door as the driver stepped out, rounded the taxi, and headed up the stairs into the hotel.

"See you in a few minutes," Brighton called.

Left alone, he swung himself down into the driver's seat. He checked the time again. If they were off by even a few minutes, they would have just wasted seven hundred dollars.

He looked out toward the street, hoping to spot the rental car.

But it was nowhere in sight. If they were late…

He tapped his fingers on the steering wheel, then turned his head toward the hotel's front doors. His breath caught.

Sheply hurried down the stairs carrying two bags, one in each hand. Brighton put the car in drive and inched forward to the edge of the curb just as Sheply arrived at street level.

"Where to, sir?" he asked, approximating an Australian accent. He thought it came out all right, though it was the product of just two hours' rehearsal the night before.

Of the three of them, Wörtlich had pulled off the accent best, but Sheply would have recognized his old friend in an instant. Sheply may have seen a picture of Brighton in the wake of the index theft, but the two men had never met in person. Brighton hoped that would be enough.

His heart thudded in his chest as Sheply made eye contact. Just as quickly, Sheply broke the gaze. Brighton relaxed. No recognition.

"The airport," the Englishman said in a clipped tone.

Brighton's eyes darted back to the driver's door and searched for a button to open the trunk. If it took him too long, Sheply would grow suspicious. Spotting the lever next to the automatic window controls, he reached out and pulled it. He walked around to the back of the car and picked up Sheply's bags.

"Mr. Sheply!"

Brighton turned to see the hotel concierge hurrying down the steps.

Sheply, already halfway into the back of the car, peered out. "Yes?"

"There's a call for you. It's urgent."

"Who is it?"

"Someone from Cairo. The man insisted I stop you before you

left."

While Sheply was distracted, Brighton lifted the bags and placed them on the pavement next to the car instead of in the trunk. When Sheply stepped out again, Brighton slammed the trunk shut, acting as though the bags were safely stowed.

Sheply walked toward the concierge, annoyance writ large on his face. "Why didn't they call my mobile?"

The concierge shrugged. "I really couldn't say."

"All right." Sheply looked over to Brighton. "Hold the car for a couple of minutes. I'll be right back."

Brighton nodded. "Sure thing."

He smiled as he watched the man climb the stairs, following the concierge back inside.

A few seconds later, the rental car pulled up next to him.

Ira hopped out the moment it stopped, a cell phone to his ear. He put up a hand and waited for a voice to answer. At the first sound of hello, he hung up, then picked up one of Sheply's bags and tossed it into the backseat.

"Hurry up," Wörtlich said from the front.

Brighton closed the doors to the taxi and walked toward the rental vehicle, still smiling.

By this time, Ira had taken care of the second bag and closed the door. Before Brighton got inside, he saw the taxi driver return to the curb. Brighton waved, a grin on his face, then climbed inside and slammed the door shut as Wörtlich pulled into traffic.

Brighton's shoulders dropped in relief as they sped away. "I can't believe that worked."

"I told you it would," Wörtlich said.

Brighton unzipped the first bag and found nothing inside but clothing.

"It better be in there, for all the trouble we went to," Wörtlich said over his shoulder, keeping his eyes on the road. The light ahead was about to turn red, but Wörtlich sped through. He ignored the insistent beeping of a car horn behind them.

Brighton opened the second suitcase and found a stack of folders. He pulled the top folder out and flipped through the papers. He didn't recognize anything, so he moved to the second folder, and then the third. The map of the bone field slipped out and landed on his lap.

"Got it!" he cried.

"Are Max's notes there as well?" Wörtlich said. "Those notes are crucial."

Brighton looked back in the folder and found a piece of paper sitting inside it filled with handwritten notes.

"It's here," he said as Wörtlich took a sharp right turn and cruised up an on-ramp. Brighton braced himself against the ceiling of the car, then looked back at the handwritten page.

Wörtlich tapped his horn as he merged onto the freeway. "What does it say?"

Brighton squinted at the page. "I don't know. The writing's pretty messy."

He put Doctor Holden's notes aside and opened the folder again, where a short stack of documents still sat. They looked like paystubs. He frowned, picking one up.

"Hold on," he said quietly, reading off the slip of paper. As he read, two words stuck out at him, causing him to break out in a sweat. "Guys—"

Wörtlich sped toward an upcoming exit. "Just wait. We are almost back."

"No." Brighton looked up over the open folder. "This is important. Really important."

Ira shifted around to see into the backseat. "Then out with it."

"Sheply wasn't here for the lecture. He *was* looking for us. But it wasn't Doctor Holden who put him on our trail."

"Then who was it?" Wörtlich asked.

Brighton hesitated, the words caught on the tip of his tongue. This couldn't be right. It didn't make sense. He looked back down at the paystub to double-check, to make sure he wasn't seeing things. But those two telltale words stared back at him.

"Sheply's been receiving checks from Creation Tech." He looked up, making eye contact with Wörtlich through the rear-view mirror.

"Where have I heard that before?" Wörtlich asked.

"It's Raff Lagati's company." Brighton looked back at the folder and flicked through the rest of the documents. "It says right here. Sheply's been on the payroll for nearly three years!"

Wörtlich slowed down. They were on the exit, about to head into traffic again. Through the mirror, Brighton saw beads of sweat forming on the archaeologist's face.

"No," Wörtlich said softly, almost to himself. "Three years? That cannot be right. That is about the time when the Institute put him in charge of the Alexandria excavations—"

Wörtlich cursed as he swerved into the motel parking lot. He missed the entrance by a few inches and the back wheels jumped the curb. He crossed the lot and parked right in front of the building. He leapt out.

"We should get our things and go," Wörtlich said. "We might have been followed."

Once inside the room, Brighton went about gathering his things and stuffing them into his backpack. Fortunately, he was traveling light.

"The Alexandria excavations," Wörtlich said aloud. Was he talking to himself? "That explains a thing or two, now that I think about it. Lagati must have used his connections to put Sheply in that job." He paused, his shoulders dropping in realization. "Except that means Lagati already had access to the index, that he didn't need us to steal it at all. What kind of sense does that make?"

Brighton slung his bag over his shoulder. "Unless he did need us to steal it, and wanted Sheply's hands to be clean."

"Perhaps," Wörtlich allowed. "Maybe Lagati needed us to do the dirty work so he would have leverage over us in the future. Or maybe the whole thing was a test of some kind, a damned test."

Wörtlich struck the bed's headboard with his fist, which probably did more to hurt his hand than the headboard. "Something about this is all wrong."

Ira stopped by the bathroom sink to splash water on his face.

Brighton heard the beginnings of rain hitting the front window. Just as he turned, the door flung open.

Sheply stormed inside, looked straight at Wörtlich, and said, "I never thought I'd find myself in a high speed chase, Emery."

Brighton froze, spotting an idling taxi in the parking lot.

Sheply offered Wörtlich a crooked smile. "But I have to tell you it was quite exhilarating. You almost lost us twice."

Wörtlich stepped forward. "Noam—"

Sheply put up a hand to stop him. "I'm sorry we didn't get a chance to connect yesterday. I realize now you must have nearly run into me."

"Did Raff Lagati get you your job in Alexandria?"

Sheply's eyes widened. He feigned surprise well. "Raff Lagati?"

"You don't have to pretend," Brighton said. "We saw the paystubs."

Sheply turned to regard Brighton. "Mr. Brighton, good to meet you. Too bad it wasn't under better circumstances."

"I always thought it was strange that you got that job," Wörtlich said, walking around the side of the bed. "You were not the obvious choice. Menefee deserved it more. Hell, I deserved it more."

"You may be right," Sheply said, conceding the point. The Englishman shifted his gaze, acknowledging Ira. "Rabbi Binyamin, a pleasure."

Ira acknowledged him with a stiff nod.

"In any event, I've been helping Lagati for years," Sheply continued. "He's been looking for some pretty incredible things. Of course, you know that more than anyone. I regret that I couldn't go on this adventure of yours myself, but with the discovery of the index I had too many obligations to take care of. Lagati needed someone else."

Wörtlich heaved a big breath. "There is something I still do not understand."

Sheply let out a derisive snort. "I would imagine there are a great many things you do not understand. Now, kindly return my bags."

Wörtlich ignored him. "We have worked tirelessly for Lagati. Why would he send you to find us now?"

"My bags."

"Answer my question. Why did Lagati send you to check on us?"

Sheply shook his head, sadly. "You don't understand him at all, do you? Raff Lagati is not a trusting man, Emery. Everything was going well, true, but he needed assurance that he was going to get what he sent you for."

Sheply reached into his coat and pulled out a gun. He leveled it at Wörtlich, who took a startled step backward.

"You brought a gun?" Wörtlich asked, incredulous.

"People are not always as they seem, no? Now, give me my bags."

Ira's right foot suddenly left the ground and struck Sheply in the side. Sheply stumbled backward, surprised enough to drop the gun. James Bond, he was not.

Brighton remained rooted to the spot for a moment, trying to piece together what had just happened.

Sheply sat up, dazed for a moment, and lunged for the gun.

Wörtlich, however, got there first.

Realizing he had lost, Sheply backed himself against the wall, looking caged. The fear on his face was palpable.

Brighton stared at Ira in open disbelief. Once again, the old man was full of surprises.

Ira, for his part, met the others' stares as though nothing unusual had happened. In a deadpan, he said, "I think we had better run. Now."

With that, the rabbi sprinted out the door.

As they raced across the second level balcony and down the concrete steps, Brighton heard Sheply coming after them.

Wörtlich reached the parking lot first and pointed the weapon back toward the stairs.

Sheply froze on the second to last step.

At the last possible moment, Wörtlich thought better of his plan and turned the gun on the waiting taxi, shooting out both front wheels. The driver dove onto the passenger seat, just in case one of those bullets missed its mark.

Brighton, finding himself nearest the driver's side, thrust himself behind the wheel of the rental car. He shoved the key into the ignition and started the engine just as Wörtlich and Ira flung themselves inside.

Wörtlich still pointed the gun, keeping Sheply from coming any closer.

"Stop!" Sheply shouted, but instead Brighton gunned the engine and took off across the lot.

"Drive north," Ira instructed as they got to the street. "We can't risk the airport, but we have to get out of the city."

Brighton pressed his foot down on the gas and felt the car speed up. His hands shook the wheel, he realized, and Wörtlich watched him warily. Brighton steadied his hands and gripped the wheel tighter.

Up ahead, he saw a crowded parking lot. He checked his mirrors, jumped into the left lane, and slowed down.

"What are you doing?" Wörtlich demanded.

Brighton glanced behind him. He saw no sign of pursuit. That had been fast thinking of Wörtlich to shoot out the tires.

"Pulling in," he said.

"We cannot stop."

"This will only take a second," Brighton insisted.

He brought the car to a stop and jumped out. Using the edge of his key, he leaned down and worked at the screws holding the car's license plate. He pulled the plate off and swapped them for those of the black four-door sedan parked next to them.

"Smart kid," Ira murmured from his spot in the backseat.

"Now we can go," Brighton said.

A moment later, they were racing north.

*   *   *

The better part of an hour passed before they got out of the city, but Brighton found the drive up the Pacific Highway relatively easy since they were heading against traffic most of the way. He looked longingly out at the view to the east, wondering if he'd ever return to these white sand beaches under less stressful circumstances.

He glanced at a sign announcing the distance to Brisbane.

"We're not going all the way to Brisbane, are we?" Brighton asked. "How are we going to get out of Australia?

"Obviously we can't call Lagati for a lift this time," Ira pointed out.

Wörtlich was pouring over Doctor's Holden's notes. "We need to figure out our destination before we can worry about getting there."

"Have you figured it out?" Brighton said.

"Well, Max did. According to this, Max had no trouble deciphering the hieroglyph." Wörtlich held up the map of the bone field and pointed to a curving arc of bones in the top left corner. "Up here is the character for equality, and on the other side is the one for contradiction."

Wörtlich moved his finger down the center of the page, crossing over a series of horizontal lines laid out next to each other with a secondary line running through them.

"In the middle... well, this is not a word or concept as much as a physical location. Max must have seen this before to understand it so quickly. Perhaps it showed up on the stone tablets he found. It refers to the Giza Plateau, he says. Or more correctly, to 'Rosetau,' which was its ancient name. Put together, it seems to read 'equal and opposite of Giza.'"

"But what does that mean?" Brighton asked.

Ira leaned forward between the two front seats. "It's very clear. We're looking for a site equal to the importance of Giza, but on the opposite side of the world."

Wörtlich held up the page with Max's handwritten notes. Flipping it over, he revealed a set of coordinates, longitude and latitude, circled and underlined several times.

"That's where we're going," Ira surmised.

Brighton looked away from the road just briefly enough to see that the location represented an island in the South Pacific. "How do we get there? We obviously can't take the rental car."

Ira tousled his hair affectionately and Brighton pulled away in annoyance.

"You forget so quickly," the rabbi grinned. "Open your eyes to—"

Brighton rolled his eyes. "Yes, the possibilities. I remember."

"The way will present itself."

Wörtlich picked up Sheply's bag and dug around inside. From beneath the stack of folders, the archaeologist pulled out a black leather pouch. He put down the notes and the map and worked the small pouch's zipper. He looked inside and grinned.

"What's in there?" Brighton asked.

Wörtlich withdrew his hand to reveal a money clip stacked with Australian bills.

Ira let out a low whistle.

Wörtlich turned to Ira. "Take out the computer. We need to find the quickest route to an airstrip."

Brighton kept his eyes forward as the two men made their plans. But he couldn't hold back a smile. Just a few hours ago, they'd had nothing, but now they knew where they were going, had eluded capture, and had the resources to get there.

See the possibilities, indeed.

TWENTY-EIGHT

Tubuai, French Polynesia
SEPTEMBER 29

Wörtlich held on to the edge of his seat, white-knuckled, as the jalopy of a plane bumped its way over the clear skies of the South Pacific. A small, green island emerged from the waters like a jewel, encircled by a reef against which waves crashed continuously, creating a ribbon of undulating blue and white.

The coordinates had led them into a wide, deep expanse of the ocean. The nearest island was called Tubuai, a remote target. Their circuitous route had necessitated numerous island-to-island hops in rattletrap aircraft. The flights weren't particularly long, but the endless jostling made them feel interminable. He had become convinced on several occasions their tiny plane was going down, but each time the plane managed to right itself and fight on.

Now that Tubuai was in his sights, he relaxed. The plane circled the island a couple of times, allowing Wörtlich to spot the *aerodrome*, as a local on the flight called it: a single narrow airstrip hugging the northwestern coast.

He felt his hair brush the ceiling as they bounced their way down the airstrip, and breathed deeply when the craft finally came to a stop.

When they disembarked, they picked up their bags where a short Polynesian man had unloaded them onto the pavement. Wörtlich picked up his luggage and followed the other passengers toward a small hub that served as the only terminal.

Unsurprisingly, no rental cars were available, but one of the airport employees offered to drive them to the hotel on the north shore. The employee described the motorway that ran around the entire perimeter of the island, a mere twenty kilometers in length. Wörtlich almost laughed when the "motorway" turned out to be no more than a dirt track with tall grasses and weeds growing wild between wheel ruts.

The motel had only three rooms, giving it more in common with a bed and breakfast—except without the breakfast. This didn't make a great deal of difference; all they needed were the beds.

After depositing their things, they walked outside to get their bearings. Crossing the motorway, they found the long, north-facing beach. Tall palm trees marked the barrier between grass and sand, their trunks swaying in the wind, their fronds whispering in the breeze. Offshore they heard waves breaking vainly against the reef.

Wörtlich took off his shoes and stood in the cool surf, which foamed over his toes and ankles. Shading his eyes from the glaring sun, he looked up and down the beach in both directions. "We are going to need a boat."

Brighton looked at him in annoyance. "Can't I have a moment to enjoy myself? We just got here."

"He's right," Ira told Brighton, water rushing over his bare feet. "Sheply may chase us here. He knew these coordinates, which means if we have any head start at all, it's a short one."

They left the small town on foot. Every once in a while, a truck trundled past, bouncing up and down through the potholes in the road. They could hear the vehicles coming a mile away.

"Over there!" Brighton called. He walked faster, pointing toward a hut built out over the water and connected by a dock.

They soon clambered onto the dock, their footsteps clipping softly on the water-softened planks. Outside the hut, a hand-painted sign offered boats and other swimming gear. Three boats were tethered nearby. One was the size of a yacht while the other two looked barely seaworthy.

Inside the hut, two dark-skinned islanders—one older, the other in his teens—played cards around a table. The older of the men—the father of the boy, Wörtlich surmised—noticed them first and pushed his chair back, rubbings his hands together.

"We're looking for a boat," Brighton announced.

The man appraised them for a moment. Apparently, they didn't get many tourists here.

"Keone," he said, sticking out his hand. His name, no doubt. *"Vous êtes en vacance?"*

Brighton froze, then turned to Ira and Wörtlich with a hopeful look in his eye. "Either of you speak French?"

Wörtlich stepped forward. *"Un bateau, s'il vous plaît?"* The words came out uncertainly. It had been many years since he'd been forced to speak French.

Keone let out a laugh, his large belly shaking.

"I speak some English," he said in a heavy accent. "I think my English is better than your French!"

"I think you are right," Wörtlich said.

"So, you need a boat," Keone said. "Going snorkeling?"

Wörtlich opened his mouth to reply, but Brighton stepped forward.

"Yes," Brighton said. "Snorkeling."

Wörtlich raised his eyes and smiled at the lie.

Keone said something to his son. The boy jumped up and ran outside.

"I have no other business today," Keone said. "I can take you to the reef, if you like."

"We're actually headed for open water," Ira said, turning to Brighton. "Sherwood, do you have those coordinates?"

Brighton nodded and pulled a folded paper from his pocket. The young man handed it to Keone, who took one look at the numbers and frowned. "This is ten miles offshore."

"Is that a problem?" Wörtlich asked.

"There is no snorkeling ten miles out," Keone said. "The reefs here are like none in the world, but out there it's just—well, water."

"Let us hope not," Wörtlich said, almost under his breath.

Brighton pulled out the money clip and displayed a handful of cash, slapping it down on the table.

Keone stared at the payment for a long time. It was probably more money than he had ever seen.

"What am I going to do with Australian dollars?" the Polynesian man asked.

Brighton looked back at him blankly. "We can give you more, but all we have are dollars."

Keone picked up the bills and counted them one by one in his hands. Finally, he stuffed the cash into the back pocket of his shorts.

"All right," he said. "Boat's at the dock."

The breeze had picked up a little and the boats bobbed up and down, their hulls bumping against the dock. Wörtlich looked over the side and found the water clear as a magnifying glass. Without kneeling to take a closer look, he could make out individual grains of sand and the sharp rocks that jutted out from beneath them.

Keone walked up to the largest boat and pulled it closer to the dock. When it was close enough, he held onto the metal railing and jumped aboard. Ira and Brighton went next.

All aboard, Keone headed up to the steering area and switched on what looked to be a GPS device. He entered Brighton's coordinates, then twisted around without moving his feet. "Are you sure this is where you want to go?"

"Very sure," Ira assured him.

Keone shrugged and started up the engine. After a few moments, he maneuvered them out into the lagoon. "I will need to steer for the channel before we get out into open water. Just relax."

Wörtlich sat on a blue-and-green cushioned seat and stretched his arms over the railing, feeling the sun warm his skin. Ira sat next to him, and Brighton across, though Brighton was staring back toward the island as they left it behind. The young man was lost in his own world, and Wörtlich couldn't blame him. The view was spectacular. Tree-covered ridges rose into rugged hills in the center of the island. The beaches glistened golden under the bright sun.

"If the ocean isn't calm, I will turn back," Keone shouted from steering wheel.

Wörtlich just nodded.

The boat cut through the water as Keone picked up speed. He swung the bow to the west, heading toward a gap in the reef where sand bar islands held ground less than a foot above sea level. Once past the reef, the ocean stretched flat across the horizon. The boat glided over the almost non-existent waves with ease. It was the perfect day for this, Wörtlich thought. If the water had been choppy, going out ten miles would have been almost impossible.

Wörtlich sighed, then checked on Ira. The rabbi's head was tilted back and his chest rose and fell rhythmically. He looked asleep, but Wörtlich knew better.

"I will not let you destroy the Book when we find it," he said softly to Ira. Keone couldn't hear over the sound of the engine and Brighton was still busy taking in the view. "It is too valuable. It would not to be right to destroy it."

Ira's eyes cracked open. "You say that because your only sense of right and wrong is determined by your emotions. You should be more careful. You can't always trust your feelings."

"Nonetheless." Looking back, Wörtlich saw that the island was no more than a thin line on the horizon now. "I'm disappointed Lagati could not be trusted."

"Oh?"

"His intentions were noble, I think. We may have been wrong to run from him so quickly. He could have offered us help."

Ira closed his eyes again. "Nothing I was interested in."

Wörtlich threw Ira a sad look. The man was so entrenched in his beliefs that he couldn't see what was really going on. "Ira, I am beginning to understand how you think, but you are still wrong. You could do much good with the knowledge you possess... but you keep it to yourself. Is that not the epitome of selfishness? If the discovery of the Book allows us to share its knowledge with the world, do we not have an obligation to do so? It is arrogant to assume your ancient traditions are more important than the betterment of humankind."

"It's not arrogance."

Wörtlich grunted. "Then what do you call it?"

The rabbi opened his eyes and swept his gaze over the watery horizon. "Despite what you think, I *am* conflicted. I've spent my entire life studying and meditating on the knowledge that the sacred writings have revealed to me. All those years have led me to what I know now—the true principles of creation and how to operate in them. Man wasn't meant to have that knowledge. At least, not right now."

"But you yourself are a man. Who are you to decide who gets the knowledge and who does not?"

"It's not my decision, Emery." He paused, sitting up straighter. "There's one aspect of this I still haven't told you."

Wörtlich rolled his eyes. *Of course there is.*

"The Watchers, the angels who rebelled against God and started this whole mess, did more than just impregnate human women," Ira said. "The knowledge they brought with them to earth, all their mysterious technology, all the secrets supposedly contained within the Book… none of it was theirs to share. The exact science behind the pyramids, the sonic key that allowed us to pass through the metallic barrier, all of that was stolen. When the Watchers taught it to mankind, that's when everything went wrong. That was their plan. Man wasn't ready for it, just as we aren't ready for it today.

"But even the Watchers didn't grasp the full scope of what they had taken from God. They were just hungry for power, Emery. Just like Raff Lagati—and I assure you, his intentions are no nobler than that. These mysteries he is obsessed with have done nothing but produce suffering throughout the ages. The knowledge in the Book is inherently self-destructive."

Wörtlich absorbed Ira's words, though most of it only made sense if he made the same basic religious assumptions that Ira did. What proof was there that God had anything to do with this? It didn't seem necessary that the Watchers had been angels; they could just as easily have been a civilization that had evolved alongside humans. Or visitors from another world.

"If what you say is true," Wörtlich placed strong emphasis on the word *if*, "why did God create the mystery in the first place?"

"These mysteries are part of the fabric from which the world was made. The things we don't understand are the invisible means that allow us to live in harmony with the earth, enjoying fellowship with each other and the creator. But the Watchers made such a mess of it. People today are making the same mistakes." He took a deep breath, perhaps to gather his jumbled thoughts. "If everyone has access to the most secret principles of creation, our world would become even more selfish and dangerous than it already is. That's why people like me strive to *protect* sacred knowledge, not to *withhold* it. I believe I'm performing a vital service."

Wörtlich puckered his brow and scowled. "It seems to me the selfish part is assuming you are more enlightened than everyone else. That you are the only one capable of using knowledge wisely."

"That's not entirely true, Emery. The abilities I've demonstrated—the truth is that they *are* freely available to everyone. How do you think I learned them? When you learn these principles through relationship with the creator, you can't help but use them out of pure intentions. But intention is everything. What Lagati is doing is intended for self-betterment. He has no interest in the creator at all."

"But why must it all come back to the creator?" Wörtlich said. "You imply that you do not trust my intentions. My intentions are good."

"That isn't for me to judge," Ira said. "I hope you someday come to understand these truths for yourself. You are a gifted man, Emery.

And I believe you're right; your motives are pure."

Wörtlich was about to make a retort when Brighton's voice carried from the bow. "We're at the coordinates."

Keone and Brighton swept their eyes across the empty horizon. Except for the smallest hint of Tubuai behind them, there was nothing.

This cannot be. Max's analysis was correct, I am certain of it. This is where the hieroglyph pointed us. There has to be something here.

Wörtlich's chest fell as he gazed out into the endless blue. "There is nothing here…"

"What were you expecting?" Keone asked.

Brighton looked and sounded just as disheartened as Wörtlich. "I don't know. Something."

"We're going diving," Ira broke in.

All eyes swung to the rabbi in astonishment. Ira kicked off his shoes, walked to the stern, and peered over the railing into the dark depths below.

"Diving?" Keone snorted. "Do you have any idea how deep the ocean is here? It's miles to the bottom."

Ira turned to the Polynesian man. "You have the gear, I presume?"

"Yes." But Keone held his ground. "This is no place for amateur divers. The pressure at the bottom is enough to kill a man."

"We're not going all the way to the bottom." Brighton rolled his eyes. "That would be ridiculous."

The look Ira threw the young man, however, made it clear that Brighton had spoken too soon.

The thing that made Ira so maddening was that he was almost always right, even when he sounded insane.

Wörtlich wanted to side with Keone, but if they left Tubuai empty-handed, there was nowhere else to look. Their search had led them to this spot. He hated to agree with the rabbi, but maybe they had to go down a few meters to check things out. Maybe this part of the ocean wasn't as deep and empty as it looked.

"Very well," Keone finally said. "But I will monitor you the whole time, and you must not go out of sight of the boat. In fact, stay within twenty feet. These waters are dangerous."

Keone disappeared below deck and emerged a few minutes later with a black-skinned dry suit with a pattern of white stripes encompassing the waist. Wörtlich knew he was going to look ridiculous in one of those.

"Have either of you ever dived before?" Brighton asked as Keone went back under, having left the suit in a heap on the boat's deck.

"Yes," Wörtlich said as he sat down to remove his shoes and socks. "Many years ago, I visited the bottom of Alexandria Harbor to see the ruins of the city's old Royal Quarter. But the harbor was shallow, nothing like this."

He looked over the edge of the boat just as a puff of cloud obscured the sun. The blue water turned an ominous shade of dark grey. Under complete cloud cover, he suspected it would have been almost black.

Maybe Keone was right. This was a foolish idea.

"And you, Ira?" Brighton asked.

The rabbi peeled off his pants one leg at a time. "No, never."

Wörtlich's spirits were only slightly lifted to see Brighton's face turn an embarrassing shade of red at seeing the rabbi in his underwear.

Keone's footsteps clanged against the metal rungs of the ladder leading to the lower compartment. He handed a second suit to Brighton, then went back down.

"Sherwood, pass me the suit," Ira said.

Brighton picked up the first suit and handed it over. The young man carefully tilted his head to avoid seeing anything he wasn't ready for.

Ira took the suit from him and inserted one of his legs down the pant leg. Once both legs were in, he removed his t-shirt, revealing a chest covered in wiry grey hairs. Ira rolled the thick rubbery material up over his torso.

Brighton likewise had no difficulty fitting into his, but Wörtlich couldn't shake the feeling he was going to be too large to fit into the third suit. He had gained a lot of weight in recent years, and had never been more self-conscious about it than now.

Fortunately, the third suit was the largest of the bunch. He shuffled off his shorts and stepped into it. Zipping it up, he turned to the others. They looked ridiculous. Brighton's suit was a garish orange. Wörtlich's was mostly red, with blue stripes around the collar.

Why are these suits always designed to be so offensive to the eye?

He supposed it was so that they were easy to spot underwater. But weren't there times when you didn't *want* to be spotted? He glanced back at the calm waters and wondered what kind of predators might lurk in the depths.

The clinging material was not as uncomfortable as it looked, but it left little to the imagination as far as his skin rolls went. The latex seals around the wrists, feet, and neck would make it impossible for water to get inside the suit, but Ira looked particularly silly in it.

The rabbi took a moment to fold up his clothes and settle them down on the bench where they weren't likely to get wet.

Keone dropped three pairs of flippers onto the floor, then pulled open a compartment holding several oxygen tanks.

Once their helmets and tanks were properly connected, Ira, once again leading the pack, ventured onto the ledge at the boat's stern. The ledge was slippery, so they held hold tight to the railing to make sure they didn't accidentally lose their footing and fall in.

"Remember, stay close," Keone warned. "Within twenty feet."

Ira flashed him a thumbs-up.

Brighton leaned toward Ira and said under his breath, "We're not going to stay within twenty feet, are we?"

"Now, we're not." The rabbi's eyes flashed with childlike excitement. "Do you trust me?"

Wörtlich's stomach turned. Feeling nauseous, he closed his eyes and reminded himself of all the other crazy things Ira had been right about.

Just as he opened them again, Brighton and Ira plunged in. Wörtlich waited a moment. Turning off the rational part of his brain, he jumped, slicing through the calm waters feet first.

Though the water was chilly, his body settled into a comfortable temperature right away. It was a strange sensation to be completely submerged and yet bone dry. He oriented himself by spotting the shadow cast by the underside of Keone's boat, then searched for Brighton and Ira.

An orange spot loudly proclaimed Brighton's presence, and Wörtlich said a quiet apology to the designers of the suits he had earlier maligned. Ira floated a little further away, a black spot in otherwise clear water. The rabbi swam fast, away from the boat and deeper into the ocean. He was already well past twenty feet. Resigned, Wörtlich swam after Ira, imagining the curses Keone was probably hurling at them from above.

They plowed against the current, which made the sickly green water smack into his goggles, forming bubbles which rose to the surface. He kicked his feet and pumped his arms until they were sore, trying to keep up with the rabbi.

A dim glimmer caught Wörtlich's attention, and he glanced over to see a soft glow emanating from a point some thirty meters away; it was difficult to gauge distances underwater.

Ira had noticed it, too, and had shifted direction toward it. Wörtlich slowed as he approached the strange glow, taken aback by what he saw.

The light didn't come from the surface, as he had assumed. Instead, it hung suspended in the water with no discernible source. The dancing light played off his goggles, creating a strange three-dimensional effect. He swam around it to study the phenomenon from all sides.

Ira floated beside him, kicking his feet casually. The moment Ira arrived, the light brightened and intensified. Its pulsating dance quickened, a haunting glow twisting into strange columns of light which pierced the depths below. Wörtlich desperately wanted to ask Ira what it was, for the rabbi did not seem especially perturbed. As usual. But he knew what Ira's maddening answer would be: *"It's not a matter of having foreknowledge, Doctor; it's a matter of expectation."*

Brighton joined them, and the three men encircled the light, forming a triangle. Ira reached his gloved hand out toward the phenomenon and Wörtlich decided to do the same. The dancing light, becoming brighter still, caressed his fingers and grew stronger as he touched it.

Within the pirouetting light, a degree of order began to emerge. Fascinated, Wörtlich drifted closer and was surprised to see recognizable shapes and patterns arising. Three horizontal lines became apparent, each of them tugging at his memory.

The hieroglyph!

He pulled his hand back and made a frantic gesture to Ira, but as usual Ira was a step ahead, having already recognized the significance of the image. The rabbi's wrist vanished into the heart of the seeming hologram. He didn't seem the least bit troubled by this.

Though Wörtlich had no idea what the appearance of the hieroglyph meant, he felt a rush of relief knowing they hadn't made a mistake. Without a doubt, they had come to the right spot.

The hieroglyph wavered and a tiny current rippled through it. The ripple started as a meandering stream of white curling lazily up through the hologram.

When Wörtlich looked down, he realized the stream came not from the hologram, but from the depths. A thin column of air pushed upward, spawning tiny bubbles.

Before he could absorb the implications of this effect, he was forced to jerk his head to the side as a flash of light struck him. Squeezing his eyes shut, he waited to see if the light would abate.

When he peeked, the light was stronger than ever, and he kicked his feet to put some distance between it and himself.

The water churned, and what had moments ago been calm seas transformed into a chaotic surge. Wörtlich kicked hard, fighting the current with everything he had, but he couldn't escape its pull.

He tried to catch a glimpse of Brighton or Ira, but saw neither, and he wondered what had become of them.

He twisted his body, a burst of pressure hitting him square in the chest and violently wrenching him backward.

Tiny streams of water snaked their way down his arms and neck, and he realized the pressure of the current was too strong for his dry suit.

Wörtlich panicked as memories of drowning flooded through him. He struggled to breathe and his arms peddled madly, but he made no progress. Something below pulled him inexorably. The stream of bubbles had widened now, and the water swirled around him like a drain.

It is a whirlpool, he realized.

Terror inundated his every thought. The water seemed to explode around him.

Knowing death was near, he closed his eyes and prayed to Ira's God. Then he relaxed and let the current carry him away.

The pressure was so strong that, though he struggled to remain conscious, he had difficulty focusing. A crack formed on the front of his goggles and water broke through. As the salty taste hit his lips, he blacked out, his body thrown like a ragdoll through the maelstrom.

His last thought was regret that he wouldn't see Elisabeth again.

TWENTY-NINE

The Pacific Floor
SEPTEMBER 29

Brighton's head pounded as light seared through his eyelids. He let out a muffled scream and snapped his eyes open to find that it had been a dream. Had it come from Barakel again?

The water had poured in from all directions at once. There had been no end to it. The current had swept him away.

He tried to move, but his muscles howled in pain, so he lay still. It was worse than any hangover he could remember.

Sleep claimed him. He didn't know how long he dozed, but he awakened intermittently, too tired to move again.

When he awoke for the fourth or fifth time—he lost count—his head lay on a mound of rich, black earth. He coughed, and some of that earth spewed out. He brought an arm up to wipe the dry soil from his face and found it caked to his cheeks. His arm didn't hurt so badly now, and with that realization he propped himself up on his elbows.

Groggy, he looked around and saw that he was surrounded by a dim light that glowed from above. He perceived the gentle curvature of an invisible barrier rising up from somewhere behind him.

It wasn't a dream.

With a start, memory of the whirlpool came back to him and he coughed again, as though to expel water. But his throat was dry. In the same moment, he realized he had lost his helmet and breathing apparatus, and his feet were bare. He groped behind his shoulders and found the breathing tube, snapped in half—who knew where the oxygen tank had gone to.

He ventured a glance behind him, then scrambled back in alarm. The dome met the ground just inches from where his head had lain, and beyond waited only murky blackness.

Where am I? The ocean floor?

Brighton sat up the rest of the way. He had fallen into a shallow depression in the ground. He got to his feet, stumbling under his own weight, then doubled over and threw up, heaving the contents of his stomach into that dark, loamy soil. He wiped spittle off his face and straightened. His muscles continued their protest, but he tried his best to ignore them and assess his situation.

He staggered up the side of the depression, taking a sudden intake of air as he laid eyes on the most incredible sight yet.

An enormous stone pyramid rose beneath the dome's center, its four sheer walls covered by a smooth and perfectly preserved encasement of white limestone upon which played dancing reflections of eerie light. Atop the pyramid rested a golden capstone.

His mouth hanging open, Brighton walked closer, trying to calculate its size. It was about the same dimensions as the Great Pyramid of Giza, he thought; perhaps precisely the same.

"Ira, are you there?" Wörtlich shouted from somewhere off to his left.

Brighton's heart leaped, and he turned from the pyramid to walk toward the voice.

"Ira!" he heard again. And then, "Mr. Brighton?"

Wörtlich was shuffling across the uneven terrain, holding one of his elbows tightly as though it had been injured.

Brighton quickened his pace. He soon broke into a jog, despite the pain he felt every time his foot slammed into the ground. At least the ground was soft. "Emery! Over here!"

A relieved smile broke out across Wörtlich's face. Seeing the archaeologist smile so broadly was strange, a side of his personality he rarely showed.

"Mr. Brighton, I cannot tell you how good it is to see you. I thought I had drowned."

Brighton rubbed the back of his neck, working a kink that had developed there.

"I don't think I've ever been this sore," Brighton admitted. "How did we survive the fall?"

He looked up again at the dome and calculated the distance from its apex to the bottom. Two thousand feet or more. His head swam, thinking of the miles of ocean pressing down on them. Why didn't they feel the pressure?

Wörtlich's gaze was stolen by the pyramid. His feet moved toward the pyramid almost of their own volition. "What is *that* doing here?"

As they neared it, Brighton made out a tall spire just ahead, like the tip of a long sword, if the hilt had been buried deep underground. It even shone like steel.

"Gentlemen, we have arrived!" Ira's voice called.

Ira appeared from behind the spire. He circled its base, closely studying the hieroglyphics scrawled upon its surface. He still had his dry suit's helmet in hand.

"Doctor," Ira said, "perhaps you should take a look at this."

Wörtlich stepped up to the spire and surveyed the inscriptions. "It is an obelisk. It seems to mark the entrance."

The archaeologist paused, coming around the corner of the spire. Right at his eye level was the "equal and opposite" hieroglyph they had seen in the surface waters. It stood apart from the rest of the writing, given special significance.

But Brighton's attention had caught something else, something stranger, lurking in the dim light. Between the spire and the pyramid sat what looked to be a massive boulder.

That's no boulder, Brighton mused as he walked closer. And indeed, it was not.

A giant's skull lay half-buried in the black dirt. Brighton knelt and stared straight into the dark, sightless holes of the skull's ocular cavities.

A chill passed through him.

"This comes from Antarctica," he called over his shoulder. "From the bone field."

"How can you be sure?" Wörtlich asked.

Brighton turned to look at the two men. "Remember what Poulson said about the skull being missing? This can't be a coincidence."

"In that case, perhaps it is a marker, a confirmation that this pyramid was built by the same people who built the Antarctic ice dome."

Wörtlich's gaze rose to meet the pyramid, apprehension and exhilaration evident in his eyes. "These were the pyramid builders. I never thought I would see such a place."

Ira put his hand against the inscriptions carved into the spire. "Can you read this, Doctor?"

Wörtlich turned back to the inscriptions, but he was clearly struggling to understand them. "I think it says that this place is—a gateway. Or perhaps a refuge. Yes, a refuge."

Ira nodded as though that made all the sense in the world. "The Watchers built this, a refuge from the Flood. You see how this dome holds the water at bay?"

"You are most likely right," Wörtlich admitted. The words sounded forced. "This ancient civilization, these Watchers, went out of their way to leave a trail."

Brighton peered back into those sightless eyes. "To lead us to the Book of Creation, as Lagati hoped."

Ira left the obelisk and approached the pyramid's entrance. The entrance itself was square, but there was no source of light inside that he could see. Brighton shuddered at the thought of marching through that entrance to face whatever waited for them.

"The Book is here," Ira said without slowing down. "The Book and all its amassed knowledge."

Brighton caught up with him. "Everything?"

"Everything they stole from God. They brought it here."

"I honestly never imagined we would find it," Wörtlich said, joining them in their march.

"Whatever we find here belongs to God," Ira reminded them. "Not to us."

"Do not get ahead of yourself," Wörtlich said, speeding up. He arrived at the entrance first and rested his palms against the limestone edifice. "There was once a limestone casing around the Giza pyramids, too, but it eroded over time. It is beautiful to see it so well-preserved."

Ira lifted his helmet and pointed its lamp into the darkness.

Wörtlich then walked in, the other two following close behind.

This pyramid's passage stood in marked contrast to the one at Giza. The space was clean and there was very little dust in the air. Glowing rocks, such as they had seen before, illuminated the way.

"We are in the descending passage," Wörtlich noted. "If the layout proves to be the same, the ascending passage should branch out in a few meters."

True to his prediction, an upward sloping passage soon appeared. To the left, the path continued downward, perhaps to a subterranean chamber. The upward passage curved up and to the right. A bright light shone from above. If that wasn't a beacon telling them which way to go—

"I think we had best go up," Ira said.

"Up it is," Wörtlich agreed and led the way.

The slope was steep for the first few feet, so Brighton had to push his center of gravity forward to avoid falling back. Unlike the Giza pyramid, there were no handrails to aid the progress of tourists.

Before long, the low-ceilinged passage gave way to a towering chamber. Brighton paused before continuing.

"This is the grand gallery," Wörtlich said, his voice echoing in the cavernous space.

Looking up, Brighton discovered the source of light: glowing slabs of rock built into the ceiling. The effect was similar to recessed lighting in modern structures. The light bathed the walls, which looked rough but felt smooth when he put his hands to them.

The incline of the passage then became much steeper. At one

point, he lowered his arms to grab the grooved stone floor in front of him, crawling. A fall from here would prove fatal.

But so should tumbling to the bottom of the ocean, he reminded himself. The thought didn't tempt him to walk any less carefully.

At the top of the gallery stood a broad stone arch, held up by two thick columns that extended down beyond the slab of rock which served as a landing between them.

Wörtlich was the first to reach the platform. Winded from the climb, he took a moment to lean against one of those columns. His chest rose and fell as he took deep breaths, recovering from the exertion.

Brighton didn't feel out of breath in the least. He had been feeling progressively more able-bodied ever since awakening.

He was about to clamber up onto the landing when the stone beneath began to vibrate lightly. He gripped the rock on either side and held himself in place.

Wörtlich turned to look into the dark depths beyond the stone arch. Ira, too, froze on the landing, listening to the vibration.

Brighton looked up at Ira. "What is that?"

Ira shook his head. "I don't know."

As they waited and listened, the vibration changed to that of a deeper sound. Alarm sped through Brighton as he realized it was more than just a sound: it was a groan.

A voice, impossibly deep, grave, and heavy with age, filled the chamber, resonating as the tones lengthened and reflected off the stone walls.

He had heard a voice like that before.

Picking out a scuffling noise, Brighton turned in time to watch Wörtlich and Ira disappear through the arch.

*   *   *

With heavy feet and an even heavier heart, Ira crossed the threshold into the chamber. He knew the Egyptian counterpart was known as the King's Chamber. Scholars believed that an ancient pharaoh had been laid to rest there, though the real meaning of the pyramid transcended an ancient burial practice.

This King's Chamber truly lived up to its name. Ira knew he would find more than an empty sarcophagus inside; this chamber held a living king.

The low voice filled the room, and as he listened he detected the subtle nuances of speech, though in an ancient and long-forgotten language. As he waited, standing absolutely still, the voice quieted and went out—like a candle's flame being extinguished.

In place of a sarcophagus sat a long wooden table, and in its center lay a gleaming scroll, bathed in golden light.

Ira's breath caught, and for the first time he was truly surprised. Despite the long journey to this place, he had never entirely prepared himself for the moment when he stood in front of the scroll and looked upon it. He had glimpsed it in dreams, yes, but this experience was so much more profound.

Wörtlich stood before it. All Ira could see was the archaeologist's back, but the temperament of his posture was unmistakable. He was terrified, frozen to the spot. Ira doubted Wörtlich could move, yet it was no physical force holding him back; just like the feelings that unexpectedly rose within himself, Wörtlich's prison was emotional. For a man who didn't subscribe to the notion of holy ground, Wörtlich was now experiencing the phenomenon for himself, and that experience obviously left him troubled and confused. What they were looking at had never been intended for human sight.

"Is that the Book?" Wörtlich asked, perhaps feeling genuine reverence for the first time in his life. The glow suffused him, casting him in silhouette. His shoulders were clenched, his neck rigid.

Ira forced himself to move forward, even though all his instincts screamed to flee. He took slow, measured steps, his bare feet clipping on the huge stone blocks below. The stone felt cool, sending shivers up through his core.

Remembering Wörtlich's question, Ira swallowed and then opened his mouth. His dry lips cracked from the effort.

"Yes," he whispered.

Ira continued his approach until he stood next to Wörtlich. He was taken aback to see a single tear sliding down Wörtlich's cheek. The man was locked in turmoil, his eyes moving rapidly across the open parchment. Was he reading? Could he understand?

Wörtlich brought a hand up to hover over the golden parchment. The hand shook. Whether it was nerves or some external force, Ira couldn't say. Ira had to admit he didn't have the answers. His experiences left him ill-equipped to make sense of something as profound as beholding the Book in person.

"Look at this writing," Wörtlich breathed. "From the hand of God Himself." The archaeologist's tone held no question.

For the first time, Ira saw clarity in the man's eyes. Only conviction. In this moment, Wörtlich was a believer. He could no longer deny the power and presence of the document before him.

"Ira, can you read it?" Wörtlich asked.

Ira could not step any closer.

"I cannot," Ira said, every syllable a struggle. He blinked, fighting tears that threatened to roll down his own cheeks. Emotion tore through him, building until his skin felt as if it would burst. Yet he could not look away.

Ira clenched his jaw. "I must not."

The sound of pebbles skittering across stone broke Ira free of his stupor, and he twisted his body to peer into the darkness behind him.

Brighton stood in the dim light under the stone arch. The young man's eyes stared into the room's darkest recesses.

Ira's heart lurched.

A living king...

Only the dimmest light penetrated this far, but Ira narrowed his eyes and focused. He dared not approach; he knew the danger lurking in those depths. His heart had dreaded it, his mind had doubted it, and now the voice confirmed it.

As his gaze crept along a crack in the stone floor, he came to what was unmistakably a plank of wood standing upright—a thick leg, a chair leg—

Every muscle tensed. Terror clutched his heart and squeezed until he was left breathless. Aaron had not prepared him for this.

Ira's eyes traveled up the wooden leg, until its outline was obscured by an even deeper darkness. He nearly jumped out of his skin when the darkness shifted, moving like heavy fabric. He made out the bottom of a cloak, and as he delineated its contours another mass of darkness emerged. Another leg, but this one wasn't made from wood. It was flesh.

Behind him Wörtlich moved ever so slightly, changing the shape of the shadows and allowing Ira to fill in a few more details of the lumbering form.

Indeed, the creature was alive. Its ancient, defiant face remained in shadow, eclipsed by the shade of its black hood, immense beyond description. Massive hands, the skin cracked in a hundred places and stretched tautly over exposed bone, clasped to the arms of the chair. Those hands had gripped those arms for an eternity, the frail fingers all but fused to the ridged grain of the wood. Deep trenches interrupted its surface.

The floor vibrated, slowly at first, but as the sound increased in volume so did the frequency. The resonant, deliberate syllables filled Ira's ears. Those words, whatever language they belonged to, sounded black and terrible. Except, the more of it he heard, the less foreign and impenetrable the words became. As the cloak stirred, the head inside it turning to observe them, those words began to make a kind of sense—

"You..."

The single word carried incomprehensible weight, a pregnant pause following it like the plodding of an elephant's step, and yet there was also a sense of verbal agility that conveyed the minutiae of ancient poetry, the raw and powerful emotion of which still resonated independent of literal translation.

The light of the parchment caught the creature's huge, cadaverous eyes. The leathery skin around them was thick and morose, a terrifying combination of beast and old man. Those gray eyes expressed sorrow and confusion, and behind them was an ache—an agony—that was impossible to express in words.

"You... have... come."

Ira remained paralyzed. Did the others also understand the language, or was it just him? He managed to glimpse Brighton, who seemed just as transfixed. The young man didn't so much as blink. Wörtlich, meanwhile, had managed to turn his body sluggishly to the side, though the battle for his attention waged on between the creature and the parchment.

"Who are you?" Ira managed after several long minutes had passed.

The weight of sadness behind the creature's eyes changed to reflect the barest glimmer of hope.

"Who... am... I...?"

Those giant eyes shifted slowly until they focused on Ira. A shiver ran up his spine as he made eye contact with this beast, this animal, this creature.

"I am..." The tone was softer than Ira had expected. "My... name... is Mahaway—"

Both Brighton and Wörtlich's eyes flared in recognition. This was the giant from the dream, from the stone room. This was the son of Barakel.

Ira tried to contain the recognition as Mahaway stared at him, those giant eyes seeming too tired to ever move again. Were they actually looking at him, or merely resting in his direction? No, he was being watched. The tingling in his arms and legs was mistakable.

"You... are... the scribe?"

Silence echoed long after the vibrations ceased. Ira found himself speechless, considering the enormity of what they were facing—both physically and spiritually.

"The scribe from the dream?" Wörtlich asked.

"He means Enoch," Brighton answered.

The giant ignored them, continuing its interminable stare at Ira. "You..."

"We have come for the Book," Ira said. He worked his fingers, trying to move them, trying to make any part of his body move. The strange paralysis persisted.

"Yes... It is... for... the scribe... when he... returns."

By sheer force of will, one of his fingers finally twitched.

"I don't understand," he told the creature. You have been saving the Book for Enoch, the scribe?"

"You must... **return**... it. In... exchange."

"In exchange for what?"

A long gasp escaped Mahaway's throat, subsiding into the stale air. *"Rest... it... u... tion."*

"Restitution," Wörtlich said. "What is he talking about?"

Ira continued to work his fingers. Two fingers. Three. "I do not know."

The giant moved again, its entire body swaying in the darkness, its skin and bones creaking with age.

"By... the blood... of your... Messiah."

Ira moved his hand at the wrist, working on the forearm. He gritted his teeth as feeling crept back up his arms, freeing him from whatever spell he was under.

"Yes, the Hebrew Messiah," Wörtlich whispered, his voice tinged with excitement. "It explains the reference to the Son of Man in the Hall of Records—"

Ira's heart sank as he began to understand, but his mind raced as it considered Mahaway's words. Mahaway had been here for millennia, conserving himself, saving himself, waiting—Ira felt crushing sadness as the enormity of the giant's task struck him. Barakel had sent his son to make amends, to make restitution, to pass along a message of penitence and regret. It explained the hope in the giant's voice.

False hope, Ira thought, his heart breaking for the creature.

The rabbi narrowed his eyes as feeling reached his shoulder and spread through his torso. "You are waiting for—" Still, he could not believe it. "—for forgiveness?"

At the word *forgiveness,* the hope in Mahaway's ancient, tired eyes intensified.

"Then it... is... true. There... is... restitution..."

"No," Ira sighed, regretting the answer but knowing the truth of it. "We are only here to retrieve the Book."

Mahaway's black cloak fell back down its cracked, exposed arm as it lifted his hand and extended a wavering finger. The finger pointed toward the parchment.

"Take... it. It... is... yours. Return... it... to the Most... High—"

Ira felt a wave of sympathy, but that sympathy was stained with revulsion. "Why have you waited so long?"

"I am... to remain... guard..." A heavy breath. *"My father... sent word... that... the Most High... had... sought... to restore... us..."*

"There can be no restitution," Ira said tightly, his paralysis fading. "You were told in no uncertain terms—"

"But... in the... fullness... of time..." The creature groaned, the sound reverberating off the walls cacophonously. *"And... in anticipation... of the scribe... I... have... waited..."*

Ira looked down. "You have waited for nothing."

"No..."

"You have waited for *nothing*."

Mahaway's eyes flashed with anger, the hope gone. Something inside the creature snapped, and the echoing voice changed, now coming down with the force of a hammer's blow.

*"I—have—waited—for—an **eternity!**"* it bellowed.

Ira backed away. Brighton also seemed to have regained his powers of movement, though Wörtlich remained in place, his eyes still pouring over the parchment eagerly, soaking up the knowledge they found there.

The planks of the wooden chair creaked, and some snapped clean as, with surprising quickness, the giant stood, its massive feet grinding into the stone blocks.

"You—are not—the—scribe!"

Towering at its full height, the King's Chamber could hardly contain the monster. Its black cloak fell away to reveal Mahaway's bare chest, stretched and exposed. The ribs, longer than any one of the three men's legs, occasionally ripped free of the chest and stuck out. Severe gold bracelets accented each wrist, the metal fused with flesh, and on those bracelets were blackened ankhs.

How had the creature remained alive so long? Its burst of energy seemed impossible—

Jehovah, protect me. Jehovah, protect me. Jehovah, protect me...

Ira stood his ground. "The scribe has come once and will never come again. The Most High's decree cannot be altered. The Messiah, his sacrifice, is not for you."

The giant produced a staff, also topped with an ankh, and swung it, its tip whistling through the air and missing Ira's throat by inches.

*"Then—the Book—is—**not—for—you!**"*

Wörtlich leapt into motion, rolling the parchment up.

"Leave—it!" The giant brandished its staff at Wörtlich.

"Emery, put it down!" Ira shouted.

But Wörtlich continued to roll the parchment, moving as fast as he could as the giant's body surged forward and took a step—then another—

"Emery!"

*   *   *

You don't have to believe something exists to find it, Lagati had said. How right he had been, Wörtlich mused, his fingers worked furiously at the glowing parchment. The table—the floor!—shook as the creature approached.

"Emery, run!"

The voice shouted at him, but his mind blocked it out. *The Book must be saved... it must!*

The thought consumed him.

"It—is—not—for you!"

As the giant raged, Wörtlich snatched up the complete scroll with both arms. Its weight nearly made his knees buckle, but he forced himself to dive just as the giant's staff crashed into the table, reducing it to splinters.

Wörtlich ran full tilt toward the stone arch, his legs moving by instinct. He would not look back, *could* not look—

He paused on the stone landing, only for a moment, catching his breath as he surveyed the grand gallery. Ira and Brighton were already halfway to the bottom.

The stone shook violently beneath him as the giant propelled itself into the archway. Stone shattered as though made of glass, rocks exploding outward, ripping through Wörtlich's clothes and lancing into his back.

Wörtlich didn't have time to register the pain. He threw himself down the incline, barely managing to keep his feet.

"Have you—not—brought enough—destruction!"

He would not look. *He could not.*

The giant's speech devolved into grunts and groans, the words once again unintelligible.

Somewhere above, he heard the sound of stone shattering, and a block of the ceiling broke free, smashing into the floor right beside him. He clutched the Book tight to his chest, closed his eyes to keep the debris from getting beneath his eyelids and burning.

He took another step, and this time his right foot met open air.

He plummeted, then hit something hard and unyielding. He heard rather than felt the snapping of bones all the way from his shoulder to his waist.

Wörtlich let loose a howl as the pain finally registered. For an instant, it was so unbearable that he didn't think he'd ever be able to move again. His chest ached with every breath. He didn't want to know how many ribs he'd broken in the fall. Perhaps all of them.

He cleared dust and grime from his eyes and oriented himself. He was stretched across a narrow ledge jutting out from a deep chasm that had formed down the center of the grand gallery.

"Emery!" Brighton wailed.

He looked up to see Brighton. The fall had only been about ten feet. The young man had gotten down on his stomach and stretched his hand as far as it would reach, his fingers flexing and grasping nothing but air. The distance was too great.

The stone Wörtlich clung to heaved beneath him, sending shoots of pain through his chest. His arms still hung onto the Book.

"I will not let go," he whispered through gritted teeth.

An enormous cracking sound echoed through the gallery again as boulders rained down, sheering the floor in front of him, widening the chasm.

"Jump, Emery!"

Wörtlich struggled to his knees, balancing himself to keep from falling forward into the abyss. "It is too far!"

Brighton scooted forward dangerously as another storm of rock came down on them. When the dust cleared, Wörtlich saw Brighton had pulled back to keep from losing an arm to a huge stone block that had crashed just to the left of him.

I am going to die, Wörtlich realized as the entire pyramid shook. It was only a matter of moments before the entire ledge would give way.

He looked down at the Book and groaned, realizing the time he had spent lusting after it would end up going to waste.

What a waste…

His heart skipped a beat.

Elisabeth.

Tears slipped down his cheek. He choked on a breath as the tension went out of his body. "Elisabeth, I should have told you sooner—"

He was cut off by another round of quaking.

The stone thrust him up, and he sailed briefly through the air before colliding with another rock, this one with a jagged point that sunk into his gut. He screamed as the rock sliced deep into his bowels. He also lost his hold on the Book.

Elisabeth must have this!

He looked up to where Brighton still reached for him, vainly.

"Take the Book!" Wörtlich cried over the sound of rock grinding into itself. "Take it!"

Wörtlich hesitated only a moment, then used the last of his energy to thrust his arms and heave the golden parchment up into the air. His breath caught as he watched it float over the chasm, praying it wouldn't fall into the depths.

He slumped backward when he saw Brighton's hand reach out a little further than seemed possible and snatch it out of the air. The young man reeled it in.

"Emery, there's no time!"

Blood covered Wörtlich's lips. It tasted like copper, coming up in a stream that threatened to choke off his air supply. He spat it out.

"Go," he managed. His chest throbbed from the effort of speaking. "Go."

As rivers of blood pumped out of his gut, splattering onto the rock and draining into the darkness below, a smile came to his lips. His broken body sagged as he remembered Elisabeth. He pictured her long brown curls, those penetrating green eyes, the softness of her skin, the taste of her lips…

Remembering, remembering everything, he smiled as a rain of stone and fury came down on his head.

*   *   *

"Don't look back!" Ira shouted as they raced to the bottom of the gallery, outrunning the deafening roar of stone caving in on itself.

Brighton blinked back tears and ducked to fit through the ascending passageway. The floor shivered beneath his feet and he wondered how long it would be before it, too, gave out.

It has to hold, he told himself. *We're almost free.*

But the truth was, it didn't have to. It hadn't for Wörtlich. Tears stung the back of his eyes, but he kept running. He kept his eyes trained on Ira's back and held the Book firm to his chest.

He momentarily lost sight of Ira as they reached the descending passageway, and in his haste he missed the extra step, tripped, and stumbled face first. He pushed himself onto his knees, feeling Ira tug at his shoulders.

"Hurry!" Ira insisted. "We haven't much time."

Brighton didn't need to be told twice. He got up, almost falling again as the floor rocked beneath him. He latched onto the wall to stabilize himself, then scurried as fast as possible up the incline.

The Book! You dropped the Book!

Without thinking, he turned around and crawled on his hands and knees, his hands splaying out on the ground in front of him, frantically searching. It had to be there. It couldn't have rolled away—

His fingers grasped the edge of the parchment and he snatched it up. He got back to his feet just as a roar told him that debris was pouring out of the gallery; he gritted his teeth and scurried faster.

A minute later, he launched himself out of the pyramid's square entrance.

"Keep running!" Ira called. "Get a safe distance!"

Brighton's feet had a life of their own as they propelled his body away. He almost crashed into the back of the giant skull, only managing to navigate around it at the last moment.

Once he felt he had achieved a safe distance, he stopped and fell to the ground. Even the ground shook. His head shot back toward the pyramid, and for the first time he witnessed the magnitude of what they had barely escaped.

The limestone exterior was cracked in a hundred places, those cracks spreading outward like a spider's web. In places, entire sections of rock had fallen inward, creating gaping holes. The entire pyramid shifted on its base as the ground beneath sunk a few feet. One of the corners of the pyramid collapsed, breaking free and sending an avalanche of rock tumbling down. Even the golden capstone dislodged, devoured by the maelstrom of stone.

"Wörtlich is still in there," Brighton gasped.

Ira leaned over next to him and watched the crumbling pyramid. "I'm afraid there's nothing we can do for him now."

Brighton sat up, pulling his legs toward his chest and holding them at the ankles. The Book lay on the ground between them. "That chasm is growing larger. We have to get out of here!"

"I know. Just relax and focus."

Relax and focus? Wörtlich is dead, damn you!

Ira's eyes briefly touched the Book, but then darted away just as quickly. He focused instead on Brighton. "Stand up."

Before Brighton could get a word in, the rabbi hurried back toward the pyramid. Brighton was about to stop him when he realized the rabbi's destination was the spire. He forced himself up and limped after Ira, once again marveling at the elder man's stamina.

Ira stopped at the spire, looking straight into the "equal and opposite" hieroglyph. He closed his eyes and brought up his hand, resting the palm on the symbol. At first nothing happened, but then the ground rumbled. The quake wasn't as strong as the one they'd felt inside the pyramid; this was more localized.

Ira was whispering to himself. Brighton tried to make out the words, but they were lost in the crashing din.

The dome around them rippled, and Brighton once again panicked. "Look at the dome! Something's happening to the dome!"

Ira ignored him, his eyes shut tight and his lips moving.

The ripple effect was strongest where the dome touched the ocean floor, and in places it looked like water was trickling in. And that trickle quickly became a deluge.

"Ira! The dome is collapsing!"

Ira's eyes snapped wide and he reached out and grabbed Brighton's hand. "Don't worry. Everything is going to be all right."

Was there a hint of doubt in that ordinarily calm voice?

A wave of water crashed through the dome, rushing inward with bone-crushing pressure. With it, further rifts appeared all over the dome, which now looked as cracked and beaten as the pyramid it housed.

Water swept in around their feet, and both men struggled to maintain their footing.

"Ira, we're going to drown!"

The rabbi gripped his hand tighter. "No."

"The Book will be destroyed!"

"So be it."

The water crashed and frothed, and in a moment it drove them off the ground. The splashing water washed over Brighton's face, salt stinging his eyes. He cried out as the water swirled around the spire, pulling them along in a circular current.

Another whirlpool, he thought as his body was thrust upward.

He stole a glimpse back toward the pyramid and realized they were already sweeping up past its highest point. He watched as the last of the walls crumbled inward, the rising dust consumed by the surging water's insatiable thirst.

Abruptly, the dome vanished, and he found himself surrounded by a rushing column of water, pulling him, prying loose his grip on Ira's hand. He clenched his fingers, but the current was too strong. Ira's hand was snatched away and the rabbi was gone.

And then, so was the Book.

THIRTY

Tubuai, French Polynesia
SEPTEMBER 30

The surf rolled up the beach, creeping closer. Ira sat with his back against the trunk of a palm tree. The tree grew out of the sand at a forty-five degree slant, angling out toward the water. Waves crashed against the reef in the distance and warm, sunbaked sand slipped between the fingers of his left hand.

"I booked my flight, like you told me."

Ira squinted up as Brighton, dressed in a blue polo shirt and khaki pants, walked up the beach. Brighton lowered himself to the ground.

"Where will you go?" Ira asked.

"I want to try going stateside. It'll be difficult without getting flagged, but I imagine there are a lot of people wondering what happened to me."

Ira nodded. "Like Rachel."

"Did I tell you about her?"

Ira shrugged and looked away. "You should make sure she's safe. Lagati will probably come after you."

"What about you?"

"I'll be hard to find."

Brighton narrowed his eyes, but didn't inquire further. It was just as well. The young man was on the right path now, but he wouldn't understand what had to happen next.

The fingers of Ira's right hand felt the contours of parchment, and he looked down at the Book of Creation, the scroll lying on the sand, its glow still present but diffused by the strength of the sun. He shifted his legs so that Brighton could see it.

Brighton gasped. "Where did you find it?"

"It must have washed up on the beach."

"How did it survive?"

Ira took a deep breath of fresh island air. "It's timeless. I'm not sure it can be destroyed."

"What are you going to do with it?"

Ira was surprised at the lack of defensiveness in Brighton's voice. The young man didn't share the same anxiety Emery had demonstrated regarding Ira's plans.

"I had intended to destroy it. But you know what they say about the best laid plans." Ira smiled. "Where I'm going, no one will ever find it."

Brighton cocked his head. "Where did you say you were going?"

Ira chuckled to himself. He picked up the scroll and placed it securely in his lap. "Mahaway was right about one thing, Sherwood. The Book should be returned, and that job falls to me now."

"But return it to whom?"

Amusement crossed Ira's face. "You ask all these questions even knowing I can't answer them."

Brighton's cheeks reddened.

"Don't be embarrassed," Ira said. "I find it... endearing."

A long beat passed, the only sound that of the waves washing in and out, a sonic seesaw that threatened to lull Ira to sleep. He looked forward to the long rest awaiting him. He had earned it.

"Ira, I want to continue searching," Brighton said, breaking the silence. "Even though we found what we were looking for, I'm only beginning to uncover what it all means."

Ira leaned his head back. "I have faith that you can make the right choices."

"Ira, I don't even know what it means to do that."

"Yes, you do. You underestimate yourself."

From the corner of his eye, he saw Brighton stealing subtle glances at the Book. A lingering question still hung between them.

"How can I contact you once I leave here?" Brighton asked.

"Not by any traditional means. I don't exactly know where I'm going. I've never been there before."

Brighton furrowed his brow, clearly finding that answer unsettling.

"But don't worry," Ira reassured him. "We'll find a way."

*　　*　　*

Brighton walked out of the motel, carrying his bag. Wind rustled his hair as he and Ira waited for the truck to take him to the airfield.

Ira had said very little since they returned from the beach earlier that morning. He'd mentioned how tired he was, but when Brighton woke from a nap two hours later, Ira was sitting just where he had left him—on the floor, leaning against the bedframe. Ira was waiting for something, though Brighton couldn't put his finger on what it was.

"There's something troubling you," Brighton said.

Ira met his gaze with that maddening smile he'd been sporting ever since Keone rescued them from the water and ferried them back to shore. At the time, Brighton had thought the smile inappropriate, considering Wörtlich's death. But he realized now that Ira's contentment stemmed from something deeper than his circumstances. Though Ira had always maintained his calm, something about him had changed. His sense of well-being seemed almost transcendent.

"I suppose there is something," Ira said. The rabbi looked up and down the road, seeing no one. "There's still something missing."

"Missing?"

"Yes. I don't know what it is, but—" He broke off, his eyes drifting across the horizon. All Brighton saw was the ocean, but Ira seemed as though he saw something more. "Everything I have come to understand, everything we've seen together, confirms the truth I have always known. Everything seems complete, seems whole..." The smile slid away and was replaced by thoughtful sobriety. "But the knowledge isn't enough."

Brighton frowned. "Haven't you always said that?"

"Yes," Ira admitted, "but on some level, I never experienced it. I experience it now. There is loneliness, emptiness... dissatisfaction that I didn't anticipate."

"Of course. To know what we know and not be able to share it."

"No, it's more than that. I feel—empty. Exhaustion has replaced enthusiasm, and I don't understand why." The rabbi recovered himself and cracked that smile again. "Maybe it should be comforting, no? That there are still new things to discover in the world? Things to discover about ourselves?"

Brighton shifted from one foot to the other. "Ira..."

"Yes?"

He looked into Ira's eyes. "Where did they go?"

"Excuse me?"

"The Watchers, the fallen angels you told us about. Their children, the giants, may have all died by now, but—but where did the angels themselves go? Surely they don't die like the rest of us."

"Once more with the questions," Ira said with a lilt in his voice.

"You're holding back. I recognize the expression now. You know something."

Ira lowered his eyes to study the grass. "Sherwood, I must ask you to drop this question. Answering it will never bring you peace."

"Ira, if they're still out there, they could pose a threat. I have to know."

"No. No, you don't."

The sound of a coughing engine stole Brighton's attention. He looked up in time to see the airport truck rumbling up the motorway.

He looked back to Ira, knowing this would be his last chance in a while to speak his mind. He dug deep to find the right words, not knowing how long it would be before they saw each other again. Words failed him.

"Ira, I don't have the words to express the affection I feel for you."

The rabbi beamed, and Brighton could tell the older man was profoundly moved. Ira reached out his hand and took Brighton's in his. He took a step in and gave Brighton a hug, holding him tight.

After a moment, Ira pulled away, patting him on the back a few times.

The truck pulled up next to them and the driver got out.

"It's time for you to go," Ira said.

Brighton picked up his bag and crawled into the passenger seat. Before the driver started on his way, Brighton turned and gave Ira one last hug.

"I'll see you again," Brighton said. "Soon, I hope."

Brighton wasn't sure if it was true, but so long as he kept telling himself that, the pain of parting didn't sting as badly.

"*Vite, vite!*" the driver called, slinging himself back into his set. He honked the horn, then gestured at Ira. "You coming?"

"Oh, no. I'm still waiting for my ride."

"Next flight leaves tomorrow, *Monsieur.*"

Ira shook his head and offered a sly grin. "Somehow I don't think it'll be that long."

The driver shrugged, then put his foot on the gas. The truck lurched off the rutted grooves as it pulled forward in a wide circle, cutting across the grass and leaving a swath of tread marks in the over-grown lawn.

Brighton leaned back into the headrest. After they had driven a short distance, he glanced out the back window. The motel and beach receded from view.

But Ira had vanished.

Frowning, Brighton turned away. He unzipped his backpack and pulled out a notebook that had been sandwiched in next to his computer. He fished inside for a pen with one hand while the other flipped open the notebook to a fresh page. He uncapped the pen with his teeth and scribbled down three words, all in capital letters:

WHERE ARE THEY?

He underlined those words with a thick stroke. Having phrased this last question, he capped the pen and dropped it into his lap.

Watching the ocean speed past, he closed his eyes and allowed himself a smile—

—and a look of determination.

EPILOGUE

Provo, Utah

OCTOBER 3

The elevator doors parted and a smartly dressed middle-aged woman stepped out. She breezed through the waiting area where Brighton sat and stopped at the reception desk.

Every woman who walked through those elevators fit the profile: somewhere in their thirties, forties, or fifties; a scientist-type—though he only had rough stereotypes to draw from—and returning from lunch. Brighton's head snapped up to study each one as they passed.

Only one could be Elisabeth.

This particular woman had to wait a few moments before the male receptionist, dressed in jeans and a navy shirt with the letters "BYU" stamped on the breast pocket, spotted her from the adjoining copy room. He held a half-eaten apple in one hand as, like all the other women before her, he buzzed her through the swinging glass doors that led into the heart of the building.

Brighton shuffled his shoes on the gray carpet. He almost hadn't come, but every time Rachel smiled at him, he wondered why he had survived and Wörtlich hadn't.

Wörtlich had only mumbled the woman's first name once before falling asleep in that cramped equipment room in Antarctica. But Brighton couldn't move on. Wörtlich had cared for a woman out in the world, and she would never learn what had happened to him.

As far as everyone was concerned, Wörtlich had dropped off the face of the earth, and in a sense, he had. Who knew what lay at the bottom of that chasm? The memory of the archaeologist, his broken body slumped and beaten—

Brighton shuddered and forced the image out of his mind. He might have to live with the memory for the rest of his life, but he needed to get better at shutting it out.

Another woman stepped up to the desk, this one a little younger, a little prettier. The clerk buzzed her through.

Brighton looked up as the elevator doors opened again, revealing a woman with long brown hair. She wore a light green blouse that complemented her green eyes, and a knee-length skirt. As she approached the reception desk, she pulled out an ID card and held it up to the reader built into the wall next to the doors.

The receptionist perked up upon seeing her. "Oh, Elisabeth. There's a man waiting for you."

Brighton sat up straight as Elisabeth Macfarlane turned to regard him. She put the card back into her purse and walked over, sticking out her hand.

Brighton was surprised to see she was younger than Wörtlich by at least ten years. He immediately felt bad for thinking it, but Wörtlich, only in his fifties, had always looked and sounded like a man somewhat older. Life had not been kind to him, and yet this woman reflected a side Wörtlich had never shown. How much more had Wörtlich kept to himself?

Brighton took her hand. "Hello, Doctor. Sorry, I didn't make an appointment."

"That's all right. Did I get your name?"

Brighton flushed. He hesitated, then said, "Sherwood Smith." He immediately regretted his choice; the name sounded fake even to his own ears.

"Can I help you with something in particular?" she asked.

"Yes." He swallowed. "Is it possible to speak in private?"

She glanced at her watch. "Sure."

A long corridor with offices waited on the other side of that swinging glass door, with labs sprouting off to either side. Elisabeth led Brighton to her office at the end of the hall.

Two lonely pictures of nature scenes, the sorts that often came as placeholders in newly bought frames, were affixed to the beige walls. The office had two bookcases, but only a couple of shelves held books, all tattered and dusty and abandoned. An oak desk sat in the middle of the room, slightly too big for the space. She had taped a photo of herself with two grown children to the desk. A stuffed dog with dark brown spots on light brown fur was perched next to it. Brighton thought it a strangely personal ornament for such an impersonal room.

"Sherwood," she said as she set her purse on the desk and flicked her hair over a shoulder. She pushed her desk chair aside, not sitting down. The chair shifted with a disapproving creak.

Brighton grabbed the edge of a folding chair, the only other seat in the room.

"Funny thing," she said. "I just heard about another Sherwood last week."

"Oh?"

She reached back into her purse and pulled out a thick stack of letters. "A friend of mine is on business overseas, and one of the men he's travelling with is named Sherwood."

Brighton rested his hand on his chin and exhaled, giving up. "Actually, that would be me."

Elisabeth looked up, startled. "What?"

"I'm Sherwood Brighton."

"You just said you're name was Sherwood Smith."

"People are looking for me. I have to be careful."

Elisabeth retrieved the desk chair she had pushed away, sat down, and leaned toward him over the desk. "Did Emery send you? Do you have news?"

Brighton opened and closed his mouth several times, not knowing how to best answer. He felt the need to put matters delicately, and yet he didn't know anything about this woman or her relationship with Wörtlich.

"Yes, I have news."

Those earnest green eyes of hers widened. "And?"

He hesitated, looking down. "He found what he was looking for."

Perhaps she picked up on the subtext of that statement. She looked at him uncertainly. "He never told me what this adventure of yours was about."

"I'm not at liberty to tell you about that," Brighton said. "I'm sorry."

She waved him off. "I understand. You are both in some trouble. Emery didn't tell me either. I suppose he was trying to protect me."

She cleared her throat, then turned her attention to the stack of letters and began sorting through them, stacking them apparently by size. "You came instead of him. What should I take from that? Is he all right?"

Brighton shifted uncomfortably. "Well, no. He's not."

Elisabeth looked up and he saw that her eyes were wet. "I presume you're here to tell me he died."

"Yes."

She wiped her eyes dry with the back of her hand, but they only moistened again. "Did he tell you about me?"

"Yes."

"The last time I saw him, I felt like maybe he had changed his mind…" Her words choked off as she went back to sorting her mail, taking the time to nudge envelopes into perfect stacks. "Well, it's not going to happen now."

"I think you were right," Brighton said softly. "In the end, he changed his mind about a lot of things."

"When did he die?"

Wörtlich's broken body, coughing blood… Brighton closed his eyes and forced the image out. "Four days ago. In the South Pacific."

Her fingers froze over a light blue envelope. She absently wiped at her face as she stared it, so completely oblivious that she missed the tears now streaming over her cheeks.

Slowly, she said, "When were you in Australia?"

Brighton frowned in confusion. "A week ago. How did you know?"

She held up the letter. No return address had been written on it, but the stamps featured the five stars of the Southern Cross.

"This is Emery's handwriting," she whispered.

Brighton's first instinct was anger—Wörtlich could have exposed them with that letter. Then he remembered they had been exposed anyway, just a few short hours later. The letter didn't matter, except, of course, to Elisabeth.

She should read it alone. The things Wörtlich wrote aren't meant for me.

"It's a funny thing," she said, her voice quivering, the letter trembling in her hand. "I never had any great loves in my life. Apart from work, I mean. Then Emery came along... but he was twice married and busy throwing away a promising career. I didn't mind. He did."

That sounded very much like the man Brighton had come to know.

"I should be going," he said, standing.

Elisabeth nodded, her eyes fixed to the letter as though it might vanish if she looked away.

Brighton turned and walked out of the office. Just as he was about to set off, he peered back through the open door. Elisabeth opened a desk drawer and pulled out a letter opener. She tore open the envelope and removed a small bundle of pages folded into thirds. Flattening the pages, she leaned forward to read.

So strange that a man's life can be reduced to a single letter. He tried to shake off the thought. *One day, I'll be reduced to that, too.*

Ira had said that once something was in a person's memory, it was possible to access it at any time. Ira's technique had allowed them to go back and examine their dreams and subconscious thoughts in a visceral way Brighton once would have deemed impossible.

As he made his way out of the building, Brighton wondered if the same pertained to people.

*   *   *

Noam Sheply sat across the polished onyx dinner table, delivering his report, and Lagati found himself only half-listening long before Sheply finished. In a way, the details of Sheply's failure were immaterial. Lagati was much more interested in the pale moonlight streaming through the tall window that looked the front of his Swiss estate. Each jagged, snow-capped peak impaled the night sky in an act of rebellion, the moon presiding over the scene like a faraway, deposed queen overlooking the subjects who had abandoned her.

"And what of the Book?" Lagati asked when Sheply finally stopped talking.

Sheply hesitated. "Like I said, all we found at the coordinates Doctor Holden gave us was open ocean."

"Then we'll go below, damn it!" Lagati shouted, surprising himself. He clicked his fingers irritably on the tabletop. "You say there was no sign of Binyamin, Wörtlich, and Brighton?"

"They definitely flew to Tubuai and stayed a day, but I doubt they found anything more than we did. They knew we were coming after them, saw what they were up against, and gave up."

And why do I not believe that? Lagati asked himself. *Because Ira Binyamin would not have given up. He would have found a way.*

Instead of arguing, he dismissed Sheply. The thought of the man remaining under his roof any longer than necessary disgusted him, so he had his driver pile Sheply into the Bentley and disappear down the winding, cliff-side road. The car plummeting to the valley floor would not be the worst thing that could happen.

Lagati climbed the mezzanine steps and strode toward the library. He cursed Ira Binyamin's name as he walked past the overstuffed armchairs he and the rabbi had once shared. How many years had he planned for this? If Ira really had found the Book and destroyed it, all his efforts would come to nothing. He had invited Binyamin to serve a purpose, and Sheply to dispose of him once he'd served it. The danger had always existed that Binyamin would get in the way, but *they* had assured him—

And where was Wörtlich? Where was Brighton?

He opened the door to the stone terrace and stepped outside, feeling the cool autumn air sweep over him. Winter would soon enshroud these heights, and he would lose his favourite meditation spot. At least, until spring.

Lagati settled into a lotus position, his legs folded tightly beneath him. He placed his palms down against his upturned feet and took long, deep breaths, focusing his anger, steadying the rhythm of his beating heart. His eyes slid closed—

—and he found himself in their usual meeting place.

Ominous cliffs encircled the well-flattened floor of a crater. He had been to Mount Hermon many times. Though this wasn't really Mount Hermon, just a memory of it.

The sound of stone crunching underfoot made him turn just as a tall, hooded figure strode in through the crater's only natural entrance, a well-worn path that winded down the mountain from the north.

The approaching man threw off his hood and revealed a severe face with hardened, blade-like contours. His lips were twisted in a sneer and his eyes smouldered with barely contained fury.

"Thank you for coming," Lagati said.

Azazel drew himself to his full height, making Lagati feel very small. "I am not summoned by common men."

Lagati cowered.

"Do you have the Book?" Azazel demanded.

Lagati's eyes rose only to the angel's knees. "There was a complication."

Azazel's eyes flashed. His long arms reached out and grabbed

Lagati by the front of his shirt and lifted him into the air.

Lagati's feet struggled to reach the ground that was now more than a foot out of reach.

"You knew the price of failure."

Lagati willed himself to depart the vision, to shake loose Mount Hermon and reawaken on the terrace. Would he be safe even there?

Azazel shoved him roughly to the ground.

Lagati landed some distance from where he'd been standing, pain lancing through his shoulder.

"Please…" he groaned.

Azazel's twisted face leered down at him. Roaring with anger, the creature delivered a swift kick that sent Lagati flying. He heard the crack of ribs breaking as he tumbled across the stony ground.

Please, wake up! Please…

He clenched his eyes as tight as possible and waited—to wake, or to die.

He didn't wait long.

To continue the journey,
visit www.thebookofcreation.net
to read from Sherwood Brighton's blog
as he continues his exploration
into the mystery of
the Nephilim.

ABOUT THE
AUTHORS

EVAN BRAUN is an author and professional editor who has been writing books for the last two decades. *The Book of Creation* is his first published novel. He lives in Winnipeg, Manitoba.

CLINT BYARS hails from Atlanta, Georgia, where he lives with his wife Sara and two children, Sydney and Reese. The author of *Devil Walk*, an autobiographical book chronicling his experiences with the demonic realm, he is also involved with Pokot Water, an international project aimed at providing clean water wells to remote regions of Kenya. Clint is the pastor of Forward Church.

CPSIA information can be obtained at www.ICGtesting.com
Printed in the USA
BVOW011556300512

291361BV00005B/15/P